TRISTAN II:
A BRAT'S TALE

Also By
S. Legend

TRISTAN

XAVIER'S SCHOOL OF DISCIPLINE

S. Legend

TRISTAN II: A BRAT'S TALE

Mockingbird Publications

Mockingbird publications

www.mockingbirdpublications.com

ISBN 978-0-9920246–5-9 (pbk)

ISBN 978-0-9920246-8-0 (epub)

Edited by: Aanchal Jain

Proofread by: Susan Keillor

Inner Book Art by: Arkham Insanity

Cover Art by: M.A. Sambre

Cover Art Design by: Chiara Monaco

For my Readers. You are the fairy clappers. You make me real. This one's for you.

DISCLAIMER

Beyond lies fiction. This book is not meant to instruct or depict any kind of lifestyle. This book does not follow any particular set of rules or morals. Although the themes are real, this should be considered a fantasied version of this lifestyle, written to create a particular feel, one the author, her readers and the characters love best. The author does not write "how to" guides. She writes for kink, for fun and entertainment, period.

Should you resonate with the themes of this book, it is important to seek guidance that is not this book.

Tags: polyamorous relationships, domestic discipline, lots and lots of spanking, BDSM, erotica, non-consensual spanking, consensual-non-consent.

"I am who I am; no more, no less."

— TERRY GOODKIND, WIZARD'S FIRST RULE

CONTENTS

PROLOGUE

FIFTEEN YEARS AGO: EAGAR KANES

I hate staring at a wall. Especially half-naked with a smarting behind.

I've been standing here for a long while. Of course, any amount of time spent standing, staring at a wall, will feel like a long time, but I know I have been standing here for at least an hour. My feet have become restless, and the ache in my backside has become more of a nuisance. After a spanking, the sting lasts for some time; the length of time depends on the implement used, but then the sting turns into an ache, the same ache muscles get when they've been worked over. The ache is more annoying than the sting, in my opinion.

"Fidgeting is not the way to get out of the corner. You're meant to be thinking," Arcade says from behind his desk.

I know that.

I would snark at him, but that would not go over well. I'd be right back over his knee. Instead, I find the calm place within myself, the one Arcade helped me find long ago and I'm able to still my aching legs. Don't know how much time passes after that, but I finally hear the words, "Come here, please."

I move to stand before my husband's desk and keep hold of my shirt as I had been instructed. Humility is part of it. Hard to explain that bit; all I can say is that it is.

"Turn around, please." Biting my lip, my heart pounding in my throat, I turn around so my husband can look upon the artwork he painted on my backside earlier. "Is this what you wish me to see as I drive my cock into you? Evidence of your disobedience?"

"N-no, sir," I say, my voice wavering.

"Turn back 'round, return your clothing proper, and take a seat."

Damn. He's not finished with me.

When I'd returned here, to the barracks, after bringing Tristan back to his mother at the palace, he was waiting for me—even opened the door to our chambers before I could so much as touch the door handle. I couldn't look at him and stood there waiting for him to speak, my eyes downcast. "What is the real reason I'm about to spank you, Eagar?" he asked me.

"The real reason? Not my muddy clothing? I know you don't like me traipsing around the palace that way unless I've been out on the field. In which case I'm to come directly here, and—"

"—that was not an invitation to spout off our rules, Eagar. You could have cleaned Tristan and yourself at the palace. I would have been none the wiser, yet you chose to come here. Why do you think that is?"

"You said you'd be gone for the day. I didn't think you'd be here. I wasn't trying to get caught," I'd explained.

"Maybe not consciously, but I have a good feeling if I hadn't come back, there would be other evidence of this mishap left for me to find."

When he said it, I knew he was right. I hadn't given much thought to what I'd do with the dirty clothes. I most likely would have tossed them in the laundry bin—on top—where he'd see them plain as day. Not to mention the baths would not have been cleaned until the next day—even if he missed the clothing, he wouldn't miss that.

It's textbook *bratting*. And I am not typically prone to brat behavior.

I know this, yet I still don't understand myself in the way I would like—there are no books on people like me in Markaytia. "I know it's hard for you to ask for a spanking, angel," he said, his voice softer.

"I don't want a spanking," I complained and sighed. It's the strangest conundrum. I never want chastisement, but always feel a world better after it. I avoid it at all costs, but it never ceases to amaze me—the ways in which I'll seek it if I need it—even ways unbeknownst to myself. *If I know this, why is asking so hard?*

"I see. Your undisguised rule-breaking is evidence that you, my love, need a spanking. You're all wound up. Come with me."

I followed him to his office. My eyes widened when I saw what awaited me, and my heart raced. Several implements from hairbrush to punishment strap, laid out in a neat row side by side. "Arcade! You can't use all of those on me. What I did wasn't *that* bad."

"I could if I thought you need it, but I have not decided which I will use. You know I always want to be prepared. I didn't mean to scare you, love."

I calmed down. Arcade has never been unfair; I should have known he wasn't about to start now.

"And yes, breaking *that* rule wasn't *that* bad; however, there is something bigger going on and I plan to deal with you properly," he said with serious eyes.

Arcade chose the hairbrush. I hate that Gods-awful thing if anyone wants to know. He bared my bottom and put me over his knee in the most uncomfortable position possible. My toes couldn't reach the ground, and I was unequally weighted, so I felt like I was falling forward. I put my hands out in front of me to catch my weight, but he wouldn't even permit that.

"Give me your hands, Eagar."

"Arcade, *please*."

"Now."

I stifled a groan as I placed my hands at the small of my back, and he held them in place. I felt all of five years old—*good job, Arcade*—but I knew better than to complain out loud. I earned this spanking, subconsciously or not.

He began with his hand. Anyone who says bare-handed spanking is nothing has *never* been spanked by my husband. I was bleating like a lamb in less than two minutes. "I'm sorry, Arcade! I'll behave proper next time!"

"You will, sweetheart."

"*Please*. I've learned my lesson."

"I'm sure you have, but you have not paid the penalty."

"But it *hurts!*"

"It's meant to."

No amount of crying or pleading stopped him. I suppose that's why I trust him the way I do. That's part of it too. Trusting him to do what's best for me despite what I want in the moment, because no submissive or brat wants a spanking in the moment. If he had stopped because I'd begged him to, it would break the chain; it would be hard to trust him to catch me when I needed him to. It's important he knows I trust him to know to stop when it's time to stop, but also never stopping *before* that point.

Tears streamed down my face, and I reached a point of clarity. Spanking is the physical manifestation of my emotions and in those moments over Arcade's lap, I reached the true reason for my disobedience. He knew. He *always* knew, and that was bloody annoying sometimes. "Having any epiphanies down there?" he said as he took up the Godsforsaken brush.

"Yes, sir. I am. Please don't use the brush. I can tell you in detail."

My pleading did not deter him. Arcade took to each of my sore cheeks with his evil, wooden paddle, disguised as an instrument of vanity.

"Do enlighten me," he punctuated with more of the same.

I kicked my limbs as the tingling turned into a throbbing ache. "By the love of the Gods, Arcade. Allow me to—*owww*—speak!"

"You're telling me that a man of battle as you are—my second in fact—cannot take a child's chastisement while speaking? I don't believe it," he continued.

"I didn't—ooowch!—come to y-oou, because I really didn't want a spanking."

"Yet here you are, getting one."

Snot was running down my face by this point, and I couldn't wipe it away, since my hands were secured at my back within Arcade's grasp. "Yes," I panted, and finally Arcade let up, giving me a break. I knew it wasn't over, so I took the opportunity to get more words in that wouldn't be interrupted by cries. "I don't like that I *need* to be spanked."

He rubbed over my sore flesh, sending good tingles to my cock, and I couldn't help my arousal. Not that I was going to get any sexual relief during a punishment, but I couldn't help my body's reactions. "It's who you are, angel."

He proceeded to spank me with his blasted brush until my voice was hoarse. When he was finally finished, I was done holding back any feelings I might have and was ready to talk. But of course, he saved the talking about the feelings part, helping me stand and directing me to the wall instead.

"I want you to think about any conclusions you have come to, and while you do, you are to hold up your shirt, so I can see your naughty, spanked bottom. Is that understood?"

My face heated and my damn cock responded in kind, hardening like a rock. *Don't get too excited, it's not like you're about to get any rewards.* "Yes, sir."

Now, I suppose, we're going to talk about the conclusions I've come to at the wall. He waits for me to speak. "Tristan is going to be like me, and it's all my fault. I should stay away from him, but I can't. I'm too selfish, and I love him too much."

He's quiet for several heartbeats. "Tristan *is* like you," he says. "But not because you made him that way. It's something you're born with, Eagar. Tristan has been the way he is since birth."

I shake my head. "He sees too much, even if he doesn't know what he's seeing. He's started to ask questions. I don't want this for him, Arcade; needing someone to decide what's best for him because he's too pathetic to do it for himself."

"Are you calling our son pathetic?" He quirks a brow.

"No. Arcade *listen* to me. Our son is going to have the same dysfunction I have, but he is made from your and Olivia's genes, not mine. He could only have gotten it from spending so much time with me—learning to behave as I do. I'm not good for him."

Arcade sighs long and heavy, pinching the bridge of his nose. "Where do I begin with all of that?"

"It's simple. Just—"

"—do you make the decisions, Eagar?" he cuts me off.

"No, sir." I shake my head.

"That's right. I'm surprised by what you've said, is all. I suspected other things, but not this."

"What other things did you suspect?"

"We shall get to those things in due time, but first and foremost, I will not be keeping you from *our* son. You are his papa, and he needs you. Let that be the end to that one."

Inside I'm relieved. If Arcade still thinks it best, then I'm glad even if I don't quite believe it. I know a father is supposed to behave self-lessly as regards his son, but I don't think I could keep myself away from Tristan, even for his own sake. I relax as much as I can; my arse hurts.

"Next on the docket—let this be said once and for all; I hope our son will be *exactly* like you. He could be so lucky."

"How can you say that? That would mean he would need—"

"—someone like me?"

Oh. Oh, right. I nod.

I know Tristan doesn't see it now, and he won't until he's older, but he could be so lucky to find a man just like his father. That being said, the boy is six. Arcade could let up on him some. It'll be a few more years before he begins training for the position of Warlord. Sure, we bring him to the field and show him some sword stuff, but he's too young to practice with the big kids. Though Tristan seems to have a way of making it onto the battlefield with them and I wouldn't be surprised if he was fighting with us sooner rather than later.

"I have some things to say about you and our son," I say.

"Then let's have it." He looks amused, not angry like I think he should be.

"I don't like the way you speak to him, and while we're at it…" I pause to seethe for a moment.

"Yeeeeees?" He's smiling now, as if he thinks I'm cute.

"You punish him too harshly for trivial things. You berated him the other day for just spilling milk," I continue.

"Ahhh. These would be the other matters, the ones I suspected were upsetting you."

"Well. Explain yourself," I demand.

"Mind yourself, Eagar," he says. There's discussion and then there's belligerence. "Tristan is the most agile six-year-old I have ever encountered. Would you agree?"

"Yes, but accidents happen to the best of us."

"Have you ever seen me spill a thing?"

"No." It's true. The man is infallible.

"That boy has more physical skill than I've ever seen in anyone his age—including me. That spill was no accident. I would think you would at least recognize that by now."

Icy tingles spread over me. "So, you already know to what extent Tristan is like me?"

"I know, and I act accordingly. Until he marries and finds a partner of his own, I provide a source of grounding or he'll get out of sorts. My role is to be that solid form he can depend on. In fact, I shall only approve of such a partner for him."

"How could you know? Why haven't you brought this up with me?"

"I know the same way you do—I recognize it because I possess the same threads even if they are a different color; there's no sign in particular. I was thinking of a way to bring it up that wouldn't upset you. Though if I'd known how much it was already upsetting you, I would have ripped the bandages off and spoke with you sooner. I should have known you'd recognize it as soon as I did."

"You're not mad about it? You don't blame me?"

"I love you. Everything about you—*especially* the part of you that makes you need me as you do. It's special, Eagar. I've already said it, but if you need to hear it again, I'll say it as many times as is necessary: No, I don't blame you. You'll be helpful counsel for Tristan someday."

"It's dysfunctional."

"I know you won't believe this now, but I'll say it anyway: Needing what you need is not dysfunctional, love. But that is something you'll have to process yourself and it's not likely to resolve within you today. Think about this: Who would there be for me, controlling bastard that I am, if I didn't have you just as you are, to complement me?"

"I'm lucky to have you understand my condition, you mean."

"No. I mean exactly what I say—we balance each other—if you are dysfunctional then I am dysfunctional, and I can't care two ways past Sunday."

I laugh. I love his confidence. "But our son, he can't know. Maybe there's still hope for him—we can change him, make him be more like you."

His eyes frown sadly, not for our son but because he wishes I would understand what he's trying to explain. "It's his nature, Eagar. We can't change him anymore than you could stop a crow flying. Besides, you want our son to be a smarmy, possessive arse?"

"I want him to be strong and in charge of his own life."

"You are both of those things."

That's true. But, "What grown man needs to be spanked?"

His eyes fill with mirth. "You. There's not much more to it than that."

"People would judge me if they knew." Except for maybe Olivia, Tristan's mother. She knows, but she reserves judgement and is accepting. Other Markaytians are not as accepting of kinds of relationships they do not understand.

"If they judge us, they judge us. People judge people for all sorts of things. There's no way around that."

I nod. "And what of our son? If he's like me, will you go easier on him?"

"I will do no such thing. Aside from the fact that I am a harsh person, if Tristan wants to be Warlord he might as well get used to it. I'm bound to get a whole lot harsher."

I nod. I know to expect that by now. I look down at my tunic and play with its edges, wondering if I'm forgiven, but too embarrassed to ask. "Come here, Eagar," Arcade says, standing and opening his arms for me.

My heart lifts and I have to say, this is probably the best part about spanking—the after spanking cuddle. "I'm sorry. I'm so sorry, Arcade."

Arcade moves my hair from my face and wipes the tears with his thumb. He's smiling. "Sorry? You know how much I love spanking your naughty bottom. I do want your obedience, but maintaining you is no chore."

I squeeze him tightly, grinning into his shoulder. He makes no apology for who he is and if Tristan has to be submissive like I am, then I shall endeavor to make sure his self-confidence is like his father's.

***

TRISTAN'S MUSINGS

To be fair, I have always been a brat.

Growing up, Lucca and I were usually in some kind of trouble. I remember the blond-haired hellion running down the hall like fire was chasing him, nearly barreling into me. It turned out "fire" was the pastry chef. "Tristan, run!"

Note, I had nothing to do with this venture, and yet I was a willing accomplice. If he was in trouble, so was I.

As he approached, I could see the two small pies he carried; I matched Lucca's pace and ran with him.

"Wait till I get my hands on the pair of you! Royalty or no, you won't steal my pies!"

But we were younger and faster than the old pastry chef; it didn't take much to outrun him. A few sharp turns and we lost him in the maze of halls, but we did need a secluded place to eat the stolen pies without someone *else* catching us. "Tristan, this way," Lucca said.

We continued to run, veering left and right, until we reached the back of the palace where there was a secret door, unguarded, we could slip out of, undetected. We carried onto the stables, knowing where to go like we had one mind and soon, we were lying against a large hog, buried in thick mud, bellies full of fresh blueberry pie. "How did you manage that, Lucca?" I asked him.

"How do I manage anything? I'm clever as sin."

Of course. I rolled my eyes at my arrogant cousin. *Lucca's father had made many attempts to temper Lucca's conceited demeanor over the years, but the task proved hopeless.* "Whatever. I'm glad you did. The pies were delicious," I said.

"My pleasure—what you want to do now?"

"We should probably go clean ourselves up before—"

"*Tristan. Arcade. Kanes!*" Papa's deep voice was followed by an equally angry, but more feminine, "*Luccalthizan Amarail Kanes!*" from Lucca's mother, my aunt.

"—before we're caught." Only we were already caught.

Upon reflection, I sometimes wonder if we wanted to be caught; as I'm learning, it's in a brat's nature to brat. We can't ask for spankings, won't, we need to be chased and we need to be made to go over a knee. I didn't understand this about myself at the time, but I do now.

We froze. "Do you think they've seen us, yet? We could make a run for it," Lucca whispered to me.

"Yes, we've seen you, and we can hear you as well. Don't even think about moving," Papa said as he came around the corner. I knew better than to disobey a direct order like that; I remained where I was with Lucca against the hog, in the squishy mud.

"You sir are a mudball," Papa said when he finally got a good look at me and he was not pleased. The queen was behind Papa, looking every bit as stunned. She ordered Lucca to her side, but I wasn't getting that courtesy. Papa walked over and lifted me, unconcerned about the sticky mud, or my six-year-old pride.

Papa was a warrior, Father's Second. When he wasn't looking after me, he was on the field, ergo the mud covering one muddy little boy didn't bother him like it had the queen.

"Let me down Papa. I'm too big to be carried." I squirmed and pushed at him, but Papa was stronger and paid me no mind, even going as far as to smack my little bum as he began walking away with me. I looked back to see Lucca, who didn't have it much better—the queen had grabbed him by the hand and was now dragging him up to the palace—as Papa carted me off to the barracks.

I had chambers in the palace, which is where Mother lived, but I also spent a great deal of my time in the large barracks, and so was given a room there as well. Papa and Father preferred to stay there, and I preferred to stay with them.

Father and Papa had a fine set of rooms in the barracks since Father was both Warlord and brother to the king. Normally, I loved being in the barracks; Mother often complained I spent all my time down there and not enough with her, but that day, I was panicking a little. Going down to the barracks increased the chances of having to tell Father of my transgression.

It's all fun and games for a brat until they're caught, and then they are left wishing they had behaved in the first place.

I tried to appeal to Papa's softer side. "I'm sorry, Papa."

Papa stopped walking, set me on my feet, and crouched down to look into my eyes, giving a wry smile. "How was the pie?"

"How did you know about the pie?"

He laughed. "It's all over your face little man." He reached out to wipe the corner of my mouth with his thumb.

"We shouldn't have done it and I'm sorry, but please don't take me to Father; he'll murder me." Papa lifted me, and I was set on his hip once again as we continued toward the barracks. "I said I was sorry,

Papa. Will you please put me down?" Life felt very unfair at that moment.

"No." He was quiet as I contemplated my certain doom, but finally, he spoke. "I should let you continue to *think* I'm taking you to your father, but I won't. I'm just going to clean you up, then we'll go back to the palace to discuss the repercussions of what you and your cousin did."

"Are you going to spank me?"

"I should." Papa sighed. "But I'm not going to. I will have to tell your father and I can't promise you he won't."

There was no question about that. Even as a little boy, I knew Papa reported to Father about all things. Still, a boy could hope. Thinking back, this was one of the many things about their relationship I never questioned, but now I see it was a part of their domestic discipline style marriage. Otherwise, I don't believe he would have had to tell Father absolutely everything. Not the small things anyway.

"Lucky for you, he's out at the moment. I came to fetch you from your mother and I am not pleased to find that you were not with her."

"Oh, c'mon Papa, don't be mad." I hated it most when Papa was mad at me. "I was, but she said Lucca and I could go off and play around the palace."

"You are much too young to be left to your own devices in such a large place."

"I'm six." I remember puffing my chest out, trying to make myself bigger. Thing was, Papa was huge, especially to the six-year-old me.

"Do not sass me, young man, you are in enough trouble as is."

I also knew well the difference between "little man" and "young man." "Yes, sir." I obeyed and shut my mouth.

Papa carried me all the way. I didn't know it then, but because I was Papa's only child, he allowed himself to indulge in things like carrying me, even when it was unnecessary, and I know he saw it as a deterrent from future misbehavior.

"You're a silly little boy, you are," he said to me when we were finally on our way to the baths near the barracks. He had to spend some time dumping buckets of water over me, to rid the excess mud before we could think about entering the baths. I'd had enough mud on me to turn the bath water into a swamp.

"I said sorry, Papa."

"Sorry until you and Lucca are involved in the next pot of chaos you stir." But he was smiling.

"Lucca's fun. I'm glad he's my cousin. You think I'll ever have a brother, or maybe a sister?"

He raised both brows. "Don't you think one mud-boy is enough for me to take care of?"

He reached down to tickle me until I was giggling. "Yeah! Yeah. One's enough!"

"There, that's how a proper boy should laugh."

The baths in Markaytia were large as pools, and the staff always kept them filled with fresh water. I jumped in, the mud spreading all around me. "Over here, please," Papa said. I swam over to him so he could scrub me down. When he was done, he was wet and dirty, and as it turned out, this was what tipped Father off. When I was towel-dried, I was sent away with a pat to my bare bum, in the direction of my small bedroom in the barracks.

That's when Father returned. "Eagar! You here?"

I froze. It was time to face the music. Papa didn't spank me, but Father would, and I knew then, maybe he'd spank Papa too. Poor Papa's shirt—totally ruined and muddy beyond repair, the water from my bath having trailed the mud everywhere, making him look just as muddy as I had been.

At that moment, the look in Father's eyes—I remember it well. *Now I know what it meant.* Papa knew he was going to get scolded, and I've been learning from my time in Aldrien what that does to ones like me and ones like Papa. We can't bear the disappointment.

Father set eyes on me and then glared daggers at Papa. "Explain, Eagar."

The trouble Papa got into was my fault, at least I thought so then, so I cut in. "Lucca an' I stole pies. We ate them in the pig pen—it's not Papa's fault."

"Yet he's the one who looks like he's been rolling in a pig pen," Father roared.

I backed against Papa's leg and then reached up for Papa to lift me —yes, after all that fuss over being carried. He scooped me up, shielding me from Father's ire. "Arcade, I was just about to clean myself up. I had to get Tristan settled, you see—"

"I can see it very well, thank you. Take the boy back where he belongs. I need you today."

"But, Arcade, I thought you had business out of town?"

"That business has changed. Go, now. Come right back."

Despite Papa's respect for Father's command, and the scolding we both knew he was going to get, I got the distinct impression that Papa wanted to pummel Father. "I just got him, Arcade. Can't we visit? Just for an hour." *Papa would plead, but he would never disregard Father.*

"No. Is taking him back going to be a problem for you? I could get one of the men to do it."

"That won't be necessary. I'll take him to his mother." Papa wasn't going to win the argument, but he was going to have some time with me, one way or the other.

"Good, but you won't go anywhere like that. Change first."

"Yes, sir."

On and off the field, Papa called Father "sir." I didn't think anything of it at the time, but now I understand its real meaning.

---

*W*hen Papa brought me back to Mother, she was only mildly surprised to see me. I've always loved Mother a lot, but when I was a little boy, hanging out with her wasn't fun. She often made me cross-stitch. Six-year-old me liked swords and violence; cross-stitching was a major snooze. "I'm sorry, Olivia. I know I was meant to have him for the afternoon, but Arcade said I had to bring him back."

A sentence like that meant nothing to me then. It was the kind of thing I was used to hearing. But I get it now. Papa had a responsibility to Father beyond that of a standard Markaytian marriage. With Elves, everyone has a designation based on their unique energy, from super dominant to super submissive. It's a spectrum.

Whatever Papa was, Mother knew.

"It's all right, Eagar," she said.

"It's not. What if you had things to do? Arcade can't expect you to drop whatever you had planned to look after him."

"You know he can. That's my role. I knew when I agreed to bear Arcade Kanes an heir, that my first responsibility would be Tristan, day or night."

I hated being talked about like I was a chore, but I knew I wasn't, not really. Father and Eagar were a married couple; Mother's only involvement was me. She was always treated with respect. The palace pays handsomely for *Mothers*, and her relationship with me was important, but she was not part of their relationship romantically. It was always clear that she was meant to look after me when they could not. Mother didn't mind that, though. She volunteered to have me because she wanted a child; she loved me dearly. She liked not having a partner to answer to—Mother had always been a free spirit. She detested travel when it involved staying in the forest rather than Inns, but she was an active socialite and loved to visit other towns. Her social calendar was limited when I was little, but as I grew so did the engagements. She vowed to keep things that way until I was fully grown, and she could meet someone who could keep up with her.

Besides, she had just as much parental say as Papa, even though Father always had the final word on Tristan. This was understood from the outset, and she was all right with it. "Your father is a good man," she'd say most of the time. She would make jokes with me and there were times I know she wished Father would let up a bit, but overall, she supported his decisions. "You'd do well to heed him, my child."

I knew Mother would make me cross-stitch as punishment once she made me tell her what I'd done. I begged Papa not to go. I wanted to stay with him. He put his forehead against mine. "Papa has to help Father," he said.

"Can't you help him, later? I just got to see you."

"We'll see what your father says, little man," he said to me and I couldn't help but think I'd ruined our time together. Mother jumped in to save poor Papa, who I know must have been feeling bad about having to part with me so soon.

"We'll see about tomorrow young man," Mother said, taking pouty, little me from his arms. "I've had an enlightening conversation with your aunt—is there something you want to tell me about pies?"

"I already apologized to Papa!"

"But you haven't apologized to Chef Andros."

"Be good for your mother," Papa said with a kiss on my head.

When he left, I asked about the situation. "Is Papa in trouble with Father, Mother?"

Mother denied it. It wasn't her business to share. "Don't be absurd, darling."

Which was weirder for me. In my mind, anyone could be in trouble with Father and that was what I knew to be normal. I'd even watched him lecture the king. Father was the eldest brother and the rightful heir to Markaytia, but he allowed the title to pass onto my uncle, preferring to serve as Warlord instead, something that Markaytian law permits. Despite having forsaken authority over the kingdom, he still felt it his right to lecture his younger brother if he thought the said brother was being a fool.

Mother proceeded to reprimand me about stealing pies. All of my parents were determined I wouldn't end up as spoiled as Lucca. I was made to apologize to the Chef even though Lucca didn't have to—he had been the one to steal the pies, I just ate them—and was put on kitchen duty every night for a week.

That night, Father made his way up to the palace to lecture me. I did ask about Papa. I didn't know the ins and outs of their relationship at the time—still don't—but I knew something was up. Father had replied, "He's fine, why do you ask?"

"I thought he might be in trouble," I said. *With you*, I almost added.

Father narrowed his eyes. "Papa can take care of himself; he doesn't need a six-year-old boy defending him."

I was annoyed, but I didn't speak out against him. I was prone to mischievous behavior, but when Father spoke, I obeyed.

He ushered me to my chambers. "Mama already punished me," I informed him, in case that could save me. Having three parents meant receiving three chastisements and let me tell you, it was not fun. You would think I'd stay out of trouble with that fate awaiting me each and every time I put a toe out of line.

"I decide if you've been given proper chastisement or not." That was Father's role, it always had been. "I'm not sure if you're sorry about what you did."

"I am, Father." But he had his spanking eyes on, and I began to tear up.

He surprised me. "I do think this has been handled properly, for once, but I don't like the frequency of this kind of mayhem. You and Lucca get up to a lot of trouble. You both need steeper consequences. One day it could be dangerous, deadlier than pig slop. You don't know what I've seen, Tristan."

"Then take me with you. I want to see," I said.

"You think I'm going to make a disobedient whelp, Warlord? No. If you don't start obeying your parents, I'll find someone else to succeed me."

Hearing that was worse than any spanking. "I'll behave. *Promise.*"

"I hope so because I've decided your training will not begin until you can learn to behave, which will be a measure of your ability to take orders. Immature brats do not become Warlords."

"Yes, sir." I stared at my hands for a while as his eyes burned into me. Father was a man of war and that leaked through his marrow, making the air ooze a mixture of authority and purpose.

"I believe we have reached an accord," he said. "Now to bed with you." With a flourish of his long, Warlord cape, he spun on his dark leather boots and stormed off, leaving cold air in his wake, knowing his directive will be carried out.

I wiped my stupid, crying face. After what he said, I knew I wouldn't be able to sleep. And I wonder as I think back on this time if a spanking would have been better for me in that instance? No six-year-old is going to admit to that.

If I were a more submissive one, I'd have gone to bed straight away, the guilt of disobeying too great to live with for long, but that's not what I did.

Have you met me? I am Tristan Kanes, Brat. Always have been, always will be.

Instead of going to bed as I should have, I slid the picture frame over. Behind was an intricate maze of tunnels Lucca and I had found a while back. The tunnels zig-zagged through the palace which we used to sneak from room to room unnoticed by our parents who did not seem to know they were there. I slipped behind the frame and into the beaten stone passageway, intent on finding Lucca. First, I would clobber him for getting me into trouble and then we'd see about the frogs down by the stream we thought might like to live with us.

Secret frogs of course. No one was going to allow us to have pet frogs and for good reason—Chef Andros almost ended up with unintentional frog soup.

CHAPTER 1

ALDRIEN ~ PRESENT DAY~ TRISTAN IS ONE YEAR IN ALDRIEN

"Good job I'm not you, Tristan. When Bayaden sees that, he'll skin you alive."

That's Tom, manservant to King Caer Gai, standing there with his smooth tuft of yellow-orange hair. He's right too you know. Bayaden probably will skin me alive—if he finds out. I take the white shirt and toss it in the fire. The two of us watch as it goes up in flames, all evidence vanishing before our very eyes.

Tom looks at me like I'm crazy and he's right; I am crazy. What I'm not is stupid. "Won't he notice one less shirt in his closets, Tristan?"

"Are you kidding me? That pompous arse has more shirts, pants, and boots than he knows what to do with. He'll never miss one plain, non-unique blouse when he's got at least seven more." My lips curl around the Elvish words and while I don't ever think I'll have command of the language like Tom does, I'm proud that I can speak Elvish fluently. It's not easy to learn.

As for Bayaden's blouse, there's no way I'm bringing it back with a large red stain on it, especially when it would be the second one this week. As long as I live, I don't think I'll ever get the hang of laundry. This time it honestly wasn't my fault. I made a point to separate the colored fabrics from the whites, but somehow one white blouse ended up with the colored clothes. I swear, it had a life of its own and made its way into the wrong pile.

"If you say so, Tristan."

I get on well with Tom, but both our royals keep us busy and we don't see each other often. It always seems to be when I run into Tom that I'm in the middle of trouble. The guy probably thinks I'm loony. Maybe I am a bit; this place can make any sane man go a bit 'round the twist. "Don't worry about me. I know exactly how to handle Prince Bayaden. He thinks he's so smart, but I'm always three steps ahead of him," I say tapping my noggin. "That's the secret."

"I'll take note," he says. I don't think he believes me.

"As you well should." I grab the last bit of Bayaden's laundry, poke at the ash that was once his white blouse with a fire poker, and salute Tom before I make my way back to Bayaden's chambers.

It's early. Bayaden is sleeping soundly in his four-poster bed while I've polished boots, gathered laundry and ordered his breakfast. I used to have to bring it to him as well, but I seem to either get sidetracked on my way to the kitchens or Meren would stuff me full of whatever goodies she'd made that day (despite Bayaden's orders) and I wouldn't be hungry enough to eat with Bayaden. It irritated him when he couldn't feed me. He likes to have me eat with him, claiming it gets lonely with just him in his chambers. I suggested he go eat with his family if he wanted company, which did not go over well. I spent that meal hanging by my wrists from a chain slung over the rafters in his chambers, with some phallic-shaped thing stuffed in my mouth as he ate divine-smelling food and lectured me on the importance of speaking to him respectfully. He also said I could either eat with him at the table, or he'd string me up just as uncomfortably every meal-time, where I could watch him eat then take my meal from the floor once he'd finished his. I kept my mouth shut after that. Bayaden can be grouchy, but if I'm obedient, he's good to me.

I take a moment to stare at his almighty form. Elves are massive. The whole lot of them. I was considered tall in Markaytia at six feet.

Baya is a good three and a half feet taller than I am. He's tangled in the blankets—he always twists them up and pulls them off me—and it allows me to ogle one of his mammoth thighs. He could crush me with his legs if he wanted to. He's threatened to, yet here I stand.

I set the laundry basket down and move to slide the curtains open. The bright sunshine will wake him—he'll hate it. I get few pleasures in life now that I'm a manservant. Bayaden's scowl when he's forced to wake with the sun is one of them. "Do that and I'll tan your pretty hide," he says before I can so much as touch the curtains.

"But, m'Lord, it's a beautiful day," I say, deepening my Aldrien, Elvish accent. "The sun is shining, the birds are calling, and the flowers are blooming. Does that mean it's spring here? Or summer? I can't tell."

"Quit your nonsense. You know it's always summer here."

"How can it always be summer here?"

"Because it is. Come." I climb onto the bed and he pulls the covers down. He's naked of course. "Suck."

I scowl at him. His eyes are still closed. "Only if you ask me nicely. I'm not your dog."

"Suck my cock, now, or I'll put a leash on you, and you'll know exactly what it's like to be a dog," he says, his dark eyes glittering. He can be such an arse in the morning.

I move to his cock. It's large. All the Elves seem to have gigantic members, the thickness of tree trunks and the length of human arms. Okay, I might be exaggerating about that last bit, but that's what it feels like when I swallow the thing into my too-small-for-it mouth.

"Mmmmm ... You're good at that. It's my favorite reason Andothair gave you to me."

I want to bite him for that. I don't though. I've only bitten Bayaden once and I'll never do it again. I don't like to think about why. Coming awake now, he pushes his hips up into my mouth, and when I hit a nice spot, he grabs the short hair at the nape of my neck, so he can move my head how he likes.

My beautiful long hair is gone, has been for some time, since

Andothair lopped it off. They won't let me grow it back. I lick up his shaft and to the underside of the head of his cock then swallow him up again and suck and suck and suck. It's not long before he's releasing into my mouth and I'm doing my best to swallow around his engorged cock. I lick him off and wipe my chin with my fist.

"Well, I guess you've had your breakfast then," he says.

"*Bayaden.*"

He laughs. *I've come to love his laugh.* "Not to worry, little human, I won't allow you to starve. Come up here."

He won't. He's oddly attentive.

I crawl into his arms and he cards his hand through my short hair, as he lazily strokes my hard cock. I enjoy. His hand is large, able to fit my whole cock inside like it's got its own cave and Elves have wonderful uses of magic for sex, like getting the body to stimulate the release of a fluid to act as lube, which he coats the shaft with. I push my hips upward, fucking his hand, moaning.

Suddenly, his hand squeezes too hard around my cock. I pant and freeze, tears spring to my eyes and I have to wait until his thought passes. "B-Baya, what's the deal?" I grit out.

"You said you'd always stay, no matter what. You made a trade: You for him."

Well, that's something we've not discussed in a while. By *him* he means Diekin who is safely in Mortouge. "I'm staying," I cry. "I'm yours, remember?"

He releases my cock, which hasn't wilted. Why not, you ask? It's just had the life squeezed out of it. But I am a fool who likes danger; it turns me on more and I'd fucking like to finish what he started. Only now he's in a mood. He climbs out of bed, ready to set the room on fire. "You aren't really mine."

"What in the name of the Gods has gotten into you? I never leave this room without some kind of marking on me."

Marking culture is rampant among Elves. Like bloody wolves they are. Of course, Bayaden has to be careful how much he marks me and where he marks me. I am a lowly slave, and he is Aldrien royalty. It's complicated.

He doesn't answer me. "Dress me, Human."

I'm Human when he's pissed and little human when he's pleased. And damn him, my cock still aches, disappointed. *He* loves it all: the dominance, the orders, and the obedience, even the violence.

If Baya wants to be an arse, I can give it right back to him. "How shall I dress you this morning, Sire?" I'm icy cold and sarcastic.

"We will practice today," he grunts.

I refuse to speak to him as I dress him for the fields. Aldrienians don't wear a lot when they fight, but at least their important bits are protected. A wide belt, with the emblem of his family crest as big as his abdomen, goes around his waist, and I help him with a baldric strap that runs diagonally across his chest so his sword can rest on his back. He'll wear shoulder armor on his right, that I will help him put on once we arrive at the training fields, and wide bands of armor around his wrists. Bayaden has a large scar that runs from his fore-head and carries down under his eye to the top of his cheekbone. He likes to boast about the time he almost lost his eye, but with magic and good healing, it was saved. The rest of it was bad enough he was able to keep the scarring should he choose to.

And of course, he did. He says it makes him look fiercer with it than without it for "striking fear into the heart of his enemies." Good Lord. Above his eye is a tattoo in Elven Script that says *Tar Jian*. It's quiet now, but sometimes he allows it to glow with magic, which helps him look like a vengeful spirit. I'll never tell him, but I think it makes him look fierce too and I often find myself running fingers over it. He's a stunning creature and when I'm not cursing his name, I'm staring at him in awe.

I like to think I know something of the Warlord after all the time we've spent living in close quarters and behind his anger is pain of a kind he isn't used to feeling. I dare to reach and move his hair behind a tall, Elven ear. He starts but lets me, moving his ear in a pleased fashion. He won't look at me. "I loved you before the oath, Baya. Do you doubt me?"

His eyes glisten when he looks at me; my palm rests on his cheek. "I do not doubt you."

"Then stop this nonsense. Or your breakfast will get cold and I'm not taking the blame for that."

He smirks. "You'll take the blame all right. You are to blame, kicking all other thought but you out of my head and monopolizing the space."

I lean in to kiss him. "Apologize."

"For what?"

"You were mean to my cock, Baya, and for no good reason."

He smiles. "Don't need one."

"At least finish the job."

He has a wry expression on his face and pulls me toward the table seating me on his lap. "Can't. You said so yourself, the breakfast will get cold."

Arse.

"Besides, I have something for you."

I nuzzle into his neck and feel him sink into the closeness. I love our banter, but I don't like fighting with him that way. It reminds me too much of the beginning and while our beginning has some comical highlights, I'd rather what we have now. "If it's another hairbrush, I decline. My arse is spanked enough thank you."

He laughs. "It's not a hairbrush, but thanks for reminding me. I haven't taken that to your backside in too long."

I groan. "What's my present?"

"After breakfast," he says, forking a sausage, taking a bite and then feeding me the other half. "But I shall give you a hint."

He lifts my hand the one the ring on it that was given to me by Papa at my coming-of-age ceremony. "It was in a bag with this."

I think about that bag. *A bag with three contents, stolen from my room the day after my wedding.* Ring. Dagger. Tunic.

Sharp pain slices through my heart. It's quick though, so quick I'm able to carry on as nothing happened.

I doubt he'll return my dagger to me. "Is it my tunic?"

He smiles wide. "Don't worry little human, it is safe. Eat your breakfast and then you shall find out."

I breathe in relief, but at the same time, a thousand sensations make their way to the surface, feelings, and thoughts stir, ones that haven't stirred in a long time. I don't allow myself to think about *him*. I won't say his name.

But the thought creeps in about what *he* would have done if *he'd* found that tunic. I bet *he'd* have done to it what I did to Bayaden's shirt earlier. I resented *him* for taking me from my family. It was *his* fault I had my title stripped, *he* never heard me, *he* did what *he* wanted when *he* wanted. *He* was selfish. Arrogant. Pig-headed.

And yet, I *loved* him.

I *love* him.

I wipe a tear from my eye.

I can barely eat my breakfast, but I do since Bayaden has this weird thing about me eating. He leaves me to finish, and heads to the back of his closets, returning with something on a hanger. "Is that my...? But it's got ..."

"Pants." He holds out both my Markaytian battle tunic and a new, matching pair of pants, proud. "I couldn't let you wear such a nice battle tunic with those hideous things you wear. I had them made in the same color as like you would have had at home."

It is burgundy.

Home. I know this sounds fucking sappy, but these days home isn't a place like it was when I was a kid, it's when the end of the day comes and I lay with Bayaden in his bed, looking at the stars out his window.

You had another home once, Tristan.

But why? Why was *he* home too? None of it makes any sense. Corrik cared about Corrik.

You just said his name.

Ugh, stop it brain. Besides, I didn't *say* it. I *thought* it, there's a difference.

"I wear these 'hideous pants' because you won't allow me anything else," I say. These pants are my only article of clothing and I'm lucky to have them at all. Receiving another article of clothing is a big deal. Not to mention, Bayaden's never given me a gift before; I had to steal the pants I'm wearing, with the only other thing on my body—the black collar bearing his insignia. I don't know what to say. I stand and rush over to him, he hands me the outfit. I hug it, and can still smell home on the tunic, a smell that will never leave it no matter how much it's washed: blood, mud, and sweat.

It reminds me of Father. I miss my father.

What would he have to say about you? You didn't even try to escape. You didn't want to. Aldrien was a convenient place to hide.

Things with Corrik were so hard though. Things with Bayaden are easy.

"Thank you, Bayaden. I have no words. This is the nicest thing someone's done for me in a long while." This tugs at the threads of me and I'm a loosely sewn cloth at best these days. "Does this mean we're boyfriends? Are we going together? What do you Elves call it?" I love teasing the giant Warlord.

"You're a hair away from a spanking," he says.

I smile and press my lips to his. "Thank you," I murmur. "This is most precious."

He inhales as I kiss him, gathers me into his arms and then tosses me onto the bed. Most slaves don't wear clothes in the palace. Being given clothes is meaningful; I've just gained a bit of status for myself.

Bayaden begins to ravage me like a madman after that. He nips and bites at my neck, sucking his way along my thigh where his mouth clamps down and I moan at the lovely pain. I release my new prize, the clothes, in favor of his dark hair, which I cling to by the root and he lets go my thigh in favor of my cock. He's only teasing me though; I know he wants to fuck me.

Before long, he's readied my entrance for him, though there's seldom a time anymore that my entrance needs much readying—*we fuck a lot.* He slams into me with wild abandon pouring the feelings he cannot say into each thrust.

We kiss. "I love kissing you, Tristan." His tongue weaves with mine, he thrusts some more, his hands are all over my body, he thrusts again and we're both breathing as if we'll never get air. He comes, releasing his seed into me, and without any more urging from my cock, I come just after him. Without stopping to clean ourselves, he flips me over and we begin again.

I don't worry over Corrik for the rest of the morning, but he's entered my sphere again and like Corrik does, his energy barges in and takes over everything.

CHAPTER 2

"*Y*ou're a happy boy this morning. Why could that be?" Deglan says.

She knows; I play along. "Because, look. Bayaden gave me my tunic back, and he had pants made for me." Donning my old tunic on after this long is an indescribable feeling. It doesn't fit as well as it used to. Even with the many months of training with Bayaden's army, I've still some size to put on before I'm back to what I was on the day of my coming-of-age ceremony, where Father named me future Warlord of Markaytia. It won't take me much longer though and I'll be back to that. I've always put on muscle easily, Papa always said it was my dragon's blood.

Deglan laughs. Her blonde hair whips with the light breeze. "Yes, Warlord. You look magnificent. I must admit, I had a hand in that. Baya asked me if he should do it and I said that, of course, he should."

"Thank you," I tell her with all my heart. I love Deglan, she's a magnificent war Elf. I might love her as much as Diekin. She's kind and her skill on the field is almost unmatched, aside from Bayden that is—he is Warlord for a reason. She is large—Elves only seem to come in size large—and fearsome when she wants to be. I'm used to Elves towering over me by this point.

She is beautiful to watch with her bow. The way she spins on a coin and can hit a target from many paces out. The graceful way she nocks her arrows with her fingertips gracing along her cheek. She angles her torso back like she's marrying with the wind and finds the path to send it toward her target.

The only thing better is watching Baya shoot an arrow or play with swords or fuck me into oblivion.

"You are most welcome. Now. Pick up your bow."

Deglan is a hard taskmaster. One of the promises Andothair made me is that he would fulfill my heart's desire, thus, I was permitted to train with Bayaden's warriors. Training on the field is the place I self-identify. I didn't know how I was going to live my life without ever picking up a sword again. *At least now I don't have to.*

The Elves here have no fear over me having the skills Deglan says I am earning. *Arrogant Elves, they are.* I swear, one day, Elven arrogance will be their doom. In any case, I'm more than happy to be out here doing what comes naturally. After having my title stripped, I was forbidden from lifting a sword. Not that I haven't, I'd been able to procure many a sword without Father or Papa knowing—they both would have had words to say about that.

Bayaden's had me fighting with his warriors since the first couple months I'd been here, though, "fighting alongside his warriors" is putting it generously. More accurately, I got beat to a pulp each day, at least when he had me try with a sword. Eventually, Bayaden thought I'd do better with a bow in my hand. It's not like fighting with a sword, but it stirs my dragon's blood and makes me feel whole all the same.

Over time, I impressed Bayaden with what I could do, enough that he gives me private lessons with a sword that aren't much easier than the ones with his warriors, but it's not a malicious beating. I look forward to those, even though I leave them battered.

"Good job, Warlord," Deglan says.

I look at her curiously. Only her and Andothair call me that. With Andothair it's mockery, but Deglan's not like that. "Why do you still call me that?"

"That is who you are."

"Bayaden is Warlord."

"Of Aldrien, yes. But you are still a Warlord. It is who you are—it's in your blood," she says. "Denying it doesn't make it any less true."

"Corrik didn't seem to think so," I say under my breath. I know she can hear me, but she only smiles.

Great. And now he is on my tongue.

"How did he do today?" Bayaden says as he walks toward us, several hours later. My arms are ready to fall off, and my back muscles have been worked nearly to death, but all my aches are good ones. Bayaden often talks to Deglan like I'm not here—he can't treat me too much like a person in front of warriors.

"He is doing well, brother, but he is tired. You need to give him a night off. From *everything*," she adds. I balk at her—she's one of the few who shows any respect for my strength and now she's acting like the rest of them do like I'm a pathetic human.

As a great warrior should, she reads my body language. "Do not be insulted, Tristan. You have much strength if you can last this long in my brother's service." She winks. "I work you harder than I do the Elves, and no human here can match your strength. But we all need time to recover."

Bayaden loves how annoyed I am. "I will take better care of my weak little human. He will have the night off."

"I don't need the night off!"

"Come." He ignores my protests, taking the bow from me and placing it on the rack. He grabs my hand, tugging me along as I glare after Deglan—this is her fault! "I'm sorry my little human. I've got to take better care of you."

"I'm not a pet, Bayaden."

"You're my pet," he says and smiles a cheeky smile.

"Oh really? Wasn't someone having a strop earlier because he thought I wasn't his for some asinine reason?"

He yanks my wrist, snapping my body to his, so he can look down at me face to face. "Mark my words Tristan, no matter where you go in the world, you'll never stop being mine. I shall always have a piece of you and that is the truth. I was being a jealous idiot before."

I laugh. "And where in the world would I go? Am I planning a trip I don't know about?"

He pulls me closer and presses his lips to my crown. His long ears twitch. "The only trip you're going on right now is over my knee."

"For *what?* I've been a perfect angel." I squeeze around his waist though. He knows me, yes, but I also know him. He's distracting himself. My heart clenches and my stomach churns. Something is about to happen, but he can't talk about it yet and I don't want to see the Warlord cry. There is nothing more heartbreaking and I'll turn into a worse mess.

"Haven't decided yet," he says picking up our cadence, holding my hand *again,* which is another sign. We're not supposed to hold hands in public. I am a human slave and he's Elven royalty. "But with you something always reveals itself, I have but to wait."

That makes me smile. It shouldn't, this is my arse on the line, but I'm on air about it. Maybe others care about having their arse spanked, and believe me, I have the good sense—most of the time—to watch which vats of oil I stick my hand in, to avoid *those* kinds of spankings, but either way, I live for the dance.

Unbeknownst to myself, I've been involved in this dance my whole life. I just didn't know how free I could be within it. Bayaden taught me how to release myself. He might regret it just a bit, but mostly he has as much fun as I do.

"Not this time," I say purposefully not thinking about the shirt I set aflame this morning.

"For good measure then," he says.

My body warms the whole way through, and I've never felt so good being Tristan.

CHAPTER 3

*B*ayaden leaves for a meeting with his father and I use the opportunity to tidy up his chambers. Problem is, without Bayaden to distract me, I'm alone with my thoughts and things creep back, like the doubts I've shoved away.

Diekin. Did he really make it out? Or was he taken away and killed? I didn't demand any sort of proof; I took Andothair's word for it.

Further back, I remember my beautiful hair, lifeless on the ground, my wrists and ankles shackled as Diekin was taken away to the prison for the first time. I stared at it and while I hated that it was gone, I felt another feeling I didn't like.

Freedom.

It's odd for a slave to feel free at the time of their imprisonment. I buried that feeling first, but it manifested anyway.

"You have no intention of returning to Mortouge, Warlord. I know this," Diekin had said. He was right. Eventually I'd bartered for Diekin's release, but I didn't even try to barter for my own. I told myself there was no hope for my release and I wasn't wrong, but that I didn't even try to, said something about me I had to think about.

"No. I already told you," I'd said to Diekin. "I can never face Corrik or Mortouge again. I can only hope I can save Mortouge and that they will still hold alliance with Markaytia."

Ha! If I had a noble cause, then my actions were still *good* by my old morals. But I was only fooling myself. I know Diekin didn't believe me, even if he tried reasoning with me. I acted selfishly. I was not thinking of my homeland, or the kingdom I was meant to serve, only myself.

My heart chose for me, even if it was heavy with betrayal.

I betrayed everyone for this slice of happiness. That I am a prisoner seems to make up for everything, at least it did, but when I *remember*—something I choose not to do—it makes less sense to me.

But when I look at Bayaden, it all makes sense again.

When he returns, he knows something's up. "What's wrong with you?"

The Elf is as rough as they come. Even being pressed up against him can be a callous experience, but so is sandpaper and what's beneath it comes out smooth—that's what Bayaden does to me, smoothens me with his roughness. "Do you remember what you first said to your brother about me?"

He smirks, remembering.

I try my best at an impression of his deep voice when it's most irritated and I use Markaytian like he did that day so I would hear him insulting me. "What is this *creature*? It's absolutely hideous. He looks like something the sea washed in."

"To be fair, the sea had just washed you in. Hadn't you come from a boat my brother destroyed?"

"I'll not stick my cock anywhere near that thing," I continue. "It's probably riddled with fleas."

He still won't admit to his treachery. "You were a scraggly ragamuffin. I had every right to exercise caution."

He moves closer to me and takes over. Bayaden has a wide frame like you'd expect an Elven Warlord to have. He's dark-haired with coppery skin, more like mine. Andothair has a sandy hue of brown to his skin, but he's not tanned like Baya. It's testament to the long days Baya's spent out in sun, much like I had once upon a time and so he's several shades darker than Andothair with a pink hue. His skin isn't weathered of course, seeing as he's an Elf—their skin forever remains youthful-perfection and not even the sun can age it before its time.

But his eyes are what always get me, they are primal, dark menaces.

"I had you bathed and unsheathed your glorious beauty quickly if I remember."

"Not before your guards imprisoned me and whipped me nearly to death."

"You were not whipped nearly to death." No, I wasn't, but still. "I came to retrieve you, didn't I?"

I laugh. "You weren't happy about it."

When he set his black eyes on me that day, I wanted to run back into the cold cell and stay there. I was sure he would finish the job the guard began.

"No, but would you have been in my position? Andothair was breathing down my neck more that day than usual and then I was called to fetch my unwanted, disobedient manservant."

"Your fault. If you'd have just given me this in the first place, all of that could have been avoided."

I rest my hand on the collar at my throat. It's thick, black leather and has a tag with Bayaden's Warlord's insignia and a pendant from the house Tar Jian. I'd tried to convince the guard that I belonged to Baya in a desperate attempt to get out of the dank place—the smell of rotting flesh and the sound of painful moans get to anyone after a time—but the guard didn't believe me.

"Right, and I'm king of the ninth realm," the guard had said because it *was* unbelievable. I didn't know it at the time, but Bayaden had never had a manservant before me and telling the guard he suddenly had one, was as believable as talking frogs.

Even when I had the pendant, not everyone cared about it at first, but once they knew I was Bayaden's manservant, they eventually left me alone. Never stopped looking upon me with contempt, but they didn't apprehend me. Before that, there were a few times Baya was forced to retrieve me from the Aldrien dungeons and I was grateful for my father's harsh ways, preparing me for such an experience.

"Tell me, what fun would that have been? Besides, you would have learned nothing. You, my little human, need a firm hand."

I can't deny it. "So, are you going to tell me why you were a jealous idiot earlier?"

He hardens. "No."

I look at the ground.

"Tristan, I'm sorry. Please don't do that. I don't want to talk about it because I don't want to say his name."

His name is already on my tongue, so I do it for him. Only now there's a discussion, which brings him sentience. "Corrik."

"Yes."

"Corrik is an ex-boyfriend. The past. You said so yourself that in time he will be but a memory."

"I was wrong. When Elves are connected to someone, like in the way you and I are—"

"—the loyalty bond?"

"No Tristan, I mean through here," he says putting his hand over my heart. "We can sense the other. Your heart still reaches out to him, even if your head does not. It's subconscious. I don't think you realize it's happening."

I tear up. "No. But I love *you*."

He smiles all the way to his eyes. "You do. It's possible to have more than one love. I know this. Your love for him does not change your love for me."

Elves are this way. More are polyamorous than not, but it is not something that I as a Markaytian am used to even though I suspect more and more that I too am this way.

I love the way Bayaden's so sure. Would Corrik say the same though? I recall how possessive he was. I'm not sure he could under-stand my love for Bayaden, despite what Diekin's said, despite the usual nature of Elves.

Because I don't think Corrik falls into any of the usual boxes.

He's different from them all and sometimes I wonder if it was his mysteriousness I loved more than him—I was always a sucker for adventure, especially dangerous adventure and it didn't take long to figure out Corrik was both those things.

"Then why can't you say his name?"

"I told you, idiotic jealousy. We Elves can't help it from time to time."

They can't. It's irrational. It's also not the first time this has come up; it's just that the last time was a long time ago.

Bayaden spins me around and smacks my arse. "Hey!"

"Get back to work. I won't have you shirking your duties."

"But I thought we were talking." In other words, I thought we were leading our way up to sex. He knows. I glare at him.

"Pout all you want. Get to work."

I try to stay mad and it should be easy for me, but it's hard when his authoritative voice soothes me so damn much. "Yes, your liege." I'm a sarcastic little fuck.

"You can do it with a sore bottom, and if I get anymore lip from you, that's what's going to happen." His right ear rises in time with his brow.

That only relaxes me further and I have the choice at this point, continue my snark and definitely get spanked, or be a good boy and maybe get spanked. "I'll behave myself, sir."

And I do, *for now*.

I often marvel at Baya when he's asleep. His lids close sweetly, his breathing peaceful, none of the heaviness of his Warlord's day to mar him. Even in sleep he exudes magnificence. How can something so rough be so smooth at the same time?

Corrik wasn't rough at all. Corrik was sharp and nothing sharp can be rough. Sharpness exacts, it carves and polishes. Corrik had his vision of me and he thought he could bring me into his life and carve me into what he foresaw. He didn't expect to have to do any work, Gods forbid he had to understand me.

Perhaps it's Elven sex magic and I don't love him at all. *Maybe that's what Bayaden feels when he says my heart reaches out?*

I move to climb off the bed, but a large hand snatches me back. "Go to sleep, Tristan," he says in his booming voice that is extra-loud against the quiet of the night.

"But I—"

"—okay that's it. I knew I should have done this earlier."

He uses his arm as a vice to hold me against him and spanks my bare arse with his mammoth hand. I can't move, at least not to go anywhere, and can only kick my legs and brace myself against him. "Owww! Baya, please."

"No. You'll take it, Tristan." As he talks, he spanks never missing a beat, while I grimace and pant, my backside throbs. "C'mon let go and take it. You've needed this all day."

I try. But it hurts. That's why pain—odd as it might seem from the outside—gets a spankee like myself to a new place. Pain is something you cannot overcome. It's an experience, and it's there and you have to deal with it. You have to surrender to the pain and let go to free your body of what it's holding onto.

You do this with your mind.

Some days the pain is too much, but then so is my internal struggle, which for me takes more pain and thus more mental strength to overcome. Bayaden spanks as hard as he feels I need in times like this. "Take it little human," he coos as I writhe in agony.

Slaps ring out, each one lighting my arse afire; I struggle more, he spanks harder.

Fighting, especially when emotionally charged, is exhausting and I give up. I accept that this is happening whether I want it to or not. I take a deep breath, exhaling into the pain allowing it to sink into me, rather than trying to block it out. My body relaxes and while the pain never lessens, instead of rejecting it, it becomes part of me. My eyes still wince a bit, but I don't struggle and take what he gives me.

His heavy spanks turn to rubbing and though I wasn't crying during the spanking, it all comes out afterward. "Shhh, you needed that didn't you?" I nod into him. "Everything is going to be all right. I promise."

It's not though. I think I know what he's up to and I don't want to say either, in case I'm wrong. I don't want to give it life. "Bayaden tell me you love me."

"I love you."

"Say it again."

Instead of using words, he hums to me, something soft and deep. His singing voice is as rough as the rest of him, which is why he prefers not to sing in words. He only sings to me. I calm down and eventually, I can sleep too.

———

*T*he grey sandstone is warm under my feet, the perfect temperature for walking on without shoes. Most of the humans and Elves in Aldrien don't wear shoes, which begs the question: why does Baya have so many pairs of boots for me to polish?

I head down to the marketplace, making sure to give a smug guffaw to the large, female warriors who stand guard and allow people from the palace into the marketplace. They don't like me much and I don't blame them, I'm cocky which is opposite to the way Papa taught me to be, but I can't help it. They scratch at my ego, looking down on me as they do. It's not even because of the human versus Elf thing. I merely think Elves moronic for that; my ego is irritated because they don't think I'm good enough for their Warlord, not even as a manservant. They scathe at the pendent around my throat.

Truth be told, they've got some points they could argue. I'm a terrible manservant. I grew up as a royal with very little education in the art of servant jobs. I was spoiled even with my parents spoiling me far less than Lucca's parents did. I thought I had it rough when I was a kid, but I didn't. If only I knew how incredibly lucky I was.

But I digress. I was a spoiled rich kid. I know nothing of being a manservant, nor do I like it, nor do I try all that hard.

I am another kind of servant though as a warrior. That's where I shine and where I feel I'm equal to Baya, even if he's way stronger than I am. I wished they'd compare me to him under those terms. Not that the result would be any different, but I'd rather be hated for what I am, than for what I'm not.

I do have to exercise some amount of respect for them though, or Baya will have my head, so I nod and smile. "Lovely day, ladies."

"Be gone with you, human."

I don't need to be told twice.

The market is, in essence, like that of Markaytia's markets—a busy chaotic mass of people, but the one rather large difference is the persistent presence of nakedness. I would be naked too, if not for the pants I was able to acquire after making a bet with Bayaden on my first day here. He underestimated me. He didn't have to allow me to keep my prize of course, but he did, which demonstrated his proclivity toward honor—even to his slave.

But the odd thing about Aldrien, in general, is that as much as humans are slaves, they don't seem to mind so much. Aldrien Elves treat humans like beloved pets.

Some Elves have leashes attached to the collars of their human, some humans crawl on all fours, some are naked, others wear scant amounts of clothing or strange harnesses, some are with their owners, but some without. Each human-Elf pairing seems to have its way of things, but the commonality is, they are happy.

Never thought I'd be one of them, but here I am giddy at the prospect of acquiring Bayaden's favorite mushrooms along with some special herbs and spices they don't always keep on hand at the palace, to give to Meren for Baya's dinner.

I wouldn't have been doing this for Corrik. Not because I wouldn't have wanted to, but I would never have been permitted. This kind of thing is beneath royals.

Ugh. I have to stop thinking about Corrik though. I've kept him locked away in a box all this time. What a time for him to spring out, seemingly larger than when he was stuffed into the box, and I can't seem to fit him back inside.

I bump into Tom and Mary. "Good day to you, Warlord. What mischief you up to?"

I smirk. Yeah, I'm a brat and I own it. To be fair, the first real adventure I'd got myself into when I was here, involved textbook bratting. I didn't think so at the time, but I can see it now.

I blame Bayaden. He brings it out in me.

Mary and Tom are both fully clothed. Mary, because she works in the kitchens and her mistress feels that makes sense, plus she likes to doll Mary up. Tom because the king tends to be a bit possessive. Well, Tom calls it protective, I call it possessive. The king is not as polyamorous as other Elves, which usually does not extend to slaves, but it does in this case. Personally, I think the king's sweet on him and can't admit it due to all the rules, which apparently, not even the king can break in Aldrien.

But it's easier for the king to find reason enough to bend the rules to clothe Tom than for Baya to clothe me. It's a symbol here—ridiculous as that is—and Baya has to consider what his warriors would think if he gave me too many Elven privileges. Besides, me naked doesn't bother Bayaden in the least. The most he allows me is some protection on the training fields.

Gods damn exhibitionist he is.

"Sorry to disappoint, but no mischief today. Just mushrooms."

"Bayaden's favorites?" Mary asks, knowing me.

Hotness flushes over my face. "Perhaps. Have you seen any?"

"Over there." She points and winks.

"What about you two?"

"I was sent to help Mary, but I've got to return to the king," Tom says.

"My usual. Kitchen errands for Meren." She looks around and leans toward me. "You should know Tristan, there's a big dinner coming up. Rumor has it, Bayaden's attending."

I raise my brows. "Bayaden never attends those." At least not willingly.

Her face says she knows and that's *why* she told me.

Baya also hasn't said a word about it, which is probably why she's being so timid about it. I'm probably not meant to know until Baya finally decides to tell me. "Thank you, Mary. I'll see you two up there, then."

I get that sensation in my gut again, like looking over a ledge.

My bare feet grip the hard dirt as I pad over to the place where Mary said I could get mushrooms, show my tag to the vendor so he'll charge the palace accounts, and carry on to the spice stands. Then I catch sight of long blond hair. Most Aldriens have dark hair, some have grey, there's even white, but blond is rare. I can't see the face, they're wearing a hooded cloak, I have to follow to find out.

As much as I didn't want to be saved, with how ardently Corrik seemed to love me, I thought he would come. Part of me considered this a short holiday from the real world, at first, because I was certain I wasn't going to be here long. But when he never came, especially after I was able to get Diekin out of here, I told myself he'd moved on too.

It made it easier to put him in a box I could store on the shelf in my mind, never open it, let it collect dust.

But maybe he has been looking all this time? Maybe he's here.

I stash my mushrooms and spices somewhere I can collect them later and follow the lone rider. The Elf is big enough to be Corrik. The ears are the right height, the shoulders are broad enough, but I don't see a sword.

Corrik wore a sword to head down to the kitchens when he thought there might be cause to, no way he'd head into enemy territory without one.

Unless there was some reason he couldn't.

My heart lifts, which I did not expect. An aching begins from somewhere deep within me and my blood races. I chase after the rider now, fuck his cover, I need to know if it's him and I'm not letting him get beyond that gate without seeing. There are limits to where I can go, my collar does not get me past the marketplace gates. "Sir! Sir! I think you dropped something."

The rider stops, turns to face me, frowning.

It's not Corrik. A beautiful Elven man with blue eyes, but not Corrik. "I'm sorry, were you talking to me?"

"Ah, no. I thought you were someone else. Sorry to trouble you."

He nods and turns to head through the gate and in short order becomes another ghost passing through my life, just like my Corrik.

CHAPTER 4

*T*he material felt scratchy. After having been naked for so many days, my body had to remember what it was like to be encumbered with every step. But the beige pants kept my cock from bobbing around and at the time, I cared that I was flouncing around naked and who would see what. They were also a prize won. Bayaden didn't think I could acquire a pair without his help, but I had.

Bayaden took me for the first time that same day.

It was a build-up of amazing sexual tension due to me being a fucking brat and Baya's Top energy responding in kind, *needing* to take me. When Elves are aroused, it's different than when humans are. As humans, it's bad enough. We get fucking horny and we crave.

Elves *need.*

Once they go down that road, it's near impossible for them to stop.

It wasn't two days into my servitude to him when I returned to his chambers to find him staring out the window, but he was quick to have me against the wall, held by my throat. My black collar was ripped off and his teeth sunk viciously into my neck. I cried out; he cupped a hand over my mouth. But my cry was only because of the pain; I wasn't scared. Fuck no. All of it was arousing, my cock got painfully hard and felt as natural as breathing; I opened my neck allowing him to sink deeper. The suctioning grip of teeth released with a squishy sound, taking some of the skin of my neck with them; the holes left behind gushed blood.

He pulled his face half an inch away so I could see the burn in his eyes, his anger, laced with pure desire, the ache of it etched clearly on his beautiful face. He wanted me and he hated that he wanted me, the flea-ridden human forced into his life. He demanded something of me in Elvish. Back then, I couldn't understand him. He was being an arse-hole, but his desire for me won out, and he switched to my home tongue to move things along. "Undress, I wish to view you."

The pants were a victory, which I still swear I saw him crack a half-smile over; they proved how clever I am and Bayaden admires cleverness. "Forget it Bayaden." I tried to push past him to my bed, which was on the floor next to his. I wanted to forget the whole day had ever happened. It had been a trying day to say the least; I was in no mood for horny Elves.

"Take them off, or I'll rip them off."

"Damn it, Bayaden!"

"Now," he said in Elvish I recognized, his ears flaring.

I was furious, but I did as I was instructed. I didn't intend on putting my new pants anywhere near him, but he snatched them from me. *Stupid, agile Elves.* "You said I could have pants if I acquired them myself." I full-on pouted at him.

He tossed the pants away; he didn't care about them; he was more interested in my hardening cock. "See, you desire me."

"I am a male Bayaden, it has nothing to do with you," I lied. I hated myself and I hated him more. *I was married, and I still wanted him.* Badly. I liked what he was doing to me, even as the blood ran down my neck. By the Gods, I'd never felt like that. My heart thumped in my chest, *it does that for him—races without rhythm—it feels like the height of battle.*

We stood breathing, facing off. I was naked, sore, bruised, bleeding, and my hard cock throbbing, but *he* was the vulnerable one, and we knew it: he was about to lose something.

"I want you to suck me," he said.

I knew that day would come. Not only is it common to fuck the spoils of war—well unless you are Markaytian—Andothair had mentioned this. But I thought I would be made to do this, tied down and fucked. I didn't expect how I felt.

I *wanted* to suck his cock.

I'd like to say that I was only thinking of Diekin's life because in some small measure I was, but mostly, I wanted him. "I'm going to bed," I said.

He grabbed me by the side of my face. "You are mine." He was fucking breathless.

"I am not yours. I belong to Corrik."

He didn't like that. He dragged me by clawing at my roots with his meaty hand and unless I wanted my head detached from my body, I was forced to follow. He threw me on the bed, not my bed, but his large, soft one. I froze. Bayaden wasn't Bayaden in that moment, he was something else. *'The Elves are creatures; they are of a different breed than us Markaytians,'* my uncle had said.

And they are.

I realized my mistake, it was one I had been making all along, even with Corrik. As much as I knew they were like creatures cerebrally, I still operated as if they were human. It's hard not to; in many ways they resemble humans and so we humans anthropomorphize them. But inside they are wired differently. I began to see it with Corrik, but it was Bayaden that helped me understand it. Arousal possesses them and they turn animalistic. When that happens, it's a *need* and it has to be satisfied; there's almost no stopping the tumble of passion at that point.

He caged me with his arms planted on either side of me and sniffed up my body slowly, inhaling my scent. When he reached my neck, he licked his thick tongue across the blood still seeping in tiny rivulets from where he bit me. The holes patched themselves over. He nuzzled his nose across the mark I could feel there, and I could sense he wanted to bite it again, but he was able to exercise enough restraint not to, else he would have killed me. As it was, I could have bled out, but he'd bitten *just* shallow enough.

"That's funny, you smell like you're mine."

I couldn't breathe. There's always been something frighteningly vicious about Bayaden everyone senses, especially me, but he's got a way with sarcastic humor that's hard to spot when you're busy being terrified, and when you finally do, it's soothing—you know he's not going to murder you; he just likes you to think he's going to murder you.

Besides, danger turns me on. Bayaden is the perfect mixture of deadly and hilarious. *Ugh.* I have a type.

I knew he wasn't going to gut me, but there was a high probability he would fuck me. His fingers trailed over my body like he was trying to figure out if I was real or just an apparition. His eyes darkened, and his mouth latched onto mine. It wasn't a kiss; he was trying to suck the tongue from my mouth.

My body bent with his. Bayaden is a force that cannot be denied and that night I wasn't going to try. It never escaped me that I was still married, but desire is a powerful influence. I can't say it was right, but it didn't feel wrong either.

I wanted him, I *needed* him, so I continued to let him. I wish I would have at least tried to say no, but I wanted him. The Gods help me, I wanted him.

Elves are promiscuous creatures, but Corrik had shown what a possessive arse he was; many times, he'd expressed how much he wanted me all to himself.

The resentment surfaced.

I was forced into the marriage, taken from my home, my identity ripped away. I dreamed of the day I would become Warlord upon Father's retirement. I earned my place as his successor, but Corrik didn't care about that. Nobody did.

Now I had nothing. I had been reduced to a slave and there was something I wanted right before me—something I genuinely wanted with no one here to take it away or tell me I couldn't have it. I didn't get to want anyone other than Corrik in order to save my virginity for him. I wasn't going to get to choose anything once we arrived in Mortouge; Corrik would have dictated my life down to the second.

I wasn't called a slave, but I would have been one all the same.

Finally, I was going to have something I wanted, something I didn't know for how long I would have it and I was going to enjoy the ever-living fuck out of it.

One thing that has always been certain about me and Bayaden is that we have chemistry, and more than one person noticed it from the very first moments. I denied it at first, but there was no denying it. I attempted to kiss him back, but he wouldn't let me and moved down from my lips to my swollen neck, gentle there, then attacked my chest and torso with bites that *hurt* but didn't break the skin. When he reached my throbbing cock, I was already gone, gone, gone.

"I did not expect you to taste so good, Tristan."

He called me, Tristan. I didn't even have to ask, and he called me Tristan.

He prowled on top of me, and I pushed my aching cock toward him. "If you're going to fuck me, just do it already." The waiting was torture.

"Is that what all this poor behavior is? You just needed a good fucking? Will that inspire better behavior, little human?"

"Unfortunately, for you I doubt it," I said, smirking at him.

I expected anger at a remark like that, but he was wrapped up in some sort of spell. "I know the Gods are taunting me, but I must have you, Tristan."

"Then do it."

"No."

But he didn't move, hovering over me, his jaw hard and eyes dancing with a dangerous mix of lust and rage. He wanted permission. I knew something of the kind of restraint it was taking to stop now that we'd started. I reached my hand up toward his face, he flinched, but let my hand settle on his sandy brown cheek. "Fuck me, Warlord. Don't leave anything behind."

He nodded, taking one hand away from the bed to undo the buckle of his armored skirt in one, swift motion, tossing it to the ground with a clang. It was the first time I saw it; his cock and let me tell you, it's huge, like *huge* and for a moment I regretted telling him to fuck me, but not enough to take what I said back. It's darker than the rest of him and it leaked pre-come, his black pubic hair falling against the wet tip. He took my leg and was surprisingly gentle as he pushed it toward my head then used his shoulder to hold it there, so he could slide a thick finger into my arse.

I inhaled and cried out when he hit my prostate. I felt myself getting wet and chalked it up to Elven magic. *Of course, they have a lubing-spell.* I had to arch my back when he got faster and added another finger. I pressed down, needing more, wanting to feel him inside me, owning me.

Making me forget.

He finally pressed the thick head of his cock against my entrance, and I looked down, watching, fascinated until he was seated all the way inside me. All that day, I'd been in a dance with Bayaden, both of us trying to prevent this very thing from happening, but it was happening and now both of us hated ourselves even more. We used it. Once he was in and I was relaxed enough I wouldn't tear, he pulled back to get enough momentum to slam inside me again. He wasn't careful with me and I wasn't careful with him. I treated the large Elf like he was a leather sandbag, used for sparing, whacking at his arms while he thrust, which remained firm as granite. I clawed at his shoulders and kicked my heel into where his kidney sat. It didn't affect him, other than to ratchet his arousal yet another notch.

He likes the raw violence.

He was equally brutal, slamming into my arse, stretching my legs too far, slapping me across the face each time I kicked him too hard. We were two Warlords in a sexual battle.

At one point, I tried to flip him. I couldn't of course, it was like moving stone, but my trying amused him. "I don't think so, you're meant to writhe on my cock, my lovely."

I bit his arm for that, and he cried out, digging his hand into my short hair the moment I released him. "You fucking brat." He fucked me harder as if doing so would subdue me.

I wouldn't be subdued.

But in between all of that was the sex and it was *incredible*. It was how I'd always pictured it might be with a future mate, except we'd be on the field in the mud. It would be after a long training session; we'd start with metal swords before we moved to our *other* ones. He'd take me roughly and leave me bruised and satiated.

Bayaden hit all my buttons as he continued to hit my prostate, while we both continued our skirmish. "Stroke your cock, little human."

I did, and that sent me over the edge. I came all over my belly moaning loud enough I was sure I could be heard several doors over. Bayaden was proud of that. "Open up," he said, and I didn't get much time before his large cock was stuffed down my throat. He was close though and, in a few strokes, he came desperately. I tried to swallow, but his cock was too large and my mouth too small. I did the best I could.

He collapsed beside me in a much better disposition than when I arrived in the room. He reached for me, which was unexpected, finding my hip and placing his meaty hand there as a sign of ownership. "I'm not done with you," he said. "Stay."

And he wasn't. He took me seven more times after that and as promised, he didn't leave anything behind.

From that moment I became his. I was Corrik's and I was also his. I didn't know how to reconcile that.

CHAPTER 5

I don't ask about the dinner. I know Bayaden well enough to know that if he's keeping anything from me it's because he either can't talk about it or because he *can't* talk about it. The former is to do with the fact he is still the enemy Warlord even if he's no personal enemy of mine, which I understand because I would do the same. I am doing the same. I won't betray Markaytia or Mortouge by revealing their secrets and out of respect, Bayaden doesn't ask.

The latter is Bayaden's issue with expressing his emotions. I get this too. I'm only slightly better because I had Papa who was a feeling, emotional being. Even Mother was a bit emotionally dysfunctional. But Papa, he was raised to talk things out and he did most of the time, which meant I was forced to even when I would rather exercise Father's taciturn ways.

So I leave it. He'll tell me when he wants to or not at all, but it doesn't stop me from worrying.

I sit by the window to polish his boots and stop to admire the marks along my arms. Baya got carried away last night and I can't be seen like this. Markings mean too much in Elven culture and so it's a conundrum. If anyone were to see these, they would know how much Baya adores me and he would lose the respect of his warriors.

Technically, Baya could heal them away, but that's the equivalent of telling me I'm meaningless; something he couldn't even do the first time it happened. The best we've got is a magical Elven healing salve that will heal them faster than if they were left to heal on their own and to be honest, I don't want them gone either.

After our first time together, I was covered in marks. Not a patch of skin was left unmarred. I ached all over, the bite marks made it hard to move without pain, and my arse was sore in two ways. That time, he had chained me to a wall by a metal collar, the chain only long enough to reach a pot to relive myself in since I couldn't leave his chambers. I was livid, ready to kill him.

But he refused to speak to me in Markaytian and wouldn't tell me what was going on.

He did show me his art via a hand-held mirror; he was so proud. Baya had never been drawn to mark someone as he had marked me and while he was angry that the person to get the best of his affections was a human, I immediately became special to him and he got protective.

But all I knew at that moment was that my fucking body felt like tenderized meat because it was and I set about plotting as to how I would go about cutting his balls off but not his cock, I loved the many wonderful things he could do with his cock and wanted him to do them again.

This time, he doesn't have to lock me in. I know better than to leave looking like this. There's bratting, and then there's courting the kind of trouble neither Baya nor I can contend with. It does mean I can't attend practice today, so I get antsy. I've already cleaned Bayaden's quarters, but I go over them again, giving them a deeper clean.

When I'm in the closet, moving things around, something falls out. Even without a lot of light, the handle glints, and I know it's my dagger. I pick it up. *Wow*, was Corrik mad when he saw I took this. I laugh. It all felt so serious to me at the time, but now, I could see it going differently. Part of being a brat is embracing it; the more I embrace that side of me, the more others will, including my husband, that is, if he can love me unconditionally.

You called him your husband, Tristan.

Fuck. The box that was never supposed to open again is not only open but has begun to grow things from it, spilling everywhere like dandelion and as we all know, that stuff spreads like fire. I sit on the floor with it, remembering him—fair as snow, unrelenting, fierce, but also sweet when he wanted to be.

Okay, I admit it, I miss Corrik. But does he miss me? Would he understand the choices I made?

I stow the dagger. I totally plan on doing something fun with that one, but I want to think about it, bide my time and get Bayaden good. I'm just stuffing it back when arms encase me. I would jump, but I know who they belong to. "Not very vigilant, Tristan. I could have had you gutted and flayed several times over." He spins me to face him.

"I knew you were there the whole time," I boast. I didn't. *Bloody Elves.* I'll never get used to how quietly they can sneak up on you.

He drags me from the closet to check my arms. "These are nearly gone."

"I know." I twist my lips.

He smiles. "Not to worry. I'll give you more. Somewhere hidden by your pants and perhaps your tunic." He starts nibbling down my neck. "I'm sorry. I know how much you hate being confined to one space. You can't cage a dragon."

"You can't and perhaps I'll even forgive you if you make it up to me."

"As you wish, my Tristan. I think I know how to do that." His eyes glint and I know he's thinking of sucking my cock.

"And then I want Meren's pies for dinner."

"And Meren's pies for dinner," he says pressing his lips to mine.

"Can I also plant frogs in Andothair's bed?"

"No." Worth a shot. He lifts me bridal style. "But I will take you for a ride and we can see the frogs."

He knows how much I like watching them jump against the moonlight. I nod and let him carry me to the bed.

The Aldrien king is a large, broad Elf like Bayaden, but he has fine features like Andothair and a long, fearsome scar, also like Bayaden, running under his eye, but instead of running across his cheekbone, it runs to his chin. Rather than making him look ugly, it gives him a grand look. All I can think every time I look upon him is what it would be like to fight a man like him. He's magnificent.

Tom has told me all about the ways he submits to the king. I've even seen the beautiful way he kneels for him with his torso tall, that graceful sway at this lower back, his chest puffed, and each toe of his bare feet pressed into the soft stone. I've seen the way his eyes look up to the king, and it's clear he's been instructed to have his gaze follow him in that way; he doesn't spare a glance for me or anyone else.

It's convincing. Anyone would believe their charade, but as I've gotten to know them, it just doesn't feel true. I don't know why; I have no proof that it's any other way. The king exudes a dominant energy at times, but at other times I pick up on a different aura. Is there a chance it goes both ways? I have heard some couples switch, which is a foreign idea to me, someone who swings so much one way; it's hard to fathom someone could be both dominant and submissive at the same time, but I think that's what the king and Tom might be.

Even if just sometimes. It would explain a lot anyway.

But Andothair is submissive through and through and it's easy to see now that I've embraced who I am. I understand why he and Corrik worked when they were together. I didn't know at first because Andothair can give a bloody good spanking.

Angry, after the first time Baya and I slept together and after my confinement that I still didn't understand at the time, I sought him out. He was with the king who thought I was an odd gift for Bayaden, but since the king has a human servant of his own, he understood the attraction and thought I'd make a pretty pet even though that day I was hysterical. I shouted at Andothair, saying things that didn't make sense. I even complained that I wasn't given jobs like a proper manservant.

"Calm down, Tristan." His voice was gentle, not hard and demanding like Bayaden's.

I was breathing too fast, trying and failing to calm myself down, begging him without words to do something to make me better.

He watched me a long time, and then said, "I know what you are, Tristan. We'll meet in my chambers tonight after dinner. I'll have Tom fetch you."

I was furious. I didn't get the help I needed, but I was without another option and so I had to wait; I was ready to set the whole place on fire. I went back to Baya's chambers and slept on my bed. To add insult to injury, I was awoken by boots dumped on my head. "The Gods' sake!"

Bayaden stood over me, looking like he wanted to set my head on a pike. "You went to my brother," he accused, his teeth grinding metal. "He says you want jobs to do, so here. Polish all my boots and when you're finished, polish them again."

"Perfect. Better than having to suck your cock." I got another boot thrown at me, which I caught seamlessly.

"I thought you didn't like being caged up—dragon blood you said? Keep this up, and I'll put you in a real cage."

I was saved from anymore of Bayaden's wrath when Tom arrived to fetch me. He stared between the two of us, probably wondering if he should call someone to stop the murder that was about to happen. "Um, sire, may I take Tristan?"

"For what?" he said baring his teeth at Tom.

Tom cowed down. "He has an appointment with your brother."

"Why were *you* sent to fetch him? You're Father's manservant. If Andothair is in need of a servant, I know just the one for him."

Me, he meant.

"I apologize, Master Bayaden, I don't know why I was the one sent. I'm simply obeying orders."

"Very well, but then I want him back here straight after. You'll return him?"

"Yes, sir."

Taking my cue, I slid past Bayaden—who was shooting eye-daggers at me—cautiously, but I didn't escape unscathed. His hand connected with my still sore backside. I saved myself some embarrassment by not complaining.

"I see you have pants," Tom said without looking at me. He was smiling.

"Told you I could have pants."

"Indeed. I am surprised he let you keep them. He must like you."

When we arrived at Andothair's chambers, he wished me luck. "This is where I leave you. Do yourself a favor and try not to give Bayaden too much trouble tonight, eh?"

"That what you do? Try not to give your master too much trouble?"

He laughed. "Oh, Tristan. I'm not a brat like you; it's much easier for me to behave."

That was the time I began to wonder if I had "brat" stamped on my forehead. "Am I that obvious?"

"To me you are." He winked and walked off.

I walked into the room without knocking. Sometimes I hate Andothair because he's so pretty. He's got the bone structure of a fair-skinned Elf, which tends to be delicate and posh, with the beautiful dark skin of an Aldrien Elf. He's not as dark as Baya who spends more time in the sun. Ando's a sandy brown copper to Baya's intense red copper. Even Ando's brow arches in a pretty way giving him elegance he doesn't deserve. His dark hair shines with strands of white twisted through it and always seems to fall over his shoulders in a perfect arrangement.

I was wrong. When I first laid eyes on Ando in the light, I thought he was young because he looks young—younger than most Elves his age. He's still young for his station as Crown Prince but he's much older than Corrik.

He maneuvers everyday sort of movements with the same grace Deglan does nocking her arrows or Baya on the field—Baya's a brute during all other motion. Arrogance bleeds of Andothair like a gushing artery and it's just as life-sucking to endure.

But sometimes I see what attracted Corrik. He has grand ideas. He's powerful. Intelligent. And did I mention pretty? I want to stab his pretty dark eyes out.

"Andothair."

"Warlord. Please sit."

I did, but only because I was tired. The nap had done little to revive me from the never-ending nonsense. Andothair has a large room like Bayaden has. There is a desk, near the marble wall by a large window, with a ledge fat enough to sit on and the same sandstone floors as the rest of the palace. He likes to conduct private business in his chambers, though I don't know why. If I were him, I wouldn't want anyone near my personal space.

"Let's get straight to the point, shall we? I'm not going to give you what you want unless you ask for it, but I will give you what you need."

"What is it that I need Andothair?"

"You really don't know, do you?"

I looked for something, a sword, a dagger *anything*. Father always taught me to be aware of my surroundings: anything and everything could be used as a weapon; plan an escape route if possible. Fight, if not.

But the strange implement on his dining table was all that was available, and I was pretty sure it was meant for me.

That's when I understood. He thought I was there to be punished.

For what?

He sighed long and suffering like he was dealing with a complete idiot. "Tell me, Warlord, what do you know of your nature?"

It wasn't the conversation I wanted to have with Andothair, but I sensed building energy in the air I knew not to deny. "Corrik. He told me I'm submissive like my papa."

"And what do you think you are?"

"I think I'm something else. Diekin called it *brat*." I enjoyed what Corrik and I did, the erotic lessons he tried to teach me, but I wasn't sure I could be *that* well-behaved all the time. Papa was always so much more well-behaved than I was. I needed to let loose.

Andothair picked up the implement and twirled it between the palm of his right hand and the fingers of his left. "You are a brat, Tristan. There's no doubt of that, one whose guilt I can feel from the moon."

Was I that obvious? Why was Papa too ashamed to talk with me about it? I glared at Andothair.

"You sought me out so I would punish you Tristan. Admit it or be gone. I don't have time for you to waste."

I wanted to storm out just to show him I wasn't who he thought I was, but even though I didn't understand it at the time, I instinctively knew it had been too long. It's not my way to ask though and my inability to behave for long becomes clear to me; it's not a character deficit it's how I'm wired—how I "ask" to be spanked. "Andothair, *please*."

"Why are you so stubborn? Were you like this with Corrik? No. He would never allow that," he said the last part half to himself. *I didn't know then his relation to Corrik at the time, but his musings make sense now.* Our stupid love triangle, which I was thrust into because Andothair couldn't let go.

But unfortunately, Corrik was the crux of my issue. Talk of Corrik reminded me of what I did, and the heaviness cloaked me. For whatever reason, Andothair felt sorry for me. "Undress Warlord and allow me to take care of you. You'll feel better."

I began to undress. "Why do I have to ask you? Why can't you just …"

"Spank you?"

"Yeah."

"Because that wasn't in the deal. This is personal, some might say more personal than sex and Tristan, my brother won't like it for long. One day, you'll have to go to him for this."

"Fine."

Undressing doesn't take long when your only article of clothing is a pair of pants. I could have removed the collar, but I didn't dare. If

Bayaden were to catch me without it, especially then, he might have taken it away and without it, my choices would have been remaining in his chambers, or risk being thrown in the dungeon, both of which I wanted to avoid. "Where do you want me?"

"I don't think so. You're not in charge, I am. You'll address me as sir while we're in these roles. Understand?"

I am military. Calling anyone "sir" was never a problem for me. "Yes, sir."

Andothair is small for an Elf, but he still towers over me, a paltry human, and when I approached his thick thighs, I felt his size. Though he's nothing like Bayaden, not even close, Andothair is imposing in his own way; it's in the eyes. He's more the calculated sort. I've always kept all my eyes on Andothair.

"It's better you go over my knee for this," he said.

My cheeks heated, but yeah, I knew he was right. I climbed over his lap, my exposed cock pressed into the smooth material covering his thighs (Ando wears real clothes unlike some Warlords I know), but believe me it was not hard, not for this. A pit formed in my stomach; I thought of Corrik, I thought of my homeland. *I selfishly took something I wanted, and I'd barely been there a week.*

"This is not punishment," he began. "You haven't broken any rules, not with me at least and you've managed to stay out of trouble."

Bayaden might have begged to differ.

"What I'm about to give you is known as a 'thinking spanking,' or a 'releasing spanking.' This is to help you let go."

"Yes, sir."

"What's eating you alive, Tristan?" He turns a tall, Elven ear to me.

"Your brother fucked me, and I liked it," I said to the floor, trying to maintain balance.

"My brother is handsome, and I wouldn't know, but rumor has it that he's good in bed."

"Ando, you know that's not why I'm struggling."

He whacked my arse. "Sir."

"Sorry, *sir.*"

"I know what you mean. But Corrik is gone. It makes no difference if you fuck my brother or not."

"So, you say. That's still up for debate. But let's say you are telling the truth and he is gone. Why has my heart moved on so quickly?"

He rubbed a hand over my bare arse. "That's your problem right there. You're thinking in Markaytian. Elves understand that you can't help who you're attracted to, which is why we are a polyamorous race —no need to choose between the two. Besides, you're obligated to please my brother in any way he requests. If you like it, that's probably better for you. Corrik would want that."

I still wasn't sure. "What about Markaytia? I haven't even tried to get away."

He laughed. "What would be the point trying? You can't. You're beating yourself up over things you have no control over. You need this spanking and probably a few more to get out of your head. I want you to let go, to stop thinking. This will hurt. After a time, your focus will be narrowed to the pain and when you reach that state of painful bliss, you'll have an easier time letting go."

He talked about it like he knew something of it on a deeper level. "Yes, sir."

His hand was crisp but lighter than Corrik's. Corrik was an expert at packing a lot of power into his swats, even while taking care that I am a human. I almost told Ando he could go harder, but that's not what one does. If he wanted to go easy on me, I was going to let him. Besides, there was still plenty of sting in each swat and after some time, my arse was tingling.

It was also embarrassing being spanked like that, knowing I *needed* it. That's a feeling that never quite goes away, at least it hasn't yet, but at the same time, it's part of where *that* feeling comes from, that special, unnamable one that lights your body abuzz and makes this whole spanking thing invigorating.

"Having any revelations down there?"

"Just that I want up, this isn't working, sir." I felt silly then. I was uncomfortable with the whole thing because I hadn't embraced it.

"I'm not whacking you hard enough, am I?"

Ugh. I was going to have to admit to that. "No, sir."

"It's the first time I've spanked a human like you," he said. "I am attempting not to break you."

"Then why *are* you spanking me?"

"Because you have a nice arse," he said, which was not a real answer, which meant I wasn't going to get one. "All right, brace yourself."

He increased the intensity and picked up the pace and okay, yeah, then it became a real spanking. I sucked wind and had to do some serious breathwork not to squirm too much. "I take it that's better?"

"Depends on your definition of better, sir," I said in sharp tones trying not to succumb to the fire that was building. But when he worked over my sensitive upper thighs, I couldn't keep still any longer and I squirmed, letting out a groan of misery. "Okay, that's. Ow. Andothair!"

For the use of his name over sir, I got five heavier smacks, and I cried out. Tears sprung to my eyes. He stopped for a moment and I apologized. "Sorry, sir. *Sir.*"

"Thank you."

And on and on it went. Andothair worked over my bare bottom at the same maddening pace and as the spanking carried on, the pain built up. The loudness of each smack, ringing off the marble in the room, defined the quiet. At least no one was around to watch, but that didn't mean someone couldn't come in at any time and there were always plenty of guards at any particular time who could hear us.

I didn't have time to give those thoughts my awareness; my world had narrowed to the pain. I breathed, and I kicked, and I squirmed, but nothing eased what Andothair was doing to my backside. The tears flowed freely, and I sobbed. Everything inside hurt too. I didn't know what had become of Corrik, and I had betrayed everyone.

I wanted Bayaden, I took that for myself.

I'm—I'm just selfish.

The tears dropped in fat rivulets and the agony that had become my arse helped me connect to a place within myself, like fire finding the wick of a candle.

Eventually, Andothair stopped and helped me stand, tossing my pants to me as I continued to sniffle. I could have gone longer. I felt some relief, but it wasn't complete. But, ugh. I wasn't going to ask for more.

"There now. I have work to do. Sharpen up, Tristan. It's time for you to move on from Corrik. The sooner you do that, the better off you'll be."

J only made it to the fifth boot before I threw it at the wall. I wanted to throw it at Bayaden, who said something scathing to me in Elvish, as I continued to pout. I also had a great need to antagonize Bayaden—I thought it would be fun to see what he would do if I grabbed that book out of his hand and whacked him over the head with it.

Would he turn me over his knee?

My bet was on that or attempted murder.

"You're not very good at that." His Markaytian surprised me.

"Course I'm not. I haven't polished boots since I was my father's squire. I hated it then too."

"I'd get used to it if I were you."

"I thought you weren't going to speak to me in Markaytian?"

He swung off the bed and I jumped a bit, *maybe more than a bit.* I'd gone too far.

The man is imposing in a deadly, beautiful way, like oleander, the flower of the underworld and even knowing him as I do now has never diminished these qualities.

I was envious, once again, of his dark hair as it swished around him. "You are driving me crazy. Why must you speak back to me? Do you have any idea what …" He tightened his hands into fists, ones I'm certain he wanted to put around my neck. I didn't know it then, but disobedience drives a Top (especially an Elven Top) crazy too. They need your submission in whatever way that manifests between the pair of you. "My brother was supposed to sort you out. Can I assume that he didn't?"

"He did. Some. Not all the way." I returned to my boot-polishing task, with renewed energy hoping if I did it long enough, he'd disappear.

He swore in Elvish. "You're going to go mad."

"So everyone keeps telling me."

"Why are you so stubborn?" He grabbed my arm and pulled me from the stool, the one that has become *my* stool. "Undress."

I pulled away from him. "No."

"You are supposed to do what I say."

He wasn't expecting it, which was the only reason I was able to do it. There was a knife on the table toward my right. I used every ounce of speed I had, snatching up the knife and putting it to his throat.

I drew some blood. He laughed and grabbed my wrist, the one holding the knife and pulled it away from his neck easily. "Good job, Tristan. If you had just stabbed, you might have injured me. But you hesitated, probably were about to attempt to threaten me—you can't do that though. I am Elf."

"And I'm a flea-ridden human. Yeah, yeah, I get it."

I expected anger, in the least Bayaden brand annoyance, but I got neither. Instead, his eyes were soft, with desperate lines wrinkling the corners. "Undress, Tristan. I want you again. I'll even let you keep the knife."

"I don't want you," I whispered, but even as I did, I felt my cock harden. His breath quickened in his large, muscled chest and he lifted me easily from under my backside as he started in on my mouth, my thick thighs wrapped around him. I dropped the knife. He kissed and sucked, and I responded, running my hands through the silk of his dark hair. He was gentle at that time.

He placed me on his bed, then ripped my pants off, the gentle slipping away, which made me feel better; the familiarity was good. He stopped there and stared down at me, looking over my body, his hand resting on my tattoo. He traced it. "What is it about you?" he said to himself, in Elvish. I was able to make the words out with the little of the language I knew at the time.

"What about me?" I asked.

"What *about* you?"

"You just asked, 'what is it about me?'"

"How would you know what I've said?"

"I know *some* Elvish."

"Your Elvish is terrible. That isn't what I said." Of course, he denied it. "Enough talking," he said. In one Elven-sized bite, he swallowed my cock, and I pushed against his head with my hands; *fuck*, he's good at sucking cock.

"Mhmmmm," I moaned, unable to help myself. *"Baya."* He popped his mouth off my cock then sucked it down again. "Gods!"

I lost track of how long he sucked, spellbound. My hips bucked in time with the rhythm of his mouth and I built to climax. Just before I could release in his mouth, he was gone, and I cursed him. He flipped me over savagely and his tongue was in my most private place. I had to grip one of his pillows tightly and slam my fist down, the sensation almost too much because it just felt naughty. I moaned again and tried to restrain myself. "I'm going to come if you don't stop that."

I felt the slippery lube in my arsehole, felt fingers and then his cock, slamming into me. When he came, so did I, both of us were left panting, him having collapsed over my back and me on the soft plush of his linens. They are so much comfier than mine. We were like that for only seconds until he was roughly rolling me off his bed and onto mine beside his. *Thud.* "Get back to work."

Arse.

I did, but only because I needed something to distract me. We'd just had sex *again,* and I just enjoyed it *again.* I polished the boots hard, channeling my mounting feelings into the task. I finished one boot and began another, but the feeling wouldn't leave me.

I polished the next boot until it had a hole—I knew Bayaden would be furious, but I smiled to myself, the itchy feeling still there, and I came to know something. It didn't matter what "everybody" said about me, it mattered what I said, how I felt about what I'd done. I have to carry the weight of my actions. If I could make the choice again, I'd make the same one, but I didn't expect to like it so much and that's what I felt I needed to repent for.

At the time I didn't know that there was any repentance for it.

I dropped the boot, the one with the hole.

I looked to Bayaden; he was fast asleep. I didn't bother to grab my pants, and crept out of the room, straight to Ando's.

"You again, already? I assume this has to do with my brother's intense sexual appetite?"

I wanted to slit his throat; I still might one day. "Please, not now," I begged. I knew the protocol and knelt before him bowing my head this time. "Will you, will you, do the thing, sir?" My voice was broken. I didn't want to ask him this; it was another way I was betraying Corrik. *Only Corrik had ever punished me quite like this.* "Spank me. Please." I had to push the words out, they felt unnatural on my tongue.

"Very well." He pushed his chair away from his desk and I remained kneeling in place like Corrik taught me; hands clasped behind my back with straight arms, arse cheeks resting on my heels, toepads pressing into the stone. "Up here, then."

Gracefully as I could, because it seemed formal, I rose to stand and placed myself over his lap. It was hard to believe that Tristan Kanes, former would-be-Warlord and Prince of Mortouge, would willingly put himself over his captor's knee, naked, *and ask* for a spanking.

But there I was.

He was business-like, not taking the time to stop and smell the roses like Corrik did; he started in right away, slapping each cheek methodically. Where Corrik might have helped me by way of a prompt, with Andothair, I was left to prompt myself. *Okay, Tristan, you can do this, why are you here? Why did you place yourself over his lap?* That was as far as I got into my "process" when I realized—*this bloody hurt!* "Oww! Okay, I've changed my mind, I don't need this, let me up. Let me up."

He ignored me and continued. The pain increased, and I started kicking, attempting to get up, figuring out that kicking decreased the pain somehow; I kicked more as I tried to escape. I threatened his kingdom, his brother, his manhood, but all he did was stop briefly to put one of his thick legs over both of mine, so I could no longer squirm and continued. I grew angry, but I received the message: He wasn't letting me up till this was over. Tears pricked my eyes over the frustration of the loss of control. I wanted it to be over, it *hurt*, I wanted to be off his lap.

I wished it were Corrik spanking me.

"We're going to be here all day if you don't let go, Tristan. Remember, my hand isn't going to get tired," he said. *That was still just his hand?*

He was right. I came here for a reason and I was getting it, whether I wanted it anymore or not. That's when I began to cry, and I used the pain to make me cry more. *Spanking is cathartic.*

I took that thought, that one seed, and used it combined with the only prompt Andothair gave me, and I now realize he knew just the right one to begin with—*let go*. So I did. I allowed myself to release the heavy feeling of betrayal for what I did with Bayaden. A small part of me felt like I was paying a price, though I knew instinctively that was not always what spanking was used for, it did make me feel better.

Elves must be born with the ability to sense when someone is content after a spanking—Andothair knew when to stop. I was in a euphoric daze. The pain in my backside flared, and at the same time I felt like I was floating. He guided me to standing and placed me in front of a wall. "Take a moment. Stand here and let the lesson sink in. When you are ready, you may leave, though I'll be at my desk if you should need anything else." He winked at me.

I rolled my eyes.

What was I supposed to let sink in? I didn't know. Instead, I let it all go. I was confused as hell and felt silly standing in front of a wall like I was a kid in time out, but it narrowed my focus to the marble I was facing so I wasn't distracted. I wouldn't have thought to do that on my own. I let all the feelings and sensations wash over me; I felt worked over, exhausted, but content. I stood there until I felt settled. I still couldn't say the feelings were completely abolished—they're there, lounging in the background—but I could move on with my day.

Until the next time.

And there would be a next time, because Bayaden and I would have sex again, and I would return until Bayaden eventually took over like Andothair said he would.

"*A*re you sorted now?" Bayaden asked when I returned. He was sitting on his bed, his back against the wall, looking out of the smaller window. He had an odd peace about him, his long hair like fresh spun silk in waves down his back. The leg against the wall was fully extended, the other bent, his bare foot planted on the mattress, an arm wrapped around the knee. I was tempted to call him soft, but I knew better.

"Yes."

"Come," he said, holding out a hand for me.

He caught my hand and pulled me to him, pressing me against his body, my back to his chest so I was looking out the window with him. The sun had just set, so there was only the last bit of glow over Aldrien before it was covered in purple darkness. "Shouldn't you be yelling at me to finish your boots?"

"Be quiet, for once."

Bayaden's body was unyielding yet being in his arms was a comfort after what had just happened with Andothair, so I relaxed into him, and stared out at the brand-new night with him. I don't know how long we stayed like that, but eventually, he was tearing down my pants. "Do you mind very much?" I said.

He didn't, and paid me no mind, checking out my backside, running a hand over the hot flesh there. When he was done, he gave my bum a hefty smack (which fucking hurt) and pulled up my pants. "Go to bed." He got up to do some things around his room

I rubbed my poor arse. *He was sending me to bed?*

It wouldn't be the last time I was spanked and put to bed, sometimes that's just the way with me.

I didn't argue and attempted to sleep, but I couldn't settle until he came to bed. I wasn't to learn his feelings for me till sometime after that, nor would I admit to mine until much later, but looking back, I suppose I can see how they were always there. He watched me, checking in on me, making sure I had enough to eat in concealed ways, taking care of me as he was compelled to do. I was comforted by him, he grounded me and in return I soothed his internal aches, giving to him with my form of submission.

We are mates and we knew it before we *knew* it.

CHAPTER 6

*W*ithout the speed of an Elf, there's a new meaning to pushing myself. The massive war Elf shows no mercy. His muscles contract and extend with power as his sword slams down like a hammer to a nail, that nail being me.

When I said without mercy, I might be exaggerating some. Bayaden has to hold back fighting at full capacity, else he will kill me. My cocky attitude over being able to best even a powerful Elf has been disproven many times over since I've been in Aldrien—a humbling experience to say the least. I pant as I heave my sword toward him, each move takes great effort. The sword alone is heavy, and it took months just for me to be able to lift it fast enough to make efficient moves. I spent a long-time doing drills Bayaden set for me.

The other warriors would make fun of me, but I didn't care. *Much.* More often, I used the anger to fuel me, practicing as many hours as Bayaden would allow.

Sweat pours off me, sliding down my skin, mixing with blood from minor cuts and scrapes I've earned practicing with Baya this afternoon. He's got a few too, but they're not from me, mere collateral as a result of our quick movements, brushing up against trees and anything else in the way.

Bayaden is a formidable fighter. There are times I pause to marvel at him, and it gets me into trouble, paying more attention to his beautiful style rather than fighting, which takes all my concentration if I am to stand any chance. His style is unique—large, lethal movements that shouldn't work, but because he's so precise, they do.

Dammit. Bayaden slams against my neck with a blow that would have been fatal, sending my head clean off my body. His face is close to mine, a sword piercing my neck. "You were admiring me again."

I smile. "A bit."

"Five lashes for that."

"Oh c'mon. Can you blame me?" His lips are close. We have to be somewhat careful on the field. Of course, Bayaden's allowed to do whatever he wants to me and everyone would welcome the Warlord showing his manservant his place as he fucked him up against a tree, but there's a difference between that and tenderness.

"You won't get better if I don't punish you. Now c'mon, up against that tree, accept your lashes like a warrior."

Bayaden punishing me, however, is good for business. His warriors approve of seeing Bayaden take his belt to me. "All right, all right. Worth it."

He's as precise with his belt as he is with his sword and I feel the imprint of each hit against my back, hissing with each, sharp *thwack*. When I've taken my five, he spins me, pressing me against the tree, alighting the stripes there with new pain, but I don't care, his lips are on me and I sink into that. I always let him lead and if he's going to kiss me like this, I assume he's caught us a moment with no one watching. When we break apart, Bayaden's got a smug smile on his face, his eyes glittering with mirth. "Do you find me that magnificent when I'm striving to kill you?"

"Don't let it go to your head."

"Too late, it's already gone to both of them."

I roll my eyes. "That it for today then?" I kind of hope so. I'm knackered.

"That's it for this. Come. We're going for a ride. I promised you frogs."

*W*e're high up. From this vantage point we can see all of Aldrien and the way Bayaden looks over his home-lands reminds me of the way I used to do the same in Markaytia. There are times Bayaden and I are like oil and water and other times I think we are the same. "Why did you bring me here?"

"Because I wanted peace."

I laugh. "With me? You know I'm not a peaceful companion."

He's lying on the grass and I move across him thinking I'm going to go off and explore, but I'm wrong. He grabs my ankle and my feet slip out from under me. Suddenly, I'm in the giant Warlord's arms, trapped. "I know how to tame you. If I want you quiet, I'll just stuff your mouth with my cock."

He smiles down at me and he's beautiful. He leans into kiss me and it's not long before I'm kissing him back with ravenous desire. I can't get enough of Bayaden. I love how large he is, I love that I can hang off of him, I love the feeling of safety he gives me. I'm the sort who can take care of myself, but there are things I have trouble handling inside and over time I've come to realize he eases that.

Like Corrik did.

The thought doesn't haunt me as much as it used to, as much as it *should.*

Elves are more open about such things than Markaytians are. It's not uncommon to see a brat running from his Top through the sand-stone hallways and many times, that brat is me. Bayaden can never officially be my Top, but he is a Master of sorts and we ended up falling into a natural brat-Top rhythm. I've asked him questions about it, I've asked others questions, and they were more than willing to share like Diekin was. It's a spectrum, with many designations and various subsets and levels within those designations.

I take pride in being a brat, especially when I've made some brat friends.

Tom isn't brat, though. He's got an inner submissive like Corrik was trying to train me to be. Tom and I relate, because we have many of the same qualities and inner wiring, but we differ in the *way* we need dealing with. Submissives need stricter guides and boundaries than us brats. They're also more likely to please and be good boys and girls.

Brats, we're a strange dichotomy. We need guides and boundaries too, but we also need room to run. And when we need the boundaries, we need ultra-firm ones, maybe even more so than a submissive, but as for the rest of the time, we need to be able to play and tease. "You need enough rope to hang yourself," as Bayaden often says, which I fought him on until it happened too many times and I was forced to consider it.

I was also forced to think back to being a kid and how Father handled me. He tended to lean more toward firm and was less likely to let my brat run free. But I think it was because he wasn't used to handling a brat.

When Bayaden releases me, he runs a hand through my hair, which is still short. I'm not permitted long hair, to remind me that I'm a slave of Aldrien and no longer Markaytian or Mortougian royalty. Oddly, I don't care much about the no longer being royalty thing, other than the conveniences it afforded me, which I admit, were nice, but now I feel like I don't belong to anyone, but myself.

Well, and Bayaden I suppose. But that I'm all right with.

I know it's odd that here I am a slave, finally feeling like I'm myself for the first time, but I do. I'm nobody, I have no larger obligations— Bayaden's boot closet notwithstanding—and after my duties for Bayaden, all I have to do is what I love—work hard at training practice.

I can be a Warlord, even though I have no army. Deglan's right, Warlord is who I am. I live and breathe those morals; I live to serve in that way. Recently, Deglan invited me to show my skill with a bow to the youngling Elves picking up their bows for the first time. My own mini-army.

"I know you're not smiling about me stuffing my cock in your mouth, what are you thinking about?"

"The kids. I love teaching them."

"I've noticed."

"You know, you do have warriors to train, you're not going to have them trained properly if you're watching me all day. Wasn't I punished earlier for swooning over you while training?"

He whacks my arse, which is now covered by the pants he had made for me. They match the tunic of my homeland, Markaytia. "You are an insufferable brat. I am Elf, I can do both at the same time. You cannot." Right. *Elves.* "You are good with them. I think you could teach my warriors a thing or two."

That is a high compliment from the resident Warlord. "Be still my heart. Did you just offer me a compliment?" It's one thing for him to say I'm good with the younglings, and something else entirely to say he'd trust me with his warriors. He nods. "You'd have a full-fledged mutiny on your hands."

Bayaden has grown fond of me, but the other warriors have not. "I could get them to obey me, but I cannot change their feelings and as you know, I need their hearts as well. A warrior cannot fight for an Elf he doesn't believe in."

"I know and I'm not offended, Bayaden. I don't care what they think of me."

He rolls on his back, so I am above him now and stares up at me. "You don't. I admire that. That's what will make you a good Warlord someday."

Wait a minute. "Bayaden, what are you … You know I'm never going to be a Warlord. Are you taunting me?" Because that's too far and we don't typically go that far anymore.

His eyes fill with tears. "No." He takes my hand. "It was all fun and games when we were just fucking, but Tristan, I *love* you, which means I cannot in good conscience keep you. I am a man of honor, what honor would I have if I didn't treat the one I love with respect?"

"Bayaden, what are you doing? Whatever it is, *stop* it." Because I'm going to start crying and it won't be just any kind of crying, but the kind that will break me apart. I know he's trying to do a good thing, but the fragile walls I've built can't handle the truth.

He takes my hand. "I can't keep you forever, but it's not time for you to go yet. Until that time."

He pounces on me and my new pants are quickly on the forest floor, his cock inside me. Bayaden thrusts into me over and over, the sounds of skin slapping together echo off the cliffside and toward Aldrien.

His tears drip softly to my chest.

---

*W*hatever happened on the clifftop, we're back to our version of normal by the time we return to the palace. I complained on the way back that we couldn't bring even one frog to which Baya replied, "If I find you've brought one, just one frog home, I will tan that pretty backside of yours good."

The look he gave me said he wasn't messing about, so I refrained from my usual bratting. I'll have to find another way to antagonize Andothair.

"Tristan?"

"Uh?" We're back in his chambers, he's in his closet and I'm lazing about. Not the sophisticated way of a dedicated manservant, but then again, I'm not a dedicated manservant.

"Do you happen to know where my white blouse went? I need it for dinner tonight," he says removing his cuffs by himself for once.

My skin prickles. *This is the dinner, isn't it?*

I hop up and begin to remove my nice clothes—the only other set I have—and change into the clean but worn-out beige pants. I've had to use some of my mother's sewing lessons to patch and repatch certain places.

Before I get a chance to answer, he looks me up and down. "Tristan, you know I am not in a position to give you clothes. It's complicated, like with not being able to have you train my warriors. Why have you not stolen more in all this time?"

I squint at him. I don't have an answer, at least not one that makes sense. "You said I could acquire these."

73

"Do you mean to tell me that's the directive you chose to obey all this time, while you've disregarded so many others?"

"I guess. I don't know. I'm complicated."

"You most certainly are. It's just as well; I like seeing how clever you can be."

"Wait, if you can't give me clothes, how were you able to give me my tunic and the matching pants?"

"I have reason enough for that if I'm asked. You train on my field and it's within my jurisdiction to grant you a uniform if I feel you've earned it. Your work with the younglings allowed for it."

"Well, I do like being clever. I shall have more clothing by nightfall."

He smiles. "Good. You should know I don't plan on making it easy for you. Now, where is my shirt?"

Shite. I haven't come up with an excuse that's good enough. "It's right there. Are you blind?" I strut over to the closet and pull any white blouse from a hanger. They all look the same to me. "Here."

His brow raises. "That's not the one."

"This one?" I try handing him each white blouse successively and even a blue one I claim will look better on him. And then, "Maybe you don't need one at all. You look handsome in your battle armor."

"Come here little human," he says figuring it out.

I briefly glance at the door before I try to make a run for it. It's easy for him to catch me and toss me over his shoulder. I kick and bang on his back to no avail; it's like beating on a mountainside. He swings out a chair and stands me before him in a ritual that has become formulaic for us. "Are you going to tell me now, or while you're over my knee, hmmm?"

I contemplate which I'd prefer, because either way, I'm going over his knee. "I don't even know how it happened. I suck at laundry, Bayaden!"

"Tristan."

"Fine. It somehow ended up with a red splotch on it, and then it became fire kindling."

"How did my fine shirt become fire kindling?" he says with a hard edge to his voice.

"Because I threw it in the fire in hopes you wouldn't find out. You have so many, how can you tell the bloody difference?"

His mouth forms a line and then his fingers are at my waistband, pulling them down, baring me for the spanking I'm about to get and over his knees I go. Bayaden knows what a warrior I am and therefore how much I can take, so he's not easy on me. His hand is leaden, coming down on each cheek in successive sets of five.

My arse is quickly on fire and I'm squirming and kicking, trying to free myself, which is a useless endeavor and happens to be something else I like about this—being manhandled, unable to get away. "I'm sorry! I'm sorry all right?"

"That's the fourth shirt this month, and I liked that one best." He keeps spanking me.

"Ow! Baya-aaayowwch! You have seventeen others."

I'm flushed in more places than my backside, it's still embarrassing getting a spanking like a child when you're a grown man, even if you need it. Any person could knock at any time and they do. Bayaden lets them stroll right in. Does that mean he'll let me up? No. If I want to misbehave, then such is my fate.

When he finally lets me stand up, after the spanking from hell, I pout at him, but I feel better even with my arse afire. Sometimes I don't even know I need a spanking until after the fact. I think that's why his shirts "mysteriously" end up ruined. He pulls me in for a kiss with my pants still down. "That was naughty, brat."

"You really do look better in the blue one, you know," is my answer, because yes, I'm a bit naughty and I can't deny it. In my defense, Bayaden brings it out in me. I pull my pants up.

"All right, fetch me the blue one then."

I race off to get it. "What's going on tonight anyway?" Bayaden is a Warlord, Warlords don't dress fancy for anything. They wear their finest armor and that's as lucky as you get.

"A dinner." So he's still not going to tell me. "I'll need my tall black boots unless you have another suggestion?" His brow quirks over a dark eye, his smile half-formed.

"No, the black boots, but with pants."

He wrinkles his nose. He's not fond of pants. "If I must."

"And your hair tied back. I'll do it for you."

"I would appreciate that. Very well. I will go bathe. You'll need to look nice too. For that I can have you done up."

"I will be presentable." I'm more worried than I was before. He's never had me come to his fancy dinners. He hates them in the first place and only goes because he is required.

"I see that look in your eyes. Don't ask questions. Now go before I think you need another spanking." Bayaden's gruff as usual—by the Gods he can be infuriating—but there's something behind his eyes.

Still, I can't allow him to talk to me like that and give him cheek right back. "Yes, my Liege."

"*Out!*"

I leave, before he smacks my arse again, laughing all the way.

---

*W*hen Bayaden is dressed for the event, I can't stop staring. He's magnificent in blue, his large biceps pressing into the long sleeves. The shirt tapers into his solid black pants, which are tucked into the boots I polished for him—the best job I've done yet—and his long hair tied into a ponytail at the nape of his thick neck that stands out under his square jaw.

I'm proud of myself for dressing him so nicely and at the same time, I'm smirking. He's like a schoolboy dressed up for mass with the way he's scowling, and I'd say so to him if he knew what it meant to go to church—Elves believe in the Gods, but they do not attend mass. He hates dressing up. "My, you look fetching," I say.

"I look all wrong. I'm a warrior, not a socialite."

"Here, this will make you feel better." I hand him one of his favorite swords, sheathed in its baldric. He straps it onto himself, so the sword sits at his hip. I realize I'm the only one who ever sees

Bayaden without a weapon. The large Warlord always has a weapon or several on his person. The only time he removes them is when he's in his chambers, or on mountainsides with me.

Having the sword does make him feel better and I can see it as soon as the sword is securely around him. "I like you naked better," he says.

"For the Gods' sake. I spent all afternoon cleaning myself up, I won't have you ruin me."

He smirks. "I suppose flea-removal takes a while does it?"

I glare at him. I know he's joking, but still. "Would you like me in nothing but my collar, sir?"

He grunts, which means no. "Tristan? Did you hope to have children someday?"

I stare at him before I can answer. First, there was his behavior on the mountainside and now this. "I wanted an heir to succeed me as Warlord until I had my title stripped. With Corrik, it was part of the marriage contract. We were obligated to have at least six, but as many as we wanted after that, or we could stop."

"Forget about all that. What did *you* want?"

What I want is a foreign concept. "I think I might have liked four, but much later. I was going to be gifted immortality. I would have liked to wait a few hundred years."

He nods. "Come here." I go to him and he pulls me to him. "We could never have children, Father wouldn't allow that, but if we did, what do you think they would have been like?"

I can't help the immediate thoughts that come to mind. "The Gods help us, they would have double Warlord in them, dragon blood, and Elven. They'd be so stubborn, and you'd be so annoyed."

He smiles. "They would obey me."

"They would, you'd be a strict Father like mine was, but they would love you fiercely like I do mine." I enjoy the thought for a moment. "What about me? Would I have made a good Papa?"

"You would have coddled our children, except for on the field; there you are a barbarous taskmaster."

I can't deny any of that. "They would have been magnificent warriors."

"*Las nah*," he says, an Elvish expression for "all is well" or "not to worry," but my heart now aches for our stubborn children. "We agree on something."

It will anger him, but I have to ask. "Baya, what's going on?"

He plays with the tag at my throat. "Don't ask questions. Just obey me for once. I mean it, Human. Best behavior or I shall spank your bare bottom right in front of everyone." He turns heel sharply. "Come."

Something is coming, something that's going to shatter me. But I follow him because however much this is going to hurt me, Bayaden is hurting several times over.

I keep close as I've been instructed. There is protocol in situations like this. I am the servant and I'm to stick by my master. I may only refer to him as Master, which Bayaden enjoys far more than he should in my opinion. I get to sit beside him though, and not on the floor as some humans are made to. Apparently, being the Warlord's manservant does afford me some status if Bayaden should decide I've earned it. But also, it's not really Baya's thing. He likes some bedroom play, but for every day, he enjoys our brat-Top dynamic over a more submissive one.

Tom kneels at King Caer Gai's feet, his perfect kneeling posture a thing to behold and admire from afar—people can look, but they can't touch. As usual, he's to keep his focus on the king and he does it well. Tom adores the king, which is the only reason I hesitate regarding the king at all. I don't know what the king's up to, but it's something nefarious. Tom's faith in him has me wondering if the king's not simply in over his head.

I'm in a new environment and I can't help what's been trained in me since birth by both my parents. I survey my surroundings and look for oddities, familiarities and odd familiarities. The first thing I notice is an Elf in a hooded robe on the other side of the room. He stands out because he's trying to blend in, and he does blend in for everyone, but not for someone like me. To me he's a sore thumb, sticking out, throbbing red. People don't notice him, because he's older, and he's attempting to come across as frail, but he isn't frail. Under those robes, he's quite large, you can tell by a person's neck and jawline. Plus, he looks like someone I know well. "Which family member of yours is he, Master?" I whisper. I'm not supposed to speak unless spoken to, which is why Bayaden gives me a glare to defeat all glares and I have the wisdom to cow. I can't help myself though, this is yet another reason I was not cut out to be a manservant. "You look like him."

"You will meet him soon enough, little human."

Little human. He can't be that mad at me. I almost reach out to touch him, but I remember just in time. Bayaden and I have lived on top of each other this past year. We're used to touching each other in some way, whether that be on the field, passing by, in the bedroom, or while eating, which he often does with me in his lap these days.

I am the spoiled pet who gets to lie about on the furniture.

It's natural for us to be within close proximity, a hand resting on my thigh, him tugging me around by the waistband of my pants, one of us dropping a kiss to the lips or some place on the other's body. I often grip onto his long hair for comfort, or just so he knows I'm there. I soothe the restless Warlord and he brings me contentment.

When dinner is over, people mingle except for Bayaden to his father's dismay. Bayaden's the kind who sits and waits for you to approach him. He really is the most anti-social person I've ever met.

Unless you're talking war, weapons, or strategy, he has no interest in you.

"Get up and talk to someone," King Caer Gai hisses at him in Elvish. "Else why did you bother to attend?"

"Was there an option not to attend?" Bayaden says, also in Elvish.

His father gives him the same look I've seen on Bayaden many times, and it usually means, *"Tristan, you're walking on thin ice,"* which are of course my words, I doubt Bayaden's ever seen ice, but either way it means that Bayaden had better get up and mingle. He stands and signals for me to come.

Aldrien has been banished from the Elven realm indefinitely. The king hosts these dinners to form alliances with other races. Even alone as it is from the seven Elven realms, Aldrien is still powerful and holds sway due to their connection to magic that comes from the ether. Of course, they still want what they can't have which is to reunite with the Elven realm, and if they can't have that, then it must be destroyed.

"Tristan, this is my uncle Taj," he says in Elvish since he can't be seen talking to his manservant in Markaytian. Baya and I move back and forth between Elvish and Markaytian. No real rhyme or reason as to why we speak which language when.

I think that may be the one thing I'm grateful to Andothair for, the Elvish lessons. After a year of lessons and immersing myself in Elven culture, I can speak Elvish fluently, even if it doesn't sound as nice as when Baya speaks it. "Pleased to meet you, Tristan," he says. I like his eyes; they remind me of Bayaden.

"Uncle Taj comes and goes," Bayaden explains, his Elvish accent strong. "He lives alone and travels a lot."

I feel it in the air: something's going on, I don't know what, but this meeting with his uncle is meaningful. I'm used to speaking Elvish to Bayaden, and others on the field, because Bayaden makes me, but I still get nervous breaking it out for others. I know my accent isn't amazing; it's embarrassing, but I give it a shot anyway. "Nice to meet you, sir." I bow my head rather than extending my hand in greeting, I'm still a lowly servant, I'm not to be so familiar.

"I'm sure we'll get to know each other well enough soon."

My head snaps to Bayaden. Because what the fuck does that mean? My dragon blood rages.

Bayaden's as gruff as he always is. "We'll speak to you later, Uncle." He ushers me away. "Don't say a word, Human."

His tone says cross him and get spanked right here, so I keep quiet, but I'm fuming. He's got something planned for *me* and he did it in secret because he knew I wouldn't agree to it. But surprises aren't done happening. The king is back, and he's brought with him the king from Dominithia and his son. The Dominithia are a race of green people. They look Markaytian, but with pastel green skin. After formalities, the Elven king introduces the prince. "Bayaden, this is Prince Sancytha, I told you about him."

Bayaden hardens. "You have, Father." He grunts a hello to the prince who does not look like he wants to meet Bayaden at all.

The Elven king forces a conversation in what I assume is Dominithia, a language I know nothing of, in which Bayaden is his taciturn-self and the Dominithiaian prince looks like he wants to vomit things his skin color. He is a handsome prince, with gorgeous dark hair (I always notice hair) but he's the kind who will break like the glass meant for these kinds of fancy parties. He's not meant for war. I don't know what they speak of, but I can tell Bayaden is not a fan of whatever's being said. Bayaden's Dominithia is as polished as the prince and the Dominithiaian king's and I can't help but admire how smart he is.

I pick up on the feel of the conversation, which is uneasy all around.

Eventually, it ends and Bayaden stalks off. I have to quicken my pace to catch up to him. "What was that all about?" I hiss at him.

"Be quiet," he snaps looking around. Right, I'm not good at following the rules.

At long last, the night ends. Bayaden is furious and I'm annoyed. I know Bayaden has no obligation to me, but I've gotten used to him telling me things that have to do with me. When we get back to his chambers, I round on him as he's shutting the door, ready to tell him all about what I think of him and whatever the hell tonight was, but when he faces me, his eyes are wet. *Crying*, but also hard, vulnerable, and filled with need. Crying has got to be the worst thing I'll ever see Bayaden do. It's at least ten times worse seeing the great Warlord cry than any other person I've met because it's more heartbreaking for some unnamable reason. We come together in a kiss and he lifts me so I can grip around his wide torso with my strong legs.

We're both wild with passion, quickly divesting ourselves of the fancy clothes we spent an eternity dolling ourselves up in and it's not long before we're dirty again, with blood and sweat and come. We fuck several times and we mark each other and when we're ready to rest on his bed in the moonlight, we're stained in each other's fluids and scent. "Did you manage to find clothes today, little human?"

"Is my name Tristan Arcade Kanes?" I remember briefly that legally, I'm not Tristan. I'm Kathir Tahsen Cyredanthem, but I don't feel like Prince Kathir. I'm not even sure I'm a Kanes anymore. I'm just Tristan and that's fine with me.

"Of course, you did. All right, it is time for sleep, we've got a big day tomorrow."

I move to roll off his bed and go to mine, but he doesn't let me leave, slinging his large arm over me, trapping me beside him. "I don't think so, you stay here. I might need you again in the night."

But he doesn't and we both sleep soundly next to each other not talking about the things that happened at dinner.

CHAPTER 7

I line up my warriors. Elves are permitted to train young, the equivalent of a pre-teen in Markaytia, but these Elves have been in the world at least thirty years. Some of them barely reach the middle of my torso, but they are Elven children and many of them can run circles around even me. I'm not really in charge, Deglan is, but she trusts me to take them through the standard training exercises without her instruction and some of my own she's approved of.

Some of these Elves will be the future archers of the Aldrien army. Deglan decides who will be presented to Bayaden's general and the general will work with that crew until she has a few Elves she can present to Bayaden for selection.

Bayaden is aware of my choices. I informed him as to who was going to make it and who wasn't. I'm certain and when I'm right, I'll tell Bayaden I told you so. I might be old and grey by that point, but I'll make a scene about it no matter what age.

It's weird to think that I'll be so old-looking while Bayaden will remain young. Becoming Elf is off the table for me now and so I will grow old and die within a regular human lifetime. I never thought too much about becoming an Elf—it was what I had to do, as part of the marriage contract. There's a bit of relief, the thought of living for so long was hard to contemplate. A human can't comprehend time in that way.

"I want fifty rounds through the obstacle course," I tell them once I've shown them what to do. I get some scowls, but they don't dare argue. I can't do anything about them if they do, but Deglan can; I reported them to her, and they eventually learned to behave for me. I'm still proud of every one of them as I watch them progress, even the ones who hate me. Not all of them think I'm human scum, though. A few appreciate and even seem to like me.

They return tired. I've gotten good at finding ways to exhaust them. "All right. You can head to the baths," I tell them in Elvish.

"Thank you for today, sir," Coldera says. "You're a good teacher."

The little guy smiles at me and I ruffle the dark hair on his head. He's the smallest of the pile and I tend to worry he won't make it. "Thank you. Happy to be of service."

When we're on, we're *on* and I don't allow for such softness. I'm more like Father on the field. But off, I'm all Papa. They know the difference. Bayaden joins me as Coldrea scampers off. He yanks me to him. "We're done for the day," he declares.

"Oh, we?" It's early to be heading off the field.

"Yes." He stares at me, his smile soft like his eyes. "I'm exhausted and my cock isn't going to suck itself."

I whack him. "Bayaden."

"It is your job."

"I'm telling your sister on you," I say.

"What's my brother doing now?" she says coming behind us.

"He's being his usual arrogant self," I tell her, still looking at him, trying to memorize him.

Something big's going to happen, my gut reminds me.

Without warning, he lifts me over his shoulder, bow and all, giving a hefty swat to my arse. "I don't deny it," he says, as I complain for him to put me down; all my demands go ignored. "We'll be occupied for some time Deglan. I'll need you to finish up here."

"I can do that." I can't see her, but I feel her smirking at me. "Good luck to you Tristan."

84

"You never liked me!" I shout.

I can't see her but her tinkling laugh imprints into my memory.

I have to suffer the embarrassment of being carried across the grounds. "Do you intend on carrying me the whole way?"

"Yes."

"I hate you, for the record."

"Noted."

We travel through the palace, no one paying too much mind to us, except for a couple of guards who love to see me in such predicaments. "What did you do now, Tristan?" one of them says to me, his fine Elvish reminding me how much I still need to work on my accent.

"Wait till I'm upright again," I curse at them.

"*Tristan,*" Bayaden warns.

I can get away with some of my banter with Bayaden because we have a special relationship, but it's not how I'm supposed to treat Elves. I settle down, having learned about creating trouble I can't handle. Bayaden is as obligated to the rules as I am. "Sorry, but they're the worst," I say as Baya continues to cart me off.

"They are."

We don't head to his chambers like I expect; instead we go to *the room*. I should have known with the way he was looking at me on the field.

It was a couple of months into my "enslavement," just after I promised myself to Bayaden forever, in exchange for them releasing Diekin that Bayaden went all territorial and brought me to this very room, chained me up and strapped me for the first time.

It feels like forever ago.

We've been back many times since for a variety of reasons, punishment being at the top of that list. I'm not a well-behaved pet.

But I know I haven't done anything to earn a punishment, not recently anyway. We're here for another reason.

He sets me to my feet and because there's no one here today, I can let him have it. "Carry me like that again Bayaden, and I'll gut you in your sleep."

Bayaden snickers. "You wouldn't. Who would you have to spank your naughty bum?"

No one is here, but I flush anyway. I don't, however, deny I need him to do that. I understand something fundamental about myself—I am a brat. Brats need handling in a different way than a submissive does and Bayaden seems to know just how. He lets me run and then reels me in with a sound spanking. He's strict but relenting at the same time.

What would've happened between Corrik and I?

He wanted a submissive husband. And it's not that brats are not submissive, we are, but it's in a different way than someone who weighs more heavily toward the submissive end of the spectrum.

Bayaden is no less strict, but there's a give there; I need that bit of freedom.

I don't mean to smile in return, but I do. "What are you going to do with me?"

His dark eyes sparkle. "Wouldn't you like to know? Undress."

The room has areas, and each area has a variety of equipment. The area Bayaden's chosen for us has a high bench with tall posts in each corner—like a four-poster bed but a bench in the middle. As I undress, Bayaden pulls out rope and my cock is hard at the prospect of what he might do, even though it's likely to be a very long time before he gets any kind of release. "Lie back on the bench," he says.

"Yes, sir." There is still a bit of protocol when we do these things, like with spanking, but it's not as formal. Bayaden just isn't the formal sort of person and it comes through in everything he does.

The only exception being when he's on the field. He takes that seriously. If he doesn't Elves can die.

My nakedness always feels *more* when Bayaden is clothed, the text-book symbol of power exchange. "Bend," he says, and I know he means my left leg. He begins tying my calf to my thigh, with the sole of my foot flat on the bench. "When I first saw you, I didn't like you much."

It's a random thing to say, he hasn't talked about that in a long time, though maybe it's not so random and maybe this is a whole lot of foreshadowing to the *thing*, the thing I can feel but can't touch. I pay attention. "That's an understatement. We *hated* each other. Passionately if I remember."

He begins working on my other leg. "Did we though? I tend to think that underneath all the dislike, there was something."

I didn't believe Deglan when she told me how much the Warlord had taken to me, but after an explosive two months of hate-sex, he dragged me around everywhere and it became clear. Sure, I'm his manservant, but no I didn't need to be attached at his hip. He doesn't even sleep without me any more like I'm some kind of fucking teddy bear.

I pretend to mind, but he knows better. I'm happy to follow him like a puppy. "There was something," I tell him. With my legs tied the way they are, I'm exposed, my hard cock throbbing at the thought of how I'll look to anyone walking in because anyone could walk in and they'd see me spread for Bayaden like this. I could close my legs, but I don't. Baya will just swat them open.

"You were such a brat, but I … I got excited to see what you would do next."

"You just liked getting to spank me."

"I'll never deny that." His smile is wide enough to show his sharp, Elven, eye-teeth. Next, he works on tying my arms open in a T-shape, flattened against the bench, but attaching cuffs to each wrist and clipping them to straps that hang from the posts. Now I'm vulnerable for whatever he'll do, I shiver.

"If someone told me I could fall in love with a human, I would have had them banished."

"Don't hurt yourself over it," I snark at him.

He swats the side of my arse. "I'm trying to tell you something if you'd behave for two minutes."

I laugh. "Shutting up, sir."

"I no longer think about humans as I used to. I never should have; you've changed me."

My heart clenches and I don't want to think about why he's getting like this. I don't even know how he'd, how *we'd* separate if we tried.

Aside from obvious Andothair compilations, I made a loyalty oath through magic. Can it be undone? Regardless, I don't want to go there, so I act my usual self. "Damn right you never should have. Elves I tell you. The lot of you are arrogant fools."

He scowls. "That's it. You're in a bad position to be so cheeky."

"Do your worst, Warlord." Something you should never say to the Elven Warlord.

"I plan to."

His fingers ghost up and over my bent knee and up my thigh. I feel every callous, every mark he left on his skin, preferring to keep the proof of his hard work rather than allowing it to heal away. He visits my cock too soon, to tease it and my hips buck off the table. "Please."

"We have a long way to go before you're getting that."

Arse!

He circles his large finger at my hole, I'm powerless to do much more than lay back, surrender, and attempt not to be too needy, but it's hard. He knows all my buttons. He whispers the spell and somehow my body makes a slick that lubes my entrance and allows his finger to slide in. I breathe through the initial burn, sighing happily when he's all the way in. As he relaxes my opening, he leans over top of me, his hot lips meet mine and he sighs into them.

I tug at my bonds, not trying to escape, trying to chase his lips, get closer, feel him.

The throb in my cock turns into an ache, the arousal already getting too much. It's like this whenever he ties me up—the sensation of being vulnerable sends me reeling. I start to get just a tad floaty. His fingers pump in and out, I feel both his calloused knuckles and can't help pushing down, spreading my legs wider.

"Bet you'd like my cock in here, uh?" he says, breathless. My moaning and writhing are affecting him too; he can't fool me.

I want to be snarky, but as he always says, I don't have to come, and I want to. "Please, sir. I've been so good."

"You have, for *you* anyway." He's not wrong. I did throw his shirt in the fire, but that's nothing. He smiles into my lips continuing to kiss me, still broadening my entrance so I can take his large cock. His fingers pull away and his mouth makes its way down my torso, sucking hickeys along my ribs, making me laugh when it tickles and cry out when he uses teeth.

A lot of our fucking is rough, as rough as he can be with a human. It leaves me marked and bruised up most of the time. In Elvish culture, the amount your lover marks you is a sign of how much you're loved—you would only mark up someone you can't resist. Conversely, your partner bears the marks proudly and can give you some of their own.

Most slaves are lucky to get any marks. It happens to Tom, who is adored by the king, but it's never been to the extent I've had.

Bayaden can't resist marking me, sinking his teeth into the tender skin of my inner thigh, enjoying my yowl. *That's going to stick around.* He uses his tongue to lick up my taint and to the base of my cock and laughs when I whimper and struggle. "Be still my pet human. I'm not done with you yet."

Ooooh!

He pulls out a soft flogger. He's intent on being gentle today—not that the tails don't hurt, they sting against the places he's bitten me— showing me a kind of worship. The flogger licks over my body, raising the skin in a pleasant way, still bringing enough pain to keep me interested, otherwise it would be too much of a snooze.

I arch and move with his continued whacks, tugging at my bonds wanting him to stop and keep going at the same time. Sweat drips off me and marks form from pulling on the wrist straps too tightly.

Finally, Bayaden can't take it anymore either, which is not like him. Usually, the large Elf can tease me into the seventh realm of hell for hours. But already, he's lining his cock up with me and sliding in. "Put your legs around me."

Starting slow, he slides in and out, picking up speed as I cling onto him with my thighs, my legs still tied. Using what little leverage I have, I pull him to me as he starts to pound hard, and it's a good thing I'm tied to this bench and have straps to grip, or I'd fall off. Bayaden's at full force, lost to lust, his sharp teeth glinting.

He's a sight to behold when he's like this; I crane my neck to watch his massive body heaving and his strong arms flexing to hold the weight of my hips since I can't take the full weight with the way my legs are tied. I love the way his long hair flies and whips with his movements.

He's magnificent.

Everything builds, all the sensations together; the hot skin, the bruised flesh, Baya's cock against my prostate. My cock is leaking. "Baya, *Baya. Sir.* Please. *Please* say I can come."

His dark eyes get darker as he bites and licks his lips. "Come, my Tristan."

I come hard and have to pull on the straps as my back arches like a wheel, Baya maintaining his grip on my thighs so he can keep me linked to him and his cock inside me. He moans in ecstasy as he releases inside me and then collapses on top of me.

I'm spent, far away on the floaty clouds of subspace as he unties me, and it barely registers that I'm free and he's carrying me (bridal style this time) back to his chambers. I realize I'm on his bed when he nudges me to drink water. "You passed out," he says.

I roll my eyes. "That's what you get for doing that to me after training."

"You enjoyed yourself, don't deny it."

I beam at him. "I did."

He feeds me fruit and we lie together a long time—not our usual. He has food brought up for dinner rather than having me go get it—and it reminds me that something's up. Horrible as I may be at my job, that's still my job.

I continue to avoid the topic knowing it's something I don't want to hear. I remember something I wanted to ask him earlier. "Will you want me when I'm old and grey?"

The creases of his eyes constrict. "What kind of a question is that?"

"I'm not going to become Elf, I'll get old and die while you preserve your gorgeous luster."

"I am gorgeous."

I whack him. "Answer the question."

"I will always want you. Even if you grow spots, or all your hair falls out."

I grab my hair like it's about to fall out now. "No. It's short enough as it is. You can't let that happen. Can't you do some kind of Elven voodoo to make it stay?"

He tilts his head. "You miss this don't you?" He cards a hand through it.

"I do. I loved my hair as much as I love Markaytia."

"That's a lot." He pauses. "Speaking of things you love, do you still love Corrik?"

And there it is. The question that's been building. The Corrik box was opened and he won't be denied any longer, it's a breathing, living thing that wants to know. My stomach tightens. "I love him. I'm sorry. But it doesn't detract from what I feel about you."

It really doesn't. In the same way a Mother loves all her children, I love Corrik and Bayaden the same. The relationships are not the same, but the amount of love is.

"Please don't be mad."

"I'm not."

"You've destroyed many things being upset about my love for Corrik, including my arse."

"I know. But in my defense only when I was aroused." Aroused Elves can be territorial. "I've remembered I'm an Elf and we Elves are polyamorous creatures. You can love us both."

"Then why all the possessive posturing?"

"Because I am. Can't help it sometimes, doesn't mean I don't understand it when I'm of sound mind."

"It doesn't matter anyway. Corrik's not here ... or is this your strange way of telling me you want someone else in on this?

He squeezes me to him, tightly. "No. No one else. It's time for sleep, Tristan."

"But it's barely—"

"—don't argue."

A bit of the old Bayaden seeps into him, the cool Warlord who hated humans. But this time I know it's because he's guarding himself from breaking apart. "You're staying with me?" I ask. I'm not sleeping by myself tonight, not after all that.

"I'm staying with you."

I nod and close my eyes.

*I*t's dark and Bayaden's shaking me awake like he often does. "Tristan, I need you."

From there, it's teeth and hot lips and bruising fingers. Bayaden is consumed with need. His dark eyes glitter in the moonlight, as he sinks into me and he's wild, flipping me over, tossing me, covering me with marks not caring where he places them.

I do the same. I always give just as much as I get when we fuck. I scratch down his back and he cries out, I bite into his flesh hard enough to draw blood. You have to bite hard to sink your teeth into Elven flesh and even then, you've got to be careful as a human. I've had my teeth mended through magic a few times from biting Baya in places that are too tough. Their skin is softer just above where the neck meets collarbone and a few other places. I also suspect some areas are specific to Bayaden. He love-hates when I bite where the inner thigh meets crotch. It makes him hard, but it also fucking *hurts* if the sound he makes is anything to go by—he won't admit it though.

It's not until I'm on top looking down on him, fucking away on his cock that I notice.

Hair. *My* hair.

It's surrounding me, everywhere, already sticky with sweat. Sex is halted while I run fingers through, admiring the silky texture. He gave it back to me, my gorgeous dark hair, only, there are improvements. Mixed in with the black are streaks of blue and purple. I stare at it in awe, relishing in the way it feels to run my fingers through it again and I never run out of hair as my arm extends to full-length; there's another solid few inches below that point which I allow to fall away from my fingertips. "It's beautiful."

I cry, the tear drops thick because if he's given me this, I know it's time to say goodbye. This means I have a station again—*can't have station as a slave.*

"Yes. They represent your colorful personality, or perhaps the colors your arse turns after a run-in with my paddle, haven't decided." He succeeds in making me laugh through the tears that stream down my face. "But really, it's so that you have something of me, surrounding you, forever. No one can cut this. Well, they can try, it will grow back by nightfall."

I bend down to kiss him, sniffling; it's a wet, messy kiss.

Bayaden must see I'm about to fall apart, he flips us so he's on top again, taking over. "Are you going to come for me, little human?" he whispers, hot into my ear. Bayaden hits my prostate just so, reaching out to stroke my cock until all the sensations are too much and I come despite my crying.

He's not far behind me, releasing his seed into me. I know it's for the last time.

The large war Elf stares down at me, suddenly turned to stone. "It's time for you to go, Tristan."

I knew this was coming, but I won't accept it. "What do you mean? *No.* I'm here with you. I stay with you. That was the deal."

"No. It was never right. Andothair should never have taken you, I never should have accepted you."

"I'm a spoil of war, Bayaden. I always knew there was a chance for this, especially had I become Warlord. All's fair in love and war."

"Love and war are never fair, no one knows that better than you and I." He can't move, he's fixed in one spot, hardening himself for this moment. "Don't make this harder than it already is."

"I don't want to go back, Bayaden. Please don't make me." I can't help the tears that keep coming, but if they serve to make him feel guilty, then good. This is a terrible thing to do.

The tears soften him some. He switches to my home tongue, to Markaytian. "You are like me, Tristan. Your first duty is to your homeland, everything else is secondary."

"Screw Markaytia. Markaytia abandoned me and shipped me off with Elves."

"No. The marriage might have been arranged, but you didn't fight it. You did so with pride, for your people. The dishonor you feel not fulfilling your side of the bargain has you burning up my shirts at two a week."

"Is this about shirts? I'll get better at laundry. I'll have Mary teach me. I'll be so good at it. They'll say 'that Tristan, he was once good with a sword, but you know what he's better at? Laundry. Stains beware.'"

He smiles a watery smile. "I'm going to miss your nonsense."

"No. You don't have to miss it; you can keep it right here."

He shakes his head. "It's tearing you apart Tristan. I understand. I am the same," he says taking my hand and putting it over his heart. "My father wants me to marry the prince from Dominithia and I'm going to. I know the prince doesn't want to marry me all that much, and I don't blame him, but Father is right, it's a good match. They are a strong kingdom. I'm pants at all the politics and the prince clearly doesn't know the sharp end of a sword. We will balance each other, it will work."

"I'm fine with that. I will service you both, happily. Tell me, do you think his come is green too? I could get on board with green come."

He laughs, then he frowns. "There's something else, Tristan. Father knows I've gotten too close to you. He was fine with it, for the time, but he says it's gone as far as he can allow it to with a human. He likes you though. You have a knack for making the most unlikely of us fall for you, which is why I got any choice at all—I am to make arrangements for you to leave, or he'll have you executed."

"What does Andothair think of all this?"

"He doesn't know. We're not going to tell him until it's done. He'll be angry, but he'll calm down since they're Father's orders."

I nod, a thousand things running through my head. You don't always get to know when it's going to be the last time for something. Today was my last day in Aldrien, that's why Baya cut us out of training early. I don't want to think of sad things, so instead I remember something else. "Wait, aren't the Domi one of the races in which the men can have babies?"

"Yes."

"You're going to have green babies," I say picturing it, but instead of it being funny like it should be, my heart is breaking. I want our stubborn, warrior babies.

"Let's hope I can teach one of them to be half as good with a bow as you are."

"Good luck without me there to teach them properly." I put my arms around him and cry. I know he's right. We're both far too duty-bound for our own good. Aside from the fact that his father would never allow him to marry his *human* manservant, his father needs that match. I am good at politics, my parents—all three of them—made it so and I know this marriage would secure strength so that if they do attack Mortouge, they stand a chance. Domi has a solid army.

"Corrik has been looking for you."

They're the words my heart's wanted to hear, but they hit different, knowing that to see Corrik, I have to say goodbye to Baya.

"Uncle Taj knows where he is. He can get you out of here and bring you to him."

I nod attempting to imprint his smell into my nostrils, and the way he feels, into my fingers. "I love you. I *love* you."

"I love you, Tristan. You have my heart. And I … I have recovered from a great many battles, but I don't know how I'll recover from this."

Regret sets in for all the moments I spent hating him, and all the moments I spent doing anything else aside from being with him because now I have no moments left. I feel them slip away. I'm going to wake up tomorrow somewhere else, somewhere he isn't, where I won't see how hard his jaw gets when I've said something that annoys him, where I can't make him laugh at my nonsense, and where he won't chase me through the soft-stone hallways, hollering at me to, *"Get back here now, Human,"* so he can spank the life out of me.

"I thought about what I wanted to give you, something your paltry human brain might use to remember me by," he says, trying to tease me, but it doesn't work; everything's too sad right now. "But Corrik wouldn't let you keep your stuff; he'll never allow you to keep anything from me so…"

"That's why the hair?"

"Yes."

"Thank you, Baya." I hug one side close to me and I can feel him.

"I like to think that maybe you'll miss me someday and your hair will surround you, bring you comfort." He tucks my long hair behind my ear. I can't move my ears like he can. I wish I could so I could show him affection in that way. It's a subtle thing, but Elves move their elegant ears in a variety of ways to display various emotions. Took me some time to learn that.

"I already miss you."

"I already miss you too."

We hold each other as long as we can until finally, we've run out of all our minutes. "It's time to go, Tristan. Pack your things."

When I'm ready, I take one last look at his chambers, the bed I used by his bed still freshly made from when I made it last, not knowing it would be for the last time. The table we ate at together, the window through which the sun shined in on us every morning, and the moonlight during the long nights we spent fucking after a hard day training in the fields. I attempt to memorize everything, knowing I'll never see it again.

I grab my bag packed with my meager belongings and together we head out the door.

CHAPTER 8

*B*efore we head off, Bayaden hands me pair of scissors. "You'll need to cut this, to get out of the gates, and then I'd keep cutting it if I were you until you're back with Corrik. Remember, it will grow back by nightfall." He chokes on Corrik's name.

I nod, unable to speak anymore. If I do, I'll start crying again. There's already an ache in my chest telling me to beg Bayaden not to send me away; I don't know if I'll be able to stop myself if I open my mouth. I pull my new hair taut and mercilessly hack it back to the length it was.

We take two horses from the stables, and it's easy for Bayaden and I to pass through the palace gates and then the ones past the marketplace, to head up to the cliffside, since we have many times. Bayaden's trying to emulate stone, but he's got tells, and I know them. "Andothair will get over it. He may not speak to me for a while, but I'll live."

"I see you're heartbroken about it."

He smirks. Bayaden respects his brother but enjoys peace from him on occasion.

We're quiet as we carry on, but eventually, Bayaden breaks the silence. "I hated you so much when you first came here, never did I imagine getting rid of you would be so hard."

"How unbelievably romantic," I say, and he laughs. "I hated you at least as much and I wanted to leave, but now I can't imagine going. My brain is still telling me we're just going on our usual trek to the mountainside, that we'll go back at the end of the day like usual."

I stop talking when I tear up again. Goodbyes are hard.

"How long have you been planning this?" I ask, to take my mind off leaving. I'll think about that when we get to it.

"Not long; I have been in conflict for a while. Father approached me, but I had some time before I had to seriously think about how I'd get you out of here and then I heard whispers that Corrik was looking for you. If you have to go, I knew that's where you'd want to go. When one of my warriors was found with his eyes carved out, I knew that was likely Corrik. I consulted with my uncle and he agreed with my perspective on things. He offered to help. Uncle Taj is going to take you to him."

I nod. "What about the war? I know Andothair and your father want to join the seven realms or destroy them."

"I don't have an answer for that one. For now, let's hope it doesn't come to that. Regardless of what happens in the future, this is what's right in this moment."

A lone rider comes into view as we approach the forest's entrance. Bayaden's Uncle Taj sits on a horse like Bayaden does, which is a comfort to me, at least he'll be with me in a way. I remember my hair that will grow back by nightfall and I'm glad I'll have it to surround me when Bayaden is gone.

Uncle Taj is quiet, watching us as we hop off our horses. "Uncle, we'll need you to perform the unbinding ritual."

I made a promise to Andothair through magic that I would not leave. Maybe that's the real reason I don't want to go and for a moment I hope so. I know we'll be saying our final goodbye in a few moments, the thought alone hurts, perhaps it will be less painful afterward. Uncle Taj nods. "Only someone like my uncle could do such a thing, Tristan," Bayaden explains. "Andothair used powerful magic."

Of course, he did.

"Come Tristan," Uncle Taj says. "I must analyze your energy."

I stand before him, after receiving silent approval from Bayaden it's all right. I don't think about it, I look up to him, used to it being this way. What's going to happen when he's not there?

I allow Uncle Taj to run his hands over the air surrounding me until he's satisfied. "Andothair wrapped it tightly. I can loosen it enough so it won't be painful for you to leave, and then it will fade over time."

"Will it be easier to leave when the spell is loosened as you say?"

His eyes shift between the pair of us. "If you mean will your heart be less heavy, then no. It will only bring you more ease physically since the spell will not stop you."

"Right then. Let's get this over with."

"Will it hurt him, Uncle?" Bayaden's voice is strained.

"Yes. I have to pull magic from him that's tightly woven into his cells. You'll feel it too, but not to the extent Tristan will. The vow was from his end, you're merely the tether."

Bayaden grabs me. "I shall hold him then."

"Ready, Tristan?"

"Ready."

Bayaden holds me to him, my back against his chest as his uncle holds his hands over my heart. When Ando did the spell, his hands were in the same place and white light gathered, pouring into me. It didn't hurt; I filled with buoyancy and was surprised by the lack of reaction. Ando assured me that the magic was conscious and if I tried to leave, it would know and stop me.

I never tried.

Now nothing is happening. Not a single thing. I don't feel pain and I don't see any white light. Uncle Taj tries harder, his face scrunches forming the wrinkles his face would have if he were a human as old as he is. Sweat pours from him, his muscle clench, but nothing happens. Then he gives up, taking a breath, sighing. He seems to be looking for something on me that isn't there. "Uncle," Baya says fed up, surely ready to call this whole thing off.

His uncle smiles, serene energy surrounds him. "Ah, I see why what I'm doing isn't working. You'll be fine, Tristan. We can go now."

Bayaden's not letting me go just yet. "The spell will crush him and once you're in … in there, turning back will be dangerous."

"The spell will not crush him because he is no longer governed by the spell. Tristan is loyal to you of his own accord, and because of the nature of this particular spell, it trusts Tristan is devoted to you and does not feel it needs to coerce him."

I tilt my head back to meet Bayaden's dark eyes, asking him wordlessly if we can trust that. I don't doubt his uncle believes the words he's saying, but is he right? "If Uncle says it's so, then it is so. I don't know anyone with a greater understanding of magic than he has—he's more powerful than Father."

I turn to face him. "Does that mean it's time to say goodbye?" I'm not ready.

"It's time." Bayaden kisses me, it's hard and sensual and I grip him for dear life. He's the one I was meant to fight on the fields with and fuck through the night and do it all over again the next day. Us warriors like the discipline in such repetition.

"I have something for you," Bayaden says.

I haven't noticed it at his hip, too distraught to perceive the non-anomaly as it's not unusual for Bayaden to have three weapons on him—the two he usually has strapped to his back are there.

But there's also a third.

I recognize the sword; my eyes widen as I take it from him to inspect. "*My* sword."

"I've been keeping it for you."

"Sure, you have. Probably afraid I would gut you more like. Tell me, how many times did you consider tossing it into the kiln?"

He twists his lips, his eyes dance with amusement. "A few. And I do not fear a little human like you gutting me." He would usually have a much better retort for me, but it's all he can muster. Instead, he looks me over, like he's memorizing every bit of me, ghosting his fingers up my arm and under my chin, which he uses to turn my head up to kiss him. Then he squeezes tighter, encircling me in his giant arms. I squeeze with as much strength as I have around his torso. When I move to pull away, he won't let me go. "Farewell my love."

I'm a mess, a fucking mess as I let go. He has to help me onto my horse. When his hand is leaving me, I grip him by the wrist. "Wait," I cry. I have to kiss his hand, his knuckles, I have to remember what it feels like to touch him forever. "Farewell, my love."

His uncle mounts his horse and starts off on his own; my signal it's time to go with him. "Go, Tristan," Bayaden says, his voice hoarse. "May the Gods keep you safe, when I can't."

He slaps my horse on the arse so that I have to scramble to get hold of her. It's the most natural thing in the world to scowl at him and when I see his face, it's smiling, despite the silent tears dripping to the ground.

He did that on purpose.

I pull my horse to stop for a moment, now that I'm several feet away, smiling back while I let my tears flow too and then I head into the forest.

"$\mathcal{I}$ 've never seen my nephew like that," the gruff Elven rider says. Bayaden comes by it honestly.

"Never?" I say, sniffling, wanting to turn around before Bayaden makes it back to the palace and beg him to run away with me.

He shakes his head. "I would bring you back to him myself if you weren't already married to the Mortougian prince. We do have to get you back Tristan; Andothair never should have taken you, my brother should have made him send you back, but he spoils the boy."

I like Uncle Taj already especially when his energy feels like Bayaden's, it soothes me, but in a more fatherly way. It also feels good to have a sword at my hip. I look at the long scar on my arm from wrist to elbow, from one of the days I trained with Bayaden's warriors. Before I took up the bow with Deglan, I trained with his warriors, or as I called it, my daily beating. I couldn't keep up with them, especially when they showed me no quarter.

Even with Baya himself showing me the technique, they were still too fast for me, but I went over and over what he taught me with sticks, with real swords, with the broom I used to sweep out Bayaden's chambers, anything I could get my hands on. I thought that if I practiced long and hard enough, one day I could raise a sword to an Elf and give him something to remember me by.

No such luck. To do so, I'd have to become Elf. I suppose that's another thing to look forward to; going back to Corrik means becoming an Elf. I try to come up with all the good things so I can stop thinking of how I won't see Bayaden when I wake up in the morning.

"Yes, sir," I say.

"That's Uncle Taj to you. You will always be family."

He's an odd sort of Elf. His shoulders are as broad as Bayaden's and when he speaks, his words are careful and heavy with purpose. His long white hair is bundled into thick sections, making it look like yarn, and he carries a presence that's quiet, but certain. "You don't live with the family?" I ask.

"No."

He's not very talkative. "Why not?"

"I should think that's self-explanatory," he says, his accent curling around the Elvish words.

"The king?"

"Yes."

I roll my eyes at his back. He's as insufferable as Bayaden, but the resemblance lifts me. Takes the edge off the pain of leaving him. We travel over hard roads and even some treacherous passes, but we don't see anyone, not a soul. *That's not right.*

When darkness falls, Uncle Taj dismounts. "We will rest here for the night and take turns on watch. Tomorrow will be the hardest part and then your husband isn't far. He will take you the rest of the way."

I don't know what to do with all that. Not only is Corrik close, but he's waiting for me. How long has he been out searching for me? How long has he been away from home?

My gut churns.

Corrik's going to be furious, he likely wants to burn Aldrien to the ground by this point; he just needs to get me out of it first. Which brings another question to the table, why hasn't anyone shown up on Aldrien's doorstep?

It's an uneventful night and thankfully warm. When I sleep, I put on a warmer shirt and use my pack as a pillow. Uncle Taj has things for us to eat—dried fruits, meats and cheese and plenty of water. He surprises me with campfire chat, maybe because I'm heartbroken. "You know Tristan when Bayaden was a little boy, he was a happy little spirit; I never had to spank him as often as his older brother. But when their mother was killed, it changed him. He stopped smiling. He threw himself into his duties. As much as Andothair is a spoiled brat, he sees people, I think his intent—if by poor design—was genuine with his brother. He knew you would heal him, and you have."

My body heats head to toe, thinking I could heal anyone let alone Bayaden. My head turns to look in all other directions, anywhere but his eyes. "He had an effect on me too."

"Why does it embarrass you so, to think you could heal someone?"

"It's not a crown I feel I wear," I say.

"You are humble is all. That's a good thing." He nods. "But you have. He hasn't smiled like that in a long time."

"Then why are we doing this? Take me back." The fire is warm on my skin, but inside my body is cold.

"Aside from that my brother will kill you, it's not right. You were taken, Tristan."

"I was taken anyway. With Corrik it was only mildly more consensual."

"Still angry about that are you? Take my opinion for what it's worth—very little these days—but while it's true the children of royals are pawns, it doesn't change that you belong in Mortouge, or your responsibility to the contract, unless … are you willing to endure the consequences for breaking it?"

I'm not. I stare into the fire, feeling like a coward for not being able to let go of my parents' expectations of me. "How will I face him, Uncle Taj?"

He smiles and pokes the fire. "Like any other battle, I wager. But that is a problem for another day, we must talk about tomorrow."

"I imagine there's something dangerous?"

"Yes. There's little I'm allowed to tell you. I swore an oath through magic. You'll need to follow my lead and have your sword out."

I nod. "I can do that."

"Bayaden wanted to come, but he thought it for the best if when you made it to the other side, he wasn't there."

"He was right." Corrik will probably want his head.

"I will take first watch. I chose this place because we are safe enough here, but once we pass through, we'll keep going until we get you to safety."

I begin the day cutting my hair. It grew back in the night and while I doubt we'll see anyone where we are, I have nothing to tie it back with and I'm no longer used to keeping it out of my face while I ride. For now, it's easier to cut away—it will grow back again by tonight anyway.

Our surroundings are eerie, the sky a purple haze, as we move into the dense forest. Nothing in here is alive, but it's not dead either. We maneuver our horses carefully through the brush, the brambles, and branches thick with thorny limbs. I get scratched to shit, I would pull my sword to cut my way out, but Uncle Taj is trying to be quiet; I follow his lead best I can. I know he can't tell me what this place is, so I don't bother to ask.

Instead, I observe and keep a watchful eye.

The necrosis isn't the only thing disturbing about this place; it's the lack of sound and stale air that unsettles me. We should be able to hear birds flitting by, or the creak of trees as tiny creatures run up them, but it's just nothingness. The breeze should bring a myriad of forest scents, but it doesn't.

There's not even a breeze.

Everything's still, like it doesn't know where to go even though it

104

doesn't want to stay, locked within this moment forever. Whatever danger does inhabit this place is lying dormant for now as we make our way through at a decent pace. After two hours of riding, we approach a large stone megalith. It surrounds a small body of water, tall stones lined up around the edge with thick ones laid horizontally on top of the vertical ones. A pathway, also made of stone, extends across the water. "Are those made from sarsen stone?" I recognize them from a book I read back home in Markaytia.

He grunts his acknowledgment.

He stands at the edge of the water in the middle of two of the larger stones and begins to circle his hands in various patterns. I've watched Bayaden do magic in a multitude of ways over this past year. Elves draw magic from the Earth using their consciousness. He does that now, and a pattern appears drawn in light forms. When he throws it, light explodes toward each stone and there is a fissure of illumination, glistening in mid-air. "We're going to walk through this with our horses. Once we get to the other side, we'll have to run full speed until we get to the forest's edge."

"Is this what anyone has to do anytime they leave Aldrien?" I ask because it seems elaborate.

"Depends on where they want to go. Not every place has Elemental Death Wolves at the end of it. Unfortunately, Corrik waits outside the other side of this particular barrier."

"Does he know we're coming?"

"Yes. I spoke with him. I have been negotiating."

"What sort of negotiations?"

"I asked him to stop killing our warriors, and in exchange I would bring you to him."

"Is he aware of the Elemental Death Wolves?"

I already know the answer from the hesitation I see in his eyes. "No, but there was no other place to meet him without him figuring out how we keep Aldrien hidden. As far as he knows, we've brought the veil around the place, which will bring him more questions than answers, but that works. There is only a problem once we're inside since they don't have the required magic to pass through the veil. We just need to get to the other side where they cannot follow us. They cannot leave the veil."

If only Corrik knew I was about to run from Elemental Death Wolves. "Is that what this place is? A veil?"

He nods. "The world and the underworld are closest at this point. We're not quite in the land of the living, but we're also not in the land of the dead.

That's fucking creepy. "How do you get back?"

"Same way. The door will be open for me until I close it. You'll forget what you saw."

"But I won't forget ... I won't forget—" I panic.

"You won't forget your time in Aldrien. That would take an amount of magic not worth the price." He winks at me and I think he has more to do with that than anything else.

We approach the gleaming door, and he steps through it. I follow after him. Once I'm through, I hit the ground running as he does. Being an Elf, I know he can ride much faster than I can, even when I'm at full speed, but he stays back so I don't lose him. The landscape is more of the same as what we left—a pile of not-dead things wound together, making up an eerie forest. It was hard enough traversing it at a slow pace. At this speed, it's more of a challenge for me, but I do my best to keep up. Looking everywhere all at once, I skip and jump my horse to the tune of Uncle Taj's lead, clearing bramble, dodging rocks.

We luck out, and there are no Elemental Death Wolves, but with the way Uncle Taj is still charging through, I suspect we're not in the clear. For now, the concern of falling off my horse is more immediate, and I'm glad we don't have wolves to worry about too.

My heart races and my muscles strain. I've taken on some challenging terrains as a rider, but nothing like this. Without the added strength and magical benefits of Elves, I begin to tire too soon. It's when I think I can't hold on any longer, I feel them surround us. Running as if on tracks of air, the white creatures appear. They're as beautiful as they are deadly. Gorgeous white fur, long and curling at the ends, whipping against the wind created by their speed alone since there is nothing but flat air in this place.

They have bright silver eyes and claws, and teeth that can undeniably rip through any part of me. Their breath is hot when they snarl. "Tristan, *duck.*"

I grip low on my horse, somehow managing to stay on her, just in time for a ball of blue flame to sail over my head and take out one of the two wolves following us. I thank the Gods and my horse, but most of all, Uncle Taj and keep going.

We must be getting close; Uncle Taj's body language gives him away. He looks ahead to judge the distance we have to close before we make it out and he looks behind to check where the wolf is snapping at my horse's hooves. Any other horse would have been attempting to throw me off by now, but this isn't just any horse, she's one from an Elven realm, which means she's got more strength and ability. She'll still scare, but not easily.

It's also not hard to imagine that with their Elven strength and Elven horses, Elves must be able to make it out of here without too much trouble. It's the human component fucking this up. I bet they all sail through here without issue. I'm slowing us down, but if I go any faster, I will fall off.

"Tristan, again!" he shouts. It must take a massive amount of energy to create those balls of fire, and I deduce how powerful Uncle Taj must be. The second ball hits the wolf snapping after me, but not before the wolf's long leg stretches out enough to catch my leg and tear through it. The wolf is sent tumbling away and I cry out as I bleed all over my horse.

Uncle Taj looks ahead, clearly trying to gauge how much distance is left, but with my leg bleeding profusely, we can't go further until it's healed. I'm gushing out blood and I won't last long. He rears his horse and signals I should stop. I do, but the sudden stop highlights how light-headed and woozy I am.

My face meets my horse and then there is blackness.

I'm being shook awake. "Tristan. *Tristan.* I need you to wake up now."

Things are shadowy at first until my eyes can receive light again. Uncle Taj comes into focus. I'm no longer on my horse, but on the ground, under a decaying tree. "Uuuhhh?" I moan.

"We don't have much time until more wolves come. We're almost there. Can you ride?"

I check myself over, looking for the gash that's no longer there. "Healed me?"

"Yes. You lost a lot of blood though, something I cannot replenish. If we leave now, we can make it out without having to ride at such breakneck speeds. You could ride on my horse if you don't think you'll make it."

"No. I'll be all right." Once the fog clears, my limbs are strong if a bit tired. Heaving myself onto my horse and steadying my gaze I nod to Uncle Taj.

"You sure Tristan? You won't survive another blood loss like that."

"Will it slow you down to have me on the back?"

"It will."

"Then I can do it. I'm sure."

We ride again at a medium pace in comparison to what we'd been riding at, and it reminds me that no, I'm not one hundred percent; the forest spins and my stomach lurches. I'd hoped to tell him we could go faster, but that's not going to happen. *Focus Tristan. Get to the end. You're fine.*

And I do all right, but when I hear the twin growls, I'm overcome with a lot of "*oh fucks.*" Uncle Taj fills with concern, I know he doesn't think I'll make it, but I'm not dying today. "C'mon," I shout to him, forcing myself to speed up my horse. I narrow my focus to his horse, and he nods enough for me to see him. He speeds up too.

Horse hooves pound as weighty as my heart, the sound filling the fetid air almost drowning out the sound of the growls enough so that I can center myself to where I can see the clearing. We're almost there. *Almost.* I dare to speed up my horse, faster than I can manage for long.

The blood loss catches up to me, I see black spots, I want to retch, I start to slide sideways, the breeze of a claw whips at my flank followed by fire overhead—another blast of Elf fire that just singes my new hair. Thankfully, it will grow back by nightfall. "Almost there, Tristan!"

There's one wolf remaining, and it's too close; I have to go faster, *faster* than is manageable. Squeezing my calves puts speed into the large Elven horse, and I hang on for dear life, no longer relying on my riding skills, praying the horse will make its own wise decisions to traverse the gnarled landscape in a way it can without breaking an ankle. Uncle Taj looks back to check on me, knowing I need help and he can either do that or attempt another fireball.

Strength begins to seep into my limbs, as if from nowhere and it gives me the boost I need to make the final push to my horse, to get us out, but we don't have long.

We don't need it either.

The front legs of Uncle Taj's horse hit sunlight first, and he's through. I'm not far behind, not a moment too soon; the snarl is too close, the large paws thump heavily as the wolf pounces and I clear the veil just as I hear it landing behind me, happy to leave it trapped inside.

CHAPTER 9

My heart is still galloping at the speed my horse was moments ago when we exit the clearing. The vestiges of death still encapsulate me, and I shake as if physically getting rid of the whole experience. I'm about to collapse, having reached the end of my endurance, my face buries itself into the silken mane of my horse. "Good girl," I tell her. "That was some stellar riding."

Uncle Taj keeps back, ready to ride into the veil and it only occurs to me now that he'll have to fight his way back alone. The massive ex-war Elf doesn't look bothered by the task, his white hair stark against his copper skin, his fierceness burning straight through his blue eyes, which are focused behind me.

Corrik is here.

His hair shines brightly as I remember, but there are streaks of white and a tightness to him that wasn't there before. He's tired in his soul and it's plain in the way he carries himself, but when he sets eyes on me, someone has poured sunshine into his cup once again. "Tristan, is that really you?"

I didn't know how I was going to feel seeing Corrik again. I've fallen in love with someone else, but the Gods help me, I still love Corrik too and it consumes me the moment I'm in his space. I don't think, I just do. I hop off my horse and run to him. It's natural when he takes me in his arms. It's like I never left, and we sink to the ground and kneel on the grass together.

That's when I hear the rearing of a horse and we both look to where Uncle Taj is. "Fare thee well, Tristan." He doesn't give me the chance to say goodbye, or even to thank him, and he's gone disappearing into the veil. *I'll never know if he makes it back okay.*

Corrik ignores the large Elf, which surprises me, focused only on me. "Tristan you … you're different."

I don't even think about it, the Elvish comes out. "Different, how?"

He wrinkles his nose, his ears turn up and he continues in Markaytian. "You have *their* accent. We're going to have to do something about that."

"But I like my accent fine," I say in Markaytian, not wanting to start trouble with him, *already*. Right, Corrik and I fight, a lot.

I'd forgotten.

He shakes his head. "It's fine. Tristan, I'm just so glad we've found you. Your hair though, it's gone, and it's got color to it."

His disappointment guts me as much as it ever did. But I can fix this one. "Wait until tonight. It will be back."

He doesn't ask how, only nods. "Right. We've got to get moving Tristan. It isn't safe here. Are you hurt?"

"Not anymore, was just healed." He winces. "I'm okay though. A bit tired." The blood loss has me a bit woozy, but I don't mention it. But right, overprotective is Corrik's middle name. Bayaden was protective, without being *over*protective.

"When we get you home, I promise I'll make it so you're never hurt again."

I'm not sure I like the sound of his words, he's too vague for my liking. Two more riders show up. I recognize one of them. "Young Warlord!" Diekin says hoping off his horse, running to me. I get up from where I am on the ground and stand to embrace him. "We've been searching for nearly a year, but we never gave up."

That's meaningful. I get it. He knows how much I worried over Corrik never forgiving me, but he wouldn't look for me all this time just for the sake of some treaty—royalty knows when to cut their losses. "Thank you for not giving up on me," I try in Elvish hoping he won't hate my accent too.

"Look at that, Corrik. He can speak like us."

"He speaks like *them*," Corrik says, his disdain clear and I decide to stow the Elvish for a bit, switching to Markaytian.

The other rider is as icy as Corrik was when we first met, and I see the family resemblance. But I know he's not just any one of Corrik's brothers, it has to be Alrik, the one I've heard so much about, the one that is the *Crown Prince* of Mortouge. He's amazing with his larger-than-life energy and even larger muscles sticking out every which way, making him broader than Corrik, which is saying something.

And I can already tell he does not like me. *Joy.* "Pleased to meet you, Your Highness," I say, trying to pull out my most respectful self.

He grunts. "Get him on a horse and do not lose sight of him."

Something in the way Alrik says that makes me feel more like chattel than I ever did as an *actual* slave in Aldrien. "He'll be riding with me brother," Corrik says.

I would argue that I have my own horse, but it's clear my opinion's unwanted. Instead, I move to grab my bag. "Leave those," Corrik says. "We've brought items for you."

I nod with a last longing look at my things. It's just poor-quality clothing I stole from around the palace, but they are the last fragments of my life there. At least I've got my pants and tunic on from Bayaden, for however long I'll get to keep them. I let Corrik assist me onto his horse and feel his weight settle in behind me.

I can't help noting the difference between him and Bayaden. Baya had warmth to his solid frame, Corrik is like ice. I remember there was a time Bayaden was too hot; I had to cool him. I hope I can use my wiles to thaw the ice prince.

---

*K*eeping my physical state a secret becomes impossible and I pass out against the back of Corrik. "Are you sure you're all right?"

I bite my lip and choose to speak to him in Markaytian. "You'll get angry."

His fists clench. "Probably, but there's nothing for it. You need to tell me, Tristan."

I huff. "The giant white wolf thing got me. I'm okay. I—"

"—white wolf? Tristan!"

He stops his horse, which alerts the other members of our entourage. In addition to Diekin and Alrik, there are several members of the guard with us. Alrik rides over, glowering. "Corrik, what's the meaning of this?"

"He was attacked by a white wolf," Corrik says looking me over. He finds nothing.

I grimace. "Corrik, I was healed. It's the blood loss that's affecting me a bit, but I'm fine."

Alrik is unimpressed. "You should have told us. You could be cursed."

"I'm not cursed," I argue. "Uncle Taj healed me; he would have told me if I were cursed."

Everything about that enrages everyone. "He is *not* your uncle," Alrik underlines. "And Rogue Elves know little about such things. I have more magical ability in my little pinky."

I would argue with that, but I think I've argued more than my allotment today. His stony gaze is intense, and I have to stifle a shudder.

"Corrik, see that he gets a proper examination. We'll stop here for the night to allow him some rest. If you can't keep him in line, he rides with me."

After he sets off, leaving the cool air behind him, I tear up missing my life in Aldrien, wanting Bayaden to spank me soundly and curl around me to sleep. Mercifully, Corrik softens as he helps me down from the massive horse. "I'm sorry, Corrik. Please don't be mad at me. It wasn't my fault."

There are more than white wolves on my mind. My gut's churning with what Corrik might think of me and yes I fell in love with Bayaden, I was torn up about it for a long time, but I came to accept the circumstances of the whole thing. I hope he will too. "I'm not mad at you, Tristan. You have no idea how grateful I am to have you back. I'm angry he didn't tell us the dangers. I wouldn't have allowed it, even if it meant you not coming back to me. You alive and out there is better than dead."

Oh.

Corrik has changed. Now that I'm not recovering from death wolves chasing me, I can feel him better. There's a calm to him that didn't exist before. I relax. "I'm sorry I didn't tell you. I wasn't ready for your anger."

"Fair," he says. "I'm going to check you over now. Lie back."

Corrik does something with his eyes closed, and his hands raking over me just above my skin. He begins at my head, tracing down my body, ending at my booted feet. It reminds me a lot of what Uncle Taj did when he was checking on the loyalty spell. "So? Am I cursed?"

"No." He looks over to Alrik off in the distance. "Don't tell Alrik I said this, but Taj is a talented healer. You well should have been cursed. Death wolves—by Ylor, Kathir." He helps me up. "You are weak, though. You'll be riding with me for a few days. We'll do some healing spells together each day."

I nod. "Thank you, Corrik."

He grips my hand and helps me up to a seated position. "I'll have a tent set up for us tonight, you need a few nights of good rest and some food." He leans closer. "And I imagine time to yourself wouldn't go amiss."

I squint at him. "Who are you?"

He looks at his hands then back to my eyes. "Tristan, there's much to tell you. I want to say it all at once, but I also don't want to overwhelm you. Give me time?"

"As much as you need, and I can have the same?"

"Of course."

I smile, a bit of warmth settling into me, maybe things will be okay.

―――――

*C*orrik has two beds set up, which is weird for me even with the year between us. I assumed things would kind of just slip back into some version of what we had, considering how we started. We went from chatting in a book to sex on our wedding night.

Things surely have changed.

Sleep does sound good, and maybe alone is for the best. I've had no chance to grieve Bayaden—Papa taught me the importance of grieving—and my body is feeling the effects of being slashed open by an Elemental Death Wolf. I get into bed and I cry myself to sleep.

If Corrik hears me, he doesn't say.

Morning comes too soon and yet not soon enough. The first thing I notice is hair. Lots of it. Mine. Bayaden. I inhale the scent. It doesn't smell like him, but I still have remnants of him left, all of which will fade too soon, but I will always have this, and I can feel him like he's here surrounding me. I roll around in the feelings, my hair silky against my bare skin.

Two violet eyes watch me from across the room. "Your hair is back."

"Yes," I say reaching for my tunic and pulling it over my bare torso. I'm not going to cut my hair anymore. It does seem to draw attention, but I'm sure there's something to tie it back with for riding.

"May I … May I brush it out for you? My brother will have kittens —as I believe the Markaytian saying goes—if you walk out of here like that."

He's so hesitant and he needn't be, but I suppose it's going to be like that until we find our footing again. I decide to make a start to that end. "I'd like that, Cor."

He frowns. "Cor?"

"Your name, shortened. It's what we Markaytians do with people we are familiar with—shorten their names."

He considers that. "I hope you don't expect me to call you Tris in return."

I laugh. "No. I mean, Lucca did at times, but that was Lucca."

Corrik relaxes, moving off the cot he's on. He retrieves a brush from one of the bags and heads to my side. Gently he takes the hair in one hand, pauses briefly—can he sense Bayaden as I can?—but carries on, running the brush through, de-knotting it, taming it some. "It's beautiful hair, Tristan. Please don't cut it again?"

"I won't."

I make the conscious decision not to rile Alrik and to stay out of his way, neither of which is easy since he's been on Corrik's case about me. After a week and full recovery, I'm still not permitted to ride on my horse, who rides lonely, beside us. Poor girl.

Things are awkward between me and Corrik, but not in a bad way. It's that shy, *does he still like me,* kind of way I used to feel about boys in my teens. I look forward to when I get to wrap my arms around him, when we're on the horse together, and sometimes, he rests a hand on mine as we ride. I come to the conclusion it might be for the best I ride with him. Even with the added weight of one human, Corrik's horse can gallop faster than I can ride my horse on my own; I would slow them down.

Just over two weeks after we leave the place where I came out of the veil, we reach the barrier dividing the seven Elven realms from the rest of humanity. A whole other world lies beyond, one I've never seen, one humans rarely get to see.

The barrier is a golden sheen, reaching far as I can see into the sky and across the Earth. It shimmers and from afar it's beautiful, but as we get closer, it resonates with energy that feels like a threat. "Keep hold around me like you are, Tristan and you'll be all right," Corrik says. "You will feel it a bit until you are Elf, and we can key you to the wards, but you will be okay."

Our entourage rides through and the golden light is uncomfortable for me. I don't like it, it's a "walking over graves" kind of sensation. "Ugh. That was unpleasant."

"Better than being disintegrated I wager," he says chuckling.

Disintegrated? Guess I'm not leaving this place until I'm Elf; I won't be able to get out without Corrik or another Elf. It doesn't matter—*where would I go?*

"This is the seventh realm," Corrik announces. "We must head North to reach the first. Mortouge."

When we get across, I forget all about barriers and leaving, this place is incredible, unlike anything I've seen before. The trees are brighter, their color appearing more vibrant somehow. Foliage surrounds us every which way and the landscape buzzes with life, creatures—some I've seen and some I haven't—flitting about.

Where there are structures, they're awe-inspiring—there is nothing as intricate as Elven architecture. I don't know how some of it holds up, built into mountainsides as it is, yet it's also perfect and solid and has likely been there thousands of years. The seventh realm is full of warm colors, which doesn't surprise me; we're still a goodly distance to the south of Mortouge where I know the climate will be different.

"We shall stay at the Inn tonight," Alrik declares, his cruel tongue wrapping around the Elvish words. "Tristan needs a proper bath; he's starting to smell."

Sorry, we can't all be Elves with built-in air fresheners. I'd really like to clock that guy, but I hold my tongue. I think Corrik's impressed with my restraint since he squeezes my hand and smiles. He's still keeping his distance in other ways though. His gestures are courtship-like, usually only touching me when necessary, or when there's an excuse to. He won't sleep in the same bed and for an Elf, he's modest doing his best to give me privacy when I have to change and when he can't, he pretends to do something else. He's continued to ask permission to brush my hair, which is as far as he's gone in the land of non-essential touching.

We haven't kissed.

After stabling our shared horse, we head inside, followed by an armed guard. It's a bit much, but I don't say anything. Corrik's paranoid and I get it. I can live with the extra detail in close proximity for a few weeks without complaint, so he can keep his mind at ease. I did think he'd cool once we entered the Realm since the barrier is supposed to be keyed to keep them out, but I suppose if Rogue Elves can get aboard a ship in the middle of nowhere, why not here too?

The Inn is beautiful, much fancier than the ones I'd stay with my father and Papa when we were on the road. Everything Elves touch seems to have unparalleled beauty. Corrik removes his shirt, leaving himself in his white pants with the gold trim, his long hair cascading down his back.

My long hair flows down too, tickling my mid-back, reminding me of Baya. I thought I'd feel more guilt about the whole thing, but I don't. I mean, I am worried over how Corrik will react, but I'm no longer as sorry as I once was. There's more guilt over my lack of guilt. "Shall I bathe so I don't continue to offend your brother's nose with my smell?" I joke. "By Gods, does he think I'm a flea-ridden human or something?" I can't help the sadness I feel thinking about fleas and humans.

"Actually, no. I think he likes you quite a lot."

I don't like what's behind his eyes. "You've got to be kidding me? You Elves. Is that how you all like someone? Pull on their pig tails?"

"Pig tails? But you don't have—"

"—Markaytian saying." Elves don't like when they like humans. It's the same story over again. I sigh. "Anyway, point me to the bath. I'll head down, won't be long."

"Just a moment. I'll come with you," he says, fetching his sword.

For a moment, it's strange to me, I'm used to popping around the palace, going here, going there, on my own. I hope he doesn't plan on coming everywhere with me. "Yeah sure, Cor."

We head down with the guard. Corrik doesn't bathe but he keeps watch, without watching me, while I clean myself thoroughly. Alrik was a dick for saying it as he did, but he wasn't wrong; I do smell. Maybe that's why Corrik hasn't come too close, though it never seemed to bother him before.

When I'm done, I smell like fresh gardenias and when I'm dressed, Corrik takes me back to the room. "I'll get us food, you relax here," he says.

"I wouldn't mind stretching my legs. I'll come with you." I almost call it a date, but I'm not sure if we're there yet. We seem to have come to this awkward place, one in which we're married, we know we've got the hots for each other, but we've got no clue how to act around each other. I doubt there's advice in the counseling books for this sort of thing.

Corrik frowns so deeply, his body frowns with him from his shoulders to the cut of his waist. He takes a breath. "Okay," he says, but he's uneasy.

"Is something wrong?

"No. Nothing. It's probably better you stay with me anyway. Come." He holds his hand out for me, his face hard as stone, he keeps the large sword strapped to his back, rather than leaving it here—he doesn't need it while we have Inn stew.

From there it's more awkwardness and Corrik looking around a lot. "You want to take our stuff to go, Cor?" Seeing him uneasy like this isn't what I wanted to inflict upon him.

"Just eat, darling," he says, but doesn't smile.

Kinda dampens the whole date feel. When the server comes 'round offering dessert, I begin to decline. "You don't want dessert, sweetheart? That's unlike you. Normally your stomach eats itself if you haven't had at least one dessert."

I love that he remembers. "You seem anxious to get back to our room."

"Ahhh," the Elven innkeeper says. "Can't wait to have your way with this one, uh Prince Corrik?"

I wait for Corrik to return the banter, instead he's annoyed. "Bring him the dessert."

The innkeeper rushes away.

"What was that all about?"

"I am a prince of the first realm and so are you. He wasn't addressing us with proper respect."

"You're usually keen to boast about fucking me, Corrik." He knows it's true, I keep hard eyes on him.

He sits back and folds his hands. "Maybe I shouldn't have been."

"It is the way of Elves."

"But not of Markaytians."

"It doesn't bother me, Corrik."

"It did."

"Are we going to fight here?" I hiss. "I'd rather not."

He calms down. "No fighting. Look I'm being ... I will relax. Please have dessert, Tristan."

I raise a brow. "Will it make you feel better?"

He nods. "I don't deserve it, but it's for the best."

What does he mean by that? He's right though. I've learned something about soothing Toppy, Dominant Elves over this year. They get riled when their mates are unsettled; things like hunger can count as unsettled. It's the same with disobedience. There are triggers and controlling their emotions as well as their guttural response becomes near impossible. It's too primal to tame, and it's better to learn your Elf rather than fight forces of nature.

This time I reach across the table to grab his hands, and he stares at them. "I will eat until I've had my fill Corrik, but you're telling me what you meant by that comment when we get upstairs."

He peeks up at me, his ears peer up with him—they move in a finer way than Bayaden's do. "You're so much older than you were. Mature."

I am and I have a theory on it. I think it's a lot to do with living my true brat nature. Father did the best job he could, I see that now, but he was not made to handle brats. His ways were good for me when I was riled up to an extreme, but not for every day. Bayaden had a way with me and it worked. I'm the most myself I've ever been, I'm scared of losing it with Corrik's ways because ultimately that's up to him now—he'll make the rules, he'll direct us. But will we flow? Or get stuck at a dam?

"Just wait till I'm comfortable, you'll see I'm the brat I always was."

He tilts his head. "Confident, too, I see. Okay, Brat. I'm game."

The look he gives me is meaningful; my heart lifts and new life spreads through me. We have a lot to work out, a lot, but if we can have that, it could work. I'm about to do my thing, but we're inter-rupted. Alrik's voice booms through the Inn. "Corrik. *Corrik!*"

Corrik's eyes tear from me to meet the solid black ones. "What is it, brother?" he says, keeping his voice low.

"What are you doing down here with him?" he says under his breath. "He's bathed. I see no other reason to be down here."

Corrik's quiet. I think he's going to argue. Instead, his chair slides out, and he raises his large form from the table, reaching for my hand. "Come Tristan. I'll have the rest of our food brought up."

I take his hand.

"I'll do it," Alrik says. "Stay put and get sleep. We leave at first light."

"*What* is up with your brother?" I ask.

"Things haven't been easy on the road. He's as anxious to get you home as I am," Corrik explains removing his sword and setting it by the bed.

I remove my tunic—my sword is already by the bed as I saw no need to bring it to the baths—and I try to put Corrik at ease. "It has been a long day. I shall eat my cake and go directly to sleep." I open the covers and collapse on the bed. "That is unless … do you want to have your wicked way with me?"

"No." That's all I get other than to watch him remove his white jacket with the gold trim. He leaves his pants on.

Truly I was joking. I know Elves have a different nature than Markaytians, but I need to tell him about Bayaden before we can do that. I did expect some banter back and forth though, maybe some flirting, but not a flat no. In any case, it's not the time to deal with that one. I revisit his earlier comment. "All right, lay it on me, what did you mean at dinner, when you said you don't deserve it?"

He lies on the bed next to me—it's the closest we've been since our reunion—when we're not riding a horse. He tries to make his face blank. "I lost you Tristan, and it was my fault. I don't know if I'll ever be able to make it up to you and yet you'll have to submit to my nature, regardless."

It's true. I know well the danger in riling Elves. I've done it enough times to have learned my lesson. "I'm not upset with you for that. It wasn't your fault."

"It was. You must know by now of the relations I had with Andothair."

Right. That whole thing. Honestly, I'm just sick of it. I don't care what ex-boyfriends he's had. "What Ando decided to do is no fault of yours. He needs to move on."

"He does, but it doesn't absolve my actions or my responsibility. Originally, I wasn't going to tell my brother, but I want you to know I went to him and told him everything. He was furious, and I was punished. We did keep the matter within the family. I'm lucky he didn't see fit to banish me. But since, I've done much repenting and growing up. I won't make the same mistakes again."

I don't see things the same way he does. Love is love. I don't think he should have been punished for caring for someone, I think they should put their centuries-old argument to rest. "I'm still not upset about it, but if you need me to say it, I forgive you."

This does not bode well for the Bayaden thing though.

"I appreciate that Tristan and I shall endeavor to make it up to you." He changes the subject. "You don't happen to remember where you came from in the veil do you?"

"I …" Huh, no. It's just gone. "I'm sorry Cor, but no."

"We were told you wouldn't, but you never know. Magic is a tricky thing; it tends to have a life of its own at times."

I know the truth of that. I remember the loyalty spell that shifted and changed into what it is now. "I'm surprised you were able to stay on the outside of the veil, waiting patiently."

"There was nothing patient about the way I waited. Ask Diekin. There was a negotiation, and we weren't to come in. We were given coordinates and told the deal would be off if we set a toe inside. By that point we were desperate enough to wait where we were told. Aldrien is gone, it's just gone. We never did find it."

"Gone? That's impossible. I assure you it's very there."

"We know, it drove Diekin nuts too, but it's not there, at least, it's not where it was. We collected you several miles northeast of Aldrien's former location. What was once Aldrien, is now flat, empty fields."

"I'm sorry, Corrik. I never even knew to ask. For me, it was there."

"It's fine. You're back now. I have to say, I'm not far off from Alrik's level of concern. I'm likely more so I just have a soft spot for you, that Alrik doesn't have for anyone. I should be more careful with you."

I laugh. "When it comes to me, careful is your middle name. I wouldn't worry."

He doesn't laugh with me.

The food arrives, I eat and then we sleep, Corrik on one side, me on the other.

CHAPTER 10

INTERLUDE

*W*e're laughing, hard and we're trying to stop, but we can't. We can only manage brief pauses, but we'll look at each other, just a look, and lose it again. "I can't—I can't b-breathe, Bayaden stop it."

"You stop it. You're the one making me laugh."

"Me? You keep looking at me, stop looking."

"No, you keep looking at me."

The fields of Aldrienian wildflowers stretch out before us as we lie in the middle of them, not a soul in sight. The grass is tall and because it's eternal summer here, it's hot and lovely. The blue sky is dusted with fluffy clouds and bees zip by to tickle my nose.

Finally, we can look at each other without laughing. "Baya? What do you like best about me?"

"Best? That assumes I like anything about you at all. You're human, what's to like about a human?"

I whack him on the shoulder. "Arse! Fine. I don't like you either."

He laughs, but it's not uncontrollable like earlier; it's "you're adorable when you're mad" and "clearly that's not true". I know this, and I still pout. He schools his features to something more serious.

"All right, it's a secret but the Warlord fancies a human. Can you believe that? A human."

The soft glow of gold from the tattoo over his right eye makes his face brighter and more mischievous. I play along. "Oh? How scandalous."

He stares. "It is. Poor bugger was blindsided," he learned that saying from me, "and it can't be said that it's his fault. The human is quite enchanting."

"How so?"

His fingers dance up my bare torso. "Well, there are a great many reasons. Like how he moves on the field with a weapon in his hand and his quick wit. It is even said that the great Warlord enjoys his sharp tongue."

"Great Warlord, eh?"

"Oh yes, I can't stress the 'great' enough." I laugh. "The human is also more beautiful than any other he's seen, more than any Elf too." His face gets soft. "But none of that's why he's enchanted. It's just a thing that is. I find I wait until he breathes before I take my next breath, I live to see his next smile, selfishly hoping I'm the cause of it, and when I kiss him the world falls away and life feels easy if only for that brief moment."

He presses his lips to mine. The memory fades. Summer's gone and our laughter is trapped in the wind.

CHAPTER 11

*I*t takes weeks to reach Mortouge, but when we finally lay eyes on her, I am impressed. The cool landscape isn't as foreboding as I thought it would be. If ice can be described as friendly then that's what I'd call it—friendly. It invites me in and even the snow crunching under my boots is a welcome sensation. Unlike the thicker, wider buildings in other places within the Realm, the buildings here, in King's Keep are thin and tall. Almost everything sparkles ice-blue and is accented in white.

Even the Elves are dressed in warm, white accents despite their midriffs showing. The Mortougian Elves seem to have built-in fire-places for the cold. I, on the other hand, do not and am grateful for the warm white fur coat and reinforced leather boots Corrik bought for me along the way. I pull the fur around me tighter.

"What do you think, my husband?" he says.

"I think that she is beautiful, but Corrik, is it always like this?"

"No. We have seasons, but it's never as warm as Markaytia. Not to worry, when you are Elf, you'll be much warmer. For now, we'll make sure there's plenty of wood on the fire for you."

"Thank the Gods for fireplaces."

We enter the gates to the palace and my breath hitches again. Some levels of the palace stretch further than I can see into the sky, with others lower to the ground and decorated with intricate patterns indicative of Elvish style. The entire structure spirals in a cochlear fashion upward, the towers spreading further apart and the backmost ones reaching furthest into the sky.

We're brought straight to the king and queen, who are sat down to dinner. The queen is up, rushing to me, taking me in her arms, squeezing me. She speaks Markaytian. "Oh, Kathir. We were worried we'd never see you again."

Even the king has to have his turn with me. "Son. I can't believe we allowed this to happen. I hope someday you can forgive us. You're all right?"

"There's nothing to forgive sire and yes, I'm all right."

"Then please, sit. Dine with us. Let's get reacquainted."

Alrik and Diekin ask to be excused. "I'll see you around, young Warlord," Diekin says before he leaves. Alrik says nothing. Corrik leads me to where I'll be sitting for meals at his side and we have a nice dinner. My stomach is happy to have something aside from the road fair.

Corrik is still uneasy around me. He's thinking about something, and of course, my mind runs wild with what. There wasn't a lot of time or privacy on the road for many intimate conversations and even when we had the time, Corrik was awkward and distant. In part, Corrik maintained a constant state of vigilance, which meant he was immovable—it was a dangerous journey. As much as Corrik wanted to get me home, we sometimes had to take a longer way so we could avoid being seen. He didn't trust that there weren't Rogue Elves out looking for me (they aren't supposed to be able to get into the seven realms, but they are). However, I knew they wouldn't be.

My insistence that no one was looking for me, and the subsequent tantrum I threw because no one would listen to me, resulted in my first spanking from Corrik since returning to him. Corrik didn't need any prodding to administer the same, believe me, but Alrik didn't care. He said if Corrik didn't spank me, he would. I kept quiet for the

rest of the trip and suffered Corrik's anxiety. I supposed he was enti-
tled to them after looking for me a year.

But I thought once we were here, his anxieties would fade. No
such luck.

When the meal is finished, Corrik asks for us to be excused, like
we are one person and I should be used to it, it's not like Bayaden ever
asked my opinion on anything, but I was his slave. I'm supposed to be
Corrik's husband, not a wallflower.

It's only the first night I'm back though. It might take some time,
me being here, uh, home I guess, for Corrik to feel comfortable. I can
give him that time. I let Corrik lead me up to the rooms that will be
ours. "I will have the palace tailor pay you a visit tomorrow. He'll
make you all new clothes. We'll also need to get you started in Elven
policy, history, and politics."

I stare at him, trying to figure him out. Something's off. "Corrik, I
just got here. Don't you think, maybe I could have some time to
adjust?"

I don't know what I expected, but anger wasn't it. Corrik rounds
on me, his teeth bared. "I thought you were a warrior? All you do is
boast about that and your bravery and your experience and now you
want time to adjust?"

He's breathing hard and all my Warlord bravery's left me. "I … I'm
sorry, Corrik. Yeah, you're right. It's probably best I get started on all
that right away."

He balls his fists. "Get ready for bed." He points to the wash-up
room and I head in there trying to process what's going on. He seems
to want me to start my life here yesterday. Is that what this is about?
Some kind of urgency to have me be part of Mortouge? Maybe he just
needs some assurance.

I walk out, expecting him to have undressed or something. No, we
haven't been together as a couple in a long time, but we are a couple
and Elves don't care about naked. Even I don't care about naked so
much anymore, but he hasn't moved. He's outside the door, leaning
against it.

Oh.

Oh, I see.

He's standing vigil. Not letting me out of his sight. Uh-oh. This can only spell trouble for me. Corrik was already overprotective. He knows I've figured him out. "Before you say a word, don't. I'm not in the mood. You're just going to have to deal with how I am now."

There is a lot I want to say, hearing him use the phrase, "you're just going to have to deal with how I am now" is worrisome, but I remember what Papa always said about leaving Father alone till morning whenever we'd have an argument. "A tired Arcade is an unreasonable Arcade, Tristan. You'll have better luck in the morning."

Papa's advice applies here too, especially when Corrik reminds me so much of Father right now. Somehow, even though he picked me and not the other way around, I managed to marry my father.

I start to undress so that I can get into bed, but Corrik stops me. "What are you doing?"

"Getting undressed for bed...?"

"There are nightclothes in the closet. Go in there and change. I will wait till you are done and then I will do the same."

"Do you even own nightclothes, Corrik?" I say, trying to be coy, trying to be fun. He's not having any of it.

"*Now*, Kathir." He uses all Elvish, which means he's not impressed with my teasing.

I want to cry. All of it makes me miss Bayaden more than I already do. If not for the treaty, I'd leave in the morning. I do as he asks, finding myself a set of pale blue nightclothes, which will be fucking weird for me. I haven't worn nightclothes since I was a little boy. I'm quick about it, sensing he doesn't want me out of his sight long; when it's his turn, I wait on the bed.

At least the bed is divine. It's very Corrik, with plush, ice blue satin and white accents. The bed is large—it can fit at least ten grown elves in it. Way overboard, but there has to be some kind of perks being an Elven prince, an incredible bed is one. While I wait, I give myself a pep talk, again trying to channel Papa. I know he had to deal with my father's moods, he was good at it. I try to think of what he might have done. Papa was very submissive.

Trouble is, I've learned that while, I am submissive, yes, I'm more a brat. True submissives are fairly well-behaved, I am not. Bayaden would pull me to him some nights and hold me still as I cursed him, letting me get everything out, and I'd get quiet. "Are you done now?" he would say.

"No."

"No?"

"I don't want you to spank me."

"Too bad. That's happening. You are a brat Tristan. You need a good spanking when you get like this."

He'd put me over his knee and spank me until I cried and yeah, I would feel a world better.

Corrik climbs into bed. He looks funny in sleep clothes; I miss his large naked body. *Temporary, this is temporary, Tristan.* But I'm not sure it is. He does climb nearer to me, which surprises me since he's being so formal, but if I'm to think like Corrik, I would say the closeness is to better protect me. He doesn't reach out to bring me into his arms.

I'm not sure I want him to anyway. I'm not feeling close to him, but I'm used to someone holding me to sleep. I was supposed to sleep on my bed, but after the first couple of months, I would magically end up in Bayaden's bed each night. He would spank me like a bad pet and then refuse to let me go anywhere, telling me to close my eyes and go back to sleep.

I want to reach out to touch Corrik, but I can't, too afraid of the rejection I'm bound to get. *The morning Tristan. This will all be resolved in the morning.* "I'm glad to be home, Corrik," I try. Hearing me call this place home should lift his spirits.

"Home? How can this be your home? You've been here hours."

"Corrik, have I done something to anger you? If I have, please tell me what I've done, so I can fix it."

He's quiet, and then he says, "No. It's nothing you have done, and it's also nothing you can fix."

Since Corrik doesn't want much to do with me, other than to make sure I'm not going to disappear, I wrap myself up in my hair, feeling Bayaden surround me like he promised, missing him as I promised.

---

*F*rom there, things get worse, *much* worse.

---

*I*n the morning, the fresh sunlight of the eternal winter day comes in through the window and I wake up to a cold bed. Corrik's gone.

It's freezing, especially compared to what I'm used to—nights so hot you don't need covers, the warm sandstone under my bare feet when they hit the ground, as I'd prepare to head off and fetch Bayaden's breakfast. Corrik thought to leave me a warm robe and slippers. I climb out of bed and dress warmly, thinking I'll head off in search of food. My stomach is already growling. I don't know the rules of this place, but if I catch it for breaking one of them, at least the spanking I'd get for it will be worth it.

When I tug on the door, I find it locked. I start yanking, pulling with all my might to no avail. I bang on the door, shouting until my voice is hoarse, but no one comes. When Corrik dares to show his cowardly face, I'm sitting at the long table, furious. "What is the meaning of this, Corrik Cyredanthem?"

He's ready for me though, and I realize it's for this moment he's been preparing—while we traveled and even last night—steeling himself for when I would take him on not as Tristan, but as Warlord. "I understand this will be hard for you, but soon you'll come to see it was the right choice."

"What is the right choice, Corrik? Making me prisoner?"

"You are not a prisoner. This is your home."

"Last night you said this could not be my home. I've not been here a day."

"I was upset. This is your home and I am your husband. I will make the choices right for us and this is what's right for your safety and my peace of mind. You will remain in this room, under lock and key until you are ready to become Elf. When you are, you will be strong enough to combat another Elf. Right now, you are too weak and fragile. You must be protected at all costs."

I don't agree with him, but he's completely convinced himself that this is needed. I don't dare mention how much training I've had with Bayaden. It's not the time and that time may never come. "Corrik, *please*. Whatever you're thinking, can't we talk about it? There must be another solution."

"I've had a lot of time to think about a great many solutions. There is no other solution. Not to worry, everything is set up. You'll begin lessons with approved and vetted instructors, and we'll have you ready to pass the tests as soon as possible. I'm certain within a year, Father will approve you and we can take you to the place where you can become Elf."

"And what if I'm not ready in a year?" I know that to an Elf, a year is a blink, but I am still human, and a year locked in a room seems like forever. Besides, how am I to know that will be enough for him? It may never be enough. There will always be some new thing around the corner, ready to get me, as far as my husband is concerned.

"Then you stay here until you are. But not to worry, you will be ready. I'll make sure," he says, smiling with true encouragement.

Last night suddenly makes a lot of sense. No wonder he was hell-bent on all the lessons. The sooner I begin, the sooner I can become Elf. "Corrik, I understand you're afraid—"

"—no you don't understand," he shouts. "You don't, or you would not be arguing with me."

Maybe he's right about that much. I don't understand what he's going through, or what he went through but when I look closer, I see how much one year of me gone has weighed on him. Elves age slowly. He's been off looking for me, worrying and the truth is, I haven't. I mourned our relationship and moved on.

I kept Corrik in my heart, but I believed I would never see him again and as much as I can be a drama queen, I'm pragmatic too.

Corrik never gave up, he had faith in us I didn't have. He suffered worrying about me while I believed he'd be just fine. I was wrong and now I've aged the ageless. "Father had a guard for me. What about something like that?" I suggest.

"So, you can evade them like you and your cousin did?" Why, oh why, did I tell him about that? "No. You will stay here. You'll be busy anyway. You have much to learn in a short period of time."

These are all things he's told himself to feel better about this. He knows what this will do to me. "What's the longest it's taken for someone to become Elf?"

He doesn't want to answer that. "You are intelligent, you already know Elvish—even if I do not care for your accent—and that makes up half the requirements. I have no doubt my mate will exceed expectations."

"How long, Corrik?"

"Ten years."

"What if it takes me ten years?"

"Then you will remain here ten years. Once you are Elf, ten years won't matter. In time, you'll see this was best for us. We'll ride through the mountains on horseback, rejoicing what we've overcome. You'll see."

He believes that, but there's something he doesn't understand. "You cannot cage a dragon, Corrik."

"Watch me." His eyes are a pure challenge, daring me to say something about it, and his ears poise themselves for battle, but I remain quiet with the hope that I can talk him out of this over a few days. Maybe once I'm here for a bit, he will thaw. When he's sure I'm not going to say anything, he continues. "I knew you weren't going to take this well, at first." At first? Does he really believe I'll accept this? "So, I came up with everything I could to make you comfortable. You can call for whatever you want, no matter how outlandish and it will be provided for you. There are several rooms within these chambers, you have access to all of them. You'll even get to keep your sword. I'll admit that I would prefer you don't have it, but Father will not budge on that point, especially after what happened.

He insists you be allowed to practice with it. One of the rooms is just for that."

He begins to talk animatedly, going on and on about all the wonderful attributes my prison will have, but I'm not the least bit interested. I cross my arms and wait for him to finish. "I even … Tristan, I knew you might not look upon me with favor after this, I have been taking care to exercise respect by not taking you like I want to. You don't know how badly I want to pull you into my arms. I *ache* for you, but I can wait until you are ready."

"You don't have to wait. Give up on this foolishness and we can have sex right now. Or cuddle or make out, anything, but *please* don't do this, Corrik," I say giving up on anger, tears flooding my eyes.

It is affecting him, but it does not move him. "This will be hard for both of us, but it's for the best. You'll see."

"I disagree."

"When we have a child, won't you want what's best for the child, even if it's something he doesn't want?"

"I am not a child, Corrik. I'm an adult, and I don't deserve to be locked up in a room."

"You don't deserve it, this isn't about deserving, it's about safety."

"Then how about the palace? I would feel far less confined if I could at least have free reign of the palace Corrik."

"Did you not see the size of this place? Forget it. It's too open like the ship was. It's much safer here. When you're Elf, you may have free run of the palace."

I don't like the way he says that. "You don't ever plan to give me all liberties, do you?" I expected that to some degree. Even as the son of the Warlord, I was confined in some ways and it would have continued when I became Warlord. My father never went far without a full guard. Warlords are always wanted, but my father could come and go as he pleased and that was the difference.

"You are an Elven prince now, Tristan and aside from that, there's the prophecy to worry about."

I barely hear him anymore, I'm too angry about it all.

"And I know this is not the best time to bring it up, but I feel it's become more urgent for us to have a child. I have been given special permission considering the circumstances."

"A child?" That reminds me of Bayaden's green babies for a moment and I almost smile. "We can't possibly bring a child into this mess, because it is a fucking mess, Corrik."

"On that we can agree, but a child would strengthen the treaty with Markaytia and demonstrate our loyalty. Your father was not impressed we lost you. As we scoured one side of where Aldrien was supposed to be, he and your papa scoured the other. We sent word that we found you, but that wasn't enough. They will be here in a fortnight to see you with their own eyes. Talk of a child is good fortune, Tristan." He speaks softly, and with the weight of a person struggling with a great many things with no relief in sight.

I almost feel sorry for him and I know he's right about this. I sigh. I hate fucking politics. "Yes. A child will strengthen that pact." And I know how my father thinks. He will want to see some formal show of alliance. It's not uncommon for the spouse in an arranged marriage to "go missing," leaving the treaty intact, but without the obligation to the missing spouse, and the other is free again to make another treaty over a second marriage. As much as Father and I don't always see eye to eye, he cares about me and wouldn't want to see me used like that.

Speaking of my father, fuck. He's on his way here. Why do I feel like a little boy in trouble all over again? Knowing my father, he's simply coming all this way to scold me for getting abducted.

"Then we agree on that much?"

"We do." *Ugh,* though. Thinking about having a child to cart around with me, is overwhelming because we all know who will be expected to look after it. This is another thing we'll have to discuss. Am I to look after the child in this room? *One thing at a time, Tristan.* "What are the rules other than don't leave this room?"

"No other rules."

"Does that mean I can choose not to associate with you?"

I've stabbed him with an invisible sword. He swallows hard like he's also swallowing that information, but I think he expected it. "You will show me respect as your husband, Kathir, but after that, no. I will not force your company."

"Then I respectfully ask that you stay away until you come to your senses. This is pure madness, Corrik, and I won't endorse it. I will obey you, but I'm not going to act like it's okay. Finding another room for your clothes and to sleep in would be best."

"I cannot do that. You must realize that we need to show we have good favor with each other, even if we do not. Servants talk. I will respect your wish and come as little as possible, but I will have to come each night for bed, to get my clothes and yes, to visit."

"Fine, but I have no wish to see you otherwise."

"If that is what you wish."

"It is."

He takes a heavy breath. "Very well, I will return for dinner."

He leaves. I hear several locks click shut sealing me in and I want to die. All I have to stop the tidal wave of anxiousness being locked in a room brings me is my anger. Even that upsets me, being angry at Corrik. I don't want to be. I still love him. It's all too much to bear.

So, I return to bed, and I don't leave it other than to attend to my studies for three days.

---

*A*fter a week of confinement, I begin to lose my mind. I had vowed not to speak with Corrik unless spoken to, but I've begun to beg him, especially when Elf studies are not easy. I'm starting to worry I'll be trapped here ten years or more. "Corrik, *please*. What if you took me out? Full guard. Not too far. Maybe just to the palace gardens or something?" That's a shot in the dark, I wouldn't know if this place had a garden or not.

"No. Do not ask again."

But I do, over and over. I come up with new ideas and ways I could be kept safe—I have a lot of time for thinking—but he shoots down every single one, growing increasingly irritated. I'm surprised there hasn't been a consequence, I know I'm getting close though.

Suffering the consequences will be worth it to get my mind off being alone.

And Bayaden.

Missing Bayaden is different than missing Corrik. There was guilt attached to missing Corrik, guilt over what I'd done and what I didn't do, regret over things I never told him. With Baya there's just missing —missing waking up with him, missing eating in his lap, I even miss him yelling *Human* at me. The more I miss Bayaden, the worse I am to Corrik, who finally does spank me, with a nasty, little wooden paddle. It's a relief.

At the same time, I know I have to be careful how far I push him and decide there are better ways to annoy the living piss out of him, ways that are less dangerous for my backside.

I notice that although Corrik has refrained from making advances on me, he'd like to. The pajamas at night are as much for him as they are for me. I'm also tired of the Mortougian style of dress. It's too confining in comparison to what I'd got used to in Aldrien. Since I've been given leave to ask the tailor to make me whatever I desire, I request an assortment of large, silk robes, with giant bell sleeves. My hair melds with the robes, cascading down them like it has always been part of them. They casually remain open and I keep bare underneath so that Corrik will have to stare at me this way if he wants to continue to visit.

As soon as he sets eyes on me, I know I've achieved a small victory. He's annoyed, but he's refraining from saying what he'd like to. I know the Elves of Mortouge are promiscuous and open about things like nakedness. The tailor went as far as to compliment me on my taste when I suggested such robes, telling me how much the prince was going to love them.

"What is the meaning of this, Tristan?" he says in my home tongue.

"Oh? You don't like them? You said I could have whatever I wanted from the tailor."

"The little Markaytian I know would have balked at such an outfit."

He's right. That Tristan would have. "I am not that person

anymore. Are you about to tell me I'm not allowed this freedom either?"

He thinks about it. He'd like to. "No. It was just a shock. They do look nice on you, Kathir."

I know they look good. My body is still in supreme shape from all the lessons with Deglan, the time spent teaching the younglings, and sword practice with Baya. I'm bigger than he last saw me, more muscles in my back and shoulders, carved legs and glutes. Plus, my gait has changed into one more like a panther, like Bayaden, which is used for hiding in the brush, so you can sneak up on your opponent easily. "Are you here to eat? You're early."

"Yes. I thought we could have dinner together, but it had to be early. We have some things to discuss, your parents will be here next week. They were brought safely into the Realm."

I suppose we need to discuss that. "I will be on my best behavior, Corrik."

"Will you?" He's doubtful, and with good reason. I have been nasty, but that's because I am still angry. I don't see an end to my anger anytime soon.

I sit at the table as he glowers at it; there's a knock on the door. One of the guards for my room announces the food and Corrik allows them to enter. He begins talking as we're served. "I think we should tell them we plan a child in the next five years. We'll use your studies as the reason we're not going ahead with a child sooner. Kathir?" he says when I don't answer.

"Are you asking my opinion?"

He glares at me, but I don't apologize. He hasn't asked my opinion on much. "I am asking your opinion."

"In that case, yes. My parents will be amenable to that. I'll even pretend to be excited."

"Pretend? I thought you'd be excited to have a child. In a few of our conversations through the book, before we wed, you told me you wanted children."

Corrik left a book for us to communicate through during our engagement period. He often used it to give me instructions, mostly concerning my cock, but we did chat too, with him getting to know me as best he could despite my resistance.

Which reminds me, this scenario playing out now, is not the only cause for me to resist Corrik. His overprotectiveness has always been a point of contention for us. It's now reached massive proportions. "I do want children, but not like this. I want my freedom back, Corrik."

"Why must you continue to make this so difficult?"

"Because I hate it and feel it unnecessary. Corrik, you can't protect me from every eventuality." For a moment I consider telling him how I could fall out the window at any time, but that will only result in him having all the windows barred up and I need fresh air.

"One day you will understand," he says, something he repeats over and over, because what else can he say? The whole thing is highly irrational and overboard. "Tell me, how are your studies?"

"Long and arduous. I never liked school much."

"You told me you did well in school."

"My parents left me no other choice, doesn't mean I liked it. Once again, just doing my duty. I prefer sword practice, Corrik, if you'll hear me for once. I'm also good with a bow if you care to know." I'm not sure I ever told him that.

We eat in silence. He seems to be thinking about something, likely a hard topic he wants to approach likely, and I just want this meal to be done, so he can leave. Finally, he gets it out. "I ... I would provide you with lovers if could, but I haven't been able to figure out how to do that safely."

"Great, so that's something I'm forced to go without too unless I want you, but I do not," I say and yes, I'm being mean (especially when I do want him), but I don't care. I'm done with this dinner.

His jaw hardens. "I am not taking lovers either. I will be faithful. I *have been* faithful."

"Which underlines that I have not been. Go on just say it." I know he knows. We haven't talked about it, but I don't doubt Diekin told him for some kind of benevolent reason.

"Yes, I know of your relations with the Aldrien Warlord. But I don't hold any anger over that," he's quick to add.

"How could you not? Your relations with Andothair were some big crime, nearly treason. Isn't this the same?"

"No. Totally different circumstances. You had little choice. If you need forgiveness, I forgive you." His eyes plead with me. He knows we have to talk about this. He hopes I'll go easy on him, but I will not.

"I had plenty of choice Corrik. I chose, and I fell in love. That's right, I love the Aldrien Warlord, *deeply*. My heart is still broken."

Then he surprises me.

Corrik has always been possessive. I expect him to lose his mind about this, but that's not what happens. "I understand the situation. It's normal to have more than one love. I can't say I love it, especially when you've withdrawn from me, but I understand it. You thought you were never coming back to me; you wanted a happy life, which is what I would have wanted for you if that had ended up being the case."

"You're saying this? You, who almost struck your uncle for suggesting he get a turn with me."

"You were my shiny new toy," he says winking. "Besides, I have seen the Aldrien Warlord, as much as I hate to admit it, he is your type."

He's trying to be coy. He's also trying in general and the empath in me wants to give into him. Truly, I know he's in a position, but he is still wrong, and we are at war. If this is the only battle that I can fight, if it is to be my last battle, I will fight it without mercy. "He is my type. I wish I were back with him. Are we done here?"

"You know Tristan, I am still your husband and I will still spank your naughty bottom when you need it. Talk to me like that again and I will."

I can't help it, I shiver. Corrik still gives me *that feeling*. The magical one. I am addicted to it. "Spank me or don't, I do not care. This has become a marriage of duty for me, nothing more. I will continue to obey you and fulfill my duty to Markaytia by acting as a loyal servant to Mortouge, but that's it."

He slams his hand on the table, the glasses jump. "Part of your duty is as my husband and all that entails. I could make you, you know. It would be my right."

I do know. That reality gives out my bravado. "Will you?"

"No. Never. My point is that I do treat you with respect."

"Gee, thanks for asking my consent, Corrik."

He is losing his patience. "I know this is hurting you and I'm sorry for that. It's meant to keep you safe."

"No Corrik. This is for you. Don't pretend it's anything other than what it is. I am perfectly fine with taking my chances out there, it's you that isn't."

"My family agrees, Tristan. I am not the only one concerned for your welfare. My parents were beside themselves. They agreed this was the safest route until you become Elf."

"I grow weary of this conversation, Corrik. I will never agree with you, so long as I live. May I be excused? I'm very busy. Social calendar is booked."

He stands and places his cloth napkin on the table. "You're excused." He walks out after that without another word, and once again the door is locked tight. I hear every bolt as it is secured into place.

I feel more alone.

---

*C*orrik doesn't return for days and when he does, he's politely cold. "I came to tell you that your parents arrive tomorrow."

He looks terrible; I take a bit of pity on him and answer in Elvish, doing my best to display a Mortougian accent. "Thank you, husband," I say. Having had a few days to think by myself, I realized I should be showing at least the minimum respect required. He is still my husband, even if I'm enraged.

He smiles. He still answers in Markaytian. "See? I knew my husband was smart. You're learning quickly. We'll be making the journey to Drakora in no time." We stand, with only two feet between us, but so much keeping us apart. "I shall go now, Tristan. I know you do not want me here."

I pull my robes around me. I haven't stopped being angry at him, but the time alone has been good for my head. I nod. "Corrik?"

"Yes, Tristan?"

"Would you allow Diekin to visit?" I haven't been allowed visitors yet, and I don't know why. Though truthfully, I wasn't ready to see anyone, anyway.

He beams. It's something I want that he can give me. "Yes. I have figured out a system for that. I can allow one visitor per day, other than me. I don't want the guards getting used to too many visitors."

It's hard not to roll my eyes, but I'm actively trying not to argue again, so I nod. Besides, my complaints get me nowhere and I'm far too excited to see Diekin. Corrik turns to leave. "Cor, wait."

"Yes?"

"Come to bed tonight?"

He's not as excited about it as much as I thought he would be. "I will do my best Tristan, but I've been working 'round the clock. I may have to sleep in the barracks again."

I know at that moment he won't be here tonight. I try not to let my disappointment show and I feel stupid for asking. I spend time after he's gone sitting at my window, a place I've taken to, a place I try not to let Corrik see me sitting at, or I'm sure he'll flip out. I spend time looking out at Mortouge, studying the stones on the side of the building, which sticks out in odd increments, making a shape I cannot decipher from this angle. I am high up, but thankfully I wasn't put in one of the taller towers and truly, I could find a way down from here. My mind can't help thinking in that way. It was what Lucca and I used to do often.

Late in the afternoon, Diekin enters like the ray of sunshine he is. We rode home together, but it's now the absence of his bouncy spirit, while I was gone, strikes me. His hair is shorter than mine, it stops at just past his shoulders, allowing the front to wave up and over to the right. He has a new tattoo over his shoulder I didn't notice before with his shoulder armor in the way. He's in nothing but a white, male shift dress with no sleeves, that hangs between his inner thighs, the sides open showing off his tree-trunk legs. It's cinched at the torso with the only bit of armor he's got on—a wide band of Elven steel.

"Warlord, it is good to see you." I haven't bothered to change; I don't bother to close my robe. Diekin appreciates my finer features. "Perhaps Corrik will allow you and I to play at some point. Ditira is a bit possessive, but she might make an exception for you."

He waggles his ears with his eyebrows, and I blush hotly and it's nice to know there are still some Markaytian sensibilities in me. I close up my robe and he smirks. "It is good to see you Diekin."

I lose my false confidence and burst into tears. Diekin gathers me in his arms. "I'm sorry, Tristan. I am the weaker mate and therefore do not get a vote in this, but I don't agree. I love Corrik and he's usually level-headed, but with you, he loses all reason. Ditira was the only one who tried to talk Corrik out of this insane plan. Unfortunately, Alrik was not only in agreement, but he also talked Corrik further into it. He does not want to waste his time going after you again and as the crown prince, he views it as his duty to ensure you are kept safe to honor the treaty. Corrik remains in conflict."

"Corrik is in conflict? No. He's all for this plan. Meanwhile, he galivants and sleeps in the barracks." I would love to sleep in the barracks.

Diekin's brow squeezes together, his ears turn down. "Corrik in the barracks? Tristan, no. He has been outside your door, unless he absolutely needs to leave for a royal duty."

"Outside my door?"

"Yes. He slept on the floor one night, but Alrik quickly caught word of his behavior and put an end to that. He sleeps in the guest room, next door."

"But, why did he refuse me earlier?"

"Things with Corrik are bad. His parents weren't happy with him when they learned of his relations with the Rogue Elf Prince, and he's still trying to make it back into Alrik's good graces. Plus, he's torn up about you. He knows what this is doing to you, but he doesn't see another way. You have every right not to feel sorry for him given your predicament, but he is struggling too. It's getting harder for him to face you."

"I have little mercy for him at the moment," I say, but the part where he's been sitting outside my door, day after day, going as far as to sleep out there gets to me. I had pictured him off doing things, like living his best life and having fun which I am forbidden from doing. I'd even take mucking out Bayaden's stables over this.

"I know, it's a bad situation. I see both sides, even if I disagree with one side. Corrik is more worried than I've ever seen him, this shook him. It can only speak to how much he cares for you. I do realize this is little solace for having to remain confined."

Wow, even Diekin is struggling. "Come, let me show you around my confines. I have to say, if I am to be locked in a tower, it's not too shabby," I tell him in Elvish, unfortunately, most of what I say is still with a lot of Aldrien accent.

Diekin doesn't care. "Lead the way, Warlord."

Diekin and I have a good time and I feel better having spent time with someone I'm not mad at. But too soon, he has to leave. "I will come back as often as Corrik will allow," he tells me.

I feel so good after the visit, I do something I haven't dared. I remove my robes and put on a single pair of pants, ones that were given to me by Bayaden, ones I'm surprised Corrik hasn't taken away yet, and head into the room that is meant for me to practice with my sword.

I have glanced at the room from afar, but I haven't been in here. It's a room without furniture, to leave room for footwork and flipping about the room. The floor is made of stone, placed at unequal levels, I imagine, to provide unequal terrain for training purposes. Against the far wall, my sword stands lonely in its baldric. I walk over to it, pick it up and unsheathe it. I can read the inscription now. I smile.

"He who wields this sword wields the fire of Dragons."

The king knows me.

I spend the next several hours practicing. I practice some of what my fathers taught me, with some of what I learned from Bayaden, and invent new moves from the combination of styles. Sword fighting is my art, it's how I create, how I feel the world.

The sun goes down, and I'm still swinging, dodging, slicing. Sweat pours off me and I relish in the feel of my hair whipping around me once again. I notice when I have a spectator. He strides into the room and pulls out his sword. "You are quite beautiful when you have a sword in your hand. Let's see what you've got," Corrik says.

My eyes gleam at the chance and I can't believe this is *my* husband saying this, but he is, and it gives me hope.

Corrik is beautiful with a sword too, and I get distracted wanting to watch him, my cock hardens as the sweat begins to pour off him, along with one of my favorite scents, the scent of a fight. I can tell he's going easy on me, but it's still too much and when my knees hit the ground, it once again drives home the point that I am no match for an Elf. I hear the ring of steel as Corrik slides his sword home. "When you are Elf, I think you might best me. You're the finest I've seen."

I beam, feeling so good, it gives me a high, my muscles are tired and aching in the best way. "You're not worried I'm going to run myself through?"

"A bit, but my vision has come again a few times since you've been away and I'm sure now, it was not by your own hand. So please try not to fall on your own sword, eh?"

I laugh. "I won't," I say, catching how nervous Corrik is. "I know I have done nothing but berate you, I shall refrain today."

He looks down at the floor. I have never, in my recollection, seen Corrik display anything close to submissive, but I see it now. He's stopped knowing how to be around me at all. He knows what he's doing is affecting me, but he doesn't see another way around this. His eyes fill with tears. "I am sorry, Tahsen."

Oh. And he feels he's an immense failure. I see that now. When my parents get here, he will have to face them as the Elf who lost me to a rogue band of Elves who, for as far as anyone knew, abducted me into sexual slavery. He doesn't think he'll be forgiven, and if he ever forgives himself, it will be a miracle.

Somehow this, his version of keeping me safe, makes amends for all that.

I take his hands. "I'm sorry too. I can't say I'll ever be happy about this, but I will learn to accept it." Thankfully, I am doing well in my studies. All I can do now is make sure this only lasts a year and hope Corrik will relax by the time I'm an Elf. My anger doesn't help anything.

"This means a lot to me, Tristan."

I notice the bits of white in his hair again. Without really looking at him, they blend in with the rest of his blond hair, looking like nothing more than highlights. I reach out to pick it up. "Is this new?"

"I was wondering when you'd say something." He smiles. "It began happening a few weeks before I found you."

"What does it mean?"

"I think it's my sadness."

That breaks my heart. "But you're not sure?"

"I'm not sure. But do not feel bad for it, my sadness is my own."

"No. I have been nasty. There's no excuse for it. You should have given me a lot more spankings than you have."

He smiles. "Oh really?"

"Should have. But you didn't. Retrospective spankings are not a thing."

"I was not aware of that rule. I'm going to have to check the book." We both laugh and it feels good not to be mad at him. "You did not eat your dinner."

"I, oh. No wonder I'm so hungry."

His laugh this time is hearty; it's a laugh I've missed. "I was going to say you're usually ruled by your stomach. Come. I shall make sure my husband is fed."

I let him pull me by the wrist to the table where he sits me down and pushes the food in front of me. He sits on the other side, casually, his large thighs splayed, his thick shoulders opened as wide as possible, his long hair pulled back in a half-ponytail with the rest of it hanging down his back, and his tall, Elven ears poking high and uncovered. He's dressed casually too, a V-neck, dark blue blouse, tucked into black pants that stop at the top of his large calves. He watches me.

"This is good. I'm starving," I realize as I say it. "So, to what do I owe this visit? More talk of my parents?"

"No. I was hoping you'd allow me to stay the night."

I set my fork down. "Cor, you should, regardless of my wishes." Corrik might not be in line for the throne, but as a royal couple, we still need to display unity from within. "But, I really would like you to stay."

"I know but, I thought just a few nights alone would be all right and do us both some good."

"Is it true you sit outside my door for hours? That you slept there one night?"

"*Diekin*," he curses. He looks up from hooded eyes. "I have."

"Please don't do that anymore, Corrik."

He nods. "As you wish, Tristan. Now please, keep eating."

"Does my eating make you feel better?" I ask, before taking a large bite.

"It does. Being able to take care of you in any way soothes me. Have you forgotten?"

I shake my head. "No, but I suppose I need to relearn what makes you feel content."

"Please. Let me show you."

He goes through the trouble of giving me a bath. Another Elven perk is running water, which we did not have in every room in Markaytia. I enjoy it though. Having him wash my hair is relaxing. He combs it out for me afterward and even hands me one of my silk robes. "My hair doesn't bother you?" I say. He must be able to sense the magical essence from it and he's smart; I'm sure he can guess whose it is. "Aren't you angry with me?"

"No. I had a long while to process and I'm eternally grateful things weren't as I pictured. Of course, I don't like that it happened, but it's better than the alternative."

Right. I'm sure he envisioned me being raped and beaten over and over. Falling in love with an enemy Warlord is definitely a better alternative. "But it has happened, and I'm going to be honest, I still long for him."

He nods. "Do you long for me at all?"

"Of course, I do. I missed you." That relaxes him. He opens the bed covers for me but before I hop in, I remove my robes.

"Please don't tease me so, Tristan. I … I want you so badly."

And when an Elf is turned on, that craving is a *need*. They can barely stop themselves. I know what I'm doing. "I want you too. Come to bed properly, Husband."

He bites his lip but doesn't wait to be asked twice. He sheds his clothes and is on top of me with the speed Elves are known for. He attacks my lips with soft little kisses to begin with that quickly turn ravenous. "My love, my love, I've missed you so much," he says.

I respond in kind, enjoying his lips, placing my hand on his large bicep and squeezing. "Do you mind if I use some magic, Tristan?" he says, panting, between kisses. "Elves don't need lube as Markaytians do. I was being respectful that it might be weird for you."

I don't tell him I'm already used to magic like that, nodding instead. His fingers go to my entrance, as he whispers the spell and when he plunges them inside, I'm wet. "You will slick up here naturally when you are Elf," he reminds me.

Fuck. His fingers feel good. I push down, trying to fuck them, moaning, writhing. He smiles from above me as he gets his dripping cock ready to enter me. He slides in slow, taking his time. Everything about this has a gentle feel I'm not used to with him. Corrik's still hesitating and I understand. Not only is this our first time since I've returned, but I'm new. He's getting to know me again. And Corrik's changed too; he's letting me get to know him.

He slides in giving me time to adjust around his large member. He starts with slow thrusts, working his way into me, not just with this cock, but with *him* and I feel all of his vulnerability. He may have talked a big game, about time healing all and how we'd laugh about this blip in time in the future and how I'd eventually come to understand, but he was afraid of losing me forever.

At this moment, I discern something.

That's the curse of being a Top—doing the things you feel are within your role to do, at the risk of your brat hating you forever. All you can do is hope that one day, they see your intent as a whole, rather than focus on how miserable they are in the moment.

A brat having respect for their Top's role is important. *I need to do better.* It doesn't mean I have to like what he's doing, but I can still have respect for his role which is to keep me safe; we need to be a team. I'm getting a better sense of what's gone on for him; his failure to protect me, the nightmare of thinking I was being abused and mistreated and risking my hatred to do what he feels will keep me safe.

All of it breaks my heart, tears begin streaming down my face. He's tearing up too as he continues to thrust into me, bringing us both closer to orgasm, until we fall over the edge of climax, Corrik spilling his seed into me, and me spilling onto my belly. He pulls me into his arms after and I enjoy being surrounded by him.

"Oh D'orhai, I was so afraid. I've never been so afraid of anything in my life."

"I understand now, Corrik. I don't like it, but I understand."

"Fair."

We fall asleep like that; life becomes more hopeful

---

*T*he next morning, we eat breakfast together, naked, as we plan for my family's arrival, which could be at any time.

"Corrik? May I have a bow?" I get the idea suddenly. Maybe he'd feel more comfortable with that than a sword.

"Is it your mission in life to see the first Elven heart attack?"

I laugh. "No, but your vision is of me with a sword, not a bow. I am good with a bow."

He leans back in this chair, his large cock standing upright, horny again, which is a feat. It was a long night of fucking and getting reacquainted. I have bruises. "You may have a bow. I'll have something special made for you. Now come here. If you're finished with that, I must have you again."

Corrik fucks me over the table, we make a huge mess, the breakfast dishes crash everywhere. For the first time, I think about the servant who will have to clean up this mess. I've lived as a spoiled brat in some ways for most of my life. The time as Bayaden's manservant has given me a new perspective.

In preparation for my parents, I get dressed. It's one thing for me to be a fucking brat for Corrik, but Father is another matter. I'm stressed about it actually, and I run about like a chicken with my head cut off. "Tristan," Corrik says in his deep voice. "Do you need a spanking?"

Probably, but I'll never admit it. "No. I'll be fine, I just ... how about you help me make my hair look nice? You're just standing there."

His eyes turn to slits before I'm thrown over his shoulder and he carts me off toward the bed. "We don't have time for this, Corrik."

"We have plenty of time."

Corrik has gotten too efficient at baring my bottom and placing me over his knee. I can't help relishing in the feel of the large Elf's thick thighs even though my arse is already tingling, knowing it's about to be roasted. He doesn't give me time to think about it for too long, his hand is coming down rapidly.

I'm too provoked by the thought of my parents' arrival to sink into the spanking, to even think about accepting it. I kick and resist and complain. "Ow! Ow, Corrik. This isn't nice."

"Is this what you want your parents to walk in and see? You having your bottom warmed?"

"No, and if you would stop, there wouldn't be any worry about it. Yowwch!" Rule number one—never get sassy with thy spanker, it can't end well. Corrik thinks my lip means I need him to spank me harder, so he does. Quickly, my arse is scorched, and I'm groaning, feeling sorry for myself.

But then magic happens. I don't know if I'll ever be able to explain it. After all the fight is out of me and the throb in my arse has reached new heights, I melt. I finally accept that this is happening, and that Corrik isn't letting me up until I let go and release the tension from my body.

It's a submission thing, and it happens when I've been spanked long enough. I don't know what else to tell you, but this is what happens for me every damn time. Even when I think it won't, eventually it happens. Sometimes it happens sooner, sometimes later. Whatever the rhyme and reason, a knot disappears, and I release a good portion of the anxiety holding me hostage. When he stands me up, I feel a world better. He looks me over. "You need another spanking, but we'll let this one sink in first."

"Another?" I complain pulling up my pants over my tender arse. "That's hardly fair. I haven't even done anything."

"Yet. You haven't done anything yet, and I'll be keeping it that way, understand?"

My lip wobbles. "Yes sir."

"Come here, my darling. Everything will be all right."

Corrik hugs me, and I grip him tightly.

He also helps me brush out my long hair as I fret over it. "What if Father doesn't like the blue and purple? Accch, who am I kidding? He's going to hate it."

Corrik waves his hand over my hair, the purple and blue vanish, leaving only the black. "Better?"

I tear up. It's like Bayaden has left me, even though I still feel his magical essence. "No. I want it back, Corrik."

He brings it back. "It was never gone. I can't get rid of it," he says somewhat annoyed about that fact. "I can only create an illusion over it."

"I'll take my chances." I can't bear to see the color gone.

He rolls his eyes at me.

When I'm dressed, I do look nice, but the clothes are confining. The fabric is white with finely detailed silver embroidery, and rises halfway up my neck, open in the center. The sleeves are long, and the garment reaches past my hips, to show off the black, cropped pants and tall boots. The look is finished with a soft green cape and a wide, silver, neckpiece, which hangs down on my chest and spans my collar bone.

Even though most of my neck is covered, it feels bare without

Bayaden's collar. I left it for him under his pillow. I don't know if he'll bother to keep it. He has a new husband to think of, but I needed to give him something and it was all I had, which technically wasn't mine anyway. It was Bayaden's to give; it was a display of his ownership over me.

I'm happy with how I look though. Corrik places a thin crown on my head. "When you become Elf, there will be a ceremony for you, and you will have another crown. But you are still a prince, and this is your temporary crown." I recognize it from our wedding. I doubt it's the same one. I'm sure most things were lost on the ship, but it's a replica.

I do look good, even if I don't feel like myself—I am more comfortable in simple things—but when Corrik comes into the library (where he sent me to stop me running around cleaning and dirtying up my clothes), I know I pale in comparison. He's put his white outfit on, his signature one, with the gold trim and open jacket to display his chiseled abs. His long, gold hair with streaks of white, is brushed until it flows, and he tops the look with his crown.

"You're stunning, Corrik." It's an odd thing to miss one man so completely while being genuinely enchanted with another. I never thought I'd be the man in love with two men, but here I am. "We ready to do this?"

"I don't know that I'll ever be ready to recount the story of how I lost you, but it must be done."

"It wasn't your fault, Corrik," I try again.

"It was." He moves the hair from my face. "I am having a hard time forgiving myself, but last night was good. I am feeling hopeful that we can move past this."

He bends down to kiss me; it makes my heart race and my body heat, and I think that we can move past this too.

CHAPTER 12

$\mathcal{I}$t's the most people our chambers have seen since I arrived. The king and queen enter first and sit at the head of the long dining table. When my parents enter, time stops for me. Father is there in the flesh, and I can hardly believe I'm seeing him with my eyes. His long hair is greyer than when I last saw him, but it does not diminish his stature and he's every bit as menacing as I remember him.

And I didn't know it before, but I feel it now; there is something Father brings me that I was unaware of—comfort and grounding. I want to go to him and feel it, but that would be inappropriate at this juncture.

Then Papa walks in. He's much better than I last remember him when we said goodbye. He looks healthy and fit, but his eyes flood with tears when he sees me and I know he'd like nothing better than to take me in his arms, but that will have to wait.

Father strides over to me, setting his helmet down on the table, beginning his inspection of me. "Tristan, were you harmed in any way?" Wow, he's more concerned than I've ever seen him.

I have to think about that. Was I harmed in any way? The trip down memory lane has me smiling. There were plenty of times

Bayaden caused pain to my backside—so many spankings—but never harm. "No, sir. It wasn't like that. Everything was fine."

That was the wrong thing to say. "Has he been hexed? Someone tell me. *Now.*"

The entire room flinches.

"I haven't been hexed, Father."

"You and I are going to have our conversation," he promises in a voice I recall from my youth. I don't look forward to that conversation. "For now, I want answers. I want to know why my son was taken."

Father is not Arcade Kanes, calm and collected brother of the king, right now. He's Father Warlord whose offspring was threatened. He goes full dragon parent. If Corrik thought he was protective, he's about to learn a whole new definition of protection. Corrik steps up. "It was my fault, sir. I am his husband and the responsibility fell to me to keep him safe."

"I have half a mind to call this whole thing off, I still might."

Can he do that? By the look in his eyes, I'm going with *he'll find a way.*

"Sir, I assure you, we've taken extreme measures to ensure his safety," Corrik says.

But when Corrik outlines those measures, Father is not happy. "You plan to keep my son locked up indefinitely? That's your plan? Tristan, pack your things." And when I don't move fast enough he says, "Now Tristan."

I'm not sure what to do, because no bone in my body will allow me to disobey my father, but it's not that simple. As much as he'd like to, he can't just take me without a discussion. The Elven king speaks up. "Arcade were I you, I would feel the same way. But I know we can come to an agreement without breaking the treaty." He stands. "Come, we will talk in another room."

Father is hesitant, but he knows he can't refuse the king. "Very well. Eagar, you stay here with Tristan."

The king, queen, and Corrik leave and I'm left alone with Papa, which is fine with me. I run to him. "Come here, little man," he says, and I don't even mind.

Everything catches up with me and I let it all out, enjoying the way he envelops me with his large, soft presence. "Everything will be all right, Tristan."

"Can he bring me with you?"

"Not really, but your father could find a way with the mood he's in. 'Eagar, if there's one hair, *one hair,* harmed on his head …'" he says doing a spot-on impression of Father. "I had to listen to that the whole way here."

"Was he that worried?"

"Of course he was. I know he's a rough man, but his love for you is infinite."

"I thought he came here just to scold me."

"He might find excuses to do that, but that's how he shows he cares. Often he has commented on how much he misses training with you."

That fills me with more pride than I've ever felt. Papa continues to run a hand through my hair and kisses my crown. "I have missed you, Tristan. Is it true he has confined you to these rooms?"

I nod.

"You must be going crazy."

"I am, but Papa, Corrik is distraught. No, I don't like it, but it's not so bad up here. I'll study hard and become Elf and then my confinement will be over," I tell him, trying to be as optimistic as Corrik about it. Naturally, I tend toward calming the worries of others, even when I am struggling.

"That I can understand, keeping the concern of husbands to a minimum. Tristan, have you learned more about …" he puts a hand over my heart, "… the way we are inside?"

I smile. "I have. Papa, it's natural as breathing for me and I've had enormous fun with it."

"You have?"

"Yes. I know it's something uncommon in Markaytia, but among Elves it's a thing, so you don't need to feel shame over it, or guilt that I am like you. I'm actually what they call a brat more so than I am submissive. Brats like me get a lot more spankings than submissives like you, Papa."

"You do?" I nod. "Doesn't it hurt?"

"Like the dickens. I try to avoid it, but it's inevitable. Don't tell Corrik this, but I need it."

He likes that, but then his brows press together. "You talk about it like you've had a lot of experience, but you've only just returned to Corrik and you weren't with him long before that."

I look down a moment and then I make myself face him. "I found another love, Papa. I didn't mean to. I thought I was never coming back. It was he who showed me more about this side of myself and helped me discover who I am." I light up thinking about Baya. "Corrik knows, and we're still working through it, but he isn't angry. Don't worry Papa, I know my duty is here. I will make Father see that too, somehow."

"Who is he, my boy? Your other love?"

I bite my lip. "Prince Bayaden Tar Jian, Warlord of the Aldrien Elves."

He pulls in a breath. "Tristan."

"It just happened, Papa. But I'm not hexed. There was a loyalty enchantment, but that's not the same as love and it's ... gone now anyway, but my love remains."

"How do you know that's all there was in the enchantment?"

"Because I fell in love with him before the enchantment was ever cast."

I part from Papa, wishing I could remove these foolish clothes. They're not me. You know what? I'm changing. I begin to undress, struggling with the stupid, fancy garment until Papa has to help me. "I believe you Tristan and I can see how much you have fallen for him. I don't think you should tell your father."

"I wasn't planning on it. I just don't want him hunting down Aldrien Elves and murdering them."

"If he wants to, there will be no stopping him. Not to worry, the king will calm him down. Your father does get a bit unreasonable when it's you, but he's always respected Vilsarion and Vilsarion has always respected Arcade."

Papa helps me dress into clothes that are more my style and we visit, until Father storms in. "Tristan, a word somewhere private," he demands, with only Corrik trailing behind him. Corrik looks worse for wear.

"This way, sir," I say leading him to the library.

I'm only just setting foot in the library when I hear the ring of steel. It's a sound I'd know anywhere, and I don't have to think about my next move, only to jump into action. Father taught me that any situation can turn into a battle, that I have to be prepared. If there's time to map out a room as to how I'd defend myself in it, then I should be going over multiple scenarios while I can. Father would often quiz me on such things and the penalty for missing anything was severe, since failing to do so could mean my life.

This is no more than another test and I am prepared.

I dive for the table and slide underneath coming out the other side with the long curtain rod stashed there. They are made of Elven steel, which makes for far better weapons than curtain hangers anyway. I round on Father to block his sword coming down at me and push him back. I use the dance Bayaden taught me, and my speed has improved trying to keep up with Elves. All my practice with a bow has improved my sight and therefore the sensory input to my brain, which results in better sensory output. I'm quick like lightning and disarm him with nothing but my curtain rod.

It does take some time, we destroy the desk and a lamp, but I do. I reach down to help him up; he, naturally, refuses. When he stands, he's beaming and I'm not sure I've ever seen Father beam so widely at me. At Papa, loads of times, but not at me. "You are my son and you are not hexed. That was incredible. Markaytia lost itself a formidable Warlord." Pride shines out of every part of him, he doesn't even have to say it and I know.

This might be the best moment of my life.

"Does that mean I get to stay, Father?"

"Much to my dismay. Tristan, are you sure you're all right? You tell me now. I want the truth now."

I may have just kicked his arse in combat, but I do not doubt he'll kick mine if he even suspects I'm lying. "I don't like the part where I'm being held prisoner in a place that's meant to be my home, but other than that I am fine, sir."

He's at war with himself about something and then he makes a decision. When he does, he pulls me to him. "You became an excellent warrior, despite Papa's blatant coddling of you, I suppose it's all right I do this."

I try to hold back tears, but I can't. "It's more than all right, Father." I squeeze him tight. I remember the times in the Aldrien dungeon— they were terrifying. I could have been left there to rot for all I knew at the time and had Bayaden not taken to me, I might have been rotting there still. Father's ways prepared me for that. I am grateful.

But my sons and daughters will always get lots of hugs.

I'm also reminded of what *this* feels like and how it's lacking with me and Corrik at the moment. Yes, he won't hesitate to spank me, but it's not the same as *this*. The thing I have in me is more than just spanking, it's a whole system. A circle. I need the soothing hugs and cuddles as much as I need to be turned over Corrik's knee. I need his solid form and to know that he's got me. I feel all of this from Father in one embrace.

When we part, he sets a hand on my shoulder. "Now that I am calm, I see that you are more than all right, you look healthy, bigger. You don't look like you've been a prisoner for a year."

"I wasn't, not really. I was treated well. I was given to the Warlord."

He's angry. "Markaytia has already declared war with Aldrien alongside Mortouge as per the marriage contract."

So, Andothair has his war then.

"Father, please. Call it off. It was all a huge batch of idiocy that was truly Andothair's fault. If anything, blame him and only him." I'm fine throwing him under the cart. Andothair deserves it.

"It's not that simple Tristan. They have committed a grave crime by abducting a member of royalty, punishable by Markaytian and

Mortougian law. The perpetrators must be found and executed. If we do not, we will appear weak."

By the Gods, this is a mess. "Father, please. I don't want them dying on my account."

"I'm sorry, my son. In time, you will see why we must do these things."

Good Gods, between him and Corrik with that line. "And the Elven king agrees?"

"Yes."

Ugh.

That is a problem for another day. "What about my confinement?"

"Corrik has given me a more detailed picture of what they face and why he made the decisions he has." This is not looking good for me. "I'm sorry, but he is right, and I would feel better about it too, with you under full protection. However, he has sworn that when you are Elf, you will be free again. There is no such thing as completely safe, but you are human in a land of Elves, you don't have equal footing. Once you do, I will feel better considering all factors at play."

I don't mean to cross my arms at Father, but I do. I had been hoping something could be done about this situation, and my hopes had ratcheted up a few notches. I can't help my glowering.

"Don't look like that. This is for your own good. People care about you."

"That's what everyone keeps saying. Why doesn't it feel like it?"

"It will. You have grown so much in a short time; this will be part of your growth. This year you will work on your inner self."

"You think it's only going to take me a year too, don't you?"

"Why wouldn't it? You did well in school."

"Because I had no other choice."

"What makes you think you have one now?"

Right. That is my everlasting problem, thinking I have a choice. I never have. I was born into royalty. Not that anyone will feel sorry for me, we get a lot, others don't get, but we are loaded with responsibility. I change the subject. "How's Lucca?"

"He is well. He'll be married next Spring. We hope the Prince will bring you home."

Home. Where is my home now? I sigh. "I doubt it, sir. Until this thing is resolved with Aldrien, which could take years, him traveling with me is unlikely."

Father nods. "I know the Gods did not give you an easy life, but it will be a full life. Even if you had become Warlord, your life would have been filled with travesty and pain. I raised you for that. You can do *this*."

I almost question if this is my father; he's so supportive and full of words. Arcade Kanes has never been one for many words, not with me. "I will continue to make you proud, Father."

"Good. Now trousers down and over that desk."

There's the Father I know. "What? But why?"

"You know why, and you know how much I like asking twice."

The answer to that is—not at all. I walk over to the desk and pull my trousers down, but I don't know why. Even when I lay over the table and hear the jangle of his belt, I still don't know. It's not till he starts, the first two stripes from his belt and the sting of it connects to my nervous system, that something comes to me. Tears prick my eyes and I do, I know what this is for. "I gave up."

"Who did you give up on?"

"Myself."

He continues, and the strapping starts to get intense. Father's spankings are like that. A short warm-up, then straight to an intensity that makes you feel like you want to die, but then it's over. Very business-like. I can't keep quiet; I have to cry out. I grip the desk for dear life and plead with him. "I'm sorry. I'm sorry! I can do better, sir."

He pauses. "A Warlord cannot give up on himself no matter what. Or it's over."

I nod. "Yes, sir. But it's lonely up here."

"That is the wrong thing to focus on. You have a task. Focus on your task. Get the work done, achieve the goal. Find peace in your own company."

He finishes strong with ten sharp ones, five to the back of each thigh—I'm going to feel those awhile—and then it's done. Even though my backside is on fire, I stand feeling better than I have in weeks. Carefully I pull up my trousers as he looks me over. "That's better. We will stay the week and then we must return."

Father's lessons are short and to the point, but they're effective. As a boy, I just thought him cruel. I'm getting to know a different side of my father. "I'm glad you will stay to visit."

We head back to the bedroom, where Corrik and Papa are sitting at the table, sipping fine Elven wine. I have no doubt they heard what just happened. I'm almost foolish enough to attempt sitting on the hard chair beside Corrik, instead, I stand behind him resting my hands on his shoulders, while my backside stings. "Oh, thank the Heavens. You look a world better, Tristan," Papa says.

I twist my lips. "Did everyone think I looked horrible?"

"Yes," Corrik says. "I did spank him before you came, but there wasn't time for the full strapping he needed."

"You're all terrible, talking about me like that," I complain, but it feels good. I'm happy to have two of my parents here. "How's Mother?"

"She wanted to come, but traveling with the army would have been too much for her. She's not used to it. She is good and sends all her love. We sent word; she will know you're safe."

The visit with my parents is a new experience. It seems now that I am married, Father is treating me more like an adult, keeping me in confinement aside. He speaks to me like an adult and tells me what to do less (for him), leaving that for Corrik. I get the sense, now that I have a husband, Father can relax and be more of a confidant. He's still *Father*, there's a line we don't cross, but he's a relaxed version of himself. I ask Papa about it when we're alone. "Your father knows he has to let go. You're not his little boy anymore, but it's been hard for him. This is him trying."

"But he was so cold before I left. After Corrik and I were betrothed, he wanted nothing to do with me."

"That's not true, Tristan. He was struggling and ended up steeling himself against you to avoid displaying his emotions. Arcade didn't want me to tell you, because he was disappointed in himself for having such feelings, but he didn't want you to go. He knew you had to, that you had a duty to Markaytia, and he didn't want to make things harder for you by telling you."

"I wish he had. I thought he was angry with me. What changed?"

"You are here now, he had to accept it at some point. He has respect for the duties the Gods have placed before you."

The week goes by quickly and my parents have to be on their way. They come up to say goodbye and I want to go with them, but I don't say it, trying to emulate Father. If he could keep silent and perform his duty to me, I can do the same for them. But my heart aches for so many reasons. "Your father has many duties, but we will attempt to return next year if you cannot come to the wedding," Papa says. "And Tristan, I know it didn't happen under the best of circumstances, but since it is, I'm glad the babe will come sooner."

I knew he would be glad. Papa wouldn't have been alive for my first child, which is hard to think about, had we to wait until Corrik reached his three hundredth birthday. This way we'll have a child born in this lifetime. For that reason, I'm happy it worked out this way too.

"As for your father, mention the idea again and watch his eyes—they give him away."

I decide to try it when I'm saying goodbye to him. I get another hug from Father. "You are still Warlord inside, and you make our people proud."

"If we have a boy, I'll make sure he gets your name somewhere."

I see what Papa means; his eyes do betray him—he's fucking delighted. "You know," he says trying to maintain stone, but failing like I've never seen him. "Arcadia would be nice for a girl too."

Oh, Gods. My father with a baby granddaughter. I might have to see that. I spend a good number of hours that night seeing if there's a way to influence the sex of an Elven baby with magic.

*F*ather's words stay with me for months. I am not becoming an Elf for me or Corrik, but for Markaytia. I delve into my studies and do little else. Corrik spends time with me, but he finds me reading or writing essays for Cupper (one of my professors) in Elvish. Finally pleased enough with my accent, Corrik no longer speaks to me in Markaytian. It's not perfect, but it's good enough to pass exams; some words that come out in the Aldrien accent, my brain refuses to let go of.

"Come to bed, Tristan," he says one night.

I purse my lips. "Yes. One more chapter and I'll be there."

"No. *Now.* Put the book down."

"Corrik, I have to get this done."

"You are further ahead than anyone thought you would be, especially you. What you need now is sleep. Book down, or I come get you."

If he comes to get me, that will automatically mean spanking. I snap the book shut, leaving it on the table and stomp toward the bed. I remove my robe, letting it fall to the floor and get in the bed, staying far away from Corrik. He doesn't stay far away from me. He gets closer to me; I move further away from him. "*Kathir.*"

"You wanted me to sleep, I'm here to sleep. Not have sex. Goodnight."

"I wasn't going to try, I meant it when I said you need the sleep. The pouting is unnecessary."

When I still don't answer him, he moves too quickly to the other side of our bed and I bolt right up because I know what that means. "Okay, I'm sorry. I'm being a fucking brat. Come back, Corrik."

But he's already got the paddle in his hand. "Lay on your stomach, head on your arms."

He remembers, too well, how much better I was after the strapping from Father and has since, employed such methods often when I'm out of sorts. I obey him, protesting little and I make a mental note that I must be riled since I employ token histrionics on principle. Corrik starts in hard and it's not long before he has me panting and my arse lit up with the fire from a good spanking. I start crying but crying during a spanking is seldom from pain. And this spanking isn't much compared to some I've had. I'm releasing pent up emotion.

When it's over, I'm sobbing and he's rubbing my back. "Shhhh, there now. You've been working yourself into the ground. Time to take a break. There will be no lessons tomorrow."

That freaks me out. "But Corrik, I can't lose a whole day, that will put me behind a week. *Please*."

"It will not put you behind a week." He pulls me into his arms, and I go, latching onto him. "Diekin can come. He'll stay the whole day. You two have leave to do whatever you want."

So long as it's not leaving this room. I know he'll be angry at me for asking, but I ask anyway. "Cor, please. Can't you take me some-where…? Surely it's unlikely Andothair's going to come tomorrow and snatch me away."

I wait for his anger, but he's quiet instead. "Children have been going missing in the villages surrounding Mortouge."

"And you think it's Andothair?"

"Yes. If they can steal our children without a trace, they can steal you. I'm not taking any chances."

I would get into the whole I am not a child thing, but it's useless. I give up on the idea, it's not happening. "Diekin it is then."

"I have a surprise for you; I'll get Diekin to bring it with him. Now, will you please sleep, my love? Your eyes have black and blue under them and you're beginning to look like the dead walking." He kisses my forehead.

I yawn, because he's right, I am exhausted, but I want out of here, badly. If I work harder than I've ever worked before, I figure I can pass the exams in six months, which means only three and a half months left locked away like this. But one night of full sleep will do me good. I nod into his chest, sleep already taking me.

"Good afternoon, Warlord," Diekin says. He comes bearing a large wooden box. "A gift from your husband."

"What is it?"

"You must have your nose in books. I'm surprised you don't have any clue. It's something you asked for."

But then I remember, and I brighten. "Really?"

He nods. "Open it."

Inside is the most brilliant bow I've ever seen. I know—from my studies, and from my time in Aldrien—the Elven bows are crafted from the wood of fifth-generation, firstborn trees, which seemed like an oxymoron to me until Cupper explained that firstborn designates its purity and not lineage. By the time a tree hits its fifth generation, the genetics are the strongest. I can feel the magic in it and recognize my husband's essence. He forged it himself. On the weapon, as per tradition, is an inscription.

"Victory."

It's one of the words I still can't say without an Aldrien accent, but Corrik knows that and I think it's my husband telling me he accepts me for who I am. My eyes tear up. "This is beautiful."

Diekin is beaming. "He worked hard on this for you, Warlord. It's his finest work."

"Wherever did he find the time?" He's been with me a lot, as much as he can. Whenever he's not doing princely stuff and war stuff. Corrik is not Mortouge's Warlord, but he has an active role with Mortouge's Warlord, Zelphar, whom I've never met, but have heard lots about.

"He made the time. You're important to him. I know what he's like, but Tristan, that Elf would do anything for you, even if that means locking you in a tower for your protection."

I roll my eyes. Yes. *That Elf*. Totally overboard. That's a thought for another time, right now I'm distracted by this shiny, new weapon. "Let's go shoot things with arrows, brother."

We go to the room I now refer to as my training room. In between studies, I never fail to train. I won't get weak or lose my skill just because I'm up here. It's not the same without another person to fight, but both Diekin and Ditira come as often as they can, separately since Corrik's only allowing one visitor at a time—the only exception being the king and queen. Diekin had wanted to introduce us. "I will someday soon, Warlord," he said to me. I'm glad Ditira visits. She reminds me of Deglan, whom I miss. I try not to think too long about those who I miss, it only distracts me from my goal.

I take the target from my training room and give eyes to Diekin that tell him all about my mischief. "You're going to get us into trouble, Tristan."

"Probably. You game? It will be fun, I promise."

"Well in that case, how can I say no, Warlord? Lead the way." Diekin has called me "Warlord," with no junior to prefix it since our time in Aldrien and he hasn't stopped.

I set up impossible targets and show off for him, placing arrow after arrow in the target. "Impressive, Tristan, but can you do this?" Diekin sets up a course of his own, adding flips and sideways jumps while shooting to spice it up. We take turns coming up with the most dreadful course we can and invent a points system. By the time Corrik finds us, we've gone rogue. The game went from target practice to us pretending we were in battle. Targets are set up all over the chambers, in every room. When Diekin hits one of my targets—my warriors—he collects points, the number depending on where he's hit them, and I get points when I hit one of his.

As we grow weary, some arrows miss their targets and end up in the tapestries, or through books, or the table. It's not just tired, it's level of seriousness too, which has gone out the window, with some of our arrows. Arrows are sticking out of every place.

"What in the Gods' names has gone on in here?" Corrik roars when he shows up hours later. "Kathir!"

But Corrik has left himself wide open and I can't resist. I let my arrow fly and it catches right where I was aiming, the bottom of his jacket, sticking him into the tapestry behind him. Not to be left out,

Diekin follows suit, pinning him on the other side of his jacket. Corrik is furious. He rips the arrows out. "Both of you better get out here, now."

We can't keep the smiles off our faces. "Now, Corrik," I say, holding a hand up to stop him from advancing on me. "Before you kill me, you said I could do whatever I wanted."

He takes a breath, remembering what he said, regretting what he said. "I will let this go," he spreads his arm toward the travesty that is now our room. "But this was too far," he adds referring to the arrows we stuck him with.

"But Corrik, we thought you'd want to play," I say. Both Diekin and I giggle.

Corrik is unimpressed. "Pants down, both of you and over the table. *Now.*"

Gods dammit. He proceeds to use the long part of the arrow, like a switch. It's a whippy little thing, and it packs a sting. "Ouch, Cor!"

After we're very, very sorry for shooting arrows at him, we're sent to clean up the mess we made under Corrik's watchful eye, our backsides complaining. "Worth it," Diekin leans to whisper to me as we de-arrow the library.

And I have to agree. It's the most fun I've had for a while.

---

*F*ather's words get me three months in before I start feeling sorry for myself again. Corrik is now having to inspire me to work instead of forcing me to take breaks. "Inspire" should be read as "spanking," and believe me, there's a lot of it.

"*Tristan*," he says coming into the room. I don't like the way he's said Tristan.

I heard him coming; I can hear the locks as they're being undone. I grabbed whatever book was closest so it could look like I was reading it. "Hey Cor, look I'm reading," I peer at the cover, "*Elven Fighting* … oh shite."

The evil brow is back. The one that gets mad at me all on its own, by the simple arching of it. This tells me a lot about what's going to happen, without him ever saying a word. I set the book down carefully. "Cor. Look, I promise I'm reading; I was just taking a break."

The problem is I take a lot of breaks.

His eyes flicker to a chair, *the* chair, the one he often uses when he's going to turn me over his knee. I don't have much time to convince him if I truly have time at all. "What did I say would happen if I caught you slacking off again?"

I get up from my seat preparing to run. "You said you would spank me with your hairbrush, but please. My arse is sore, Corrik."

He takes a step closer knowing I'm about to bolt, hoping he can get close enough to snatch some part of me before I get too far away. "Funny. If your arse is so sore one would think you would behave yourself. Come here."

I take a step away. "No. I don't want a spanking. Okay, I'll study. No more breaks—got it."

Corrik analyzes the distance between me and him. "Now, Tristan."

There are several heartbeats while we face off and then I run for it. I don't know why I do. Locked in this room as I am it's a case of "I can run, but I can't hide," and running prevents him catching me. He is Elf; I am human.

Yet running seems a viable option.

I head for the library where there are tables and knock over chairs to act as obstacles.

He's close on my heels and I *just* clear the first table, diving over it when he catches up. "Come quietly and I won't make you stand in the corner."

Tempting. "I promise I'll behave. I swear it."

He's not buying it. I look around for an exit as his thick arms cross over his chest. "I won't have it, Tristan. Then you'll be crying in my arms about how you didn't get enough studying done."

Apparently, me crying is a war crime—he can't handle it. He wants to crush whatever's made me cry. If it's due to my own behavior, he'll spank me until he's sure spanking is the only reason I'm crying.

"I won't be upset."

"You are getting this spanking, my love."

I've reached the end-stage of negotiations. There's no more, "if you come now, I won't …" because I've earned all the things by stalling. Soon we'll enter the stage of, "you've also earned yourself a bedtime spanking, delay anymore and you won't be sitting at all this week." I should give up, but I am Tristan Kanes, stubborn fool.

He steps toward me and I see an opening. It's enough that I can slide through and return to the other room. I make my move.

But he is an Elf, which means he's a lot quicker than I am. He catches my wrist and I'm unceremoniously flung over his shoulder. He gives a spank to my arse for good measure and with his arm across my legs as it is, I can't even kick them. Instead I whack his back. "Put me down Corrik! I'm not a sack of potatoes."

I won't stop fighting today which speaks to my mood. Corrik knows. "It's like that is it?"

He's calm as he walks to the dreaded chair. He spins it around with his free hand so that it faces away from the table and thus gives him ample room to put me over his knee. He does without preamble. He smacks at my bottom without rhythm until he's said without words how displeased he is. "I'm sorry, Cor."

He helps me to stand between his legs and his expression doesn't budge. "My hairbrush. Go get it, *now*."

I don't know if I'll ever be able to explain the difference between now and moments earlier. Maybe it's the shift that's happened from the short spanking I've just received knocking sense into me, maybe it's that I've realized how done he is with my behavior—that's always piercing at some point during the process—or maybe it's the simple act of dominance, appealing to the deeper part of me who innately responds to such things.

Maybe all of it. I don't know.

Whatever the case, now isn't the time for running, even though I could. I'm quick to retrieve the nasty little item and return, my face aflame, awaiting to go over his knee. He takes the brush setting it on the table behind him.

Whoa. The tummy drop sensation I get from all of it—knowing I'm about to go over his knee, standing before him shamefully regretting my behavior, how unbending he is.

It's humiliating when he slides his fingers under the waistband of my trousers and pulls them down in a way that's deliberate and meant to humiliate. That's part of it.

Having my pants pulled down for a spanking never gets less humiliating, and I imagine it will always make my cheeks rosy no matter how many times it happens, and how much I know I need it.

Corrik levers me over his lap so I'm off balance and I can't gain purchase on anything. "Tell me what you're meant to be doing between the hours of late morning and dinnertime."

"Studying, sir."

"And were you?" When I pause he smacks my bare, upturned rear. "Tristan."

I don't want to say. "I wasn't, sir."

Without the cover of my trousers, the spanks have more impact and I'm squirming and kicking, scrabbling for something to grab onto. There isn't anything. I hiss as his hand awakens the misery there from the yesterday and let me tell you, it's hard not to attempt an escape.

He pauses, and I release a breath I didn't know I was holding. "I'm sorry, Corrik. I've learned my lesson," I'm quick to say. It's my plea for him to stop. We don't need the brush; we don't need the brush!

"I don't think so. You ran. You know better than that. When I tell you to come for a spanking, you obey me Tristan."

"Yes, sir," I groan. I regret, oh how I regret.

I hear the wooden brush scrape across the table and then the warm wood is circling my tender backside raising gooseflesh there. "Any last words?"

And that, that's the reason I maintain there's a little brat in every Top, in every Dom, in every Master. Corrik is serious, but he's also cheeky and I know why. He's well aware I face the hairbrush with certain doom and he's rubbing it in. "You're a horrible person!" I say.

"Am I? Perhaps you'll remember that next time." He's not sorry.

Corrik Spanks Tristan with Hairbrush by Arkham Insanity

The devil thing makes contact with my arse and I cry out. I'm overly dramatic today, pushing at the chair leg, arching my back and kicking. My eyes water and I have to work to catch my breath as swat after swat descends, echoing through our chambers. I make some childish noises, some woe-is-me noises, some whining groans and huffing grunts.

After a time, my skin trembles before the brush hits it, knowing how much it's going to hurt. The pain increases as the spanking continues. My focus narrows to the pain—it's all that exists—until I have no fight left in me. I collapse over Corrik's knee, still wriggling to move the pain around, but no longer struggling.

The brush clatters to the table and his hand is soft on my poor arse, rubbing it for me. "To the corner with you." He removes my trousers, which were half off anyway, the dance of spanking released them from my right foot.

I want to complain, I do, but the throb in my arse prevents it. I move to the corner with my pants down and place my hands atop my head—proper corner time protocol.

The chair scrapes across the floor. His clothes crinkle and shift as he sits, his boots creak as he crosses them, and though I can't see him, I know he's laid them on the table and has leaned back in his chair so he can keep both eyes on me.

The throb in my arse makes standing still difficult.

"Tristan," Corrik warns.

I halt my fidgeting allowing the ache to run through me unhindered and think about how I'm not going to slack off anymore. I don't know how long I stand there—corner time always feels like it's forever—but at long last, Corrik calls me over for the best part of spanking.

The after spanking snuggles.

I race across the room, climb into his lap, spread my legs to either side of him and let my red arse shine toward the room behind us, as I nuzzle into his chest. "I'm sorry, Cor. I'll behave myself."

He hugs me close and I breathe in his scent, content for the moment. "For your arse's sake I hope so." He kisses my lips.

But I've lost steam, I've fallen way behind my projected six-month goal, and something in me has been craving Bayaden. I wonder if he has a green husband, I wonder if he's expecting his first green baby, and I wonder if he misses me, or if I was just a naughty fetish he's long since stopped thinking about. And yes, I realize it's not been nearly enough time for any of those things to happen, but the Aldrien king seemed urgent about it; I wouldn't be surprised if he rushed the wedding.

I sit in my robe on the ledge reading a book, with my looking device nearby. It's something magical I can view great distances with, another gift from Corrik. With it, I have discovered a band of Elves way out, past the marketplace, who practice with swords and bows, who are a form of Elven militia and I love watching them. "They're farmers who hope to become warriors," Corrik told me when I asked about them. "It's how some of our warriors begin their service to Mortouge until they are chosen for one of the advanced guards."

It's an odd idea to me still, even though it was this way in Aldrien as well. The way we do things in Markaytia is different. A lot of it is different. Women are not allowed to become warriors like they are in other territories. I always wondered why, especially when I still remember little Asha Tucker kicking my arse when I was seven. I was sore about it and seven-year-old me was secretly glad she wasn't in the running for Warlord. She moved away the next year anyway, but that was the first occurrence that got me thinking about women joining the military.

But even if women in Markaytia were allowed to fight, or if she were a boy and not a girl, she was a servant's daughter—servants cannot become warriors. All of my father's men are of special lineage. They don't have to be royals, but they do have to prove there is a warrior in their blood somehow.

I like the idea that anyone can work his or her way to warrior.

In my depression, I've taken to hours of watching them. They are actually very good. I can see where they need pointers, but it's a good crew to work with. "What are you doing? Come away from there," Corrik says.

I usually hear the door open; there are several locks that keep it closed and two guards in front, but I was enthralled in my farmer-warrior watching. Corrik does not like me sitting on the large window ledge with my legs hanging off it. He comes over to help me, giving a smack to my already sore arse, and shuts the window.

No.

Something goes off inside me, a switch, the animosity I've been holding inside so I could get what I needed to get done bursts free. "No. *No!* You take everything from me." I mean that in a lot of ways. "If I want to sit on the ledge, I will sit on the ledge. And you know what? Screw becoming an Elf. I don't want to anymore. Do you hear me? I'm not becoming an Elf."

"You have to become an Elf, Tristan. It's part of the contract, you know this."

"Oh, I know," I say the words like a dare. They always underestimate me, *Elves*, and I would love to show them why they shouldn't. Bayaden learned how clever I was. He believed in me. The limitations I have, he recognized them in a real way, but instead of keeping me locked up, he helped me find ways of overcoming them. "Open that window back up now, Corrik, or so help me, I will find a way out of here, and you will never see me again."

I've metaphorically punched him in the gut. But he does move over to open the window wide, while his eyes burn icy cold at me before he storms out of the room and I hear all the locks get done up with finality.

Victory. I climb back onto the ledge and contemplate how I might get down.

Things become uneasy between me and Corrik. He stops spanking me for things, which even I admit he should be spanking me for, and this is not good. I need to be spanked like I know Father spanks Papa, but I'll never ask. Corrik visits less, and I begin to resent him for that too, along with everything else. I know that this time, he's not sitting outside the door for me. What I said hurt him, but I'm angry again, and my anger won't allow me to apologize. *I am right*, my ego tells me, and there seems no other way out than to manipulate him.

I hate myself for it, it's not how I operate, but my options seem few and I just want a day out of this room. One day, that's all I ask. I try not to let Corrik see me cry, but eventually, he does. "Tristan," he says, climbing onto the bed.

"No. Stay away from me," I sob. "This is your fault. And I'm not going to reach my goal, and I'll be stuck up here longer."

It is breaking me apart. If only Father could see me now, he'd take back everything he said. *All it took was locking him in a room and the Great Tristan Kanes was defeated*—that's what the books will say about me.

He pulls me toward him anyway. He's shirtless and I'm naked, his skin is cool against mine, but I like it. I need him even when I hate him. He lets me cry against him. "You're so close, Tahsen. It's just a little longer and then we will have to travel."

Travel sounds exciting. I sniffle. "To the East?"

"That's right. Mountains far to the East. This is where you will have to pass the final test and then you will become Elf."

I nod.

"I am sorry, my darling. I never should have implied that I was going to board up the windows. I saw the fear in your eyes, and you reacted in kind." His ears move with the lines of his face, it makes my chest pang with sadness. He does try.

"I was horrible and hurtful. I'm sorry too, but yes, I was scared. I've never been so defenseless in all my life."

"You're hardly defenseless, Tristan. Half of my protections are to keep *you* from breaking out. I know if you really wanted to, you'd find a way."

That makes all the difference. "Thanks, Cor. The worst of it is thinking about how weak you think I am."

"No, my mate is strong. But we all have things we cannot fight and for you, that's Elves." We're quiet for a time and I enjoy him running his hands through my hair. "Tristan, could you leave me so easily? I mean, in your heart. Of course, you could figure out a way to leave, I believe that, but could you turn away, never come back without a single thought?"

One of my biggest character flaws is saying things like that, hurtful things I can never take back. But the problem is, I did mean it at the time. "I could not leave easily, Corrik, but I could leave if I needed to."

"You won't though, because of Markaytia, not because of me."

It hits me. I still haven't told Corrik I love him. There has been too much going on, making my feelings go everywhere. I've been waiting for a pure time, but there hasn't been one. I don't want to say it to him out of duty or obligation, I want it to come out freely, but something keeps blocking it. This means Corrik still doesn't know, especially when he knows that while I have shelved my outward resentment about his "protection plan" it is still there. Plus, with all the turmoil, it must be hard for him to feel my love on his own, without the words for more certainty.

"Ultimately the reason I will stay despite what you choose to do is because I have made an oath in the name of Markaytia. But if that reason didn't exist, then I'm sorry, but my love for you would not hold me here, which has nothing to do with how much I love or don't love you. I have to love myself first Corrik; being confined like this is dampening my soul."

"I can understand that. It's not forever."

"I know. It's just hard." I take a breath. "I will get through it. *We* will get through it, but Corrik, don't doubt that I love you. I've never said it, so I'm saying it now. I love you and I just want everything to be as normal as our lives will ever be, so I can enjoy you."

"Me too, though, you must have known even before we married, life here won't be the 'normal' you are used to."

"Yes. I know it's different here. That you are deviant creatures," I say. "Which I have wondered about. There have been no lessons of the kind you tried to teach me on the ship."

"That is a time commitment, I knew you'd want all spare time to study and shoot arrows into our fine tapestries," he teases me. I laugh. "Did you enjoy those lessons, pet?"

A shiver runs through me. "When you weren't whacking me with your crop, I did."

He smiles wide, but it fades. "Tristan, I'm not sure how submissive you are. You're a brat and I worry that outside of here, there will be an all new prison for you to have to adapt to and hate me for. I love you, more than I have words to tell you and seeing your heart break, is breaking mine. I'm starting to think that … that I should never have taken you from Markaytia. I was selfish and arrogant. I had my vision and assumed that it meant all it was prophesied to be, that you would love it here. But now, I'm not sure you will. I fear the Gods are playing tricks on me."

"No. If the Gods say it's so, it must be so, but wasn't it you who told me marriage is work? Maybe getting there isn't easy, but once we arrive, it will be worth it."

"Once again, my wise husband saves the day. It is decided then, we shall succeed because we will work with what the Gods have given us."

CHAPTER 13

I do a lot of thinking. I have been experiencing emotional whiplash—something that happens when someone stops the horse too quickly and your head snaps back and forth, then back again. I need Corrik to be Corrik, but I've ruined that. Corrik holds guilt over his protection methods—not enough to end them, just enough to second guess himself at every turn.

I even threw a brat-fit one day over nothing. It was a cut and dry, Tristan-needs-a-spanking, situation and all I got was a token scolding, which did nothing to soothe my itch and only pushed it further toward the brat button, needing more of *that* feeling.

Corrik has to know. He's too far toward the dominant end of the spectrum; he can sense what I need a mile away, but he won't do anything about it.

This has the brat in me scheming.

Of course, I sit on the open window ledge where Corrik doesn't like me. He won't shut the window, but he will spank me for it, won't he? I almost hope he'll come in and catch me, *almost*. I toy with the idea of jumping off the ledge to a spot where I'm sure I can land. It's not far and with the way the stones have worn and tapered down, I could probably make it all the way to the bottom. I know exactly where the guards are stationed and at which times they switch off.

Corrik is sure I'll be abducted again, not believing how much the Aldrien king wanted me gone, but I know, and therefore I know I'm safe from that fate. I could go out for a stroll, get some outdoor time, climb back up and Corrik would be none the wiser.

As if he can hear the idea brewing in my head, I hear the locks to the door begin to open and I'm quick to jump down from the ledge and hop onto the bed with my book, and by the time he comes in, it looks like I've been reading on the bed all along. "How are your studies?" he asks me, a smirk playing on his lips.

My studies have become *the* topic. At least it seems he wants me out of here, half as much as I do. "Horrible. I don't get any of this stuff and therefore I can't remember it."

When I take the time to notice, I learn things about Corrik, things I adore, like the careful way he considers me and how he'll approach my struggle so he can help me. He sets his sword down against the wall near the armoire where his stuff is kept, his long hair shimmering, purple eyes glinting. "I will help you, my darling," he says.

"I'm sure you have better things to do," I tell him. I know he does. He's a very busy prince. His brother Alrik, whom I've not seen since we've been back—he's even busier than Corrik—keeps him occupied.

"I have no better thing to do. You are my first priority."

I'm an arse. I'm acting like a child. Everything Corrik does is for me and he's asking one thing, a big thing, but *one* nonetheless and I can't do it gracefully. "It's about magic. This book claims you can't conjure something from nothing, but I've seen it done."

"Tell me when, maybe you just think you have."

I don't want to give an example, but I do. "When Bayaden made this hair, where did it come from?"

He runs his hand through it, in awe of it because it's attached to my head. "Bayaden is talented, that is clear. To do this, you have to pull from the ether. The ether is Earth's energy field, something that can be felt, but not seen and from there you can pull things or energy from other things via the quantum field."

"What about the part where the enchantment cannot be removed?"

He nods. "Again, something only the most talented and powerful can do." I get a proud feeling in my belly because Bayaden is mine and I am proud of what is mine. "An enchantment is a living thing; it is attached to your life force now and cannot be removed easily. I know he told you it can't be removed, but I believe all magic, or at least most magic can be reversed. But you can bind magic to other magic; think of the ether like a thread, and intent like a sewing needle."

"Ah. Intent. That's the bit I was missing. Why does it not say that part in here? Seems kind of important. Perhaps it wouldn't be so difficult to become an Elf if the instructions were better, hmmm?"

Corrik laughs. "Tell Cupper I said to update the book. Things like that are intuitive to us, we forget others won't have that knowledge. I would still argue it's not so easy to become an Elf, even with better instructions."

"Agreed. It isn't Corrik."

"The exception is you though, my love. This is meant to be, Tristan. It will happen."

I roll onto my back and stare up at him. As proud as I am of Bayaden, I'm equally proud of Corrik. His mother claims he isn't kind, but that's not true. He just has a lot of sharpness to him, but I appreciate his sharpness; it's what makes him a good Top. "Cor? Was Andothair very submissive?"

Corrik nods. "He was. More than you."

"There are times I can be," I say, suddenly wanting to be as good as Andothair.

Corrik's onto me. "You did very well during lessons, but I think I knew even then it's not who you are. I don't care, Tristan. I love you. I've even learned to accept that you have half an Aldrien accent." He reaches out to toy with my robe.

I decide something. "I still want to take the test in two months."

"You think you'll be ready?"

"Yes."

"That's the spirit, Tahsen."

I grab his large hand. "I think that we can be *we* when we get past this part of the story. Right now, there's too much conflict. And one of mine is my heart. It's broken Corrik, and that's where some of my conflict lies but it's time to move forward. You're my forever, I want you to be. Beyond the treaty, or Markaytia. I have been selfish too. I committed to this marriage, and the moment it got hard, I left it."

"You have every right to be upset, Tristan."

"Yes, but to continue to be upset over what I cannot change is foolish. Father tried to tell me that and I listened for a while, but then I reverted to old patterns."

"Things will be better, I promise. And they're not so bad now, are they? You've had some fun? I even overlooked the other day when you and Diekin decided to play your arrow game again."

"You're not as sly about hiding your anger as you'd like to be."

"And you're not as good at hopping from the window to the bed as you'd like to be." He arches one brow, his *Dom* brow.

It gives me the best shiver, but just because it's a good shiver doesn't mean I don't take heed. "What? How in the Gods' names did you know?"

"Your racing heart, and quickened breath."

"Damn Elf senses."

"I can't keep letting things go. I won't from now on, or you'll get more and more out of sorts. I know something of brats."

"We're way more fun than submissives."

He smiles fondly. "I agree, though a brat is still a kind of submissive. There's surrender in it. There is still much to teach you, husband. But for now ..." Corrik traps me between his knees, his cock is out quickly and he's sliding into me. "I'm going to teach about our ways you know," he says into my ear.

"Please, Cor. Stop teasing me."

"That's no fun. Teasing you is the best part." His large cock slides in and out, I moan gripping his husky shoulders. He laughs and his face breaks into one of the best smiles I've seen since I've returned. "I can't wait for the days I can put you in chastity and you'll suffer so sweetly for me."

Unfortunately for me, my cock likes the sound of chastity, aching just a little more at the thought. *You know that's going to be torture, don't you?* But it's two against one as it often is, my cock and Corrik teaming up against me.

"Mmmmm, like the thought of that do you?" he says.

"I never said that."

"Not out loud you didn't, but I can read you pretty well, my darling." He slows down, pumping into me at a maddening pace. I try to push down longer, to feel him against my prostate more, but he won't let me move. "After three days of chastity, all I'll have to do is give you a look and you'll obey me, wanting release."

"I want release now you bastard!"

He laughs some more, pausing his ministrations to kiss me. "All right," he whispers. "Come for me, Tristan."

He grabs my cock and strokes, fucking into me again, long and slow, timing the two movements perfectly, so his cock hits my prostate when his hand reaches the base of my cock. Come spills over his hand, as I let out a desperate cry. He's not long coming after me. Corrik is captivating when he comes, his blond hair tossing back, violet eyes glowing, mouth open in pure ecstasy.

He's not real. He can't be real. I don't know how the Gods managed to make a creature like Corrik; breathtaking and dangerous all at once. "I love you most, Corrik." Tears fall sideways down my cheeks.

"I love you most, Tristan."

We make love several times till morning. We've reached that enchanting place again, the one we had just before I was taken. Things feel resolved, but that's not a good thing in my life. It means it's time for the next adventure to begin and like with all adventures, it begins with a radical happening.

CHAPTER 14

*H*is hand crawls up my thigh and I bite my lip as I wait to see what he'll do with it. It makes its way to my crotch and Corrik fiddles with my balls, squeezing them until I hiss. "When you are Elf, I'll lock this up and you'll have to be very well-behaved before I'll let you come. That will curb your brattish ways." *Fuck.* That turns me on a lot more than I want it to. Corrik notices and beams like he's found all the gold in Markaytia. "A bit of a chastity fetish, Husband?"

"I'd say more of a humiliation one. Either way it works out miserably for me." Unfortunately, miserable in the best way.

He strokes my cock until I'm pushing my hips into his hand. "Corrik, *please.*"

"You're so beautiful like this, my darling. I could watch you struggle between coming and not coming for hours. But that is for another time. You have studying to do, and I have appointments," he says, sliding into me.

Corrik interlaces his hands with mine, my arms in a cactus position against the bed as he fucks me hard and slow, kissing my lips, my neck, sucking hickeys on my shoulder. I wrap my muscled thighs around his torso and squeeze, urging him further into me.

"When we make love, everything feels like it will be okay," he says after.

"It does," I agree. Something in the way Corrik and I make love always brings us back together and I finally feel I can ask him one of the things I've wanted to ask him, something I've been avoiding, even in my head. I've been back and forth on how to ask him, in the end I just out with it. "Corrik, on our wedding night, did you use sex magic to make me fall in love with you?"

"What?"

"Sex magic."

He starts to laugh a little at first, but then really hard. "Oh, by the Gods, you had me there for a second, Tristan. Sex magic."

"I'm serious. You said we bonded via flesh and magic on our wedding night, I heard thunder in my head. Andothair said a human could not bond with an Elf in that way and then he went on about some kind of other Sex God magic. He was negative about the whole thing, but you two believe very different things when it comes to magic and humans."

Corrik gets quiet. "If I tell you, you're going to be angry. I am finding it harder to bear your anger, Tristan."

"Corrik, you're going to have to tell me."

He huffs, and it's clear he doesn't agree he *has* to tell me, but once again, he's doing it to avoid my anger. Good. "I did cast a spell that bound you to me through flesh and blood, but it wasn't a love spell, it was a location spell. If I ever need to find you, all I will have to do is cast another spell and I can get your location. A lot of good it did me when you were in Aldrien though."

I relax. "That's it, a location spell?"

"Yes, which might be why you heard the thunder."

"And you believe you can create such bonds through magic with a human?"

"I know I can. I've been able to feel you since that night. Other than when you were in Aldrien. The moment you left wherever Aldrien in currently, I could feel you getting closer to me; waiting was agony. If Andothair doesn't believe in Human-Elf bonds, he's either living in denial, or he's not as skilled with spells as I thought he was."

"There's also option three—he lied to me."

"Possible. What did you think I'd done?"

"Asked the sex Gods to make me fall in love with you."

He squints. "How would that even work?"

"I don't want to say what I thought."

"Oh, c'mon. Tell me."

"You'll laugh."

"Maybe."

Ugh, fine, but only because he's too damn adorable when he's charming. "I thought each time you had sex with me, it strengthened the spell and made me fall a little bit more in love with you each time." That sets him off, he laughs uncontrollably. "You have to admit, that's kind of what was happening."

"Oh Tahsen, this is the best thing I've ever heard."

"Yeah sure, laugh it up."

I try to roll away from him, but he won't let me. "I'm sorry, but it's a bit funny. I should tell you that if there was a way to ensure you would fall in love with me, I would have done it without any shame over it, but alas there was not, and I do not possess a magical cock with which to fuck love into you."

He laughs at his own joke. I respond by trying to push him away, but as usual, it's like pushing granite. He's smiling at me, in adoration and I can't stay mad at him. "I'm just glad it's not true."

"I'm glad you love me," he says like it's the best day of his life.

"I do, Cor. I love you, deeply." I realize at that moment how deeply. It doesn't matter what he does to me, or what he'll do to me. No matter my anger, I can't stop loving him. Sometimes, I'm unbelievably furious with him, but something in me, a little voice whispering, never wants me to let him go.

We both jump up when we hear the locks to the room opening one by one. Few people get to pass that door, and all of them either have Corrik's permission first or have at least made Corrik aware they will be by to visit. Only the king and queen have the authority to do the latter, but they tell Corrik when they plan on dropping in as a courtesy.

Corrik has his sword in a flash, which means he has no clue who's about to come through that door. "Tristan, stay there."

I want to move to the other room to grab my sword and bow, but I don't, flicking my eyes toward the curtain rod, already playing the scenario in my head of what I'll do if this goes wrong. But when the door is finally unlocked, it's nothing come to kill us, it's Alrik, the only other person allowed to drop by unannounced but who I never think about since he *never* drops by.

He doesn't spare me a hello. "Corrik, we need you to come immediately. You will have to leave your bride for a while I'm afraid."

"Why you ... *mmmph* ..." I'm stopped from my tirade by my husband who grabs me and muffles my words, probably saving me a beheading. I may not know Alrik well, but I know he is not tolerant.

"I will dress and be there immediately, sir."

Alrik peers at me like I'm a problem he wishes would vanish even though I know that's not true. I'm well aware now that since I've been married into the family, my safety is paramount if only because of the treaty. He was Corrik's number one support in his Keep Tristan Safe plan.

I'm the problem he wishes he could make go away, that he has to make sure never goes away. "Kathir, what's the matter with you? You cannot talk back to Alrik. Ever."

I nod. Yeah, he's right, but still. "He's an arse."

"I agree, but unfortunately he's an arse who is crown prince." Corrik slides off the bed to dress. "I'll be back as soon as I can," he says fixing his large sword over his back. He kisses me. "Last night was good, wasn't it?"

"It was," I say pulling the thin blanket around me, my hair splayed everywhere. "I love you, Cor."

"I love you too, my naughty, but delicious dragon." His eyes are sparkling—Corrik's the happiest I've seen him in a while. "I have something for you. I've been waiting for the right time to give it to you."

From his side of the closets, he pulls out a book I recognize. A buzz fills my body. "Cor? Is that...?"

"This one belongs to another set, like the ones we used during our courtship. Unfortunately, the set we used is likely at the bottom of the sea."

I never thought I'd be so happy to see another book of its kind. I was forced to use it to converse with Corrik the year leading up to our wedding. The book I used in Markaytia was collected to bring back to Mortouge. Corrik had his with them, so he could converse with me as they traveled to Markaytia. "Did you give the other to whom I think you did?"

"Your parents have the other. I was not permitted to leave the book in Markaytia beyond our courtship. Father is uneasy about Elven relics left outside the Realm. Special permission was given for this considering the circumstances."

I take the book from him. "It seems we have been sanctioned a few special permissions due to the 'circumstances' as you call them."

"Father and Mother are still embarrassed over losing you. Plus, they have developed a great deal of trust in your family."

The book is heavy and as I remember, exudes a powerful energy. It's finely decorated, with white-gold trim, heavily jeweled in each corner and at the spine. "I was waiting for the right moment to give it to you. Its companion was given to your father, but your papa was authorized by him and my father to hold the position of guardian over the companion."

I hug the book to me, my heart full. "Thank you, Corrik. This means a great deal to me." I can't see my family, but I can converse with them. I set the book on the bed and jump into his arms demanding to be picked up. He obliges, lifting me from under my bum so I can wrap my legs around him and kiss him soundly.

"I'm glad you are pleased, my darling. I must go now. Behave today. Get work done. I'll be back soon as I can."

do all of those things and it's a long day worrying about what's going on because something *is* going on. But of course, the first thing I do is check my new book to see if Papa's left any messages for me yet. I suspect he might have done; I'm glad to see I'm right.

Dearest Tristan,

It was good to see you. I'm glad you and your father finally got to have the discussion you should have had before your wedding. You must know how dearly your father loves you and that whatever you are and whatever you do, he is proud.

By the time you receive this, you will be ever closer to becoming an Elf. I can't wait till the next time I look upon you with tall, Elven ears. You will be as beautiful then as you are now.

But Tristan, find ways to be true to yourself, within the confines of your duties, or you will break apart. I could already see the cracks in your veneer.

Everyone here wanted me to say hello, your uncle, Lucca, Mother, and Father. We all love you and miss you every day. Keep well, Little Man.

Love,
Papa

I'm tearful. I never thought I'd have something like this. If I hadn't been abducted, I wouldn't have. My time in Aldrien, something that could have been bad, brought a lot of good with it.

Papa,

I will make all of you proud. I'm closer to becoming Elf. I can feel it and not a moment too soon, I need to be out of here. I know I should be stronger, that being locked in a room shouldn't be the thing to break me, but it might if it's for much longer.

How's Lucca? Is he allowed to write in the book? Corrik didn't say. He had to leave on a mission and now I'm feeling some of what you must have when you couldn't go with Father and had to stay home with me.

Tell everyone I say hi as well.

Lots of love,

Tristan.

Finally, I hear the opening of locks opening, and my heart lifts in anticipation, but it's Corrik's twin, Ditira. She's nearly as tall as Corrik and almost as muscled albeit in a more feminine way. Her hair is long and blonde, tied on top of her head, and then wound into a tight ponytail, with streaks of purple, like Corrik's used to have. She looks fierce. I haven't seen her fight in battle, only to help me practice, but I know she must be phenomenal on the field. "Hello, Tristan," she says.

"Hello Ditira," I respond, and attempt to make my Elvish curl as nicely around the words as hers does. I can only assume she has come to tell me bad news about Corrik, or Corrik would be here himself. I'm sure the worry is written on my face.

"Corrik sent me. He won't be back tonight."

"Any idea when he will be back?"

Her lips turn down. "No. I'm sorry Tristan, it could be awhile. Days? Weeks? We're not sure."

My heart sinks to my gut. Selfishly, I know this means me, alone, for a lot of the time. But that's not the only thing I'm churning about. This sounds dangerous, what if Corrik doesn't come back?

"He will return, Tristan. It's a rescue mission. Several children were taken from the surrounding villages. Alrik wanted him on the case because he's good at location magic. Originally, he was to locate the children and send the army in, but it's proved difficult. He's staying on the case until its seen through. He had to head into the Unbroken Mountains." Her voice is dark.

That sounds bad. But like the warrior I am, I accept what he has to do for duty. Besides, I don't want to think about it, especially when there's nothing I can do about it.

"I understand, Ditira. I have much to do anyway, probably better without distractions," I say, but Corrik being out there, where I can't actively participate is a distraction. I should be beside him, watching his back.

"That's the spirit. I will visit as often as I can, but Alrik has me busy too. Unfortunately, the same for Diekin. All our efforts will be put to this."

I take a breath. "Very well. I will work hard on my husband's behalf and do him proud so that when he returns, we can leave to make me an Elf."

"Good. I am here for a short time, to relay the news—he wanted it to be me that told you where he was headed—I want to get back to him."

She stays for a quick cup of tea, but too soon, she's gone again and I'm alone.

———

*T*wo months pass with no word from Corrik. It gives me the chance to miss him again. I miss waking up next to him and his fingers running through my hair, I miss his laugh and his giant presence. I even miss his scolding voice and all the things he'd tell me not to do. Yeah, figure that one out. I realize I live for finding and pushing against the boundaries and having Corrik yank me away from said boundaries.

I go deep into my studies, learning all I can to make the basic requirements, with plans of Corrik and I riding off into the mountains, where I need to go to become an Elf.

But when I reach month four, my endurance has long waned. I've learned what I need to and have been going over things on my own, only calling for my designated professors and Cupper when necessary.

The other change has been Alrik. He stops by to check on me

often, which is not as endearing as it sounds. And while Corrik thinks he's taken a shine to me, I believe he thinks I'm the scum you would scrape off scum. I hear the locks being undone, and it's likely to be him; my tummy churns. My other regular visitors, Diekin and Ditira are gone too. For that part I'm glad. They are with Corrik and I want them to keep him safe.

I'm right. In he strides, bringing the cool air with him and his dark presence. His hair is long and white, and he has a large scar on his face, which travels from temple to chin, which only serves to remind me of Baya, with his gorgeous eye scar that ran from his forehead to the bottom of his eye—he was so proud of that scar since he thought it was handsomely garish, plus he could show off what an accomplishment it was to keep his eye—he could have lost it.

Alrik's scar is either one he's chosen to keep since Elves can be healed in most ways or one he got from a time in which he was ghastly injured and could not be healed in time to prevent the scarring. It makes him look deadly. Especially when his long white hair flourishes around him. He's like a being from the underworld come to life.

I haven't attempted to use my Tristan charm on Alrik, figuring there's no point, but since these meetings are becoming more frequent, I decide on being friendlier. He does not pay me the same courtesy. He sits at my table without asking to be invited and stares at me for a length of time without speaking. I would greet him, but I've been told that I'm meant to wait to address him until he deigns to speak. I'm surprised he hasn't told me I'm to prostrate before him. He folds his hands on his belly. "Have you been attending to your studies?"

"Yes, Your Highness," I tell him. "I'm working this very moment." There isn't much time for relaxing with Alrik as my keeper.

He grunts, which I think means good. He stares some more and then he lays it on me. "Kathir, Corrik isn't coming back. We can't find him. He went deep into the Unbroken Mountains, both Diekin and Ditira went to look, but they came out with his horse and no Corrik." He delivers the news with a heavy voice.

"What? No. We have to keep looking."

He shakes his head. "Corrik wouldn't want that. It's dangerous and we could lose others. We've already given him longer than we would any other Elf in a similar situation. Mother and Father have decided it's time to accept his fate."

I know it's not Alrik's fault, but he gets my anger. "What? That's crazy. Get me a horse. I will go look for him if no one else will."

"Don't be stupid. You're not going off to go missing too."

I detect the note of regret in his voice—he'd like to go too, but he won't disobey Mummy and Daddy. Believe me, I get it, but some things are worth facing their disappointment over. "Leave me to mourn my husband in peace," I say. I'm not ready to give up on Corrik, but I would like him to go.

"Very well." He moves to leave.

But then I have a thought. A selfish one. "Wait. What will happen with me?" No more Corrik does not mean the end of the treaty. Markaytia has paid its price, which is me; however, without Corrik, there isn't much reason for me to be here. I could be sent home.

He takes a breath and if I didn't know better, I'd say he looked nervous. Alrik is a rock; I'm pretty sure rocks don't get nervous. "Mortouge has promised to look after you and so we shall. Especially after losing you to Aldrien, Mother and Father were quick to a solution on what would be done with you to show Markaytia are honorable people. Therefore, it's been decided, *we* will marry."

My blood goes cold. At least I can tell he doesn't want it either. "To appease a sense of honor? I'll speak to my parents and my uncle personally. Your honor will not be tarnished."

"It's not just that. Mother and Father are stricken with grief over Corrik's loss. He loved you so, he had visions of you becoming an Elf and bringing great things to our people. They think it's only right you stay in his honor and fulfill your destiny."

Technically, I belong to Mortouge now, and they can do that, I just hoped they wouldn't. "But why you? Aren't there several thousand other Cyredanthems to marry?"

"Believe me, I'm just as excited to marry you as you are me. Not to mention it's a foolish choice. My marriage should be used to secure another alliance, which is part of the reason we've been waiting so long. In any case, you're supposed to stay in King's Keep, and I am the only Cyredanthem available who can offer you proper status and protection. In other words, I'm the only one who's at the equivalent of Corrik. In terms of status, I'm several realms up from Corrik and more than enough to satisfy the treaty. When we marry, you will not simply be Prince Kathir, you will be Crown Prince Consort Kathir, and should I become king, you would be King Consort. You're receiving the great honor; I'm merely fulfilling a duty."

At least we both understand this is just duty. "Fine," I say. I want to burst into tears, but I won't let him see me cry. "When do I become Elf?"

"After the wedding, which will happen in Winter."

"That's another four months away. Do I have to stay up here? Couldn't I be allowed into the palace?"

His brows press together. "Don't be ridiculous. You can't leave here, not with everything going on. My duty is to keep you safe. Securing you up here was one of Corrik's better ideas, though I will be making some changes for extra security. You will also need to learn proper Master-slave etiquette before I'm willing to be seen in public with you."

"Slave?" Slave is another kind of designation, like being submissive or brat. On the brat-submissive spectrum, it's brat, some versions of brat in between, submissive, some versions of submissive in between, and then slave, one of the deepest forms of submission. Slave designation is much different from the kind of slave I was when I was in Aldrien. That was enslavement, this is another context in terms of your internal wiring.

I'm not surprised. Alrik is dominant to the nth degree, of course, he'd need someone with a deep level of submissive energy. "I'm not slave, Alrik. I'm brat."

"I don't care, Tristan," he says using my Markaytian name. "You will be what I tell you to be. You will learn to behave yourself as I say you must, or I will beat it into you. Do you understand?"

My lip wobbles, but I will not show any weakness. "Yes, Your Highness."

He grunts again. "At least you are male. I could not fathom trying to fuck a *human* woman."

Oh right, he's going to want sex at some point. I will too for that matter. At least he's not hard to look at, but it's not what I want to think about right now. "I would like to be left alone, now. Please."

He slams his fist on the table. "You do not dismiss me, I dismiss you."

When I was a warrior, I feared nothing, perhaps foolishly, because at least I could fight to the death. That bit of power gave me the control I needed, even if there was no guarantee I'd win any said battle. But this defenselessness, being at the mercy of someone who has no mercy and bound by my dutiful morals, I'm consumed by anxiety. I shake. "I'm sorry, Highness." I keep my eyes bowed, showing submission.

"Better." At least he used words. "Your schedule will be strict. I won't have you embarrass me when I take you before the Lady of the Lake. And there will be no more visitors. Corrik was foolish to allow that. It's too much traffic coming and going from this wing. We already have all your instructors and the servants to keep tabs on. That will also be reduced. I'll have your meals delivered once per day. Magic can be used to keep the food."

He continues to list new protocols, but I don't hear him; I've already gone numb. Corrik's gone, hope is gone, everything is gone. "Did they ever find the children?" I ask when he stops talking, needing to focus on something else.

He shakes his head. "No. They too have been pronounced dead. We assume that they went where we lost Corrik. If Corrik couldn't make it out, they would not have made it out either."

It gets harder to hold back and my heart breaks; a few silent tears bleed down my cheeks. *Where we lost Corrik.* I wish he would go. I have nothing more to say.

"I will allow you to stay here until after the wedding. Everything is already set up in this wing and I have no use for you in my chambers until you are Elf."

Fine with me. "Of course, Your Highness."

Finally, he slides out from his place at the table. "I will return tomorrow, but don't expect me every day. I have better things to do."

I love that he thinks I care if he comes or not.

He storms out but leaves all the darkness he brought with him. When I hear the last lock click shut, I fall apart. I don't know anything for a while; I sob till my throat hurts and my eyes burn until I feel like I'm drifting out to sea in a fog.

CHAPTER 15

*T*here are good things and bad things about my new keeper. For the bad, definitely the part where I'm not sure I'll ever get out of here. I'm the dirt on the bottom of his boot, he has no use for me other than whatever husbandly duties I'll have to perform and the ones for Mortouge as Crown Prince Consort.

He decides I should learn proper *slave* protocol, but he's not going to teach me—that's beneath him—and so he sends the most terrifying Dungeon Master Elf, Strobavik, to do it for him. He specializes in training slaves.

At first glance Strobavik is terrifying, even though he's not as broad shouldered as Baya or Alrik. His muscles are lithe like Corrik's but he's thinner, leaner and in general smaller by comparison.

He's still a lot taller and larger than I am.

He wears black leather everything—black pants, an open leather jacket and tall boots. His long blond hair is wavy, and his tall Elven ears are decorated with earrings and jewels. Also, I'm pretty sure he's wearing black eyeliner under his vivid blue eyes. "Put this on," he says, tossing a pile of leather and buckles at me. "Lose the robe."

His accent is different, he can't be from this part of the realm.

I approach him like I would any battle—I don't know this guy; I don't give benefit of the doubt. Not with the mood I'm in.

The shock has far from worn off, I'm still processing Corrik's disappearance and my subsequent engagement to the crown prince. And now there's this guy.

As much as I'm a fucking brat sometimes there's another side to me, one that needs to please.

There is a theory that we respond and react to energy, this notion is even stronger with Elves. It doesn't occur to me to disobey the Elf, especially when I know where his orders come from. Even Corrik was quick to obey his brother.

I snatch up the pile of leather. It turns out to be the smallest pair of black leather shorts I've ever seen and a harness, which means I have no clue how to put the fucking thing on. I've worn a harness before, with Baya, but he was the one to dress me in it.

I'll give it my best shot. How hard can it be?

Turns out, really fucking hard.

After watching me struggle with it for several excruciating minutes, visibly growing annoyed, he stops me. "I will show you how to put this on," he says in his thick accent. "I expect you to take note. Next time you will be punished for delay and ignorance."

Jeez, this guy.

I'm quiet as he prepares me, looping the crisscross harness onto my body. It carries around and down my back, cinching with a single buckle in front. It's covered with rings.

The shorts *just* fit over my arse and cover my dick, but they're comfortable, and I can move in them surprisingly well. "Tell me you know how to kneel properly," he says like I'm the most uncouth creature he's ever encountered, and I guess to a Mortougian Elf that is the epitome of uncouth.

I didn't kneel for Baya, not really. It just wasn't that way between us. Yeah, we did some kinky stuff and there were formal times when kneeling was appropriate, but it's not something he spent time training me to do. We used "the room" for spanking and bondage type stuff rather than having me spend a lot of time kneeling for him, like Tom did for the Aldrien king.

However, once upon a time, Corrik taught me how to kneel.

"I know how but I'm rusty, sir." Even I can hear the sadness in my voice.

"At least you know how to use 'sir,'" he says continuing to buckle me in.

I should be throwing a fit, in the least protesting against this but something much deeper's longing for it. "I am an avid learner, sir." I push my chest out and stiffen my lip.

He analyzes me and I hold my breath as his thoughts seem to pierce through to my soul. I grow frustrated and analyze him right back, the Warlord in me taking over, burning through me. He cracks a half smile and there's a smirk in his eyes. "All right Tristan, if you will work hard, I will work just as hard for you. I'm going to hold you to your word."

Strobavik doesn't have the innate disdain for humans most Elves I've encountered seem to, but he doesn't like his time wasted either, even if it's under orders from the crown prince. I know he's going to push me beyond endurance, but it will be because he thinks I can take it. That earns him the mark of my respect.

"I am here to teach you non-sexual, Master-slave protocol, but Alrik has given his consent for you to learn some sexual protocol as well. Even though it's within his rights to make such a decision for you, he says you are of Markaytia and that it's important I acquire your consent on the matter. I do not have permission to penetrate you anally, but we could do some things involving my cock. We've also got use of a large range of toys. If you consent, the organization of such things will be up to me and you won't know what we're going to do until we do it. You will still be expected to obey."

I consider all he's said. I'm surprised Alrik has given me the opportunity to say no, and for a moment I consider saying no out of spite over the whole thing. Then I remember a conversation with Corrik; we haven't carried on our special lessons because he's wanted to leave time for me to study so that I could become Elf and be released from confinement sooner.

I refuse to believe Corrik's not coming home. I prefer to believe that any day, he'll waltz in the door and then wouldn't it be a nice gift for him, if could I submit for him in all the beautiful ways Elves submit?

It would also show him how much I trust him, how much I'm devoted to him—I haven't been good at that. Yes, I had a right to be angry, but I took it out on him and that was poor behavior. It hasn't escaped my notice that when Father agreed that keeping me locked away was what was best until I became Elf, I didn't argue. I didn't like the idea any more than I had, but I worked to accept it. I didn't even try for Corrik or for what was between us.

Corrik must have noticed, but he didn't say anything about it.

It's time for me to do something for him.

Engaging in sexual acts with Strobavik won't be a hardship. He's beautiful and terrifying, which is one thousand percent my type. "I consent, sir. I would like to learn both protocols."

He nods. "Then do you agree to obey me?"

"I do, sir."

"All right, then we shall begin. From here on out you will refer to me as, Master Strobavik. You will be punished if you do not."

As promised, Master Strobavik teaches me things like formal protocol for the royal court, formal protocol for meals and even relaxed protocol for semi-formal meals. There are informal meals too, like what Corrik and I had with his parents when we first arrived, where protocol is not required and can be instituted or not at the Dom or Top's discretion.

I am surprised to learn there are special allowances for the king's consort, even though in some cases protocol is more restrictive. For instance, when meeting with dignitaries from beyond the realm, I'm permitted full dress should my husband allow it, versus the half or "no dress" protocols at other levels of the royalty hierarchy.

Strobavik explains one of the marked differences between slave designation and submissive. "You will exist for his pleasure and his pleasure only, Tristan. This is the way of things with Master and slave. Someone who is slave inside doesn't need to be told this, it's what they long for as well."

"Then why are you telling me, Master Strobavik?"

I get one of his piercing glares for that, because yeah, I'm being cheeky. I'm not supposed to speak unless I have permission. I'm not good at following that rule and often earn punishment for my big mouth.

"That. You are not slave. You are brat."

I don't need a reprimand to look to the floor for that one. He tilts my chin up to look into his eyes. So far, it's been learning how to kneel for long periods of time and being tied up in various positions so I could build endurance. Master Strobavik warned me that today he plans on taking it to a new and sexual place.

Training hasn't been as bad as I thought it would be. It's not been easy and Master Strobavik is a grueling taskmaster, but instead of inspiring despair, I'm driven to do better, to get it right. Most of the things we do bring me to a calm and grounded place. It reminds me of being on the field with my father.

His declaration is true and previously I had been proud of my brat status. I love everything about being a brat but when I'm striving to be the perfect slave or submissive, locking the brat in me away, it's difficult. I've had the wish that my inner brat would just go away. "I know you are doing the best you can," he says in his thick accent, "but you need to fake it better. The prince will not be pleased if you talk out of turn like that."

"Yes, Master Strobavik."

"That doesn't change what you are. This is why I'm telling you so you can work to create it within you."

There's a lot I want to say to that, but I don't, behaving like a good "slave" should.

"But you know, naughty kitten, just because you are brat, this does not mean you don't contain aspects of both slave and submissive within your character. You can get to levels of deeper submission—

you have the skill for it, I've seen glimpses. I may not be the one to bring it out in you but it's there."

I'm not sure I agree with that. Yes, I've reached some intense levels of subspace, but could I go deeper than I have?

He lets go of my chin. "Today we move on. From here on out, you won't be allowed to orgasm unless you have Alrik's permission. I have been given the guidelines as to how you will earn that permission. You will have to satisfy the guidelines and please me as well. Do you understand?" His ears move with the sharp edge of his voice.

Ugh. That's gonna be tough. All of this submission stuff turns me on. Humiliation is my thing and I find everything Master Strobavik does to me embarrassing enough that it lights up my cock whether I want it to or not. "Yes, Master Strobavik."

I'm kneeling at his feet, my arms are behind my back, hands linked to opposite wrists. The stones are cool under my toepads and I recall the warm sandstone under my feet in the hallways in Aldrien—those days seem so long ago.

"Today we begin to build your endurance to that end. When you are with Prince Alrik, you won't be allowed to orgasm often. When he permits release, you must show him proper respect for allowing you such an honor."

It won't come to that. Corrik will be home any day now. I envision him stalking through the door like the predator he is. I'll serve him in the ways he likes, ways that are far less constricting than Alrik's demands.

"Up on the bed, on all fours."

I crawl over to the bed—he didn't tell me to get up, I'm not getting caught out on that one again—and climb onto the large mattress as gracefully as I can. I remember Tom moving from kneeling to standing positions, he was damn near artistic with his movements. I am nowhere close to that.

I get into position and sure enough, Master Strobavik's crop is landing sharply on my arse. "Arse out, Tristan." *Crack!* "Not good enough." *Crack!* "Arch your back." *Crack!*

I bite my tongue because yeah it fucking hurts, but complaining only gets you more *whacks* from Strobavik's crop. When I'm finally in position to his liking, I've got several sore patches of skin complaining at me and my eyes are wet in the corners.

"I'm going to pull down your shorts, Tristan, and then you will hold position."

His fingers reach under the waistband of the small shorts brushing against my skin and I shiver—this is happening, it's really happening. I continue to focus on my goal here, which is to serve Corrik in the best way I can. Strobavik is a talented dungeon master, I can learn a lot from him. The cool air hits my skin as he peels the shorts to my mid-thighs, my cock springs free ready to party. *Sorry buddy, you're gonna need to calm down.*

Instead of the spell to help my human body make the lube-like substance I'm told I'll make as an Elf, he lathers my arse with lube from a bottle, massaging it into my crevices, making the area warm. "Mmmmm," I can't help moaning, and I imagine the way his face scrunches when he's displeased since I can't see him from this angle.

"Tristan," he scolds.

"Sorry, Master Strobavik."

"Mmmhmmm."

I'm not supposed to be so responsive for Alrik. This is more to do with his personal preferences than the Master-slave relationship in general. Though I have noticed, that while Strobavik began as an anal bastard who would not allow me to get away with anything, he's softened just a bit.

Only a bit.

He's still unrelenting and I don't get away with much, but for a response like that in the past, he would have broken out his special wooden Tristan Paddle. That's its name. He had it made specially for me because with the slaves and submissives he trains, they usually don't require something so juvenile—he didn't have one on hand. But I am a fucking brat, and he's known this since before he spoke out about it. He knew he'd get nowhere with me without using some of the things my brain and body respond to.

It's what they understand.

I start when his finger dips into my entrance, he smacks my arse hard with an open hand for that and after the sting dissipates some I relax. "That's it, Tristan. Take what I give you. The key is to open yourself for receiving. This will make you pliant."

His finger sinks in past both knuckles. It's long, and the burn feels good. I resist the urge to push back but fuck do I want to. My cock is unhappy. He wants someone to touch him, but no one's going to do that, at least not right now.

"That's it, my naughty kitten can behave when he puts his mind to it."

I twist my lips at him but only because I know he can't see me do so. Naughty kitten is a name he gave me because I cannot behave like a proper slave should. Sometimes I feel insulted by it but more often I think it means he's fond of me.

As much as others will bring out a specific energy in me, my brat energy brings out the playful energy of most I engage with no matter how rigid they are.

Would I be able to do that with Alrik if I tried?

"Is this aching, Tristan?" he says reaching under to grab my cock.

"Fuck," I mutter. "I mean, yes Master Strobavik."

I swear I hear him laugh. "When you are with Alrik, he will put you in chastity as most Masters do. There won't be any need for this to be out, bothering you."

He strokes it again but then thankfully leaves it alone. With stroking and his finger in my arse, I'm not sure how long I would be able to hold back from orgasming. What he's said has me curious and I find I am forever curious about all things in the fetish realm. I also can't help remembering Corrik talking about chastity—fuck, Corrik has a chastity fetish too, doesn't he? "Is chastity a common kink among you, Elves?"

"*Tristan.*"

I've spoken out of turn again and I didn't bother to use the appellation. Dammit. "Sorry!"

His magic hands are gone and when he returns, he has the dreaded Tristan Paddle. We both know why I'm being punished. He lays down several firm whacks to my arse, and I have to fight not to tuck under or move away. Each smack brings a fresh set of tears to the corners of my eyes because that thing's fucking sting-y, and with the force Strobavik uses it always takes my breath away.

"Thank you for correcting me, Master Strobavik," I say when he finally sets the paddle aside, my arse on fire.

"You aren't behaving yourself today. You need to focus. I'm afraid you already don't meet the requirements to earn permission for an orgasm tonight. You must do better before I can allow it."

Gods dammit. "I will, Master Strobavik. I *am* sorry."

He must hear the earnestness in my voice. "I know you will, but I also know you can do better. You're distracted."

"I am but … permission to speak, Master Strobavik?"

"Go ahead," he says, returning his evil but delicious finger to my arse.

"I'm so curious. I want to know about these things. I want to know everything."

"You have a brat's curiosity, but you also know the appropriate way to ask questions. It is my decision as to whether or not it's time to discuss things or if it's time for you to focus on the task at hand. You will follow the rules if I have to paddle them into you."

"Yes, Master Strobavik." I hope he can't see me smirking.

"To answer your question, yes. It's common with Elves. We do like chastity, *a lot*. But don't deny it, you do too. I can tell by the minute way your body responds at the mere mention of the idea."

I am *not* telling him how right he is. Smug bastard.

It gets harder to hide my responses to his finger. It's slow and deliberate, which means it's slowly and deliberately driving me mad. It takes all my energy not to give in like I want to, and I thank the Gods that when it's Corrik doing this to me, I'll be able to let loose.

Because it *will* be Corrik and he will come home.

As strict as Strobavik is, he's good about praise. "That's better. Focus, naughty kitten."

I didn't know there were cats in Mortouge, another question I asked out of turn when Strobavik first began calling me that. After he spanked me for it, he told me about the cats in Mortouge. They sound more ferocious than the cats we had in Markaytia.

As soon as Corrik is home, I'm demanding a tiny killer kitten.

Strobavik adds a finger, I whine. "I know, but you can do this. I am pushing you today, but I know you can take it. Think of how much it means to please Master Alrik, or if you need to, think about pleasing me."

I'm supposed to spend time focusing on Alrik, thinking about worshipping and pleasing him, but I'm too angry with him. I know none of this is his fault either and he must act in the ways he feels the crown prince in his position should, but I need someone to take it out on and Alrik's it. Strobavik knows I have a harder time when thinking of Alrik and will sometimes allow me to think of him instead since we have built some rapport between us.

I want to please Strobavik, I want him to tell me I've done well but I don't use him for my muse either. I use Corrik. I pretend it's Corrik behind me, adding another finger. At first this only serves to torture my cock further, but when I think about how much I'd like to please him, how much I want to give him this power over me, the edges of the world disappear. I float off into another world where this is still torture, but I can do it.

I complain by way of an indeterminate noise. "I want to keep going too," he admits, "but then we will be beyond what you can handle. You know I don't promise fair but I'm not a total arsehole."

"That's debatable, Master Strobavik."

He smacks my arse for that. "You need another spanking, but you pulled it together and have done well for your first day so not getting the spanking is your reward."

Only I would have "not getting spanked" as a real thing on a list of rewards. "Thank you, Master Strobavik. Are you sure there isn't something that says if Tristan goes on to behave himself, he can orgasm?"

"I am sure that if Tristan doesn't stop trying to circumvent the rules, he's going to end up over my knee and lose his orgasming privileges for tomorrow too."

I don't even grumble about that—a feat in and of itself.

"In addition, you will spend one hour like this, thinking about how you can improve for next time and focusing on how much your cock aches."

How is that supposed to help me? Answer is it's not. It's supposed to subtly make me hornier. *Fucking sadists.* "Sadists get to have fun too," Strobavik often says, which only strengthens my assertion that they have brat in them too.

Which makes me think. *Yeah.* We all have a portion of each of these designations within us, but it's the amount that teeters the balance and makes us spin out as one classification more dominantly than the other. It doesn't mean an aspect can't be brought to the surface from time to time.

I get it now. This is what Master Strobavik has been trying to teach me.

---

*T*he next day, Strobavik brings an assortment of toys. "We will work hard today, Tristan. I hope you are prepared."

I tilt my head from the spot on the floor where I'm kneeling for him, already dressed in the shorts and harness.

"Don't look at me like that. I'm going to use your pretty mouth, and we'll see how long you can go with one of my special dildos."

My cheeks heat at the mention of dildos and it's nice to know I have some Markaytian sensibilities left in me. But I want to know what Strobavik's cock looks like and I'm good at sucking dick so it can't turn out to be a terrible day. Plus, I vow to get just a little bit of payback for the torture he's put me through even if I end up in a meeting with his Tristan Paddle. It'll be worth it.

"We'll begin there," he says, untying his leather pants and pulling out his cock to sit erect before my lips.

Like all Elven cocks I've seen, it's thick and long. His alabaster skin allows the veins to show through, dark in contrast and the head is a thick mushroom-shape, covered by foreskin. I look it over, analyzing it, planning my attack. First, I'll show him I'm not a total idiot. He hasn't taught me the protocol for this, but I can guess from what I know.

Not to mention, I need to orgasm pretty badly by this point—I could use some good favor.

I gaze large eyes up at him. "May I suck your cock, Master Strobavik?"

It's hard for him to school his expression; the corners of his lips twitch. "Someone wants to come tonight. Very good, Tristan. You must always ask to do anything, even if it's implied." He grips my hair by the roots. "Go ahead, suck my cock, naughty kitten."

I peer one eye up at him.

He smiles. "That's your name whether you're behaved or not."

Arse!

That's fine. He's going to regret everything he's ever done to me. I know revenge by cock sucking doesn't seem like the dastardliest plan since he will enjoy the fuck out of this, but he'll be weak in the knees and that will even the score somehow.

I don't use my hands since I've not been instructed to do so. That would require breaking form and I've already caught on that breaking form is to be avoided at all cost, unless given special permission.

I'm tempted to swallow him down whole, but I want to be more devious than that. I pretend it's hard for me to reach his cock, even though I'm adept at contracting my core ab muscles enough to bend forward without falling out of position. I want him to enjoy this in every way, while I drive him a little crazy. I put all my focus into the task.

I begin at the tip licking my tongue around the top. I don't get much response from him, nor do I expect it. I'm sure he's had his cock sucked a billion times over and has conditioned himself into placidity. But I'm not trying to reinvent the wheel here, I'm doing what I know ones like Strobavik and Alrik like—becoming a pliant toy who's ready to please.

Working with Strobavik, I've learned a thing or two. Those who fall into the slave designation enjoy the feeling of being consummately controlled, sometimes down to the smallest of tasks. Strobavik recounted how one of his client's slaves needed instructions such as which leg to slide into his pants first and exactly how many peas he should eat from his plate.

It's even better for slaves when their Master can do all the things they aren't permitted to do, furthering the divide between roles—this divide creates the feeling they both want. Sometimes the tasks seem unfair—like having the Master clothed while the slave is naked.

In some ways, brats are similar, but we tend to resist, we need help to surrender. This is why we aren't made for submissive positions, but I'm beginning to see that we do contain similar inner wiring. Given the right environment, it's inspired from us.

The edges of the world blur as I enter subspace—the earliest I ever have with Strobavik.

I'm committed to this and do all the things I presume he'll love, using my tongue to lathe down his shaft, wetting him so the cool air can hit the warm spots and make him shiver.

He does.

Next, I cover his cock with my hot mouth, taking him in all the way to the base where my nose nuzzles up to his neatly trimmed pubic hair. As I pull back, I swirl my tongue along the base sucking at the same time. When I hear him panting, I know I've got him—he's enjoying this.

I use my tongue like a snake wrapping around a pole as I suck down his cock and do the same as I suck up, opening my throat, allowing as much of his cock to slide into my mouth as is possible. Baya was large, and I learned to take him. I don't have a problem with Strobavik.

I carry on like this, my head bobbing over his cock, periodically peering up at him—Tops love that. His body is as relaxed as it can be while standing upright, his head tosses back occasionally and some-times he stares at me with wondering eyes.

I speed up my ministrations and reveal how far forward I can lean without losing perfect posture. As he's about to come, I slow down, and he grips the roots of my hair. My scalp complains, but I keep going. "Careful, Tristan," he says. "I know what you're doing. You don't control this, I do."

Fuck. Wow. More than the edges blur, everything is blurred and I'm on a cloud. Floating. "How can I please you further, Master Strobavik?"

He moans. "Open your mouth, keep it open."

I do, he fucks into it, I keep my teeth out of the way. He moves at a medium pace—not too slow, not too fast—but when he gets to the end, it's hard to keep up with him and when he comes, some of it dribbles down my chin.

He wipes the come from my lips. "Even when you are deep into subspace, you're still a naughty brat, but that was divine. Now, bend over the table, it's time to put you in your place. You're going to pay for that."

And I do.

He's relentless with his collection of dildos, starting with smaller ones and working up to the largest ones over a few hours. Halfway through, when it's obvious I'm going to come no matter how much I try not to, he wraps a leather cock ring around the base of my cock, which leaves me rock hard and unable to come. My balls feel heavy and I have to bite my lip to keep from begging.

"That's it, Tristan. When Alrik takes you, you'll receive him just like this," he explains pushing the dildo into me and pulling it out slowly.

I don't know what Elves make their sex toys out of, but it's soft and pliant and it does a good impression of a real cock. I can feel the veins.

I hold position over the table best I can, but I'm tiring out. My hands are flat on the table, arms extended and wobbly. My arse is out, legs spread as wide as they'll go, close to buckling. It's a humiliating position, which means my cock is extra interested. "Master Strobavik, *please*. I don't think I can hold back any longer."

Instead of a firm 'whack' like I got the last time I pleaded, he's soft, cooing at me. "C'mon my bratty kitten, you can do this. I know you have it in you. Just a little more."

I want to do it; I want to please him.

The world blurs further.

When he's done with me, he carries me to the bed and lies beside me. "Was I good?"

"Tristan," he sighs.

Oh right. "Master Strobavik."

"You did very well," he says, running a hand through my long black hair, his vivid blue eyes study me.

I smile. "This mean I get to come, Master Strobavik?"

"It would, but what you did initially forbids me from giving you such privileges."

I groan, but then I curl my lip. "I am good at it though."

He frowns at my cocky behavior but even he can't stay mad. "I will say, you are excellent at sucking cock—at least your chatty mouth is good for something."

Whatever. I don't even hide my smugness. "Master Strobavik, may I?" I reach out to him. I don't know what other brats, subs, slaves need after all that, but I need to snuggle.

He wants to say no, I can tell, but he can't. "C'mere, Tristan."

I wrap around him still lightweight from all the stimulation. My cock remains hard and leaking. Poor thing.

We lay together, and he runs his hand through my hair until I fall asleep. When I wake up a short time later, he's packing up. I'm harness and shorts free, which means I can be a little more casual with him.

Of course, there's no such thing as fully casual with your dungeon Master. The energy that builds between you both always maintains an edge of power exchange.

"How are you, Tristan?"

"Good, sir. Well except for this," I say, motioning to my hard-on from the seventh level of hell.

He smiles a smirky smile. "Behave tomorrow. Unfortunately for you, you've given away just how good a submissive you can be."

Dammit.

"I will expect more from you. Do what you did today without attempting to Top from the bottom, and you might make a good companion for the prince yet."

When he leaves, I have some time to sleep before the tutors come. My body aches in places I didn't know existed but it's the good kind of aching, like when I've been fighting in the fields all day. I look to the side where Corrik sleeps and miss him in the purest way I've ever missed him. I know he's an Elf, and it's harder for Elves to get cold than us humans, but I think of him cold and hurt somewhere and how much I want him warm beside me.

Is he scared?

I'm not sure the large war Elf can be scared of anything but I am. I'm scared I'll never see him again and for the first time I consider the possibility that this marriage to Alrik may happen.

---

*W*hen Strobavik arrives the next day, he has a spreader bar, cuffs and a good length of chain. He raises his brows. "You have only yourself to thank for this. Originally I was going to wait until a few more sessions in."

Being suspended by chains is not new for me. I raise my arms overhead. "Challenge accepted, Master Strobavik." I'm already in my harness and shorts, kneeling for him on my pillow.

He rolls his eyes at me. "Only you could achieve cheeky while being perfectly obedient," he says attaching the cuffs.

My brows turn down. "Have I lost coming privileges already?"

"No, but speak out of turn like that again and you will."

Coming has become a need over a want, though I very much want. Today I'm grateful for cock rings and welcome chastity if I'm going to spend this much time with blue balls.

Strobavik uses magic to hang the chains from the ceiling beam and when my arms are fully extended, he attaches the spreader bar to my ankles. The bar holds my feet apart as wide as they'll go and when my shorts are pulled down, I'm horribly exposed.

And just as turned on.

"Bear down," he says.

As I do, he pushes an egg-shaped something, coated with lube, into my arse. He comes 'round to the front of me and watches. Eventually, the egg vibrates, and I only just remember to school my reaction before all my muscles contract at the sensation. I'll never have zero response, but my wince is minute enough not to earn correction, and my heavy breathing is acceptable.

He brandishes a long whip. "I want your pain today Tristan, and you will give it to me. Do well and you can have the orgasm you long for tonight."

When he dangles that carrot, I know I'm in for something. I feel the pulse from the toy against my prostate, which he controls via his magic and I have to fucking bite my lip to keep from responding. He enjoys my suffering.

"And Tristan? It will please me greatly should you succeed today."

Fucker. He's got my number.

It's a long session indeed, and he's relentless. The toy pulses without rhythm so I can never get used to a pattern. He lashes so that I have the buzz of pleasure and sting of pain rushing through me at the same time. They are opposite things to deal with, I have to exhale with the whip and inhale with the egg—an exhausting balancing act—all the while *not* coming.

"Yes. That's it, naughty kitten, c'mon. You're okay."

Tears sting my eyes when the whip lands against my flesh leaving behind hot pain. Bliss radiates through as the sensations hit my prostate, but I keep my responses minimal. I want to cry out, to beg, I ache to moan, I miss screaming, but I want him to be proud of me. Keeping that in mind drives away all other thoughts—of Corrik, of studying to become Elf, of another marriage—and narrows my focus to Strobavik's whip and toy.

It's freeing.

The world blurs. The whip slices my skin raising a wake of welts and my body reels when the egg vibrates against my prostate. But all I want to do is give to him, give him me. The exchange of energy is tactile, seeping into my skin like hot rain. I struggle, arching my back until my spine is inside out but that sensation of giving never wanes.

"That's it, kitten. I want just a little more."

His hand moves to my hair, his fingers run through the sweat-soaked strands and my muscles relax. Until the egg vibrates again. I have to bite my lip to keep from crying out. I have to twist in my bonds, muting moans to breathy murmurs. I want to come, I want to come, I want to come and yet, I want to please him more.

Somehow, I don't come. "Your endurance has improved," he says unhooking me and carrying me over to the bed.

I'm spent; can barely move. "That's not going to buy me anything good, Master Strobavik," I grouse. He'll only push me harder.

"Ah. You're learning I see."

He takes care when removing my shorts and harness. I have stripe marks everywhere and I relish in being marked again, it brings me comfort. I miss Baya. Without thinking, I reach for the magical, Elven healing salve in the drawer. "What do you think you're doing?"

"The salve, Master Strobavik."

He tilts his head. "You don't want these healed away?"

I squint at him and then burst into tears. He slides in behind me. I think I must drive the hardened dungeon master to distraction with how often he's had to be soft with me. Though I suppose he never *has* to do anything, but for whatever reason he does. "What's the matter with you?"

"Do I not rate keeping these? Have I not earned them?"

"I see. You understand the marking culture of Elves."

It's not a question, but I nod anyway. I didn't get the chance to earn many marks from Corrik ... What if I never get the chance?

"You may keep them if you wish, but I'm not your mate and so you are not obligated."

"But I rather hoped I meant *something* to you, sir." Maybe that's very Markaytian of me but it's what is. I cling to him and cry.

He pulls me close and runs fingers through my hair. He doesn't answer for a long time. "You have come to mean a great deal to me, naughty kitten—I fear you have. Stop crying now. You may keep the marks, but no complaining tomorrow when you don't like how they feel underneath what I'll add overtop."

"I won't." Except I probably will. I wouldn't be me if I didn't.

"You'll be pleased to know you've earned an orgasm. Well done. But it's only one and there are parameters."

"Oh?" He's blurry through my watery vision. I sniffle.

"You're to sit in that chair naked and after dinner. Not before, *after*. You have an hour to complete the task, if you don't come in that time your chance to come passes."

I should have known there would be some parameters. "Won't be a problem, sir."

Strobavik smoothens salve into my skin. There has always been good aftercare with Elves as much as there has been violence and pain. When he's done, he gets behind me again, but I flip to face him and wrap my body around him in a Markaytian death grip—not so death-grip-like to an Elf, I know, but still. He hesitates, I know he's thinking about telling me to turn back around but he sinks into me too, kissing my forehead.

"You know Tristan, you do have some submissive in you. You are not slave, but you have need for some stricter submissive protocol from time to time."

I scowl into his chest—he smells of sweat and wildflowers. "I am brat. You've said so yourself." But I'm only so angry because I'm worried it's true.

"Okay, okay. I didn't mean to offend you, just sharing what I see."

I don't know how many fierce ex-Warlords cry in front of their scary dungeon master Doms once, let alone twice in one day, but that's what I do. I cry again. Just when I think I know who I am, it changes. "Sir? I don't want to marry him. I want to go home."

That's not true. I'm not sure I'd be happy in Markaytia anymore. I'm not who I was. I wouldn't make sense there and I don't make sense here.

Nothing makes sense without Corrik.

I haven't even been able to write to my family since Corrik's disappearance because I don't want to tell them—telling them makes it true. The book is the only way to relay information quickly across such a distance. It's a long way to ask a messenger to travel or to merit sending a bird that may or may not get there. It would only a courtesy at this point anyway—Mortouge owns me. They can do with me as they wish without permission. No one has said whether word has been sent or not and so I've assumed not. I don't want to ask.

Strobavik should spank me and leave me. I doubt he's supposed to be this familiar. Instead, he whispers something to me in Elvish that doesn't translate to Markaytian well—a language I don't speak anymore. Corrik was the only one who still said the odd thing to me in my home tongue.

The best I can tell anyone it means is, *"The Gods give us strife so we might have a moment of happiness."* I enjoy the way his accent curls around the words.

"I know. *I know,* sir."

He lets me cry till I'm done. I haven't resolved a thing, but I'm renewed—the doubt and anguish washed gone out with the tide.

He sighs. "Okay. No more sadness. Enjoy yourself. I'm proud of you for today. And Tristan? I will know if you disobey me."

I peek an eye at him. "How?"

I get a smack to my arse for leaving off the "sir." "Because I will ask and you are a terrible liar."

---

*S*omething happened today and I'm not sure if I like it because I *liked* it. Yeah. Make sense of that one—I certainly can't. I spin my fork on the wooden table, the pokey end stabbing into the tender pad of my pointer finger. The welts from today's session still burn, but they surround me like a cozy blanket. I sink into them.

What am I?

When I was with Bayaden, it was clear to me that I'm brat. And I am. But maybe there's more to me?

What happened today was natural and electric.

My stomach stirs at the thought of what I'm about to do. I've been given a little magical device that will tell me when an hour has passed. In Markaytia, we had sun dials to tell us the passage of time, but they are not precise enough for sex games, apparently. I only have an exact amount of time to make myself come.

My lips twist at it, but my cock springs to life. "You do not help," I say to my crotch. It won't be a sword that defeats me as Corrik's vision predicted, it will be my penis.

Before Strobavik left, he placed the chair where I'm to sit. "These are not my orders," he said. "They are Alrik's. You will follow his directives categorically. And Tristan? You will think of him this time."

Initially my dragon blood raged. How can that Elf expect me to pause my grief over Corrik to think happy little thoughts of him so I can get off? Sure, I'm not actually grieving, not yet, but he can't know that. Can he? Even still, I am mad with worry and I think that's enough of an excuse thank you very much.

But I suppose that's very Alrik.

I don't believe Alrik's doing this for me but Alrik, like my father, has many responsibilities. He knows neither of us have the luxury of grieving especially if I do become Crown Prince Consort. He probably views us moving on as a duty to our people.

Strobavik gripped my chin his hand. "Remember that this is a reward from him. He is pleased with you, Tristan. He's said so a few times."

He has?

Fuck, that got me. I'm a fucking sucker for pleasing someone. Especially when that someone is a piece of jagged rock—the harder they are to please, the more I want to. Yes, I know, but I'm complicated.

I can do this.

Done with dinner, I get up. "You're to strip naked," Strobavik said. "Then you'll sit in that chair with your legs spread wide as they'll go."

I remove my blue, silk robe and sit, my bare arse hitting the cool leather of the chair. I swear to the Gods everything in Mortouge is cool.

It occurs to me that I don't *have* to do this. It's a reward. I can refuse a reward, but fuck, I need this. Particularly after today—my poor cock deserves this. I spread my legs as far as they'll go. I'm conditioned to please Strobavik. I imagine his smile of approval—unlike some Elves (Alrik) he actually smiles—when I tell him how well I've followed orders.

Thinking of Alrik is an order. How am I going to do that? He's a pompous ass.

He's also attractive. All Elves are but Alrik is something else. He's a good foot larger than Corrik and nearly as tall as the doorframe. Back home in Markaytia I was considered tall. I am nearly as tall as a Markaytian doorframe, but here, I'm lucky to reach halfway. With Alrik, it's like looking up the side of a tower.

His hair always glistens, and its whiteness speaks to his age. I wonder if it was once blond like Corrik's? It's hard to imagine him without any bit of aging. Of course, he doesn't have any wrinkles, but his skin has some mild weathering and several menacing scars. There's no way Corrik would ever allow a scar on his perfect face. Alrik takes pride in them like Baya did.

I wouldn't mind falling asleep on Alrik's chest. Not that he'll let me, but it's broad and barreled and the skin looks soft. As we rode home from where I came out of the veil with Uncle Taj, my eyes were drawn there more than once.

Plus, he's a human shield.

He dove in front of a wildaboar intent on eating me. Corrik had gone off to pee which meant Alrik was responsible for me, and he made me sit near him. The thing surprised our entourage coming out of the brush at full tilt. Wildaboars are magical creatures known for sneaking up on prey, even an Elf if he's not paying attention. Alrik was. He rolled across the path in front of me and stuck his sword clean into its chest.

I couldn't help it—my heart raced, and my cock sprung to life. Sure, I take care of myself, but I would not have heard the creature coming. I would have been Tristan pâté. Watching something as massive as Alrik move as smoothly as he did … Corrik could have done the same. I know how formidable he is with a sword but combined with Alrik's abrasive energy I was ensnared. There was something desperate and powerful there too.

He had to do it. *Had to,* I repeated over and over to myself, but Corrik's mention of his affection for me has echoed beside the memory of it.

Works for me.

I grip my cock with a lube-slicked hand and the magical timer begins on its own. I don't know how it works, I don't know how it knows I've grasped my cock, but it does. Elves have far too many magical sex toys and gadgets for their own good.

My heart rate speeds up as I stroke with a firm grip. I almost forget the other things I'm supposed to do, one of which is to fondle and tug my balls. Honestly, how bloody controlling? I can't even masturbate how I want to; it's scheduled, approved, granted and dictated by Alrik.

I cry out. That's, that's, *Gods.* It's—why's that so fucking hot?

"You're allowed five quick strokes before you slow for ten," Strobavik said. At the time I thought nothing of it, I was so fucking horny I expected to be done within the first few tugs. But I'm not and this pace is maddening.

I haven't had someone direct my masturbation session since … well since Corrik before our wedding and that seems so long ago. I'd forgotten.

This time, as I think of Alrik, it's an escape. I leave sad and horrifying thoughts in a box for later. I break from melancholy. His dangerous form tumbles gracefully across my mind, his battle cry echoing in my head. I spread my legs further—would he like that?— and stroke at the pace I've been granted. Five fast, ten slow.

"You will keep proper decorum. Enjoy yourself quietly as if Alrik was stroking you under the table at a fancy event," Strobavik warned. "Your arse will remain on the chair and your feet on the floor."

I want to moan, I want to mumble all kinds of gibberish, but I don't. The restrictions strike me more than usual. My blood is hot as my orgasm builds. When I slow down, the building orgasm wanes, still sending scorching flames through my body but keeping out of reach.

Worry that I won't orgasm in time creeps in, which doesn't help.

I'm tempted to think of things that Corrik and Baya have done to me. *Stop it, Tristan.* It's not like Alrik's not my type. I imagine his massive hand stroking my cock. Him towering above me. I imagine his deep voice, the annoying, commanding one saying, "Good boy, Tristan. Behave like that, just for me."

Alrik would never say any of that, but this is my fantasy and I'll imagine what I want to.

"Spread your legs wider. No, don't move your hips. You'll take what you're given, boy. Yes, like that."

My toe pads press into the ground, I'm in the middle of the room on a chair, exposed. Let me tell you, it's much different masturbating like this than tucked away under blankets. No one is here. No one is likely to come in (and besides I'd hear them in time to stop and cover myself with how many fucking locks are on the door).

But my brain can't help thinking, "What if they do?"

They'd see me desperate to come, tensing so that I'm behaved, obeying Alrik's orders. I want to fuck into my hand so badly. That would help. It would really fucking help.

"No. Control yourself for me. I want to see how prettily you can behave."

The Gods help me, that's what makes me come of all things. *Gods, I want to behave prettily for him.* Come spurts from my cock as my belly contracts and I exhale slow and shuddered. Hot come seeps down my hand as I recover, head back, eyes closed.

I open my eyes to the thrill of the tiny, magic timekeeper. I've spaced out. I forget where I am for a second but then it comes barreling back—I'm on a chair in the middle of my room. My limbs are whippy-wisps that could blow away with the wind, and my head is hollow like my brains have been sucked out.

I don't want to admit that I liked it.

But I liked it. I'd do it again. *Okay Strobavik, you win.* I've got a spark of submissiveness in me. It can be called forth with the right energy and the right cues. Still a fucking brat though.

And if Corrik would just come home, I'd fucking crawl to him with a hairbrush in my mouth so he could spank me and put me to bed.

I fall into a rhythm with Strobavik. When I'm following orders, I don't have to think. It brings me some amount of peace. Thinking leads me to thinking about Corrik or even Bayaden. Thinking also leads me to thinking about what awaits me in a life with Alrik. So I've discovered I have a submissive in me after all, but do I want this for every day, all the time?

No.

At least Alrik gets the reports he wants to hear—I'm a well-behaved pet.

"You still have no heart in it," Strobavik says to me one day.

It breaks my heart because I've been working hard, but I know he's right. "Am I doing something wrong, Master? I can do better."

"Silence," he says using his whippy little stick to carve a line in my back. I don't respond as wildly as I used to. My two lovers adored my responses, but Alrik will not so I've learned to take what I'm given quietly. "I'm not sure you'll ever have the heart for it. If I were you, I'd learn to fake it."

I don't know what that means, but I take his advice seriously. "Yes, Master Strobavik."

When my training is done and my studies for the day are finally over, I collapse on the bed I once shared with Corrik. I'm also coming to a new understanding of duty. I didn't realize how lucky I was with Corrik. Corrik loves me and I love him. The duty aspect sometimes convoluted the love we shared, but in truth it wasn't duty that bound me to Corrik.

This, what I'm doing now is a duty. It's what my father raised me for though and I will see it through, no matter how much it kills me inside.

Even the king and queen have not come to see me, and I'm told there was a ceremony for Corrik, one I, of course, was not permitted to attend. I didn't even bother to ask. So far, I've succeeded in not angering my new husband-to-be, and I'd like to keep it that way. I wasn't concerned about going anyway. I won't believe Corrik is dead yet—I'm not making the same mistake twice—it wouldn't have made sense for me to attend a funeral for someone who I do not believe to be dead.

I go to my book. The message from Lucca makes me smile. He's trying to be lewd, but since Papa doesn't trust him with the book on his own, Papa stands over him, stopping him when he gets too inappropriate. He's learned to use a bit of a code only I would understand. I'm not as embarrassed as I once was by his sexual jokes.

I finally bring myself to tell Papa about my situation. He knows Corrik's been gone, but I haven't told him of the disappearance, or my upcoming nuptials. There's nothing he can do to help me. Aside from my own feelings about all of it, I haven't wanted to worry him, especially when I've been hoping Corrik would suddenly show.

I attempt to make things sound like they aren't a big deal, but Papa reads right through me.

> Tristan, I am so sorry. I know how much you loved Corrik. I wish we could be there with you. Please, keep me updated. Write to me more often, I will check the book every night.

Even Papa's acceptance of Corrik's death is immediate. I wish I could speak to Diekin; he'd see things my way, but Alrik won't let anyone up here.

Alrik starts visiting though. It's weird and I'm not sure whether I like it or not. I don't know how to feel about him sitting at a table meant for me and Corrik, when Corrik can't be here, at the same time, his energy brings me comfort whether I want it to or not. This is the way with Top and brat energy. "I am told you are doing well in both your studies and your training," Alrik says. "I must admit, I expected a lot more pushback from you."

What would be the point? "I am Markaytian. I will fulfill my duty and do it well."

"Maybe it was Corrik then. You needed a firmer hand, one only I could give. You may make a fine husband for me after all."

I don't like him talking of Corrik that way and a familiar sensation burns through my blood again. A fire I haven't felt in some time. I have to quell it though, so I look at the floor and do my best not to give away what I'm thinking. "To what do I owe the pleasure of your visit, Highness?"

He stares at me for too long, like I'm a puzzle he can't solve. "You have earned some leniencies with me. In private, you may refer to me as sir or Alrik." He reaches out to brush the hair off my face. I try not to move. "You're much prettier without all this covering your face. At least tie it back."

"Yes, sir." I'm not sure if it means anything good earning leniencies from Alrik, but I suppose it's better than earning his ire. It's nerve-wracking that he finds me attractive. For some reason, Elves do. He swore he'd want nothing to do with me until I was Elf, which is only prolonging the inevitable, but I was glad for that; it gave me some time to mourn not being with Corrik. The more he's attracted to me, the more he'll be tempted to share a bed even beyond his wants and desires.

Elves need. If arousal stirs in him for me, resisting will be nearly impossible.

"Alrik," I say trying out our new level of familiarity. "Do you miss him?" I know their relationship was rough, but so was mine with my father and as it turned out, it was how he showed he cared. Knowing if Alrik misses Corrik is important.

He surprises me, standing abruptly. His presence dims and I realize now he carries light energy with him, which makes up part of his fierceness. "Corrik was my baby brother. We didn't get along because I was hard on him. Of course, I miss him. I wish I'd told him … Never mind." He storms out.

Despite my fear—that I'm going to end up sleeping with Alrik sooner rather than later—I decide that Alrik is not inherently bad, even taking into consideration his treatment of me. It's not personal. He does what he feels he has to for his people and unfortunately that means how he looks and how he comes across. He believes Elves to be a superior race and, in many ways, they are, but that does not mean he should treat those weaker than him as inferior.

Though I must admit, Markaytians are no better. We do the same with creatures and other races we feel are below us. It's a good lesson for me.

But with Alrik, I understand his commitment to duty and yet he's trying in the only way he knows how.

Duty is a running thread in my life. I am beginning to see where it's faulty.

I lie on the bed and read my nightly entry from Papa. His note isn't even particularly sad, but it makes me cry.

I haven't picked up my sword or bow since Corrik disappeared. I can't. Everything tied to those two weapons is too painful. He never wanted me to hold a weapon again, but slowly, he allowed those things because he knew how much they meant to me. Yes, the sword was because of the king, but eventually, he condoned it too. The bow, a beautiful gift, fashioned by him. I'd forgotten it was sewn with *his* magic. I patter over to my training room and pick it up, just to feel him. I can't bring myself to use either item, but I bring the bow to bed with me and hold on to it all night, falling asleep with it gripped tightly in my fist.

CHAPTER 16

*O*ver the following weeks, I resolve to practice again. No matter how tired I am from slave training, no matter how much I want to lie down after all my lessons—much more rigorous now, advancing to higher, royal protocols I originally didn't need—I practice. My muscles ache again in the best of ways.

Nothing has changed, but I feel more like myself. Strobavik notices. "I almost believe you, Tristan. The Crown Prince is harder to impress. Keep working at it." I start to think that maybe even Strobavik likes me.

I carry on, but not for Alrik or even Markaytia, I do it for me. Even sitting on the window ledge, watching the warrior-farmers as I call them, is part of the training for my mind and my heart. I pretend I'm their Warlord and give them pointers, saying them out loud to no one. I realize that without Diekin or anyone to call me Warlord, even that identity dropped away from me. Saying it to myself calls it back.

I'm careful not to let Alrik catch me. He's worse than Corrik was about protection, not because Corrik cared less, but Corrik was swayed somewhat by my happiness. My happiness is not important to Alrik, only that he fulfills his end of the treaty by taking care of me. Corrik also cared if I was put out with him, he didn't like me angry with him. If I told Alrik what I told Corrik, I have no doubt Alrik would simply take further measures to make sure I never escape, even if that meant using restraints of some kind. Elves are creative when it comes to restraining a person. Strobavik has shown me plenty of that.

As I become Tristan again and the sharp edge of my grief recedes, I remember something. The last strapping I received from my father was because I gave up on myself. I'm doing it again. And I get something else. As much as Father is as duty-bound as I am, he was willing to take me out of here when he thought I was placed in the hands of irresponsible Elves and had become a lamb for slaughter.

He did that because he loves me, he loves me because he loves himself. When it came down to it, Arcade Kanes chose his son over duty.

It hits me hard: I can't stay here. It's time for me to go. I don't know how I'll do it, but I'm going to find Corrik.

I had to leave one of my mates behind for duty. Bayaden. That situation is complicated, but in that one, leaving was what had to be done *for* the other and myself.

With Corrik, it's different. It's hard to say how exactly, other than we are bound in some way that seems to go beyond this world. We're an unlikely pair and yet we are inseparable. I have to find him. When it was me, he never stopped looking, he cared little for duty, he came for me.

Now it's my turn and I'm going to do the same.

If anything, Alrik's rules make it easier for me to leave. If I leave at night, I can take food from a whole day's worth with me. Few people come up to my suite now. Once I'm done with slave training and lessons, I'm alone for the night. I know the exact moment the guards switch over. I've watched them for months and if I time it just right, I could be out of here with none the wiser until morning and by then, I'll be long gone.

There are a few obstacles once I'm out of my confines. The biggest one being that I'm human. I'll need to cover my head and my ears. There's a chance I could pass for half-human, half-Elf, which come in different varieties in Mortouge, according to what I've read; I have no real-world experience in this area. I'll also have to get by the market-place guards, which won't happen at night. It will be easier during the day when I can squeeze out with the other people who come and go all day.

But before all that is the palace wall.

My heart races at the thought of my escape. If I get out, I'll have other problems to deal with, if I don't, not only will Alrik punish me, he'll take drastic measures to make sure I can never leave again. This is my one chance.

I pull out my pack, something that's in the back of our closet, stored here almost a year ago. It's one Corrik purchased for me on our travels since he made me leave the one I'd brought with me from Aldrien behind.

I make note that I'll need to cut my hair again.

I place everything I'll need in the closet, ready and waiting for me; my bow, my sword, a set of boots Corrik had made for me I've had no reason to wear other than when my parents came. I'll need pants and something warm, so I pull out the fur Corrik bought for me on our journey here from Aldrien.

The next day is long. I'm also more distracted than I've ever been, and I earn a full punishment spanking from Strobavik. It's not the first I've had from him, but it's the first in a while. While it fucking hurts, it's worth it for how calm I feel afterward. "I'm going to have to tell Alrik of this," he warns me.

By the time I would have to worry about Alrik, I'll be gone, so I'm not worried, but I attempt to show fear, looking to the ground, making my body position somber. "Nice try, naughty kitten. I know you too well. You need to do better. Alrik will know you don't care, and he'll make my punishment look like a gift from the Gods. Kneeling position. Two hours. That'll teach you."

Two hours? *Fuck.* I'm barely capable of one. Not only is the position grueling but focusing on nothing but Alrik for two hours is unbearable. Strobavik has special magic within him though, and while he cannot tell *what* I'm thinking, he can tell if I'm *not* thinking of Alrik. It's based more on feel—he explained to me—than mind-reading.

I assume the position because I don't have another choice. I splay all ten of my bare toes on the floor, pressing them into the stone floor, and sit on my heels. My back is tall, with my hands resting, palms facing down on my thighs and I keep my head bowed, my eyes resting on the floor in front. Part of submission is worship. I already learned that from my time with Bayaden, I naturally did that with Corrik. In a Master-slave relationship, worship is taken to a whole other level. You sleep, eat and breathe your master. Your existence is to please them. It's why Strobavik always spends some amount of my training doing this, having me kneel and focus on my Master.

But never for two hours.

This means the usual stuff won't do and I have to come up with something about him I can *really* get on board with. I decide the way he pushed my hair back over my ear was nice, *kind* even. It was a gentle gesture, and he meant comfort by it, even if he half-scolded me. He was also giving me something akin to a compliment. I replay that moment over and over. I remember the hardness in his face, the way his eyes crinkled, I trace my memory along his scar. I think about how sad he was when he talked of how much he missed Corrik, sparking new questions in my mind about Alrik.

Two hours fly by and Strobavik is impressed. "That's what I'm talking about. You've done well Tristan and have *almost* made up for the other two hours of nonsense, which I'm still putting in your report, but I will add this as well."

He makes me kiss each boot and thank him for the training and he's finally gone. Then it's lessons all afternoon. I'm exhausted by dinnertime and I consider leaving tomorrow night, but that's one more day I could be finding Corrik and I feel the urgency to get to him. What if there aren't many days left to find him? No. It must be tonight. I decide to have a nap before I eat dinner though, then I shall prepare to leave. The guards have their first change over in the evening, prime time to get out of here.

I lay down on the bed, just in time to hear the locks undoing. What the...? Alrik steps into the room and he spies me on the bed. I should get up and greet him, that's what a proper crown prince consort-to-be does, but I can't be arsed. I'm too tired. He doesn't look angry, which is what he usually is when he arrives at my chambers, instead he's … I don't know, but it's unnerving. "Tristan, have you eaten?"

Tristan? That's not good. He rarely calls me Tristan, and it usually doesn't bring anything good. "Not yet, I was going to have a nap before dinner, Your Highness."

"Remember what I said? You don't have to be so formal, Tristan. We'll be married. I can't have my husband calling me 'your highness' when we're alone."

I don't mean to say it, but it comes out. "Really? I would have thought that was a fetish of yours."

His head snaps up, and he searches my face to see if I'm serious. I'm somewhat serious, which is what makes the rest of it so funny. The stone man cracks a smile. "Perhaps a bit," he admits.

"Aren't I to call you Master, isn't that what I'm being trained for?"

I should not have said that. He flushes with arousal. "Yes, but even that will have its time and place."

Oh Gods. What is happening? Is Alrik aroused by me too? What is it with me and meeting Elves who have surprise human fetishes? I'm so done with that nonsense.

"You should eat," he says. "Come sit at my feet. Show me how well your training is going."

Bloody fuck. Can't I just embark on one perilous journey that works out smoothly for me? This has been a day of disasters. I know arguing will get me nowhere, so I go to him in the graceful way Strobavik taught me and kneel at his feet in the same position that's already made my thighs sore. My training has paid off. Strobavik always instructs me to think of Alrik in some way and I do now, it's automatic. My expression must come off as worship.

Alrik reaches out, but his hand pauses before he lays it on my head then takes his time as he runs his fingers through my hair. "That's it Kathir. Very good. I'm surprised you can be so well-behaved." He slides the covered tray over, which contains my dinner.

I should keep my mouth shut, let him say what he needs to say, get this over with so that I can leave. But Tristan, thy name is fool. "What other choice do I have? I have no wish to be beaten like a pell, Highness."

His hand cinches to my roots and I have to breathe through the pain to keep from crying out. I also may have just fucked everything up. If he makes true on his promises, I won't be able to climb down the side of the building. "S-Sssorry, Master," I say hoping the whole "Master" thing will remind him of his cock, which could also go another kind of sideways—a much better kind.

I luck out. He lets go. "I'll let that one go because I've been pleased with the reports. Strobavik isn't easy to satisfy, and he speaks highly of you." He does? That man's as prickly as my mother's cross-stitching needles. "But I'm not a lenient Elf. I will beat manners into you, and I won't harbor any remorse about it."

I take a breath. *I have to find Corrik.* I'm sure, somewhere out there, the perfectly obedient creature exists for Alrik, but I am not it. I nod and resume my obedient kneeling. He starts cutting up my meat and holds it out in front of my mouth with his fingers, so I have to lean forward to take it from him. I'm not stupid, he's testing me. You're not supposed to break form and if you do, it's supposed to be as little as possible unless you have been granted permission. He's holding it too far away for me not to break form. But I'm nothing if not competitive; I won't let him win. "May I, Master?"

He smiles, impressed. "You may."

Now I can lean forward and take the meat from his hand. The slave protocols are much more stringent than the ones Corrik was teaching me. And I don't dislike them per se; at times they're appealing in a humiliating sort of way, which turns me on. I just need more room to play. Some thrive like this in a twenty-four-seven slave relationship, but someone like me can do it only for a short while at a time. Eventually, I'll act out, it's just the way I'm wired.

And it hits me. In a snap I fall into subspace, the fastest I've ever fallen. A serene presence takes over, everything is light and pleasing Alrik comes easy. He takes me through several protocols, testing me. I pass, reveling in his praise.

Do I have a submissive in me after all?

Of course, it's Alrik to bring it out in me most.

I'm more out of it than I realized while kneeling and when Alrik instructs me to stand up, I stumble. *Shite.* I'm supposed to be a graceful bird or something else Strobavik says. "Sorry, Highness."

"Now *that* wasn't your fault," he says. "Come with me."

I can hardly believe what I'm experiencing as he *helps* me over to the bed and he's gentle, so much gentler than I ever thought he could be. "You've hit deep subspace, Tristan. I'll be honest, I didn't think you were capable, but wow, it's like you were born for it."

I was? This has never happened before. I don't have time or desire to blame him at the moment.

"Lie back, it's only right I take care of you after such a thing. Then you will sleep."

Take care of me? What does that mean? I assume he means sex but am relieved when he starts clinically massaging my thighs. It's nice and paired with the floaty bliss I'm in, it's easy to drift off. I'm not sure, but I swear I feel a set of lips press to my forehead.

I wake up with a start. It's dark—*fuck!*—and I've missed my chance to leave when the guards were switching off. If I leave now, I'll have to contend with them. Not impossible, but harder. I consider it again, what's one more day? But it's already been too long. If Corrik isn't dead, how do I know he's not hanging by his last threads? A day could mean the difference between life and death.

I have to go now.

I dress and don my boots quickly; I grab my pack and then I hop onto the first ledge.

CHAPTER 17

J've looked down at this maze of stones almost every day for the nine months. When you get used to being inside, the outside world becomes foreign quickly. Your brain plays tricks on you, things that weren't scary before, seem scary even though they haven't changed.

You have.

Looking down, about to *climb down*, is altogether different than the idea of it. I feel like there's a war inside my belly, but I take a breath and get calm thinking only of Corrik who needs me. I hop to the first stone that protrudes from the wall and then I almost slip to my death, only catching my balance *just* in time. Gods dammit, it's a bit icy. *This is a terrible idea Tristan.*

My heart pounds faster.

I look up. I could go back, it's not too late. But the fresh air fills me, I'm outside, I'm not in that room. I'm not going back, I'm here and I'm moving forward. I hop to the next ledge with a little prayer. It's not slippery, thankfully, but others are, and I nearly glide off the third. I've lucked out though, the ice hasn't layered over the whole surface of the stones, only in some patches, and my fingers can grip where the ice isn't.

I'm successful in getting to the halfway point, where I have to stop, this is where I'm more likely to be seen. I look up, it's a long way up, and without proper climbing gear, or magic, I realize that at this time of year and icy conditions, getting back up is an impossibility. Fuck, I am not used to this ice and snow stuff.

There are exactly two guards at this point, which means there will be more ahead, but two is a good number for me.

I didn't want to have to create distractions at this point, alerting the guard could result in a check-in on me—that's what I'd tell my crew to do were I Warlord looking after the situation—but if I distract them in just the right way, they'll deal with it themselves and won't report it till morning.

Using an arrow, I slide it into my bow and calm my breathing until I feel I can release the arrow with precision. The trick to shooting arrows is not to feel the let go, for it to happen in time with your exhaled breath. I shoot it several yards off and into a tall tree. They won't climb up, but they will investigate, which will give me enough time to climb the rest of the way down and move around the perimeter of the palace in the dark.

"Did you hear something?" the guard with the white hair says.

"Sounded like it went off over that way," the guard with the red hair says.

"You check over there, I'll check this way."

When they split up, I make the rest of my descent as carefully as I can while being quick about it. I'm still at a decent height and if I fall, I won't die, but I'll break something, and my adventure will have been short and very over.

I'm ready to pounce to the next stone, feeling more confident, getting used to how the ice looks on the stone, so I can grab for the iceless part of the stone, but it's dark and it's hard to judge and I'm unable to catch the ledge. I scramble in the air trying to grip for anything, but the wall is too slick with ice.

I get a bit of luck, landing hard in the brambles below rather than the hard ground. A quick check reveals nothing's broken, but I'm pretty beat up. The old Tristan, he could have done this, but I'm starting to think the Tristan I am now cannot. Nothing's going right. Then, I hear the footsteps come, but they're not from a direction I expect. *There's a third guard? But how?* I have never, in all my scouting seen a third guard. This has got to be one of Alrik's additions.

Well, that's it, I'm done for. I won't be able to directly overpower an Elf unless I use my sword, which has fallen a goodly distance away. It's over before it's begun, and this will not fall under Alrik's definition of well-behaved. He's going to kill me.

The third guard approaches. "Tristan?" he whispers.

My heart lifts—happy day!—it's Diekin. "You've made palace guard already?"

"Only just," he says puffing out his chest, his ears growing taller. "Told you it wouldn't take me long. Though, unfortunately, the decision had a lot to do with Corrik not being here. I am one of the best, they needed me here. I wanted to protect you." His eyes consider me— I'm out of my prison with two feet planted on the cold ground—and both brows arch, doing a good impression of any Top worth their salt. At the same time, I detect lack of surprise. He's more likely to wonder why I haven't done this sooner versus why I'm doing this at all.

I look at him deeply. What I have to ask him, he may not give. I don't have much time to convince him. "Diekin, I have to go. No one else can."

He gets tense and his look darkens. "Tristan, I can't let you go on a suicide mission no matter how much I want Corrik back."

"Do you think he's dead?"

His eyes flicker upward for just a second then back to me. "I don't know. I hope it isn't true."

This is old ground we know. We've faced this together before and just like before, I had to do what I must. "I'm going one way or the other, Diekin." I make my stance solid, willing to fight him if need be. I see the moonlight glinting off my sword on the ground and an opening to slide through to grab it. I say a silent thank you to my father again for all the hard days of training.

"Diekin," one of the other guards, shouts. "Anything over there?"

My heart picks up the pace as Diekin assesses me. *Will he give me away?* I have to wait two long breaths to find out. "Nothing's over here. Go back to your station," he says.

'You're in charge?' I mouth to him. He nods.

He holds up three fingers to me, which I take to mean there are three guards ahead, and signals for me to stay on the side of the palace where it's darkest. On the other side of the wall, surrounding the palace on this side is a long drop down into icy water. I can't go over; the only way is through.

Diekin walks with purpose toward his crew on this side. "It was nothing," he assures them, and they return to their posts. I follow along carefully, worried that at any moment they could catch movement. Elves have tremendous eyesight.

When we get to my sword, Diekin kicks it toward me along the grass and I snatch it up, keeping it out. I follow along where Diekin moves, careful to remain in darkness until we get to an area free of guards where I can run out from the shadow of the palace and into the trees. I know the risk he's taking for me. He puts a hand on my shoulder. "I can't fathom what you've been through. I wanted to come to see you, but Alrik won't let anyone. Of course, the king and queen could overrule him, but he's convinced them he knows what's best."

"It's okay, Diekin. I understand, but I must go."

"I can see that, Warlord." There's so much I want to say, but there isn't time. I also note my title is back and I like to think it's something in the way I'm carrying myself. "That sword belongs in your hand. If I might give you some advice, Warlord?"

"I always welcome your advice, Diekin." A good Warlord always hears the advice from his trusted counsel.

"You won't get out of the palace gates without a fight, they're too heavily guarded. The only way out is the south-east wall. It's the weakest point in our defense. The trouble is the climb down requires equipment you don't have."

I feel like turning back. It's hopeless.

Diekin's eyes brighten. "I will help you, Warlord. Come." He holds out his hand to take one of mine and recites ancient Elvish until there's a soft glow. "You'll be able to stick to the wall, but the spell won't last forever, and it will still be dangerous. I don't need to tell you to be careful."

"Thank you, Diekin." He nods. "Once I'm out, I was going to hide until morning and walk out with the morning crowd."

"That is a good plan. I would also cut this," he says referring to my hair. "They'll be looking for you by then."

He's nearly shaking, I know he's scared for me. "Diekin, even if I don't make it, do not feel guilty. Dying doing this is better than never having tried, and always remember, I have one failsafe."

"Dragon blood?" He leans back to get a good look at me.

I smile.

He nods. "It seems I'm always saying goodbye to you like this, Warlord. Please make it back with Corrik. You need to become an Elf, there are more adventures for us to have together, yet."

"We will have adventures again, Diekin."

"Last, I'm sure you know the Unbroken Mountains lie west in the second realm, but when you get to the entrance, proceed with extreme caution and start northeast. Corrik is that way. Somewhere. After that, you're unfortunately, you're on your own, there wasn't anything left of his tracks, all signs of him wiped away."

That's his way of telling me I'm on a bit of a fool's errand. "Thank you, brother. I will find him." We embrace and I thank him and then I'm gone in the night.

---

*N*one of it's easy. Even with Diekin's help, I almost slip to my death twice and I realize how much of a prisoner I really was. If not for Diekin, I would have been shipped straight back to Alrik. Perhaps the Gods were smiling upon me after all. Being a human among Elves is hard. My bandana helps, but my copper skin does not. Even the humans here are almost as pale as the elves and I stand out. I had to keep covered the whole way through the market.

Once I made it past the marketplace, I had to stay sharp. I knew there would be a hunt for me by that point. I kept to the trees like my father showed me and I continued moving like Bayaden taught me.

I had to steal a horse. I would replace her when I return.

I stay off the main roads as often as I can, and so far, I've had no issue, but now, I have to travel on the main roads. I know warriors will be on the lookout for me, and I don't know what I'll do if they find me. They are my kin now. I can't kill them; if they catch up with me, it's over. I just need to stay ahead of them.

I ride into a small town on the outskirts of King's Keep and spy a beautiful set of tall Elven warriors from the palace, questioning people. I ride into an open stable and hop off my horse, thinking I'll hide here until they pass through, but as usual, things aren't going to go the easy way for me. A massive Elf jumps down from the loft, staring right at me and I know not to move. I do think about the sword at my hip, maybe I could incapacitate him long enough to get away, but it would alert the palace guard outside. I'm kinda at his mercy if he has any. "Jagarbendir, come and have a look at what's in here."

The Elf studies me as I scrutinize him. He's different than any Elf I've seen before. Most of the ones I know are either royalty or have served royalty. Even the staff serving royalty have a particular sort of presence about them. This Elf is the equivalent of a farm boy in Markaytia. It's a bit odd. I realize even as a servant to Bayaden, I lived a royal lifestyle. "Those are fine weapons you have, *human*."

Fuck. He knows I'm human. Does every kind of Elf hate humans?

An older looking Elf enters. His age does nothing to take away from the edge of steel in his eyes or the presence of power in his sinewy body. He's got that look about him that says he's ancient and a healthy collection of scars that say he's had a rough time but has thrived, regardless. For an Elf to look remotely old, he's got to be ancient, like the king, maybe older than. This must be Jagarbendir. "Aye, a human? There are some guards out there looking for a someone about your description," he says, with the hint of an accent I've never heard before—a bit regal, but also timeless, suggesting that he has come from another time and if he's old like I suspect, he has.

"Please, don't let them find me," I whisper.

"You in some kind of trouble, boy?" I nod, pleading with my eyes. "Come with me."

He leads me into the house, lifts the carpet to reveal a secret door, which leads underneath the house. The man could be sending me to my next prison, but I quickly devise getting out of this prison will be a heck of a lot easier than breaking out of the palace, and I already did that, so I head down the stairs not too worried. The guards come, I hear voices above me and then sounds that make me think they're carrying out a search. They are here for a good twenty minutes and then they're gone.

It's a long while before the door is opening again and Jagarbendir is inviting me up. I'm relieved I don't have to fight my way out of this situation, but I know it can't be so simple; there's going to be a catch for their assistance. "You must be hungry," the old Elf says. "Sit."

He's the kind of Elf who's used to giving orders and having people obey them. "That's very kind, sir. But I must be on my way."

He shakes his head. "I insist, *young Warlord*." Fuck. See? It's never that easy. "Sit."

A stare down takes place until I do. I purse my lips and give him my best Warlord face. From the corner, the other large, but younger Elf, watches with a cool countenance. He's shirtless, I can see all of his muscles contract and stretch, I can see all of his scars too. His mouth almost smirks at me. He knew who I was too. "What do you want?"

The large old Elf begins taking things out of the cupboards—he *is* going to make food—and the other crosses his arms. "We heard about the loss of our prince. Am I to assume you're on some foolhardy rescue mission?"

"I'd hardly call it foolhardy." I try to make myself look bigger and more Warlord-like.

"You're going to get yourself killed and you're not just a prince anymore, you're engaged to the *crown* prince."

"Not if I can help it. I already have a husband thanks; I'd like to get him back."

"If he still lives. For now, things are as they are."

"If that's how things are, then you're in very big trouble helping me hide. We still haven't got to the part about why you helped me."

"My son was one of the children taken. Salamir. This is my other son, Aldagir. We both train the men around these parts. We weren't invited to go with the royal entourage, but we believe Prince Corrik was headed in the right direction to whatever's been taking our children and if you know the direction he went, we'd like to accompany you. I want my son back."

"Wait, you're the warriors I've seen from my window." I look back toward the palace, which is a speck in the distance. *Wow, my looking device can see this far?* They're both looking at me funny, rightfully so. I change the subject. "Where I'm going is said to be dangerous."

"We're willing to risk it," Jagarbendir. "It's doubly dangerous for us. I have a whole crew of men willing to go, but we've been ordered to stand down so no more of us are taken. Aldagir and I will accompany you and offer our protection and hope it's enough for your future husband to go easy on us. Regardless, we'll suffer whatever consequences we're given. We need to at least try to get Salamir back. You will need our help Warlord. I mean no offense by that, it's just the way it is. You're a human, these lands are full of magical creatures you'll need help with."

As much as I don't want to admit to my human weaknesses, they're true. I hear the desperation in his voice, how can I turn him down? Isn't this exactly what a Warlord is made for? Plus, our plights are the same. It's just, "I'm sure you realize the chances Salamir is still alive are grim."

He nods. "About as grim as the prince being alive. But Salamir was the child taken, just before we lost the Prince Corrik. We hope that means there's still hope to be had."

"All right, you may join me, but it's imperative we leave as soon as possible."

"We'll eat and have our gear together within the hour and then make one quick stop."

The three of us look a sight, riding across the small town, but I get the sense this town has an unspoken solidarity, with Jagarbendir as their unofficial leader. We ride a goodly distance, still outside the forest, but further into the countryside, where the larger farms are. We approach one farm in particular and a little boy runs out to meet us. "Papa! Papa!" The boy looks young, but that's relative. He could have lived twenty summers by now, yet he looks the age of a four-year-old Markaytian boy.

Jagarbendir lifts the boy to him. "I suppose you expect to be carried everywhere. Where is your mother?"

The boy doesn't answer, popping a thumb into his mouth, eyeing me. I'm sure I'm a sight. I'm still a little beat up from my fall down the side of the palace and while I had Diekin's help sticking to the side of the tall wall surrounding the palace, there were cold places where my skin stuck, by the time I got down, I needed bandages for my hands, not to mention all the dirt and grime that must be on my face even with the bit of clean up I attempted while I waited for Jagarbendir and Aldagir to put together their things. Now that he's still and I get a better look at him, I notice something I didn't before—the boy is half-human.

A pale-skinned human, with golden hair rushes out after her babe. Her hair shimmers in an otherworldly way, she may be human, but the humans in Mortouge are not quite as human as I am anymore. Maybe they were thousands of years ago, but since then they have evolved and changed, perhaps having absorbed some of the magic from their Elven kin.

There is an uneasy relationship between the humans and the elves of Mortouge. In Aldrien, the humans are slaves, but in all seven of the realms that make up Mortouge, lives a different race of humans, one that began long ago when humans were permitted to enter. Since the ban, the humans who already existed here were allowed to stay and carry on their lineage, but like with every differing culture, there came some amount of prejudice. Human-Elf children are known as halflings, not considered Elf, not considered human. A breed of their own, and arguably experiencing the most prejudice.

In Aldrien, human-Elf marriages are forbidden, it would be the equivalent of marrying your pet; you love your pet, and you take care of him, but you wouldn't marry him. Humans weren't considered equal to Elves, yet there was little mistreatment of them. It was even all right to fuck them and mark them. You just couldn't enter a proper marriage with one.

The king wasn't stupid; he knew I was more to Bayaden than his pet, but so long as Bayaden understood that what we did was all we would ever have, he was fine with our, what he considered *games*. When it was time for Bayaden to get serious, he had to flush me out with the tide.

I like that Jagarbendir does not hold such prejudices. "Highness, this is Cilrilda, my forty-seventh spouse, my fortieth wife."

The number astounds me for a moment, but I remember the polyamorous nature of Elves, except for the two Cyredanthem brothers I know and their sister. My Corrik never seemed to want any other but me, but I never thought to ask him. Getting-to-know-you time has not been a luxury for us, something I vow to change once I have him back. "Pleased to meet you, Cilrilda. Just Tristan is fine."

"Oh no, I couldn't, Highness. Especially not after the news." Ugh. These Elves work fast, Corrik's not even gone a year and the word's out I'm to be Crown Prince Consort. "My condolences for the passing of your first husband."

They are the first condolences I've had. Other than the servants who are not supposed to get too friendly with me, I've only had contact with Alrik and Diekin. Alrik, who was going through his pain about Corrik and Diekin, who believes as I do, that Corrik is out there somewhere. I'm not sure how to respond. Thankfully, Jagarbendir saves me. "Save your condolences, my dear. We're off to find him."

Her body lifts and her features fill with hope. "Does that mean you're off to find Salamir?"

"We are," I say, feeling proud to be on this mission.

She cries. "Oh, thank you, thank you, Your Highness."

"Tell no one, Cil," Jagarbendir warns.

She nods and her expression gets serious. "Jagar."

"We will get him back."

"Then what of you? Have you asked Suki if you can take Aldagir?"

Apparently, the wives watch out for each other. "Aldagir is a man," he says, his voice becoming stern.

"Say that to his mother and see what she says."

"I do not have to ask her permission." His eyes harden.

Aldagir is quiet as they talk about him as if he's not there, which I can relate to; it reminds me of home. It was like that with my parents, the three of them bickering over what's right for Tristan until Father told them what would be.

She seems to remember her place, which to Elves is not gender-dependent, even for humans; it is based on your designation, which is dependent on how you are wired within. Aldagir is clearly dominant, especially if he can handle forty-seven spouses. Seven of them must be men. I remember he's likely lived a very long time to have so many. I have a lot of questions for him not covered in my study books. I hope he's prepared to talk.

It's fascinating. I do love Elven culture even if I think the lot of them are arrogant.

She nods stiffly, her chest out and lips pursed. "Forgive me, Jagar."

"I understand your worry, my dear, but Aldagir came to me. I would dishonor him by leaving him here." Placing a hand on the side of her face, his small boy still hanging onto him, he tilts her chin up to kiss her lips.

"I will tell Suki. Come here, boy," she fondly says to Aldagir. "*Now.*" This woman is no wallflower.

Aldagir blushes but suffers her affections as she pulls him into a hug. "*Em* Cilrilda," he complains. It's entertaining watching the large stoic Elf, embarrassed by the small woman.

"Never mind." She kisses his head.

Even though Cilrilda isn't his mother, she's due a particular amount of respect similar to that of a mother. Em is used to designate a category of mother in Elvish, Om is the prefix he'd use for his father's husbands. Jagarbendir kisses the boy. "All right, to your mother with yah." Cilrilda takes him. "We'll be back before you know it."

I'm not sure if she believes him, but she has no choice but to have faith. "Thank you again, Highness. I know you'll help keep them safe."

It means a lot to me that she believes I can. "The Kanes family are descendants of dragons, we are bred to keep people safe. I will look out for them both."

"I'm glad you will become King-Consort one day. You are good for our people," she says. I know she's being respectful; I understand that currently, my status is only a notch below Crown Prince, but it's not a label I want, and I hope this journey ends with me absolving that title.

"Thank you, my lady. I will always do my best no matter which title I serve under.'

*W*e set out for the second realm, and I am glad to have them with me. And while I still think locking me in a room was way overboard, I start to see why Corrik was paranoid. These lands *are* dangerous. They may have been banned for humans, but the Elves cannot keep all magical creatures out. If not for Aldagir and Jagar, I would not have made it far. I once threatened Corrik that I would find a way to leave if need be. That he believed I could tells me he always did think I was fierce and I begin to feel more sympathy for his prophetic vision.

There are also the patrols. We have to stay off the main roads, which means a harder ride through the thick forest and the land heading into the third realm filled with obstacles my army of two know how to traverse well.

It's not all bad. I get to know my travel companions. They are impressed with my skill with a sword and a bow. "You don't have any spouses yet?" I ask Aldagir.

"Father will not allow it. He's a bit old-fashioned," he leans in to explain.

"I heard that," Jagar says, smiling. "A proper Male Elf should reach his three-hundredth year before choosing a mate."

That's what the royal family believes too, usually. They made an exception for me because I'm a regular human—not the kind residing in Mortouge, who live a lot longer—and Corrik was permitted to marry early.

I can't help the contentedness I feel hearing the firmness from Jagar. Aldagir doesn't harbor any true resentment over it, he respects his father's word, deeply. I relax missing my father and his firmness. Never thought that would happen. "Of course, Father," Aldagir says.

"I suppose I've married quite young and look at me, on my way to a second husband," I say.

Something in my tone causes Jagar to frown. "You do not wish to marry our crown prince."

It's not a question, but I answer anyway. I shake my head. "We're not suited. I know that doesn't negate my duties, but I would prefer the husband I had."

"You love him."

"Very much."

"If he's out there, we'll find him," Jagar says and I appreciate his fatherly tone.

I need to change the subject from Corrik and marriages. "How did Salamir go missing?"

Both Elves get serious. "Many of the halfling children began disappearing last spring. It took me some time before I could get the attention of the Crown Prince and then, nothing for a long while. We never found the first four children to go missing, but then it stopped until a couple of months before Alrik put Corrik on the case. My Salamir went missing after Uric and Stemnary."

"Only halfling children are being taken? What could be the reason for that?"

"I don't know, and I don't like to think about it. My Salamir, he's still very young, I know he's terribly frightened."

"If Corrik is there, he'll look out for him."

"I hope so, Warlord."

⸻

*T*relay Diekin's directions and they seem to know what it all means, leading us over dangerous terrain, through rivers, and finally to a ridge, with tall stone slats that reach high into the mountain. I get off my horse. "This is it," I say. "This is where Corrik went." I don't know how I know that, but I feel like he's nearby, my heart bubbles in my chest.

"What should we do, Warlord?" Jagarbendir says.

Jagarbendir is a few thousand years old; he has more experience than I could fathom. There's no way I'm going to have an answer over him, he's giving me the respect he thinks I deserve because he feels it's my mission since I'm royalty. But it's just as much his.

"My instincts tell me to go in carefully, but I know little of magic Jagar. I'm hoping you can offer me, counsel, here."

He nods, and his eyes seem to belay respect. I'm sure he's not used to having royalty ask for his opinion, even when said royalty doesn't have half the knowledge he has. "There is magic all around this place. The area is shrouded in it. If we go in there, I'm not sure we could hide from whatever's set the traps."

I nod. Magic is something I've had little experience with. As Markaytians, we don't deal in magic. I have a small amount in my blood, being a descendant of dragons, but it's not even comparable to the small amount the humans of Mortouge have. I certainly don't feel confident in deciding about it. But once again, because I am royalty means the responsibility automatically falls to me.

I recall when Father encountered new situations. I always thought he wasn't afraid of anything, but Papa would tell me that was not the case. "He has to muster all his bravery, be extra vigilant and do it anyway, Tristan," Papa would say.

"I say we stick close and assess as we go. Whatever took Corrik surprised him, it was more powerful. I am welcome to anything you want to add, Jagar," I say, knowing he won't interject his opinion to a royal unless given permission.

He nods. "You're different," he says. "I like it."

I smile. "Compliment me when I've gotten us safely through this, my friend."

"Lead the way, Highness."

CHAPTER 18

*A*s much as I want to storm in, swords blazing, we can't. If whatever's taking halflings could take Corrik, it's something powerful. We leave our horses and head into the clearing on foot. On the other side of the slats of the mountain is more forest, leading up the mountain. There's a reason these are called the Unbroken Mountains, at least. Only the strong can survive ventures in this direction and people don't generally travel this way, even Elves.

I might not have the same ability to sense magic as the Elves do, but I can feel the eerie presence of it. Whatever's got hold of this place, it's strong and bad. After traveling for half the day, we have to start thinking about making camp for the night, which is not good. We still have no idea who or what we're tracking, how to track them, or if we're just heading to our deaths. I try to remain optimistic, envisioning finding Corrik, keeping that in my mind, praying to the Gods for good fortune. "Let's find a place to make camp, no fires tonight, we'll take shifts on watch," I say.

"Highness, I insist that we take all the watch shifts. You should get full rest."

Father and Papa always took a watch shift, unless it was imperative they get full rest for good reason since a lot of the decision-making fell to them. "No. I will take the first one and then sleep the rest of the night." I don't trust them to wake me up. It's hard to put the edge of Arcade Kanes into my tone, toward someone like Jagar (I've always been taught to give elders a particular level of respect) but I manage.

"As you wish Your Highness, but please, don't hesitate for anything, even if you think it might be nothing," Jagar warns.

"I won't, promise."

We walk for a few more hours, with no luck, no signs, nothing, and then we pack it in for the night, eating sparse amounts of the little supplies we have. Jagar and Aldagir turn in for a few hours. I take a spot up in a tree, on a nice fat branch as Deglan taught me, watching over them with my bow at the ready. My body is alive with electricity as I watch over them. I also spend a great deal of my watch asking for a sign, something to tell us where Corrik is.

I have to believe he's out there even when things are looking grim.

Two hours pass, and it's about the time I should wake one of them. I'm about to climb down the tree, when I hear a sound beside me. I remain still, turning my head ever so slowly toward the direction of the sound. It's dark, but moonlight shines dimly on my tree hideaway. I don't see anything, but I feel something climb up my arm. It's small, but it's got claws.

I don't know what it is, or what it will do if I alarm it. I let the claws pinch my skin through my clothes and it continues to climb up my arm, toward my neck. When it gets there, it nips my skin. "*Ow*," I complain quietly at it. By this point, I get the sense it's not dangerous, but still, it's probably wild and wild things don't like sudden movements.

I have an idea of how big it is, and I think it could fit on the back of my hand, so I carefully move my hand toward it and nudge at it some. It hops and lands, cinching its claws into my knuckles. I hold the little blighter up to the largest patch of moonlight and though I've never seen the likes of it, I know what it is.

I recognize my kin.

"My word," I say like Papa. "You're just a little thing."

The tiny dragon coos at me with a little trilling sound. "What are you doing here?" I ask.

I don't know if it will understand me, but my bloodline is supposed to be able to speak to them. Instead of answering me, it tucks its legs under, curls its wings around its body and closes its eyes. Great, it's asleep. I stow my bow and climb down the tree doing my best not to disturb his or her majesty. They don't even move. I roll my eyes. "Jagar," I say quietly. "We have a visitor."

Jagar wakes, keeping quiet so as not to disturb Aldagir if he can help it, but sleep on the road like this is rarely deep unless you're Lucca, who can sleep through a stampede of horses. "Tristan, what is that?"

I smile at him finally feeling comfortable enough to call me Tristan. "A dragon."

"Dragon?"

"Yes." Dragons have long since left Markaytia, but legends always place them in other realms. They have popped up in stories from time to time but these stories are thought of as tall tales. Most Markaytians don't believe in dragons anymore.

"You're sure?"

"Sure, as the Kanes blood running through me."

"What's it doing?"

"Sleeping."

As Jagar inspects it, Aldagir wakes. "What's going on?" he says.

"Nothing too alarming, except that Tristan's found a dragon," Jagar tells him.

"I think it might have found me, actually."

"Well, whatever it's doing here, it's not going to tell us tonight. Perhaps you should sleep too, Highness? I'll take the next watch."

I should, but both Aldagir and I are like little boys who've just found a puppy except that puppy is a dragon. "Do you think it's male or female?" Aldagir asks, looking it over with wonder.

I reach out to the dragon with my inner senses, my blood, to get a feel of it. "I think it's a he."

"Well then, he's kind of an arrogant little thing, falling asleep on your hand like that."

"He might be but it wouldn't be the first arrogant creature I've drawn into my life. I think he knows he's safe with me."

"Go to sleep you two," Jagar says before he heads off to take his post. I'm surprised he's given me a direct order, but it must be hard for him to resist what is natural. He's incredibly dominant, I am brat. There's no doubt he'll be worried after my care.

Both Aldagir and I suppress a giggle for the light scolding, but it feels good.

Jagar realizes what he did. "My apologies Highness, I did not mean to tell you what to do. It's just ... well what would Prince Corrik say to you?"

"Say? He would not *say* anything. I would be placed over his knee and soundly spanked for not obeying him the first time." I wink. "I don't mind Jagar and I'm surprised it took this long for me to pull it out of you. I need it, but that's the only time you'll hear me say that."

He smiles. "Get to bed then you two; you can play with the dragon in a few hours."

---

*T*he sun is barely rising when Aldagir wakes us both up. The tiny dragon is not where I left him last night. "He flew over there, Tristan," Aldagir says. "I think he might be waiting for us."

How odd. And he is waiting for us, perched on a jagged tree stump.

"Which way should we go, Highness?" Jagar asks.

"Northwest," I tell him, he raises his brow. "That little fellow, that's the way he's staring. I think that's the way to go."

Without much else to go on, since Diekin's instructions have long ended, we follow the little dragon keeping our eyes peeled. The forest gets eerier, things feel tainted in this region, and it makes me wonder what this little guy was doing in here and where he came from. As we move, the dragon continues to fly ahead of us, resting on this tree or that, until we catch up. We follow him up the mountain for hours until we reach the mouth of a cliff that leads into a cave.

Surrounding the cave is some fucking weird stuff—an abandoned firepit, piles of clothing—children's clothing—and a white coat I recognize. "Corrik," I say quietly. We don't know what's around here. I look up to the dragon whose sharp eyes peer directly at me and then he takes flight disappearing in the strange, purple sky.

I look over to Jagar who's investigating, he shrugs when he doesn't find anything. I point to the cave, letting him know I'm going to head in, but he shakes his head, urging Aldagir to go with me. I wait and before I head in, I take a breath. I let it run through me.

Did I come all this way only to learn of Corrik's death?

This place was abandoned a while ago, but something heinous happened here. I use all the strength I have left to go into the cave, doing my best to hold my bow steady. I chose bow over sword today, knowing it's the only way I can be nearly as fast as something that isn't human and if it took Corrik down, I know it couldn't have been human.

Aldagir squeezes my shoulder just before I step in.

The stench alone almost brings me to my knees. Something's been dead in here a long time. Light pours in from overhead and I can see a body on the ground. It's one I'd know anywhere, curled protectively around another, smaller one. Toward the back are more small bodies and the carcass of something hideous hanging from the ceiling of the cave. I'm not concerned with any of that for the moment. I race over to Corrik, tears flooding my eyes. *Please don't be gone. Please don't be too late.*

When I place my hand on his bare arm, it's cold, but shaking him elicits a moan. Moaning is good. Moaning means alive. I shake harder. "Corrik! Corrik!"

"Tristan?" Corrik says, his voice is weak. Corrik is worse for wear in nothing but a ripped pair of pants, barefoot and his hair badly disheveled. From whatever it is his captors did to him, he's not healing, his skin is marked with bruises, and broken open in places, dried with blood. His hands are bound together with black cuffs that have strange writing on them and I see that his ankle is shackled and attached to the wall of the cave; his shackles have enough slack to allow him to move about. I notice the other forms in the cave, the small ones, also attached to the cave wall in balls, unmoving.

"It's me," I say, almost mouthing it afraid I'll wake the carcass of whatever's rotting close by.

"I thought I'd never set eyes on you again." He speaks quietly. "You should not be here. Leave. Now." His eyes look up to the thing above. It reminds me of a cocoon with its wide, cylindrical shape and its light brown covering, only unlike an insect cocoon, it looks to be made of something thicker than silk and it's oozing a sickening green-yellow pus. It pulsates, wriggling and writhing with some kind of fluid rushing across vein-like vessels.

"You can't be serious. Corrik," I say and fix him with a glare.

"I'm very serious, Kathir. I have made every possible escape attempt. There's no way out of this and I won't allow you to get caught up in it too." He's still speaking in hushed tones.

That pisses me off. I attempt to push him and when I still can't— he's weakened, but not weak—I whack his shoulder. "This is so typical of you. Screw you, Corrik. You're coming with me if I have to drag you out of here. Not only am I *not* marrying your brother, but I love you, you idiot." I manage as much venom as possible while still keeping quiet.

He smiles. "I love you too, Tristan. Wait, marry my brother?"

"Everyone thinks you're dead. Your parents, in their grief, wanted to keep me and honor the treaty. I am now Crown Prince Consort to be. People are treating me differently, it's weird Corrik."

He's amused, but then his face hardens again. "Good. My brother will take good care of you."

"Your brother wants to force me into the *slave* designation. I am not *slave*, Corrik. I'm a fucking brat and it's only so long before he makes true on his promise to attempt to beat that out of me."

"You keep telling me you're a strong Warlord, you'll be fine. And look at you, disobeying everyone. You should be in your room where it's safe." He is truly angry about that, but there's something else there and I think he might be jealous of his brother.

I'm fucking using it.

"You're right, Corrik. Kiss me then and I'll be on my way."

"It's for the best," he says leaning in, pressing his rough lips to mine.

"You know, Strobavik said I have real talent for being *slave*," I tell him.

"Strobavik. You've been training with Strobavik, but he's—"

"—a terrifying, Elven Dungeon Master? Yes. He's trained me for months and like all things I undertake, I worked to master the skills."

Corrik's imagining it, maybe me on my knees for him, maybe me tied up with my legs spread, cock hard and begging for him, but having trouble, because of the gag he would have put in my mouth. I can tell he's affected even in his state. "I will be kneeling for your brother now. I will become Elf just after the wedding and he will release me from my confinement, then he will want to show me off. I'm sure I'll be kneeling at his feet, adoring him, waiting for instructions while he deals with pleas brought forth to the Great Hall. My cock will be so hard," I say in his ear. "I'll be whimpering as it leaks, but there'll be no relief for me until I earn it."

Corrik licks his lips and thankfully I can trust a male Elf to be ruled by his cock. "Gods dammit. Enough. You win. What's the plan?"

Victory. "First, to get you out of these," I say.

"Your sword should be able to cut through. They are enchanted, a spell is inscribed on the surface. It prevents me from using magic, which is why I'm so weak Tristan. You'll die trying to get me back to Mortouge."

"Don't worry about that for now. Meanwhile, you're about to find out how precisely I can stick a blade, First Husband," I say. I've been wanting to call him that for some time now.

"You have been studying, First Husband," he says in return.

Before I get all sword-sy, Aldagir rushes over. "Prince Corrik is … is he…?" he says, inquiring after the small body Corrik was wrapped around.

"He's alive, but barely. You see that up there? That's a witch wyrm. When it finally went into its cocoon a few days ago, I gave him as much warmth as I could. But unfortunately, that thing had been feeding us as well, neither of us could procure much food with it unavailable."

The boy stirs, barely there, but still alive. "Salamir," Aldagir says. The boy's head lolls back and forth. "And the others?"

Corrik shakes his head. "The only reason we're still alive is because we're the most recent abductions. The others were already nearly sucked dry when I woke up here."

Fuck.

"Stand back," I say once Salamir is out of the way. I use my sword to first break the chain between Corrik's wrist shackles and then I work on cleaving them off. I break both Corrik and Salamir out of their ankle shackles.

When Corrik is free, he gathers me in his arms. "I thought I'd never see you again." He kisses my lips.

Jagar rushes in at that point. "I heard loud noises."

"We were just breaking our cargo free," I tell him.

Jagar sets eyes on his boy. "Salamir." He rushes to him, checks him over and then waves his hand over him head to toe. White light envelopes him and then he starts coughing; his eyes open. "Pa-Papa...?"

"Oh, my boy. My sweet, sweet boy. Papa's here." Jagar takes Salamir from Aldagir.

"Friends of yours, Tristan?" Corrik says.

"My apologies Highness, we're being rude. I do believe we've made your acquaintance before. I am Jagarbendir and this is one of my sons, Aldagir. There are no words to express our gratitude for what you've done for our boy."

"I just wish I could have saved the others." Corrik's eyes frown as he surveys what's left of the others.

"Are there any more of those things?" I ask.

"I think so, but I don't think one will appear for another few months. There is little in the lore about them, but I've had plenty of time to think about how these creatures work based on what I know and what I've observed. They live on Elven blood, but they take the halflings because they are easier prey containing enough Elven blood —and Elf is better, but a halfling is enough—to get them to their next phase of development. Feeding makes them stronger. That one captured me by pure luck. It took me by surprise. I will tell you the whole story, but for now it's enough to know they feast until they are strong enough to make their cocoon. This one will hatch, and it will be a more powerful version."

"Then we have to kill it before we leave," I decide.

Corrik's eyes worry. "I'm not strong enough, Tristan. The best we can hope for is to get away before it hatches. I was meant to be its food when it did. Perhaps without its post-cocoon meal, it won't make it."

"Not good enough," I say. This thing, it killed children. I'm going to make sure it never kills again. The ring of steel announces my sword's arrival.

"You can't kill that thing, Tristan. Put your sword away *now*. I'm still your husband and you will obey me."

I can't help it, his words run through me like icy nectar and I shiver. It's been a while since I've heard him speak like that. I won't disrespect him by questioning his word in front of anyone. There are many reasons to keep appearances, but he's crazy if he thinks I'm walking out of here without making sure that thing's dead. "Corrik, may I have a word with you in private?"

We proceed to have a five-minute stare down in which we blaze fire at each other, but he refuses to move.

Jagar quickly devises what's going on. "Your highnesses, if I may? Perhaps my son and I can be of assistance?"

Corrik, who can barely stand, who's leaning against me, is now leading this charge. I can't help the unfairness I feel. It's especially jarring to have command ripped from me so unceremoniously. I'm used to deferring to my superiors, but there was still a modicum of consideration over my opinion. I'm being left out of this entirely. "Do you think you two can kill the witch wyrm?" Corrik says, his voice weak.

"I do, but I think it wouldn't go amiss to have Prince Kathir ready with his bow." Corrik twists his lips. He doesn't like it. "As you know, Your Highness, witch wyrms continue to feed on Elven children and when they reach their last phase of development, they can take on a full Elven adult easily. They need to be slaughtered now when they're most vulnerable."

Corrik huffs. He knows Jagar is right, that doesn't mean he wants to let me do it. "All right, but you're only back up, Tristan." He grips my face with his hand. The usual strength isn't there, he isn't well and now he's using whatever energy he has left to worry about me.

"Just back up, my love. They probably won't even need me. They are both fine fighters." I press a kiss on his cracked lips.

"Hopefully they won't have to fight at all. Please, allow me to continue to keep your boy warm," Corrik says.

"You're going to fall over, Highness," Jagar says. Aldagir's quietly sizing up the massive cocoon.

"I can do that much. Tristan, help me sit against the wall and I will take him."

There's no convincing him otherwise, so I help him sit and Jagar settles Salamir with Corrik.

"Father, one of us is going to have to climb up there and slice it down."

"Do you think you can do it, Aldagir?"

"I do, but it's going to fall, and I don't know what will come out," he says.

Jagar nods. "I'll be here."

Jagar also looks at me when he thinks Corrik is distracted; normally Corrik never is, but with him so low on lifeforce, Jagar's even able to send me full messages with his eyes. I understand. He doesn't just think he'll need my help, he knows he will, and he's sorry for it. I nod enough for him to see so he can know I'm ready. I get my bow set up, and I quickly check my sword is clear in its scabbard—I think I'm going to need it.

The cocoon mass writhes every so often and the pus-like secretions drip and sizzle hot when they land on the stone floor. Aldagir has to traverse several heights of ledges to make it to the place the cocoon's plastered to the ceiling. I have no idea what the thing's made of, but it must be as good as steel, holding the massive weight under it at the height it's at.

"Ready?" Aldagir calls down.

"Ready," Jagar says.

Aldagir's able to heave his massive Elf sword and hack clean through the attachment point; when it falls, there's a loud *crunch-splat* and then silence between the second it hits the ground and the brief moment in time it takes Jagar to swing his sword. He hoists it mightily, and it sinks deep into the mass.

Then nothing.

We wait, knowing that was too easy. Sure enough, the mass starts writhing over its surface like a thousand worms are crawling through it. Jagar yanks his sword out and continues to stab at it, but it's not enough. We've fucking disturbed it and it's going to come out and let us know.

When it rips from its slumber, the brawny material of its cocoon is loud as it peels away. It's pissed but also hurt, bleeding dark blood. When Corrik called it a witch wyrm, I expected some kind of worm, especially with the whole cocoon thing it's got going on, but it's not. It looks more like a human shadow and its draped in black robes. Although it doesn't have a clearly defined face, it's got consciousness beyond a mindless killing creature and I remember Corrik's cuffs and bindings. Nothing mindless would have imprisoned its victims in a calculated way, it would have simply consumed them.

But there's a method in the way this creature operates.

Right now, all we get is the creature side of its personality, we're not going to be able to reason with it. It's enraged and wants to kill us all, letting loose an ear-splitting screech to tell us so. As Jagar swings, I release an arrow, which strikes true, but unfortunately pulls its attention toward me. I don't mind that, but Corrik might have something to say about it later if there is a later. I can't think of him right now, I have to focus.

Aldagir is making his way down from the top ledge, sword in hand and two things happen at the same time. He takes a leap and catapults himself sword first toward the witch wyrm. The witch wyrm gets its bearings, recognizing that the imminent threat from Aldagir is real, and begins to move its claw-like hands in a circle, gathering some kind of black dust seemingly from thin air, swirling in a cochlear pattern.

I don't know what it's doing, but three guesses say that black dust's fucking bad. I can't let it hit Aldagir and I'm just that much closer; I'll make it before he does. In one, fluid, motion, I reach for my sword and pull it out, the ring of steel announcing its arrival into the stale air. Spinning in an arc, I lob its head clean off, and manage to slip out of the way before Aldagir's sword gets me.

The head sails across the floor and the rest of the witch wyrm crumples in a heap. There's dark purple light and then the life vanishes from the witch wyrm.

Everyone's staring at me, none of them move. "Is it - is it dead?" I ask, also in shock feeling bits of slimy pus leak down my arm, and sticky blood splattered over my face. I didn't expect this sword to make such clear work of the witch wyrm, but I remember the king made it special for me, embedded with powerful magic.

Corrik is quiet, staring at me like he's never seen me before.

Jagar nods sheathing his sword. "It is dead, can't sew its head back on," he winks at me. "I'll light it on fire to make sure and then I suggest we get out of here, before anymore take its place. It's going to take some time to reach the bottom of the mountain as it is; the prince and Salamir need food and water badly."

Corrik nods. "We lucked out and a little water's been coming in just back there, probably from the top of the mountain, but it isn't much."

I pull the canteen from my pack. "Drink this for now. I'll get more."

Corrik drinks half of it but refuses the rest. "I can wait until we get out of here and our friend is right, it's best to leave quickly. I've been here long enough."

I nod. "C'mon."

After we do a quick check of all the bodies, hoping for at least one more miracle (there wasn't one) I slip myself under Corrik to give him assistance walking, and we get away from this place as fast as we can.

---

*J*agar helps Corrik, by way of magic, healing away some of his injuries and giving him a bit of strength to lean on, so we can get down the mountain. It's treacherous for someone fully able-bodied, weak as he is, it's hard. And unfortunately, Jagar is unable to give him his lifeforce back; that has to return on its own. He does the same for his son, but his son won't wake up yet.

"What about the ones that came before this one?" I ask.

Corrik is grim. "I don't know, and I don't know where they've been going, but I understand they use the same breeding ground. The other question to answer is, who's conjuring them? My guess is Rogue Elves."

Of course, it is. I sigh. "And if it's not?"

"Then I'm clueless. I didn't even know I was tracking a witch wyrm. I thought they were an Elven bedtime story parents told their children to keep them from wandering off. They're like parasites at first; not human, or Elf. They must be created in this form and then they feed to be reborn into a witch—a White Witch."

"I gather they have some level of consciousness," I tell him. "You were chained up in specific kinds of cuffs."

He nods. "They possess a survival-base level of knowledge specific to their prey—Elves. They also have a solid command of magic. It created those chains. It had enchantments to cast over them, so it could trap me. It was born with certain magical capabilities, enough to feed and protect itself, so it could reach the next phase of its development. It's like a worm turning to moth. I should have been able to kill it with ease, but I was arrogant, I should have waited for back up, but I went in on my own. That's when it caught me by surprise. Now all those children are dead because of me. They … they suffered, Tristan, while I watched, my sword nearby, unable to do a thing about it."

Corrik is defeated. Losing those halfling children is weighing on him. Jagar must sense it too, he changes the subject. "Highness, why don't you tell him who guided you here?"

I've noticed Jagar has switched back to Highness, exclusively, not daring to call me Tristan in front of Corrik. Even referring to me as Kathir would be informal; Tristan is damn near intimate.

"A dragon appeared and showed us the way to go. We were headed in the wrong direction. If not for him, we wouldn't have …" I get choked up and my vision is watery. We were within days, maybe even hours of saving Corrik and Salamir. I get it now, why Corrik wanted to lock me away. I want to do the same with him. At minimum, demand he takes full guard with him wherever he goes.

"Come here, my love." He pulls me to him, and I relish in the feel of him. "So, a dragon you say?"

"A very tiny one," I explain.

"I was a little boy the last time I saw any kind of dragon Tristan. They don't come around often, even to the Elven realms."

"It was quite special, Prince Corrik," Jagar says. "You've got an extraordinary mate there."

"I agree," Corrik says.

I lean into his thigh. I want to attach myself to him, so fucking grateful I came when I did. There's no way I'm going to be able to sleep yet, so I insist on taking first watch. Corrik's still too weak to argue with me about it, but he does tell me he's staying with me, even if it's only to lay near me. There isn't a bone in my body that can tell him no, both because I'm not ready to have him away from me and weak or not, he's still my dominant husband.

Aldagir and Jagar set up so they can keep Salamir warm and Corrik and I stay by the fire. I lean up against a tree with my bow nearby and Corrik lays his head in my lap. I enjoy running my fingers through is his hair, and over his skin, all things I took for granted. I'm never taking them for granted again.

"Corrik, I'm sorry. I get it now, why you were so protective. I'll be better about it from now on."

"No. I've had a long time alone with my thoughts, scared I was never going to see you again. I'm not keeping you locked away anymore, you will be by my side. I almost fell into old habits back there. I can't help wanting to protect you and you're going to have to deal with a bit of it I'm afraid but watching you today with the witch wyrm reminded me of my silent pact. You fight with me from now on. You were brilliant, my love."

I smile. "You're not worried about the prophecy, or Rogue Elves?"

"I'll never stop worrying about the prophecy, or Rogue Elves, but I can't allow what *could* happen destroy another moment with you. When my mind was going mad with the pain of heartbreak—because it felt like I was losing you even if I was the one dying—I hated knowing how much I hurt you. It's one thing to protect you, which I will continue to do, but I stripped you of everything important to you. That's why you were so angry with me, even before, when I took you from your home."

"Yes," I admit.

"I don't have the power to make you Warlord, that belongs to my brother."

"I doubt he's planning on giving me such an honor."

"There are other roles for you that require a sword."

I shake my head. "No. I couldn't do that knowing your anxiety over the prophecy. It's important to me that you feel safe and comfortable too, Cor."

He takes my hand and kisses it. "We'll figure something out. A compromise."

"I was unaware you knew the meaning of that word."

He smirks. "My husband is a wise teacher, besides, perhaps another vision will come to bring clarity to my first. Tristan, I'm feeling an immense amount of faith in the future unlike any I've felt before; an amount that makes it easier to surrender."

"It will be bright, Husband."

"So long as Alrik is relieved he won't have to marry you and reinstate me as before."

That's worrisome. I hadn't even thought of that. "Why wouldn't he?"

"I never would." There's the arrogant Corrik I know; it's comforting. "If I won you any which way, I'd keep you forever."

I laugh. "I doubt Alrik wants to keep me," I say, but I remember how he was the night before I left. I had no choice but to serve him. Through that, I found out he has some softness to him and I daresay he has some amount of care for me. But enough to go through with a marriage? No. He said so himself, marrying me would be a waste—he could forge a whole new treaty with a kingdom more important than Markaytia.

"I suppose I can't imagine anyone not wanting to keep you."

Corrik shivers, he's still healing, the fire isn't enough. I lean away from him so I can remove my fur. "*Tristan.*"

"We'll share it. I will be okay in the fire for a bit and then when we sleep, we'll warm each other with body heat under it. Please, Cor. For me?"

"That isn't fair."

I shrug. "I never agreed to play fair, and neither did you."

"Which is ironically fair. All right, *for you* I'll wear your fur for some time, but then I'm giving it back. I look forward to meeting you under it."

---

*T*he road home is hard, but uneventful. Corrik heals faster than Salamir, who is halfling, but Salamir is more alert and I work a few smiles out of him by the time we reach the edge of Mortouge. Corrik makes friends with Jagar and Aldagir; I can tell he's protective of the little one he was taking care of. I'm shocked to learn how good Corrik is with children. "Have you always liked children so much? You never mentioned it," I ask him.

He smirks. "I envisioned having many children with you, Kathir."

"Yes, but who was going to look after all those children in your vision, hmmmm?" I widen my eyes and raise my brows. I know it was me.

"You say 'was', like it's not going to happen."

"I'm game for the ones we *have* to have as per the treaty to begin with and go from there, my husband. Answer the question."

"All right, I did envision you looking after our brood, but that's the way it's been." He looks off to the palace in the distance then back to me. "I wouldn't mind a more active role, but Tahsen, I have no idea what to do with an infant."

"You think I do? I've been playing with swords since I could hold one, I have just as much experience as you do."

He nods. "Then the woman who carries our baby for us, she'll have to do most of the work."

I whack him good in the arm. "Corrik."

"I'm only teasing. We'll have to learn together."

"Right, together. So, we'll start with one and see how that goes."

He leans into kiss me, nodding. "Let's do that."

"I guess this is where we part ways," Jagar says. "Unless, you want us to come with you, Highness?"

Jagar has been uneasy because he knows hiding me from the palace guard is a punishable crime. Embarking on a mission with me, while not itself a crime, always held the potential that he would feel Corrik's ire, especially under the circumstances. "That won't be necessary. Bring Salamir here," Corrik says hopping off the horse.

Salamir is still not well enough to walk. Corrik puts a hand on his head, white light bursts from Salamir in rays and then vanishes. When Corrik's done, little Salamir can stand, he wraps his arms around Corrik's leg. "Highness," Jagar says, his eyes popping as wide as they'll go. "You did not have to use your powers on us. You're still healing."

"I am healed enough. We are in debt to you, but unfortunately, I'm not sure all will see it that way. Best we try to keep this between us."

Jagar gives a curt nod as Corrik runs a hand through Salamir's golden hair. I wish I could see Cilindra's face when she gets her babe back, but Corrik and I must head up to the palace. I jump down from the horse. "I know I'm forever in debt to you, sir."

"Highness, please don't be so formal with me."

I know I've made him uncomfortable, but I want him to know I respect him. "And Aldagir, hopefully, there will be an opportunity for that pint of mead we talked about."

"It would be my pleasure, Highness."

We part ways and I start to worry about what's going to happen when we get up there. I'm not bound to escape trouble so easily, but I'm holding onto hope that the king and queen will be so overjoyed with Corrik's return, they'll go easy on me.

Alrik.

He might be another story.

---

*W*hen we return, he's not back anyway. He's still out, looking for me. He went personally? That was unnecessary.

It ends up being a long day and a long night, but it ends with Corrik and me up in our room under heavy guard. For once, I'm fine with it. Corrik spends a long time washing. I help him with his hair, and I get him one of my white silk robes and wrap him in it. He's still not one hundred percent.

We collapse on the bed together when we're both refreshed. It feels like we've traveled a long road to get here. The window's open and the cool Mortougian air drifts over us as we lay entwined together beneath the covers. "What do you think will happen to us, Cor?"

"Nothing we need to worry about. Alrik will concede. I know my brother. He's been saving his marriage. He gains nothing politically from marrying you and he's far too pragmatic to do anything else."

And a few thousand years is a long time to save a marriage, but I guess when you have so many other sons and daughters to marry off, it's possible.

We pass out and it's the best sleep either of us has ever had.

CHAPTER 19

Two mornings, later Alrik is a monsoon flooding in our door. By the look of him, he's still in the heat of battle, his sword out and having already tasted carnage this morning. Blood is slashed across his wide chest; it mars his handsome face. His white hair is matted with it and it drips from the ends. *Fresh blood*. His massive form competes for space with his anger.

My cock hardens at the sight of him, even half asleep as I am. *Not the time, arsehole.*

Corrik and I weren't awake, but we are now, *barely*. I stumble out of bed, every bone in my body still sore from our journey and Corrik still has some healing to do. We both pull on robes, trying to prepare for whatever news we're given. Are we going to be living up here for the foreseeable future? Or is it time for me to become an Elf? Will I marry Alrik? Or will my marriage to Corrik be reinstated?

Alrik stares at his brother and I hold my breath. "Corrik. You're alive."

Corrik nods.

Alrik gathers him in a hug, soiling Corrik's white silk robe. Ugh. Royalty. They have no idea how hard it is to get blood out of things. Sometimes it never comes out. Bayaden was mostly shirtless when he trained but it was his pants that got mucked up, and he expected me to erase the blood stains—'twas a nightmare.

"You," Alrik says, turning dark eyes on me, reminding me too much of Elemental Death Wolves. Sure, they had yellow eyes, but they look just the same as he does now before they sink their teeth into your thigh.

I forget all about how I'm a fearsome Warlord and hide behind Corrik. Looks like I'm not getting a welcome hug.

"Do you have any idea the trouble you've caused? I've had warriors looking up and down the realm for you. I've had search parties looking for your body in the water below the castle. You made Mother cry."

For a moment, I wish I had fallen into the water below the castle. All of that's horrible. I never meant to impact so many people, I just wanted to get Corrik back. "I'm—I'm sorry, Your Highness."

"Sorry won't cut it this time, Tristan." His breathing is heavy, his anger sizzles through the air, the heat of it pinkening my flesh.

I swallow, but it's like swallowing chalk. I stare. His rabid state affects me in ways it shouldn't. There's no way I can speak. I nod and force myself to look away from him.

"Some good news for the pair of you. After a lengthy counsel with Mother and Father, it has been approved for Kathir to travel to the Lady of the Lake, so that he may become Elf, but we all agree Corrik must reach full health before you set out. I have given up my rights to Tristan," he says using my Markaytian name again and I detect some sadness.

I can't hide my happiness. I am glad to be rid of the Crown Prince Consort title. It was a kind of responsibility I've never wanted.

"There's only one glitch." My stomach drops. *What now?* "Corrik was pronounced dead, which means the marriage ended. You two are no longer married."

"You've got to be fucking, kidding me," I say.

"Corrik," Alrik warns, which means control him.

"Kathir," Corrik scolds pulling me to him. "Okay, so we remarry.

That's not a problem. Bring someone this afternoon. We already had our big wedding; we don't need another."

"Mother and Father think it's better you do. The people will want to see it," Alrik says.

Corrik sighs. "Fine. We'll do it as soon as possible."

"You'll do it when Tristan is Elf. Not before." He turns his attention to me and the full force of him swirls around me, like the eye of a storm. "Kathir, you are free of this room. You will be punished for publicly for running off like you did, but you have shown that you have ways of competing with great enemies. You will still have the standard restrictions any member of the royal family must bear, of course, and a few minor additions while you remain human, but they are minor."

Not looking forward to whatever that public punishment's going to be, but my freedom is worth it. "Thank you, Your Highness."

Our eyes lock. His features soften the most minute amount they can, but with all the rage funneling through him and at me, my heart doesn't race any less.

"I want to leave today," Corrik says. "For the Lady of the Lake."

"If the healers clear you, by all means."

Corrik knows the healers won't heal him just yet. I don't care about any of it though. All of these things are wins. We'll be married again soon enough, we're both as free as we're ever going to be and most importantly, Corrik and I are together again.

"Brother? Did you talk to Mother and Father like that?" Corrik looks him up and down.

"Of course not. I was under the palace looking for *him*. I spoke with Mother and Father yesterday. This morning I was with Zelphar and his army. Training."

Some training. Alrik's wearing most of the warriors he trained with.

Even Corrik can't speak anymore. He nods, pulling me closer.

When Alrik leaves, the door remains open for the first time since I've been here. Corrik is devastated. "Tahsen, I'm sorry. I'm one disappointment to the next for you. But I will get better quickly, we will make you an Elf and we will marry again."

"Honestly, Cor? I'm happy for the break. It sucks that we're not married anymore, but I think the wedding this time will be better. I'm not marrying a stranger. I'm marrying my love."

Corrik smiles. Then he frowns. "I lost the ring."

"We'll get a new one."

"That was your wedding ring."

I did wonder about it, but things were such a mess. "We'll get a better one. Aren't we super-wealthy?"

"I have a confession."

"Oh?"

"When I lost you, I put a spell over the ring, I doubted if you loved me or not. The ring would tell me when you put it on if I was your one true love."

I turn around and walk back to the bed.

"Tristan. I'm sorry."

I shake my head. "It's not that, I don't blame you for doubting—I was breaking it off with us after all by sending that ring back, and I hadn't even told you I loved you yet. But it's time for us to deal with something that is between us."

"I already told you, I accept your love for Bayaden," he guesses.

"What if he were here right now?"

His jaw clenches. "I wouldn't like it. But only because I am selfish with you and want you to love me best and I do not think you love me best."

In a race of polyamorous creatures, mine had to be the most monogamous one, which still doesn't make him monogamous by far, just more so than the other Elves. "I love you both the same for different and similar reasons. I can't change that."

"I know, Tristan. And you chose me anyway. That's good enough. Soon, this will be a small blip on our timeline. Now, how about I order up breakfast, fuck you into the mattress, and then I finally show you around Mortouge, hmmmm?"

I smile. "Okay, Corrik."

*C*orrik does not get cleared by the Elven healers which angers him. They tell him it will be at least two weeks. I distract him by saying we can make wedding preparations. "I hate not being your husband, Tahsen."

I convince him to take me to see Jagarbendir and Aldagir, so we can check on little Salamir. He's game for that. We're pleased to hear he's making a progress each day and that he'll make a full recovery. "I think we should ask them to accompany us to see the Lady of the Lake," I suggest. "They're men we can trust."

"You do not trust the warriors of the palace?"

"I do. But they're not like our friends."

Corrik smiles. I'll bet he's never made friends with commoners before.

Around the palace, I'm expected to follow etiquette even though we are suddenly unmarried. I did not lose any of the status I gained and still rate a seat at the table, unless I'm expected to sit at Corrik's feet, which is not uncommon. The upside to the months I spent preparing for the marriage with Alrik, was my submissive training. I'm still no *slave*, but this much I can do. I know the kneeling posture and I'm conditioned for kneeling at least the duration of a meal. We're expected to act as a couple courting, which is much different than a couple courting in Markaytia.

Markaytians are much more conservative; you don't have sex before marriage. The Mortougian Elves are far more promiscuous, thankfully. We can have all the sex we want. My own Markaytian sensibilities have waned. I enjoy Corrik's cock up my arse far too much to tell him I want to wait.

Something I did not enjoy was the punishment I got from the king and queen, or rather the punishment set by the king and queen. It was all quite formal. First Corrik had to bring me before them. "I had wanted to give this to you under other circumstances," he said, "but you will need this."

Corrik presented me with his collar for me. It's white leather, with white gold rings fortified with Elven magic at the front and back. Set into the leather is a plate with the crest of Cyredanthem engraved into it. "I have something else for everyday wear, but you'll need this due to the formality of the occasion."

I wore only a pair of pants, boots, and the collar when Corrik took me before the king and queen. He led me in on a leash and I was instructed to kneel on a large, purple pillow before them, so they could hand down my sentence. I knew to bow low from my lessons with Strobavik. They weren't just lessons on sexual etiquette, but general Mortougian decorum. "Thank you for coming, Kathir," the king addressed me. "This is a punishment I don't want to give out, but I must. Please understand how grateful we are to you for bringing our son home, but you broke several rules, and we cannot overlook that. However, in light of your service to our kingdom, I can exercise some leniency. You will take thirty-five with the punishment strap to your bare bottom publicly rather than the standard fifty as per protocol for such a transgression. We're not angry with you, but we were worried."

Their worry more than anything is why I was punished, I'm sure of it. It was a bit of a *'never run away from home again,'* spanking.

I was brought to the wall on the south side of the palace, which was high enough it kept me out of the crowd below, but low enough to be witnessed by anyone who wanted to see. My pants were removed, and I was placed over and strapped to a leather-padded bench. One of the straps holding me down was thick as my waist— figures it would be total overkill with Elves—and my wrists are cuffed and secured, extended to two separate columns attached to the bench.

Not how I wanted to spend my day, but I was grateful the king let me off lightly. I've had a strap taken to my arse plenty, but this partic- ular strap was thicker and meant for formal punishment; I knew before it touched me how much it was going to fucking hurt. Plus, it was embarrassing. Everyone was going to see my arse scalped.

Corrik remained by my side, his face sullen. I knew he felt this was his fault. Corrik's never lost any sleep over me getting discipline for anything, but this was different, just protocol and not earned in his opinion.

Alrik had another opinion. "Ah, there you are, laid out nicely for me," he said rubbing my bare arse with his large hand.

"What are you doing here, Alrik? Come to gloat?"

"Oh no. I'm here to dole out your punishment." I caught sight of the nasty looking strap in his hand, wide, thick, brown leather, unforgiving. "I requested it because I knew only I would give this punishment properly."

I worried a little at that point, a pit forming in my gut. With all his threats of what he'd like to do to me, I was concerned that now would be his chance to exact revenge. But as we all know, I'm the stubborn sort and I wasn't going to let him see my fear. I did set my eyes to scorching though.

"Everyone else—Mother, Father, even Corrik—has agreed that this is only to satisfy a formal penalty, but I disagree; this was earned. Maybe they don't know it, but deep down, you do."

"What are you talking about, Alrik? I saved your brother. If not for me, he would be dead." Even in that moment, saying it did something to me. It does something to me still, it breaks my heart to think I almost didn't have this time with Corrik.

"Do not misunderstand me. I will be forever indebted to you for returning my brother. I'm glad it happened, but I was responsible for you and I trusted you to be where you were told to be. You don't yet understand what that means to an Elf, but you will. Corrik, tell him. Even if it cost your life, would you have preferred for Tristan to remain safely where he was?"

Corrik was quiet, but eventually, he nodded. "I can't help it, Tristan. I'm sorry. I would not have chosen for you to risk your life for me. I'm glad you did, but the truth is, it would not have been my choice."

Alrik's face was smug. "There you have it. You will not do this again, Tristan. You will stay where you are told to stay, or I will happily discipline you."

"Then I gladly pay the consequence," I told him.

"You do, but it's more than that. You long for this Tristan. A broken rule is a broken rule to you. You've done a noble thing, but you broke the rules to do it and that doesn't sit right with you as much as you'd like it to. You know others suffered, while you left without a trace."

I hated him in that moment, absolutely loathed him, because he was right.

There's a score to keep and my body does it well. I knew how people would feel about me racing off as I did, and the Gods help me I had to do it, but I didn't like who I had to lie to and deceive in the process.

His cool hand reached for my balls and I jumped. He secured them in leather. "Don't want these nice bits to suffer any damage, even if we can heal them."

I'd been stunned into silence. No more litigious snark came from my mouth; I was only in awe of him. I learned that day what a complicated creature Alrik was. He's not who everyone thinks he is; he sees people, understands them, but because he's a huge arsehole a lot of the time, it's easy to forget all the dimensions he has to his character.

He ran a hand into my hair and gripped me by the roots. He bent down by my ear. "Relax. This will hurt, but only as much as it's supposed to. Do you remember your lessons?"

"Yes, sir."

He nodded. "Good. Breathe and you will be fine. I want you to count and thank me after each one. Ready?"

"Yes, sir."

I heard the strap whistle through the air. *Thwack!* It took a moment for my brain to tell me that hurt, so my cry was delayed, but the pain came hot and shocking. "Ahhh! One. Thank you, sir."

The pain was unlike any before it and while I still wouldn't think twice about saving Corrik if need be, I will forever be cautious of earning that strap and pissing Alrik off.

I pulled on my bonds, trying to get away, but I couldn't. His hand came to my back. "You didn't breathe properly."

"Because it fucking hurts, Alrik." That so wasn't protocol; I'm still surprised he didn't add to my total for that.

"Shhhh. Inhale when you hear me pull back, exhale as it lands. It will still hurt, but distantly. Breathing will help you let go and then you'll be in a place where this will be easier to manage."

I nodded. It took all my will to do as he instructed and not think of the wild pain that thing unleashed, but I did it. The second time it sailed through the air I inhaled, then exhaled when it struck. The pain radiated from my arse down my legs and while it didn't feel any different, he was right, it was easier to take.

Still, knowing I still had thirty-three more was daunting, and the tears came early.

Crying during a spanking, or even a strapping is seldom about pain, but that day it was a little about the pain. The other part was thinking about how much I'd worried everyone, whose trust I'd broken, who I'd betrayed, and the boundaries I'd stepped over.

"Two. Thank you, sir."

Alrik continued and while the pain never lessened, the cadence he set made the punishment feasible. I caught onto his rhythm and how he would pause long enough to let me collect myself. I learned that he's a talented disciplinarian and couldn't believe I was complimenting his work as I was still being worked on—*but he's that good.* The breathing helped pull me through and I did begin to float away into the wonderful land of subspace. I know from working with Strobavik, a Dom or a Top could keep you out of that place if they so wanted to. Instead, Alrik helped me get there.

He established trust with me that day. He was within his rights to give me a lot more, he could have abused his authority, but he gave me only what he felt I'd earned, no more and no less. He also established a role; Alrik was not to be disobeyed and after that strapping, I knew it. "You've got four left Tristan, and these are going to the backs of your thighs."

"No! *Please.* Please don't."

"Shhh," he cooed. "You can take this. You are strong. You'll feel better after."

I calmed as much as I could, but my legs were shaking; I was worn out by that point.

"I'm going to do them quickly, so they'll be done, but it will not be enjoyable."

"Really?" I said, my cheekiness surprising even me. I think I heard Alrik laugh, but I'm still not sure. I know Corrik did.

"You do not have to count these. Brace yourself."

There was no breathing through those, they just fucking hurt, but I realized immediately what a kindness it was to have them done and over with, in the way he had. I collapsed when he was done, I barely felt myself being released from the bench, but I heard the crowd going wild behind me. I looked to Corrik confused and sleepy-eyed. Honestly, I had expected jeers and taunts, not admiration, especially with the way Elves look upon humans. "They're impressed my love, you took your punishment honorably. Plus you're their hero, you brought their prince home."

With an arm slung around Corrik's neck for support, I looked at my adoring fans, smiling a lazy smile as I waved. "Okay, c'mon you. Let's get you out of here," Corrik said scooping me up bridal style.

Alrik stopped us. He grabbed my face into one of his meaty hands, turning my head to and fro, examining me; I was still a bit floaty and boy did my arse hurt. "You took that well, Tristan. Corrik, make sure he gets some salve on that. I'll be by to check on him."

Corrik brought me to our room and took good care of me. "You have an arse of Elven steel, my love," he said. "And you need it."

I passed out shortly after. When I woke, I knew I was in a different place, wrapped around a different Elf before I opened my eyes, still a bit groggy. "What you doing here, Alrik?"

"You know."

I did. *Elves.* Especially dominant Elves. They are compelled to care for you after such an ordeal.

And then Alrik went back to the avoiding-me thing he does. I haven't seen much of him since. My arse is almost fully healed.

"Come, Tristan. There's somewhere I want to take you today," Corrik says. He's nervous.

"Don't do something you're not comfortable with, Cor."

He shakes his head. "This isn't about my comfort this time, it's about who you are. Unfortunately, there was only so much I could do. You might not be marrying my brother anymore, but you've made an impression on him and he's become protective. The prophecy is still a concern."

Great. Now I've got two of them.

We travel across the palace grounds on foot. Corrik was advised to get light exercise. He was told that it would help with his healing. We take our time, enjoying the sights I'm still getting to know. People recognize me though. They distinguish me as mate to their young prince. It's cold here, so we have to bundle up. Normally, Corrik would rely on his Elven powers for some warmth, but because that has to go to his healing, he wears his large, white fur.

My fur is white mixed with bits of grey, and it matches my long, dark hair. I've got my sword, strapped to my back like Corrik does. Corrik's sword is much larger of course, which means it's a lot heavier. I complained about that, saying he should leave it until he's well again. "Carrying it will help me get strong," he said. There was no arguing with him.

The walk is a distance, and we bump into a familiar face. "Master Strobavik!" I'm surprised at how much my heart lifts.

"There he is, the extra naughty kitten." He's, of course, referring to my most recent disappearing act.

I can't help but feel like dropping to my knees, it's what I was trained to do for him.

"I think we have an appointment," he adds.

I shiver. "We do?"

"Yes. Did you think you could run away like that and not end up over my knee?" While I stand with my jaw half-open, he turns to Corrik. "Highness, I am delighted you are home, but he was under my care at the time."

This means something to Corrik who needs no further explanation. "I understand."

"Cor!" I am betrayed—of course Corrik is more than happy to allow me to be spanked. I try to plead my case. "The king and queen have already had me punished."

As if he didn't see it.

"I don't see what that has to do with me. We have our own score to settle. I will be by tomorrow at noon."

Ooooh! "Yes, Master Strobavik."

"Oh and, Tristan? I'll be bringing my paddle which now literally has your name on it." I can practically hear his self-satisfied smirk as he walks off. I'm still slack-jawed.

"That's right," Corrik says, remembering. "You had sexual training with him as well."

"I did," I reply getting shy.

Corrik pulls me to him for a kiss. "I want to see."

I get excited when I see the edges of the training field. My eyes are wide, filled with little boy excitement, no wonder he was nervous. I can't believe he's brought me here. "Tristan, this is our Warlord, Zelphar Virkalyn. Zelphar, this is Tristan."

He's massive. I could never hope to compete with someone like him. He reminds me a lot of Bayaden with how thick he is, and his ears seem to reach up taller than even Corrik's. He's wrought with scarring on all the skin I can see—face, arms, the bit of his chest poking through his shirt. I never had the chance to earn my scars. Sure, I've got a few from the time I spent in Aldrien, but they're not from a real battle and therefore I don't count them.

Immediately, I get more respect than I did in Aldrien, but I suspect it's only because I am royalty, and to appease Corrik. If I want respect from this Warlord, I'm going to have to earn it. "Pleased to meet you, Highness," he says to me with a shallow bow.

"Tristan was next in line for Markaytian Warlord, until I stole him away," Corrik says, only marginally sorry about it, which is at least more than before.

Zelphar has long, dark hair like mine, but his is shorter in front and sticks up tall over his right ear. He's uninterested in this conversation, likely wanting to get meeting the new *human* prince over with so he can get back to his much more important duties. "Will that be all, Prince Corrik?"

"No. Tristan will train with you. I want you to work with him one on one. He's shown great skill, even as a human. When he is Elf, I expect he'll be something even more magnificent."

"Forgive me, Highness. I understand he is your mate, you're bound to sing his praises, but I recommend you bring him back when he's got real ears over those stubs." The Warlord moves to turn away.

I'm not surprised at his attitude, this is what Warlords are like. To add to that, most Elves have a negative view of humans. "It has been ordered by Alrik himself. You will do as you are told, Zelphar," Corrik says.

"Fine. Be here at dawn." He turns away after that wanting nothing to do with me.

Corrik isn't pleased and I can tell he wants to go after him, but I stop him. "Don't worry about it, Cor. I'm used to Elven arrogance by now. I'll delight in showing him up."

He pulls me in for a kiss. "He has no idea the trouble he's in for. You'll still have to obey him I'm afraid, he is Warlord, and he must command the field, or the system doesn't work."

"I understand, Corrik. I can behave myself for that long." I wink at him.

---

*CW*hen Strobavik shows the next day, I drop to my knees like I wanted to yesterday. A chord of guilt sings—I don't have this innate pull when I'm with Corrik. Should I? What does it mean that I don't?

Strobavik has come to mean something to me. We are not lovers, we are not friends, we're somewhere in between. He'll always be my dungeon Master. You kneel for your dungeon Master.

My head is down, eyes focused on the stone floor. I keep the perfect amount of sway to my back—at least I think I do—and my arms are behind me, a wrist gripped in each hand. I'm in my black, silk robe since I no longer have the items I wore for Strobavik; my black hair surrounds me. "You may look at me, Tristan. Your punishment will be handled formally but we can both relax some."

I look up, relieved to have the chance to stare at him. Strobavik has striking beauty. His blue eyes are sharp and appear darker with the black eyeliner he has under them. I found out it's not actual eyeliner—of course Elves don't have use for such things like Markaytians do—but a tattoo. His white-blond hair has a natural wave to it, and it tumbles down his body in an airy fashion. Strobavik is smaller than either Corrik or Alrik and even Zelphar, but he still towers over me. I might reach his chest if I'm standing tall enough.

I smile.

"Don't think you can charm your way out of this."

"I don't, Master Strobavik. It's just good to see you."

"The Gods help me. Get up, come over this way," he says pulling out a chair and setting what I know to be the Tristan Paddle on the dining table. Gods that thing always looks so heavy even as it sits there trying to look innocent. It's not innocent. "Where has Corrik gone?"

"To see the healers. He was sorry to miss this." Corrik has obsessively been to the healers since we've returned. He wants to know the moment they approve him for travel so that we can make our way to Drakora. According to him, the sooner I am Elf, the sooner we marry again—he won't rest until he's my husband again.

He smirks. "I would have loved to have shown off for the prince. Perhaps I should wait."

I grit my teeth. "Sir!"

"There he is. My naughty kitten." A proper submissive would have said something like, *whatever should please you, Master.* "I know what it means for a brat to have to wait, and I should make you anyway, you would deserve it, but I haven't been feeling right either. I'm just as anxious to get this done."

He sits in the chair and pulls me toward him. I don't say a word. I'm not sure what I am right now or what I'm supposed to be. When he trained me, I was meant to embody *slave.* I think those lessons are done, now that Corrik's returned—though no one has said as much—and if they're done, we're done. Strobavik trains slaves. He's familiar enough with the other designations, but they're not his specialty. These are our last moments together like this.

I will see him, of course, but it won't be as before. Strict as he is, I adore him. I understand him. I'll miss him.

I'll behave myself for him today. Mostly. I've only ever behaved myself, mostly.

He pulls me between his legs. "Tristan, when it was discovered you'd left, I went mad with worry. I'm not made for long treks, but I found myself ready to mount a horse. Prince Alrik assured me it was unnecessary, that he was personally seeing to the matter and that I was better off here in case you returned."

"I'm sorry, Master Strobavik."

"I believe you're sorry but not sorry enough not to do it again." His eyes are hard, I duck my head. He uses his long fingers under my chin to make me look at him. "That's why you were a mess that day, because you were planning to leave. I remember how you behaved. You earned yourself two hours of kneeling time which means that even you were conflicted about your decision."

"How do you know I wasn't just scared? After all, I was about to embark on a perilous journey, Master Strobavik."

His smirk is back. "You would be a fool not to have any amount of fear, but you live for perilous journeys. That did not cause the chaos in you. Even if you didn't know it at the time, it bothered you to have to disobey so many people."

I nod. He's right, and it echoes what Alrik said when he punished me. Knowing what must be done and who will feel betrayed so you can do what you feel is the right thing, isn't easy. None the of people who would have forbid me leaving (had I told them) would have done so out of malice, but care.

"Yes, Master Strobavik. It did. It was not my wish to betray anyone."

His facial features relax. "You may understand better when you have children to leave behind to grieve you. You think a little longer over such things."

I'm not so sure I would have in this case, awful as that might sound. "Wait. Do you have children?"

"*Tristan.*"

Dammit. The appellation. "Master. Do you have children, *Master Strobavik?*"

He twists his lips. "Better." But then he gives a proud smile. "I do. I have a son and a daughter so far."

In all our time together, I never got to learn much about him beyond his role as dungeon Master. Strobavik is older than Corrik by far and he would be married. I like the thought of the terrifying man with tiny Elves in his arms even though I doubt they are tiny anymore. I must know. "Are they both grown, Master Strobavik?"

"Erik has just entered his seventieth year." That's like a teenager in Markaytian years. "But my sweet D'ayawin is just four."

He's smitten. I have a thousand more questions.

"Enough chit-chat. It's time for your spanking. I see what you're doing."

"I promise I'm not trying to distract you. Okay maybe a tiny bit but I'm mostly curious."

"I know all about the curiosities of brats. Remove your robe, naughty kitten."

I hold back my grumbles as I let it slip off me, unsheathing my naked body beneath. I look good if I do say so myself. I've leaned out over the duration of the aforementioned journey and have acquired some lovely scarring. Corrik wants to heal it all away, but he's forced to save his energy to heal himself if he wants us to travel to the Lady of the Lake anytime soon. I suppose he could send me to the Healing Centre, but he hasn't.

With no further delay, Strobavik pulls me over his knees, my bare torso meets his thick, leather-clad thighs. I flush at being in such a position, even after all this time, shifting, attempting to find comfort. But there isn't comfort to find.

"You disobeyed me, naughty kitten and naughty kittens get spanked," he says sounding suspiciously like someone scolding a brat rather than someone practicing slave protocol.

The hotness runs through me at a reprimand like that and when his heavy hand meets my bare flesh, I cry out like a brat would. "Ow, *ow!* Master, that *hurts!*"

"It's meant to. I don't feel sorry for you. Running off. Nearly getting yourself killed. You're still a human and what you did was reckless."

The truth of that sears through to my heart. I didn't mean to worry him, but I did.

There's also that word. Reckless. Had I become Warlord, there would have been large risks involved in the job, but there's a difference between calculated risks and sheer recklessness.

I understand why Strobavik's cross with me.

I need this spanking as much as he needs to give it—not that I'll admit it out loud. The risk was worth it to me, but I need to repent for hurting Strobavik or it will drive me crazy. He needs to honor his end of the bargain since he was one of the people responsible for me, or he'll go crazy.

Strobavik is relentless with five smacks to one cheek before moving to the next cheek. Done this way, the burn and sting build to epic proportions and while one cheek does get a break while he works on the other, it's a state of constant burn and sting because there is no real break.

At first, I attempt to exercise the lessons he taught me. I bite my lip only letting go the tiniest of whines. I tense my arse muscles, and cling to the ground with my finger pads to keep from squirming like I want to. The sting gets too much though and I'm losing the struggle to remain silent. If he were Corrik, I'd be kicking and flailing by now. I should get a bloody reward for the effort this takes.

Finally, *finally*, I get a break. I collapse over his knee and breathe, letting the burn in my arse wash over me. Fuck I wish I could reach back to rub, just a tiny rub. Couldn't I have just a tiny one?

Not likely.

"You were under my care," he says. "I was responsible for you. I missed every cue. I couldn't have been watching you closely enough."

"You can hardly be blamed for my malfeasance, Master Strobavik."

"I didn't say that. It doesn't change my role—at the time," he adds too quickly. "This is what can be expected each and every time for disobedience, an extremely sore bottom."

"And an extremely sore bottom it is. I've learned my lesson. I'm sworn off trouble for good! Please, Master Strobavik."

"We're not nearly done." There's a sound to my left, and I'd know it anywhere. It's the sound of wood scraping against wood as Strobavik picks up the dreaded implement. He circles the back of it on my tender cheeks; they waver with dreaded anticipation.

The paddle is the "special" one he had made for me. The wood is a dark, Elven bonaii tree wood and let me tell you it's sturdy. The thing about anything wooden, yeah it leaves the best marks, yeah it makes a nice shade of red, but fuck it hurts more than other implements. It's about the size of his leviathan hand which begs the question, why bother with it?

He lays down two firm *whacks* that make accepting the punishment peacefully difficult. Overtop of my already throbbing arse, the blaze across my backside is too much for me to keep still. I shift my legs as marginally as I can, I release a hiss rather than a cry. "Please, Master Strobavik. I'm sorry."

He keeps at my arse with his devilish paddle. I get no relief, only a scolding. "You, my naughty kitten, will learn to obey one way or the other. This time things turned out, but what if they hadn't? It was foolish behavior. I expect more from you."

The word "foolish" in Elvish is crisp, a much harder version than the Markaytian one you can receive in a gentler way. It belays his hurt and his frustration. My throat thickens, tears cloud my vision and the knots in my stomach cinch. *There it is.* You can't make someone cry during a spanking unless the idea already lives there—you can only uncover it.

I tend to obsess. I'm guilty of forming plans, often conceived from an emotion, and racing off to give life to my obsession without considering some of the outlying collateral. "You run off without thinking. It will ruin us all, Tristan," Father's voice rings in my head.

That was my father's one hesitation in making me junior Warlord but I learned to quell my impulses enough to satisfy him. Warlords need some amount of emotion. It's not something to vanquish which is why another Warlord tenant is to always hear the wise counsel around you—so that your passion won't rule your ability to reason.

Strobavik whacks my arse alternating cheeks, this time with no break at all, and while I want to please him by maintaining silence and stillness, the combination of the ache and the knife-edged emotion choking through me bubbles over. I kick and scrabble, working the combination through me like Chef Andros used to knead bread-dough. The pain is unbearable, but he continues.

I feel all of it. We work through the emotions together.

He doesn't scold me for my break in form, only holds me to him firmer and puts a strong Elven leg over both of mine like Corrik would. I'm at his mercy and I let go.

When he's done, even he's panting above me. My hair is sweat soaked, dripping into my brow and my arse throbs miserably. The urge to rub it rises again, but I know better. He does rub my back and I turn to oatmeal mush.

In a smooth move only an Elf could maneuver, he flips me so that I'm bridal style and carries me to the bed. I whine when he moves to leave me. "I'll be back. Just retrieving your robe."

Right. Our time together is officially over. My emotions are too close to the surface—spanking does that to you—and I'm liable to sob over anything. Fresh tears spout and trickle warmly down my cheeks. When he returns, he's got my robe but also his stupid, Tristan Paddle. I sniffle. "Get that thing away from me, Strobavik. Do I get to throw it in the fire now that we're through?"

I earn his darkest look and suffer it as he covers me with my robe. I want to hide under the robe. "Did I not spank you hard enough? I admit I'm ill-practiced at giving a brat-spanking, but your arse is mighty red. In the least, I thought I did well enough to cool your flip-pant tongue."

A brat-spanking? Is that what that was? But why would he...?

"I'm not letting that lapse in appellation go. Once we're done with our chat, you can spend some time in the corner. Perhaps you can hold my beautiful paddle between your teeth—that'll teach you to speak to me like that."

I peer at him. "What chat? Are you going to lecture me some more?"

He sighs, frustrated. I drive him to the end of his wits with my nonsense. "No. That's all done. I wanted to talk about us."

"Us?" He nods. "Isn't this over now? Corrik is back. You only train slaves."

"Ahhh. That's what the pouty behavior is all about." I scowl at him. He ignores me running a hand through my sweaty hair and I can't help relaxing into his gentle touches. "Do you remember I told you I engraved your name on this paddle?"

I twist my lips. "Yes."

He shows me. It's there in perfect Elvish, in pretty Elven script. I've never seen *Tristan* written in Elvish before. When my name is written formally, it's usually as Kathir. I touch it and trace it several times with my fingers pressing the pads into the sharp engraving. "Does this mean something, sir?"

"Originally it meant I missed you. I was worried it might be nothing more than a memento of our time together." My heart clenches. "When I heard of your return, I hoped it could be my first gift to you."

Oh. *Oh.* "Are you asking me to be your student?"

Dungeon Masters in Mortouge are permitted to choose a collection of students. They gift them things, like implements and cuffs and other kinky trinkets. I have half a mind to refuse his nasty paddle and ask for something nicer.

He smiles, relieved. "I am. Prince Corrik has already approved it, pending your final blessing. But you should know, Tristan, I also have a teaching role for you in mind as well. I'd like to use you for demonstrations which means I would be learning too. As you know, I specialize in slaves not brats. I was hoping you could help the other brats who come to the school."

I tilt my head to get a better look at him. I can't help wondering if he's joking. "Why me?"

Strobavik blushes and I will forever be telling the story of how I made the chilling dungeon Master blush. "You fascinate me, Tristan and I adore you."

Now my cheeks heat. "What about my other duties? I am committed to Zelphar every day from sunrise to somewhere in the afternoon *if* he lets me go." I haven't had my first day, but I know how practice will transpire. I'll be worked into the ground and I'll be lucky to get out in time for Elvish high tea.

He waggles his brows and his ears brighten. "If I know you at all—and I think I've come to know you a little—as much as you love training, you'll also need an excuse to leave some days."

"You can pull rank on Zelphar?" Because that I'd like to see. Seriously, that guy needs taking down a peg or seven.

"No. But both of your Cyredanthem men do and barring something imperative, he'll be instructed to let you go for the time I need you. It'll only be up to twice a week."

Both my Cyredanthem men? Must have been a slip of the tongue. He was training me to be Alrik's slave-husband-whatever, after all. "What would you teach me? You know I'm not slave."

"Did you not notice my lack of scolding during that spanking?"

I did squirm a lot. "That was an unfair spanking if you expected silence and stillness. You know I don't have that kind of endurance, sir."

"I do. But as I said, it was meant as a spanking more suited for brats. I wanted to show you that's how I would punish you, with what you're used to, but I could help you work on finding that bit of submissive we've discovered if you become my student. At the same time, you could be a mentor for other brats."

I like the sound of that. "Corrik can't help me find my inner submissive?"

"He can and I imagine he will, but submitting is the same as with anything else. Different Elves can show you different aspects and nuances since we've all had different experiences. You have beautiful potential Tristan. I could bring that out and it would add to what you and the young prince will create together."

"All right. I will but on one condition."

"*Tristan.*"

I ignore him. "I want to meet D'ayawin. And Erik."

He rolls his eyes. "You can meet my children." I'll ask about his mate or mates later. "Is that a yes?"

"It's a yes."

"Good. Hold out your wrist." I do and he snaps a thick leather cuff around it he's pulled from his pocket. "This marks you as my student. You may remove it to bathe only. It's protected with magic—it will be all right to leave on for when you practice."

It's black and etched with Elven designs with a large blue jewel, the same color of his eyes, in the center. It says *Strobavik's Apprentice Seven* in Elvish. "I am number seven?" His eyes turn into slits. "Master Strobavik." I want to roll my eyes. I don't.

"You are number seven."

"I was worried that was our last time together ... like that. I'm glad it's not."

"We'll see if you say the same thing come our first lesson. I know of your talents. I will not go easy on you."

"I expect no less, Master Strobavik."

---

*D*iekin was punished for assisting my escape. Thankfully, he's too needed to be removed from palace guard this time and he was offered clemency, as I was, since the kind and queen were too happy Corrik was brought home. He received a public strapping as I did with more strokes since he's Elf but that was the end of it. We rejoiced in being reunited once again and attempted an outdoor version of our arrow game in the woods adjacent to the training fields.

Corrik, to my great surprise, joined us. "It is a fun game. And I'd much rather you engage in your nonsense outside rather than in our chambers."

That's Corrik for the game is now banned from our chambers.

The Elven princess, Ditira, also joined us and Diekin introduced her even though we'd already met. "Tristan," Diekin said. "I didn't get the chance to introduce you myself as I would have liked to. This is my love, my wonder of the earth, my mate and my Mistress—Princess Ditira."

Ditira's blonde hair whipped in the cool breeze and the scent of Elven cherry flowers permeated everything. Against the blue sky and sunlight, she glowed, and her violet eyes gave a mystical twinkle. She is a war Elf. She trains hard, and it shows through each striation of her sinewy body. Without her armor, only one breast was covered by her white outfit and her tights traced the outline of her thickly muscled thighs.

Her massive sword captivated me, my eyes transfixed, wondering if I'd ever be able to lift something that magnificent—I couldn't wait to see her fight. Like the rest of the Cyredanthems, she towers above me. I hit the height of her chest.

Diekin was proud, kneeling at her feet, staring up at her like she was the only thing that existed. She did the same in return.

Watching the pair of them, how they moved together, it inspired me. *I want that with Corrik.* But we have our own way of doing things and I got an idea.

"Diekin and I are paired together," I said. "You and Ditira against us."

Corrik peered down at me, a firmness to him unlike any other and shook his head. "No chance of that, my love. You are paired with me. You are always paired with me."

It was what I hoped he'd say.

"If I must be." I smiled as my heart swelled and made him lean down to kiss me.

CHAPTER 20

$\mathcal{C}$orrik and I develop something new, again. We've been advised by the healers to have him take it easy so he's not doing a lot of work for Alrik, he's not even allowed to spend full time on the fields. At first, he hung around, lazing back, watching me but he could only bear so much of that without stepping in—he can't help it, it's within Elven nature to protect one's mate.

Now that I've met the requirements and earned the king and queen's pendant, Elven studies are not as time sensitive and therefore don't take up my every waking hour, leaving me free time to spend with Corrik. We spend early mornings, before I leave for practice, in bed waking up together. He lies on his side facing me, a hand pillowed behind his head, the other tracing lines onto my skin. "I heard you did well in your training with Master Strobavik," Corrik says.

"Does that mean you have plans for me?" I knew this was coming.

A serene smile spreads across his face and I swear the sun hits him at precisely the right time to make him look like he came from the heavens. I often suspect that Corrik does have a God assigned to him because I'm certain even the Gods cater to his wants and needs. "I do."

"The healers said to go easy," I remind him. I may not be an Elf, yet, but Markaytians have their own brand of protectiveness.

"I will obey my healers. You becoming an Elf is my priority. What I have in mind will be easy for me, harder for you, good for both of us."

His smile moves from serene to devious and that dangerous brow of his arches high. "I'm in trouble."

"You *are* always up to something."

"You know, Tops have a bit of brat in them too," I say sharing my theory.

He takes my hand and kisses the knuckles. "Oh?"

"Don't deny it. It's in the impish manner with which you torture and plot."

"Perhaps a bit, but only a wee bit. The rest is all an insatiable need to own and dominate." He attacks me, his lips descend on my neck and I'm surrounded by his curtain of blond hair as he slips into me slowly, the burn of his cock in my arse sweet. Soon, his savage desire takes over, his hips slam forward consuming me like always.

"Tomorrow you're mine," he says after, while I get ready to head down to my daily beating under Zelphar's tutelage. "Tell Zelphar you won't be there."

"Yes, sir."

---

*W*ith Alrik as my Master, things would have been draconian. Corrik isn't that way. He's strict, but I see that he's got a strong playful side like I do. Perhaps we're more well-matched than I thought. Now that he's learned to quell his overprotective Elven urges some, things work better between us, even this.

In many ways I like the control, I crave it. Unable to follow my heart's desires was what I found suffocating even beyond being locked away in a room for a year.

Corrik feeds me as I kneel at his feet at the breakfast table. In this position, and under these circumstances, we're not allowed to look at each other but like on the ship when he attempted to teach me, I catch him casting furtive glances my way (because I'm also breaking the rules). "Corrik," the king scolds. "I know he's pretty, but you know better. Keep your eyes off him."

Corrik shifts uncomfortably. "Yes, Father."

The king smiles though, I think he likes our not-so-covert flirting even if we're breaking the rules. We are semi-formal today anyway which means he can allow some leniencies. I have no doubt Corrik would be the one to scold me were this a formal event—I swear, he lives to scold me.

Corrik opts to feed me, rather than invite me onto his lap, which he's allowed to do. It's about position and timing of the position within a given meal. Any Master or Top may invite their person up to their lap or to the table at any time during in the meal so long as the host has finished whatever order of business that needed taking care of.

In this case, the king is the default host. Role of host during a family meal goes to whomever at the table holds the most authority. The host also determines the formality of the meal. Thus far, the king has ranged from casual to semi-formal when I've been in attendance. Corrik's shared with me that his father is not one to have formal meals often, reserving formalities only for particular guests.

Alrik, however, is another story. He prefers formal meals and when he's the host that's how it goes. There are the standard rules, and the host will announce if there are any additional rules—Alrik always has additional rules. I want to roll my eyes at him just thinking about it.

Once Corrik and I have had enough to eat, he pulls me up to his lap facing the table. By this point my cock is hard. The idea of kneeling before this many people, even with the others who are also kneeling, is humbling enough my body buzzes with arousal. Corrik teases me, dragging one finger along my balls and up my cock. I glimpse to the room, which means not all my focus is on Corrik where it should be.

"Kathir," he says. "Don't worry about them, worry about me."

That only makes it worse for my cock. "Sorry, sir."

"You will be. I'm counting that toward your total."

"Total?"

He smirks. "I know of your grand performances for Strobavik. You're good at this. Do well and I'll reward you, fuck up and I'll punish you."

Devious bastard Elf! He did his homework. "Yes, sir."

Two can play at this game though. He wants obedience? I can be super obedient. I want a reward just as much as he'd like to punish me. I'm not giving him an easy excuse.

And so it begins.

I don't imagine he'll make it easy for me either if he's aware of just how good I have been with Strobavik. Originally, I was attempting to meet Alrik's standards, and that was altogether more serious. It's not that this isn't, it's just as much about control and dominance, but Corrik and I have another side to us. I'm used to slipping into our playful banter which will be counted against me today so I've got to remain aware.

I focus on him but I'm distracted with the others around us, and the smug bastard knows it. Three fingers graze my cock, my hips buck forward and it requires demanding effort not to check to see if others are watching. Of course, the Tops have more liberties, they can watch what Corrik does to me and we can show off. Perhaps not with this particular crowd, they're family and less likely to want to watch what Corrik will do to me, but if there were guests, they'd be able to see and to watch at their leisure.

I can't help thinking things like, *what will they think of my reactions?*

I remember belatedly, reactions aren't always wanted but Corrik hasn't said they were unwelcome, nor has he scolded me for them. Just in case, I mute whatever I'd like to do. When he strokes my cock under the table, I hiss into his ear rather than cry out and when he circles my entrance with his finger, I don't move but I do look into his eyes and smile.

Eventually, the edges of the world blur and Corrik is all I see. "You're doing well, my Tristan. Keep this up and I'll hardly get to spank you at all."

Corrik's purpose in life.

When he's done teasing me and breakfast is over, he leads me by leash out of the dining hall. I hope we'll head back to our chambers so Corrik can ravish me but that is not to be. "I think we'll go for a walk," he says as if it's an innocent idea. "You'll keep your eyes on me. From this point forward, you won't speak without my permission, understood?"

"I understand, sir." He's throwing me a curveball—Strobavik and I couldn't practice this because I couldn't leave the room and he hasn't called me for any lessons yet. But how hard can it be? I'll show him.

I keep my eyes to him as we walk through the halls with me naked save my white leather collar and my apprentice's cuff, him fully clothed—this deepens the chasm of power exchange between us. Such a simple act makes a difference, and it keeps me in that floaty place known as subspace.

At least I have my hair to surround me. I stick my chest out and focus on Corrik as my bare feet pad along the smooth marble of the palace hallways. It's warm in the palace but still cold outside—it's always cold here, I miss the heat of the sun. I feel the burn of many eyes on me and I flush with embarrassment, my cock remains hard.

I work to please him. My arms are behind my back, clasped at the wrists, my eyes to Corrik's back, keeping pace so that I'm two steps behind and the leash never goes taut. I'm kinda hoping we don't bump into anyone I know. The world sharpens again and I lose my grip on subspace. "How are you doing back there, my Tristan?"

I'm sure if I told him I was cold—which I'm not—he'd give me his jacket and I would be clothed, but I want to give him this. I take a moment to appreciate how the large Elf towers over me, his blond hair flows over his shoulders to the thick of his thighs, his violet eyes glow and I know how happy he is to show me off. "Splendid, sir."

"*Tristan.*" He can tell I'm being cheeky.

I smile. "Will that be added to my tab, sir?"

"What do you think?"

I whine but I might not mind a spanking today. I'll likely sing another tune later but now it would be a relief. We carry on through the halls, Corrik stops to greet other Elves and I have to kneel at his feet and wait at perfect attention. I try to recall how Tom did this, he excelled at maintaining enough sway in his lower back to give him the grace of a swan. I doubt I'm anything like Tom but I can tell Corrik is pleased. He chats long enough, my thighs ache, the floor is unforgiving and my toes are going to cramp if he doesn't hurry it up. I breathe through the twinges and complaints from my body. The more I do this the more conditioned I'll get—that's what I tell myself over and over. It's not unlike conditioning to train on the field. Training hurts. The strain of lifting a heavy sword, the burn of muscles overworked. Even afterward, I often soak in a hot, salt bath to minimize the aches.

Each new activity brings a new, unique ache. Training for submission is no different physically.

Mentally, there are challenges as well. Pushing myself to be fast as the Elves requires more than the physical stamina I possess. My mind has to be strong to break through to the next level. Submission is the same. It's a physical, mental battle.

I get distracted.

I'm supposed to continue to focus on Corrik but I can't help wondering if this is what he'll want all the time now—me on a leash, obeying all commands whether verbal or non-verbal, naked and on display.

I can't deny how much I like it. My cock is both a happy participant and admirer, leaking its approval. Apparently, it's down with the blatant humiliation. But would I want this all the time? I guess my cock would but that bloke's always had it out for me.

When Corrik's finally finished the conversation, I do my best to peel myself off the ground and unfold like a fan, but I think I only succeed in imitating the way I'd unravel Bayaden's linens when I had to make his bed—not near any definition of majestic. Corrik doesn't add demerits like Strobavik would have.

I see Diekin and Ditira before they catch sight of us but only because they are intent on another direction. Corrik brightens. Gods dammit—it's the perfect test for me—see if I can behave myself with Diekin present.

Lucky for me Diekin's in a similar predicament, only his cock is locked away in a fancy-looking Elven cock cage. All of this I'm not supposed to see because I'm meant to be focused on Corrik but of course my eyes stray. "I'm counting that against you, Tristan. Eyes to me and only me."

"Yes, sir."

That means no hello to Diekin at all. Fuck. This one is hard. I want to greet him, I want to see what his posture looks like as he kneels, I want to see how Ditira gazes at him with adoration. I've drifted further away from subspace, I'm not even in the realm of it. "I will spank you here, Tristan," he reminds me.

He will.

I readjust my posture attempting to make him proud. Now's my chance to use the lessons I've learned along the way—all of them. I gaze up at him like I remember Tom doing with the Aldrien king. Tom's adoration for King Caer Gai was something that sizzled through the air, it burned in the space between them and the king was just as drawn to return affections. Because I'm a brat, I tried to distract Tom from his duties to the king—it was at the beginning of my stay in Aldrien when I didn't understand.

He was too practiced, his eyes never strayed and when I asked him about it he said, "Does a summer's day ask you to worship it?" He made even less sense.

But one fine day it happened with Bayaden. Just happened. There was no resistance, my mind didn't lament on questions, I didn't worry over what else was around me; there was only Baya's voice and his touch.

I look to Corrik. *Does a summer's day ask you to worship it?* No, it doesn't. It's just there and you give yourself to it. Corrik, is he beautiful? Yes, but that's not all. He's a genuine source of awe. Of all his siblings, (that I've met, there are so many I may never meet them all) I'm sure the Gods have shined most upon Corrik. Even on the days he pisses me off most, I'll seethe in a rage until I take one look at him and become transfixed by his energy. It's solid and deadly and yet somehow pure—like a good spirit come to visit from the heavens.

Corrik is affectionate and attentive. Sometimes a little too over-protective for my liking but he's toned that down significantly since we've returned, even though I can tell it's hard for him. He does it for me because he knows a dragon has to have freedom. I can't wait to see him with the army, I already know he's brilliant with a sword but him commanding them is going to be something else.

The blurred edges return. I'm mesmerized by Corrik and I give myself over.

He leads me to the Great Hall and we enter via a private entrance so as to avoid the line of people seeking audience with the royal court. Most of the time it's the king and queen and Alrik handling these kinds of affairs but Corrik has been known to fill in if needed. Corrik is one of the youngest Cyredanthems and prefers to spend more of his time with the Elven military, but he's also one of the few Elves who receives powerful visions. Technically any Elf has this potential, but not all of them do and some possess the skill to a greater degree than others. Along with this gift of Corrik's comes an added sixth sense about things, and the king and queen will often look to Corrik for council because of it even though he lacks experience.

I keep my eyes to Corrik but catch Alrik in my periphery—I might not be an Elf yet, but I have excellent peripheral vision. He's been avoiding me. I don't expect him to spare me a glance, imagine my surprise when he does. I know I'm not hard on the eyes and with my bright white collar, firm around my neck, the sunlight glinting off the golden trim, I assume that's too much for ones like Alrik to resist.

Add my human "condition" (or illness, I'm not quite sure how much of a disease Elves consider being human) and I swear I'm some kind of Elven fetish.

Corrik gestures toward a purple pillow to the right of his throne but it's also left of Alrik who's the only one looking after the Hall today. I obey, gliding into position, kneeling to the soft silk. I knew this was coming, I knew Corrik would end his kinky exhibitionism tour here so he can show me off, but I thought I'd hate it.

I don't. There's plenty of embarrassment coursing through me, being on display as I am, making my cock throb, but I feel pretty and

I'm honored to be Corrik's, kneeling for him like this. He's let go of the leash, so it dangles from my neck, the slack curled in a pile next to me. "What are you doing here, Corrik?" his brother says. "You weren't scheduled to be here today. This is the royal court, not a place for you to play games with your toy."

I want to bite his shin for that, but if I do, it will only further prove how disobedient he thinks me already and I will submit beautifully for Corrik if it fucking kills me. I tense without moving, my head bowed, letting my long hair surround me. Unfortunately, I lose my grip on subspace, the edges of the world returning—Alrik's too much of a distraction for me at the moment. "Tristan is in training, brother."

"Train him on another day—when I'm not here."

Corrik sighs. "I apologize. I didn't mean to upset you. Come along, Tristan."

But before I can move, the man who was next to approach Alrik shouts, "Prince Corrik, oh Prince Corrik! Thank the Gods. I was hoping you'd be here today, but I knew you might still be healing. I've come to speak about the abducted halflings. I have information."

I can't see them since they're both behind me but I know Corrik must be looking to his brother for permission. Not only have we been kicked out, but Corrik's supposed to be healing not worrying himself over the witch wyrm case. "You may go speak with him," Alrik says.

"Tristan," Corrik leans to my ear to say. "I don't know how long I'm going to be. You may relax until I return."

I know that doesn't mean get up; I do adjust myself so I'm leaned to one side and sitting on my right bum cheek rather than kneeling. He kisses my lips, and he's gone. I watch him head into the crowd to speak with the man, privately admiring the way Corrik moves. Corrik is as graceful as a dancer. One so large shouldn't be so nimble but he is, and truthfully most Elves are, but for Corrik it seems the air parts for him to make movement that much easier than for the rest of us.

When he smiles at the man, I smile too and my heart swells with love for Corrik.

Alrik ruins everything. "I wouldn't have allowed you to have a break. You don't need it."

I'm not "in form" at the moment so I spin my head to glare at him. "If you don't mind, Your Highness."

"But I do."

"We'll leave as soon as he's done and then you won't have to look at me anymore."

"You're annoyed."

"Of course, I am. You're antagonizing me on purpose." Plus, he's been avoiding me I don't say. It's not the time to have that conversation and maybe I don't want to—I wish I could avoid him too but that's not allowed because he's the stupid crown prince. Totally unfair.

"Antagonizing you? I thought you'd take that as a compliment. I read every report from Strobavik, I know what you're capable of."

That nearly shocks me into silence. Nearly. I cross my arms at him. "Why are you complimenting me, Your Highness?"

He tenses, snarling which is all the answer I get. His dark eyes look black especially with the way his long white hair frames his face and hangs over his shoulders, imitating the experience of looking into a cave and finding two glistening orbs that want to kill you. Alrik is stunning. Everything about him is unforgiving—his expression, his body language, the energy swirling around him. Alrik seldom wears a shirt, and it's weird to me, especially with him being the authority figure he is. He's scarred to hell, not shy sparring with Zelphar's warriors or joining a battle when he's needed and choosing to keep his markings—long raised deformed flesh, marring the landscape of his pristine skin. If Alrik didn't piss me off so much I might like him.

Just a little.

I've spent so long staring at him, I don't realize he's been doing the same to me until he snatches my wrist, the one with Strobavik's cuff.

"What's this?" I yank my wrist back or try to. It doesn't move, locked in Alrik's stone grip. His fingers dig into my flesh and I expect bruises. "Tell me, now."

I flinch. "I am Strobavik's seventh apprentice." Or I will be. We haven't had lessons yet.

"No one asked me. Why wasn't I asked about this?"

He finally lets go of my wrist. I rub out the ache. "And why should you be? Corrik gave his permission."

Alrik clenches his fists—Gods I piss him off—his nostrils flare. "Somehow, you manage to do things without my knowledge despite my best efforts. You're a thorn in my side, Tristan. I don't know why the Gods have cursed me with your existence."

That's it. I've had enough. I'm going to punch him square in his perfect teeth. He'll throw me in the dungeon, but it will be worth it.

I fume at him, planning my attack, how I'll reach that high, but thankfully Corrik returns to save me from myself. "Tristan? Are you all right?"

"Dandy. May we leave, sir?"

He looks between me and Alrik. Alrik shrugs. "Let's go, my love." He picks up my leash and we exit the Hall.

As soon as we're far enough away, Corrik presses me against a marbled wall in an alcove where we can be hidden away and then thrusts himself against my body. I enjoy the pressure of his weight and the soft material of his white and gold coat. He kisses me long and hot and I would forget all about Alrik, but Corrik brings him up. "I'm sorry about my brother. But he's taken with you Tristan."

"What? No. No! I won't believe it. No more Elves taken with Tristan. Especially no to him. He's a total arse, Cor." I speak quietly so Alrik doesn't have me thrown in the dungeons for treason should someone overhear me and rat me out.

Corrik smiles and then nuzzles into my neck. "He's not good at feelings and he's sure you despise him."

I huff. "I do."

"You do not. I know you better than you think I do, Tristan."

"Enough, Corrik. Either fuck me or take me to play with swords. I'll hear no more of this nonsense about Alrik." I open my neck to him and enjoy the way he nibbles at it.

"I do not wish to upset you. Come along. There are still things I wish to do to you."

e return to our room. I've calmed down, my mind is onto the things Corrik will do. "Fetch my strap," he says once we're inside.

"What? Cor. I wasn't *that* misbehaved."

His eyes darken, brows frowning. "Not a request, pet."

Oh. *Oooooh.* But still! I really wasn't that misbehaved. I throw all proper submissive behavior out the window, storming over to the place on the wall where he keeps his strap and remove it. I carry it to him and hand it over, still not exercising any kind of proper protocol. He's amused as I stand arms crossed, awaiting further instruction. He approaches, the strap held in one hand, his other slides to grip my face. "Well now you're just asking to be spanked, my darling."

"You win, Corrik. I suck at this. Just whip me for being a "bad pet" or whatever and be done with it."

He pulls me to him. "Oh no you don't. We were interrupted but we're going to get back on track. That's why I've pulled out my strap. You're not in trouble—*yet.*"

I peer at him. "What about the demerits I've racked up?"

He grins. "I will have my fun with those of course, you'll remember to behave properly the next time we do this, but you're still not in any real trouble. Lie yourself over the bed, spread your legs."

This is territory I know. And maybe I need this spanking, not that I'll admit to that out loud. I take position on the bed, my torso pressed against our cozy comforter—the one I love wrapping myself against Corrik under at night—my feet planted on the floor, legs spread. I imagine what I must look like for him, my arse upturned and ready, the crack visible with how wide my legs are, my balls dangling between my inner thighs. Thank fuck for Elven precision—I wouldn't want the strap landing anywhere near my nuts.

Corrik's large hand with the slender Elven fingers rubs my arse. "You've been in and out of subspace today."

"You could tell?"

"I could tell." I slump further into the mattress, I thought I was going to impress him. I wanted to impress him. "None of that. I enjoyed every moment, I'm going to enjoy more moments now. I didn't do a lot to help you—that part's on me—but I knew you weren't ready to surrender yet, which is your part. Submission cannot happen without that commitment."

"But I was committed, Cor. I wanted to surrender to you."

"You wanted to best me."

"I'm a brat Corrik, it's what we do."

"Exactly. Brats do that and I'm not asking you to be someone you're not, I want you to tap into another aspect of your character. This means I've got to show that side of you I'm worthy of it."

"That makes no sense. I know you're worthy. I spent my time learning from Strobavik so I could kneel for you. Most of the reason I said yes to him was so I could learn more for you."

"All of that is nice in theory, my darling. But submission is felt deep inside. All your barriers must go—not disappear forever," he says when I tense. "Just melt away for a time so I can enter. We'll develop this over time."

I'm still confused. I pillow my head in my crossed arms. "B-But Alrik. I practically fell into subspace with him. There's no way I trust him more than I do you."

"No, not generally," he says laughing. "But the submissive part of you does. Energies can sync if they are of similar vibration, it happens at a subconscious level."

"Stop trying to set me up with your brother, Corrik. It's weird."

He laughs and pets my arse, letting a finger slide between my cheeks. I inch toward it. "All right, I'll leave it."

But I think of something. "Why don't our energies mesh like that?"

He freezes, but then continues his ministrations. "They do but, Tristan? I am getting the sense that our shared vibration will truly hit its stride when you are Elf."

"Is that one of your other senses saying that to you?" While Corrik may have held just as much prejudice over humans as the next Elf in the beginning, that's changed. I know that's not where his feeling is coming from.

"It is. This is not to say we don't mesh now, I feel you in my bones, my heart beats with your name."

I smile into the sheets; my skin gets hot.

"But the Gods have placed challenges before us. Sometimes to entangle you must struggle, this only makes for deeper entanglement though—I'm not worried."

Corrik's never ending faith in us.

Thinking about it makes me slip, the edges of the world blur again. Corrik notices. "I'm going to strap you because it should please me, Tristan but also to teach you better focus. I won't have you count this time. I want you to let go. Don't hold your responses back either—I love them."

That lets go another knot. That's what's right for us, for our energies together.

The strap whistles through the air, hurtling toward my arse. *Thwhack!* "Ahhh!" The pain sears through me, I sink into it. Another *thwhack* from the strap, this time it's a muffled cry. He moves to strike my arse again. Corrik paints stripes across my bare cheeks (many) and some across the backs of my thighs.

He keeps a particular cadence for this strapping, one I can't track, making it difficult to anticipate. Without knowing the outcome it's best to simply let go. The intensity builds and burns, when the next *thwack* comes, my flesh feels the pain before I'm struck, it's a struggle to stay put. My fingers claw the sheets.

The next stripes have me bucking and crying out. I forget to breathe, Corrik reminds me. It's a new kind of strapping, one where I'm releasing—as I've done before—but I'm also giving. This is for Corrik. I give him my pain, my cries, I give him the tender parts of me. The end of it doesn't even cross my mind. He can have as much of me as he needs.

I flinch when he touches my throbbing backside thinking it's going to be the strap again. The combination of his gentle touch and the sting tickles. I giggle and curl into the sheets, still floating. "That was divine, Tristan. I'm ... wow. I'm experiencing a spanker's high."

"I'm glad, sir."

He helps me up, I buzz all over. "I'd like you to kneel for me. You're going to suck my cock all pretty like this."

"Yes, sir."

He places the velvet purple pillow on the floor for me—purple must be his thing, like his eyes—and I kneel feeling like maybe I was as graceful as Tom. I plant my toepads, pressing them into the pillow and hiss when my sore arse comes into contact with my heels. It burns, endorphins race through my veins, my heart beats an excited rhythm. I secure my hands behind my back and look up to him.

Corrik's still dressed, a bulge the size of a melon at his crotch. He pulls his pants down just enough and his giant Elven cock springs out. "Suck."

He shoves his cock into my mouth and I taste the sweet Elven pre-come. I don't know what other come tastes like, I've only ever been with Elves, but it's sweet and sometimes salty after practice on the fields. I open enough to accommodate his width and gag as he shoves in, tears prick my eyes, my cock wakes up ready to party at the humiliation of it.

I hum around his cock and suck as Corrik fucks my mouth. I admire the way his jaw tenses, his mouth open and his thick thighs squeezing. When he comes, his hair waves like a gust of wind's come up and he moans loudly, pushing his cock toward the back of my throat as I work to swallow as much as I can. He pulls out and come drips down my chin. I keep my wrists clasped behind my back, resisting the urge to wipe the come away.

He's not done with me.

He yanks me to standing. "Keep your wrists together," he says and with a bit of Elven magic, they stay that way. When he applies a cuff that wraps around both wrists, I complain that it's unnecessary. "This is not just about binding you. You need decorations."

Of course.

More cuffs are attached, one wrapped onto each ankle and then he leads me to the bed again, only this time I'm told to kneel onto the mattress. "Lean onto your shoulders, bring your hands through toward your feet."

Using a length of chain, he secures the singular wrist cuff to both of the ankle ones and now I'm bound with my arse in the air. I don't get to see him undress; I know he's naked when he's hot skin is against mine. For a creature who lives in a frozen kingdom, he's hot a lot of the time.

I'm aching with need. My cock has been in and out of hardness all day and this position has me exposed and vulnerable—a deadly combination for my arousal. "Sir, please. Please fuck me." My voice is whiny but I can't help it. I'm worked up and worked over at this point. I need him filling me, pounding into me.

"Oh? You think you deserve my cock, do you?"

"I do, sir. I've been a good boy." I have, for me. It's all relative.

He slips a finger inside me. "You were a little naughty but not you-don't-get-my-cock naughty."

Thankfully he can't see my self-satisfied grin.

"That doesn't mean you get to come." Dammit. "But I'm in a good mood, I could be persuaded, if you beg prettily enough."

"I can beg, sir. I'll beg as much as you want." My usual Tristan pride is gone. I want to come and I'll pay any price. My cock leaks onto the bed, Corrik whispers the words of the self-lubing spell and slides two fingers into my arse, twisting them in and out.

They only just reach my prostate though, barely enough to massage it. Fucking tease. "Please. Please sir."

Cool air from the window breathes across my skin, chilling the sweat dripping down my freshly strapped thighs. The reminder of what Corrik's looking at makes my cock ache more—I wish he'd fucking touch it. I can't. My hands trapped as they are, it's even too difficult to buck my hips. "Please."

"You need my cock badly don't you, Tahsen?"

Arsehole. I'd think that was apparent by now. "Yes, sir."

He swipes his wet fingers across my balls and along my cock, fulfilling my silent wish for it to be touched but it's only more torturous. How I must look, trying to follow his fingers with my cock, desperate and needy. "Sir, I'll do anything. Anything at all, please fuck me."

"Anything? You should be careful who you promise anything to, especially if that someone is a sadist. All right, I'll bless you with my cock," cocky bastard, "but you're going to hold your orgasm for me."

I groan into the sheets.

He laughs. "Still interested?"

The Gods help me but I am. It will please him, he'll be proud. I want to see that gleeful smugness on his face—the good spirits only know why. "Still interested, sir."

I feel the head of his cock line up with my entrance and then it's pushing inside. I have to relax to make room for the thick shaft. Corrik hooks his fingers into the crease where the bottom of my hips meet the top of my thigh, he snaps back and then forward and sinks deep, finally pushing against my prostate.

"Mmmmm, nggggggghhh. Feels good, sir." I breathe and I enjoy, floating on my happy little cloud of subspace as he pumps in and out.

Corrik says he doesn't think our energies will truly mesh until I am an Elf, but right now I feel meshed with him.

"Sir, sir! I'm gonna … gonna come if you keep that up."

"No. You're going to hold back for me aren't you, Tahsen?" Even the way Corrik's Elvish accent curls around the words is erotic. How does he expect me to hold back? "You're doing so good, my darling. Come on, a little longer. Just a little…"

Corrik releases into me and by the Gods the sounds he makes. I don't like not getting to see his face. The nice thing about Elven magic is that he has me unraveled from my confines and has his naked body wrapped around my sweaty one quickly. He sucks on my neck and I close my eyes riding out the bliss of subspace with a hard on from the deep, dark depths of the underworld.

He massages me, rubbing healing salve into my arse and thighs but he doesn't heal the markings. My heart beats into a hickey he sucked onto my neck; I run my hand across it. Slowly the edges of the world become crisp again and I'm just tired rather than 'away'. "Don't worry, you'll get to keep that my darling."

I smile and pull him to me, breathing him in. "You don't mark me enough, Cor."

"Since when does a Markaytian become more addicted to marking culture than Elves, hmmm?"

"Maybe it's like everyone keeps saying, I'm destined to become one so maybe it's already there."

"Maybe." He kisses my head from behind. He's spooning me again and I intend to have him lay here with me for the rest of the day.

"Is that what you want all the time now, Cor?" Strobavik was training me to be slave for Alrik which was a twenty-four-hour-a-day, seven-days-a-week gig.

"No, not all the time. I like the more playful relationship that's grown between us and don't wish for that to end. I will need your submission some of the time, Tristan. Or something like it. But I'd rather we let even this expression of us grow organically too, like we did with the other aspects of our dynamic." He fiddles with my collar.

"Me too. But how will I know when you want…?"

"When you're Elf, you'll sense it. For now, I'll simply tell you when you're mine for the day."

"I'm yours every day."

Corrik glows. "You'll know the one I mean."

"How long do I have to suffer with this?" I try to reach for my cock, he stops me.

"Till after dinner. If you behave yourself, I'll take you in my mouth how you like."

"Corrik." Yes, I'm whining. "You're evil—that's a long time to behave."

"You'd think it would be easy after a strapping like that."

"I am Tristan Kanes, arse of steel," I tease.

He turns me to face him. "I love you, Tristan Kanes. I can't wait to make you a Cyredanthem again."

"I love you, Corrik." I place my hand on his chest. "You're my favorite."

*T*raining with the Mortougian army is different than training with the Aldrien one. It's limited of course and it's not going anywhere—I'm forbidden a post in the army, even when I'm an Elf—but it's better than my previous situation.

The only unfortunate aspect is I've made a new enemy—Zelphar. He does not want a human training on his field. He couldn't give a fuck as to said human's past as junior Warlord, or who the order has come from for me to train with him; he's determined to prove them wrong. It's unsaid of course, and it's only something the two of us know. I could, of course, tell Corrik that the reason I return beat to shit every day is not because I'm human, but because I'm worked beyond what I should for my capabilities, but I won't. Because Zelphar would win if I do. Instead, I take the beatings and let healers heal me so that Corrik doesn't have to and all his power can continue to go to healing him (apparently the magic he uses during sex is small enough, it doesn't negatively impact healing—of course it doesn't).

When I was in Aldrien, even Bayaden got tired of watching his men beat me nearly to death each day, and it's wearing on my husband-non-husband, faster. I try to hit up the Healing Centre before I let him see me, but I have a curfew to keep and if I'm going to be late, I have to notify him. This brings him to the Healing Centre where he can view my battered body and after one too many of those days, the request comes.

"*Tristan.*"

He doesn't have to say it, I can see it in his tired eyes. "I will take a break," I say heaving my sword off my back to set it against the wall. I stride across the room, cursing Elven Warlords in my head. He won. This is exactly what Zelphar wanted, but while there are some things I can push for from Corrik, this is not one of them.

Corrik pulls me to him from behind and nibbles on my neck. "I would appreciate that; besides, I have news. You need to get ready to travel my love."

I turn to face him. "The healers have cleared you?"

"The healers have cleared me. We can leave for the Lady of the Lake and she can make you an Elf."

Good and then I'll really show Zelphar.

"For now, it's time to spank you and put you to bed."

"What? Spank me? I've been on my best behavior." In an effort to allow him to heal, I've denied myself many a brat delight.

To prove how well he is, he slings me over his shoulder. "Corrik! Put me down."

He laughs. "As you wish." He dumps me onto the bed though, where he proceeds to divest me of my trousers and underthings. "To answer your question, good boys get spankings too and you need it."

"I beg to differ."

"Brats always do."

But if Corrik says I'm getting a spanking, I am. Aside from being much stronger than I am, I've learned to trust him on such things. I'm like Papa this way; I need spanking to balance the chaos inside me. Corrik works over my arse good. I delight in knowing it's a firm arse. Between the travel to save him and the daily workouts on the field, it's got the tight bounce it once had, back. You can only get so much firmness working out in a room.

Even good boy spankings *hurt*. If not, they're a snooze for someone like me and pointless. At the same time (between cries), I'm soothed. He's got his thick wooden hairbrush (his favorite) and I'm over his knee, off-balance, my hands pawing at the ground. Corrik's sitting in the chair he likes to spank me in. It has the appearance of something entirely non-threatening but it's threatening, let me tell you. If you see a chair with no arms and a soft cushion (for the spanker, heaven forbid their arse experience discomfort) beware. Head for the hills.

When wood smacks flesh, it makes a crisp *thuck* kind of sound, a bit like if you muffled hands clapping. Corrik has as steady *thuck*-rhythm going on my arse and it doesn't take long for me to kick and move and fuss. "Corrik that hurts!"

"I know, my darling. Let go."

"You let go of that infernal hairbrush and we have a deal."

I swear he laughs—it's a quiet laugh, and the brush is loud on my poor arse, but I have excellent hearing—but he spanks harder and shifts enough he has a firmer grip on my thigh.

By the time Corrik's done, my woes have up and wandered off to wherever spanking takes them and I'm ready for sleep. He carries me over to the bed and I think I'm going to close my eyes and head into dreamland. "Oh no you don't, not yet." He slips his cock between my reddened cheeks—something he can't resist.

I collapse on top of him when he's done with me, feeling a world better than when I came in and for some reason, it pours out of me. "Elves don't like me Corrik. I'm not sure they're ever going to like me."

It was almost better in Aldrien since I didn't expect them to. I'd hoped here things would be different. "I'm sorry, Tahsen. I can't promise it will get easier in that regard."

"Why do they hate us so much? I don't get it."

"Prejudice isn't logical."

"I doubt it will change when I'm an Elf. I see how the halflings are treated, I don't see a human turned Elf getting much love."

He runs fingers through my hair. "No."

"Do you think something could be worked out so that I might visit with the friends I have made?" He knows I mean Jagar and Aldagir.

He frowns. "We can work out another visit, but it won't be permitted on a regular basis. They are commoners, there are rules." Yeah. I've never much cared for rules though. "I see your wheels spinning. It's not my rule, but you need to obey it all the same."

I often wonder why I was born into so many levels of royalty; I get along far better with 'common folk'. I change the subject. "What about the witch wyrms? Have any more children been taken?"

I'm not an idiot. I know the "send Tristan to training camp" was largely to keep me from that mystery. It's been successful in keeping me busy, but not out of my mind. We discussed the information Corrik was given by the man in the hall the other day, but it was more hearsay than fact, hence not helpful.

"So far, no more children have been taken, but there has been no word on who has been conjuring the creatures."

I nod not liking any of it. I feel the draw to be out there, looking. If it is Aldrien, I could find that out.

"No to whatever it is you're thinking, Tristan." He knows me too well.

"I won't," I say. "I can't change that I want to, but I won't. I worry that no one will care enough, because they're halfling children." Which was the problem in the first place. They'd been going missing long before anyone did anything about it. If they'd been Elven children, I know the calvary would have been sent immediately.

"I care, my love."

"A lot of good that does. You're banned as much as I am." The king and queen are still not over his "death."

He smacks my arse a lot harder than any of the spanks from earlier. "Watch yourself. That's a mighty attitude, my darling."

I hide from his darkening eyes by burying my head in his chest. I like him put out with me less and less. I'm finding my brat energy isn't as strong with Corrik as it was Bayaden. I'm still submissive with him, with a shade of brat, but I want to be good for him more than not. "I'm sorry, Cor. I'm just frustrated."

"Me too. I might not have permission to go yet, but I am on many councils. I will push and I will watch over this problem."

"Maybe we should wait then, to go. Otherwise, who will oversee this while we're gone?"

"Ditira. She's as invested as you are. Alrik respects her more than he does me."

"Alrik respects you more than you think." From the way he's had nothing to do with me, other than to terrorize me in the Hall, I suspect giving me up to Corrik was not something he wanted to do and because of how much he adores his baby brother, he's stayed away.

Corrik's eyes begin to close, but I've got my second wind and there's something I need to do. "I'm not ready for bed yet, Cor. I'll be back in a bit."

"You were nearly asleep moments ago," he mumbles. Thankfully my stomach has good timing. I can always rely on it as an excuse; it makes itself known. "Your stomach, I swear. I spend more time feeding it than anything else. Come back soon."

I kiss his lips, dress, and head out of the room.

———

J have free run of the palace now. I don't require guards for inside, or across the grounds, but the moment I leave that boundary, it's a full guard, and that is non-negotiable. Hence, I don't leave much. I've never liked that requirement—it wasn't different at home—and sometimes, I think about running off like I used to, but I've grown up some and I think about others now. Especially when I'm starting to see the wisdom in it.

And the punishment I got from the kind and queen for taking off.

I'll never regret it. I got Corrik back, but the look in the eyes of my Elven parents, well, it's not the first time they've 'lost' me and they're getting pretty tired of losing me, even though they were just as happy to have Corrik back. They've both come to care for me deeply.

I gather my courage. Talking to Alrik's never been easy. It has a lot to do with his energy. He's a Dominant supreme and while I'm still not submissive enough to be with him, my energy does react in kind. It's hard to be anything but compliant.

But I have to ask him a favor.

I know he likes to hang out in the armory this time of night. It's well past my curfew for leaving the palace, even to head over that way, but it's not enforced by a guard. I'm expected to keep it. I usually do, and I know I'll be reprimanded for this, but I also know I won't catch Alrik at any other time.

Sneaking up on him isn't an option, so I don't bother. He knows it's me without turning around. "Tristan," his low voice says. "You are not supposed to be out at this time. You might not be mine, but I still have leave to spank you if need be."

I carry on over to him. He's polishing his sword like he does most nights. Alrik is rough around the edges. If Bayden was the sandpaper that made things come out smooth, Alrik is the jagged rock breaking your skin, so you are forced to heal over—you're stronger, but healing over never leaves a clean canvas behind. I understand why people fear him, but I tend to think if you get to know someone's motivations for things, most people can be reasoned with. I didn't like him at first either when I was judging him. But when he got vulnerable with me, I saw that he did have a heart and I can't forget that.

I watch him for a little while, admiring how meticulous he is. He doesn't send me away, so I sit and continue to watch him. I'm not kneeling, but it feels much the same as kneeling makes me feel. "Are you going to tell me why you're here at some point? It must be something important if you're risking a spanking from me."

"It is." I take a breath. "I need to make sure you'll look in on the halflings case while we're gone."

He doesn't speak for some time, continuing to polish, but finally he asks, "What makes you think I'll be here?"

"Won't you?"

"No. My place is looking after you."

"Alrik—"

"—do not take that the wrong way. I have a responsibility to you. Nothing more."

Horseshit, at least if Corrik's suspicions about him sweet on me are anything to go by. Gods I hope not. "Corrik and an entire army will look after me. I also imagine Zelphar will be there to my dismay. You will be of more use here, Your Highness."

When he doesn't answer, I move to leave because clearly, he's not going to listen to me, and I really am hungry. I plan my route to account for stopping for a meat pie on the way back. "You're impossible," I add.

"Sit there," he says.

I slump back down in my seat. He doesn't say anything, and I have to wait. And wait and wait and wait. Until finally, "We are still engaged to be married."

"*What?*" Brilliant. Bloody fucking brilliant.

"I did not tell my brother because he will flip out. It's a legality glitch that will go away when you become Elf, since it's like being reborn."

"That doesn't make any sense. Does that mean the marriage between Corrik and I would have been absolved when I became Elf anyway?"

"No. It doesn't work like that. If we wanted to, we could still keep the engagement, but the opportunity to absolve prior commitments of a specific nature is on the table. Marriages and engagements being two examples."

"How could Corrik not know about this?"

"Do you have every in and out of Markaytian law memorized?"

"No."

"Well, there you go. I didn't know either until we tried to annul it. Therefore, you are still my responsibility. I am coming and that's final."

I would argue some more, but not only will he follow through with turning me over his knee, when Alrik sees you as his responsibility, he's bound by his code of morals to look after you. He's one of my new keepers whether I like it or not.

It's not unwelcome. I don't know that I understand it myself, but the Gods help me, I like the idea of having Alrik's protection.

"I will tell Zelphar he needs to leave a special force of guards around the lower edges of town, will that appease?" I nod. He smirks. "It will have the bonus of giving Zelphar more work."

"More work?"

"I know you'd like to get him back for his treatment of you."

"You know about that?"

"I told you, you are my responsibility. I have received a report on you each day and checked myself on other days. Corrik will have done the same. You can't hide things like that from us, but I commend you trying." He's so fucking smug.

"Why have neither of you intervened?"

"Because you are not in mortal danger and you can take a beating. Not to mention you would have thrown a fit."

"I was totally adult about taking a break when Corrik asked me to, just tonight in fact." I'm indignant. How dare he? "Besides, no one's ever worried about the fits I throw."

I get a quarter smile out of him. "So, you admit to throwing fits then?"

Gods do I want to punch him. "Oh, forget it. May I be excused, now, or am I to suffer your company for the rest of the evening?"

"You're the one interrupting me. You may go after you come here a moment."

He suddenly seems bigger as I approach, and stronger as his meaty hand makes sharp contact with my arse several times. "Ow!" My arse is still sore from when Corrik spanked it.

"That'll teach you. Stay where you're supposed to."

It hurts, but I know it's nothing compared to what he could do, he's gone easy on me. "You never want company, while you do this? I'm good at this kind of stuff." I used to pass Bayaden's standards.

"If you want to come down here after curfew, I'm not opposed, but you'll have a member of the guard bring you down. Understood?"

"Understood, sir."

"Then you are dismissed."

I pause a moment. I want to ask him why he was so angry over my commitment to Strobavik. He's the one who set me up with Strobavik in the first place. He doesn't make any sense. But my stomach growls, and that's a good enough excuse for me to chicken out of asking.

I leave and stop at the kitchen for a meat pie. The staff is sparse, which is good since they don't like seeing me around here much. It makes them nervous even though they needn't be. I'm on my third one when Corrik appears. "I told you to come back quickly. It's been over an hour."

"I'm hungry," I say between bites. "You want one?"

"No. I want you in bed snuggled against me. Come along."

He doesn't wait for me to follow, slinging me over his shoulder and carrying me off to bed.

CHAPTER 21

*I*t takes over a week for our entourage to reach Drakora, the mountain of source, where it is said that Elven power was born. The place we seek, the Pillar of Varys, is buried deep in the forests at the mountain's base. It's the place we can summon the Lady of the Lake. We've got several warriors with us, much like we had when Corrik and I traveled from Markaytia and Alrik and Zelphar, along with Brylee, Zelphar's second and his mate. Diekin was permitted to come as well and I get my wish to have Jagar, Aldagir and some of their men from the village. The journey isn't a long one, but it's treacherous.

Regardless, it's been the most fun I've had since arriving in Mortouge. Brylee is a brat like Diekin and I; in fact, he might be worse than both of us, which still baffles me—Zelphar is strict like my father. Aldagir is not a brat, but he's not a Toppy-type either and he can't resist engaging in our fun. Our final night before we head into the forest at the base of Drakora is spent on sore arses from one hell of a hiding we got from Corrik, who'd had enough of us.

They all had, but Alrik, Zelphar, and Jagar insisted on doing a proper parameter check before we rest for the night, so only Corrik is around for the last straw. We got into a sword fight, after we'd been warned of the importance of keeping quiet. All of us knew this, of course, but brats distract one another and influence the abandonment of good sense. We got carried away and Corrik got pissed. We were made to pull our trousers down and touch our ankles, while Corrik embossed just how displeased he was onto our arses with a whippy little stick he found in the brush and I swear he fortified with Elven magic.

We're quiet when the rest return. Brylee can barely look at Zelphar. "What did you do?" he says running a hand through his long red hair.

"I've already been taken to task, Zelphar."

"Not what I asked you."

"Fine, we got too loud. Prince Corrik had to spank us."

Zelphar isn't pleased and Brylee's turned straight over his knee for another bare-bottomed spanking in front of us all. I feel lucky Corrik is my mate and that I'm not being dealt with twice until I get a look from Alrik that has me cowing. *He wouldn't? Would he?*

I suppose technically he's my husband-to-be for the moment and unfortunately, I think I know the answer to that. I remain quiet hoping he'll forget about me. Things have been odd between us. He's always got two eyes on me, but he's been respectful of Corrik, keeping his distance. There's no way Corrik doesn't know, but he hasn't brought it up. *Elves.* I'm not sure I'll ever understand how they work.

Corrik takes me away a short distance, where we're still under the watchful eyes of our protection, but we have the illusion of privacy. "So, my love? You ready to become an Elf?"

"I am. More than I thought I would be, but I'm a proud Markaytian Cor, part of me worries that will be scrubbed out."

He shakes his head. "It can't be. This is an addition to your personality. It won't change the core of who you are. But you will have pointy ears," he teases. "I want you to know, I would keep you as a Markaytian if I could, but you'll grow old and die too soon for my liking."

Something hits me in that moment, something I've never thought about before. Once I'm an Elf, everyone in my life's going to grow old and die and I'll long survive them. They'll become a blip on my time-line, but I'll still be around, missing them. Eventually, I'll be so far away from them in time. I think of Papa, Father, Mother, Lucca. *What if it's like they never existed?*

On the inside I panic, on the outside, I keep my game face.

Your thoughts are irrational, Tristan. Everyone will get old and die before you anyway, well, except Lucca. It's not a big deal.

But it *is* a big deal, and I can't get the thought out of my head.

Corrik pulls me in for a kiss by the nape of my neck. "How's your arse, naughty boy?"

I blush. "Sore."

"Gods I want to fuck you, Tristan," he says kissing me again. He yanks my thick thigh up against his torso pressing his pelvis into me.

I'm all for sex right now, it will get my mind off things that don't matter, like second thoughts on becoming an Elf. There isn't a choice, it's part of the treaty—I'm meant to serve here for more than a life-time—and even if there was a choice, my opinion matters very little. I'm low in the hierarchy of command.

Corrik spins me to face the tree. "Put your hands on the tree," he says, already pulling down my travel pants and underthings. "Spread open for me, darling."

I spread as wide as my travel pants will allow and he murmurs his spell to conjure lube-like substance, so he can slide two fingers in. The other warriors are nearby; when I cry out, they'll hear me and the thought of that arouses me further, my cock beginning to leak. *"Please,* Corrik."

His cock sliding into me is much better than his fingers. I love feeling the weight and length of it inside me. I grip the rough tree bark with my fingers and sink into the sensation against my prostate. I move my hand to reach for my cock, despite the rules. "Ah, ah, ah. I don't think so, my love. You can come on my cock, or not at all."

"Bastard!"

"You're the one bratting off with your brat friends," he says hot in my ear.

I think he likes that I have brat friends though. He knows my struggle making friends in general, which is not my fault, and everything to do with Elven prejudice against humans. Even humans at the palace aren't super friendly, also preferring to fraternize with Elves, like being friends with their race will tarnish their reputation. Plus, I'm an outside human, which to them is somehow worse than their kind of human.

"You gonna come for me, Tristan?"

"Yes, sir."

Later, we wash up in the small body of water behind us. It's nearly ice-cold, but it's refreshing, and I'm brought back to the present where I remember I'm about to be given eternal life.

Even though an Elf can be killed, the life of an Elf is considered immortal because they do not die of 'old age'. Elves are used to such things; they're born into a life of immortality and think nothing of it. To a human, it's a vast landscape with no map. With so many other things to think about, and with so much hinging on me becoming Elf, getting to this point was pivotal. Now that I'm here, I feel like I'm on a ledge looking over, too high up to see what's below.

When we return to camp, and Corrik offers to see about our sleeping arrangements, Alrik has words for me. "Even without my title behind your name, you have a responsibility to act with decorum. My brother is too young to deal with you properly and if that's going to continue, I will."

Yeah, bet he'd like to.

"He dealt with me fine, sir." I grit my teeth. No, I should not be talking to him like this. Yes he's right, but if Corrik has an issue, *he* can take it up with me.

Unfortunately, Alrik sees my backchat as a further sign I need to be dealt with and it's my turn to be spanked in front of everyone over Alrik's knee. Even Corrik's careful about lipping his brother off and maybe I was asking for it anyway. My trousers are pulled down for the third time in the past five hours and I'm soundly spanked by Alrik's heavy hand. Tears prick my eyes. "I'm sorry, sir. I don't mean to be a lippy brat," I say from over his lap.

"Oh, you mean to. But you will behave yourself, understood?"

I nod and sniffle. "Understood, sir."

"You're a Cyredanthem now. I expect both you and Corrik to represent the name."

He spanks me some more and the tears flow but the spanking is a relief, especially with the thoughts running 'round in my head tonight. I release it all, wondering all the while if I am a Cyredanthem anymore. I'm not married to anyone, even if I'm technically engaged to two Cyredanthem brothers.

After one helluva spanking, Alrik helps me to stand and places me into Corrik's arms. "What did you do?"

"Other than he wasn't pleased with my behavior from earlier, I got lippy."

"*Tristan.*" But his eyes are glittering. I think he likes that his brother spanked me.

The fresh tingles from the extra spanking helps me sleep.

I haven't gotten one watch on this journey, and it's like it was traveling from Markaytia to Mortouge. I'm told I'll need all my strength for what I'll have to do with the Lady of the Lake. I don't stay asleep and end up waking when the moon is still out. I get up to pee, slipping out so Corrik isn't disturbed.

I pick a tree and look over to see Aldagir just off in the distance. He acknowledges he's seen me. I spot the two other guards on watch.

"*Triiissssstan...*"

I snap my head around. "Who's there...?"

It sounds like a man's voice, but it's too low to say for sure. I wait for an answer, but I don't get one. I hear the voice again. "*Trisssstannn...*"

I shake my dick off and put it away, looking around, but don't see anyone. "I'm getting real tired of weird shit happening," I mutter. I check in with one of the guards. "How's the area?"

"Secure, Your Highness."

Satisfied, I decide it must be my sleep-addled brain inventing ghosts. I finally fall into a fitful sleep, where I dream of Bayaden and his green babies.

When I wake, most things are packed up. "I let you sleep," Corrik says. "It's a big day for you. You become Elf today, my love."

I don't bother to talk about my apprehensions; what's the point? I can do this and deal with my feelings later.

We head out from camp, the day is misty and thankfully we don't have to head up the mountain, but we do have to slog down into the sloshy bog, heading deeper into the forest.

Knowledge of the way to the Lady of the Lake is passed down, like the way a recipe is passed down; the most secret ingredients told only to a select few. Corrik and Alrik, being part of the royal family have been gifted with this knowledge and can only show the convoluted route to other members of the royal family. This means Corrik, Alrik, Diekin and I must carry on past this point alone. "We will set up camp here, and look forward to you joining us as Elf, Tristan," Jagar says, keeping the expected, respectful distance he didn't need to maintain when we traveled less formally. I appreciate his words in the way I might appreciate them from my father. Jagar is a less hostile version of him and I can't help feeling surrounded by his care for me in the same way I do Father's.

We move on foot, leaving our horses with our entourage.

After an hour of trudging through the rough forest, hacking our way through the ungroomed path, clearly not traveled by anyone or anything and we come up against the side of the mountain. Once we're there, we stare up at the sheer size of Mount Drakora. "Right, we carry on this way," Alrik says.

It's exhausting moving through the brush, at least for me, trying to keep up with three Elves, but I refuse to complain. When I start to trail behind, Corrik slows for me, only some, not wanting to insult me, but I'm frustrated. That will be an upside of becoming Elf, keeping up.

"Triiissssstan ... Trissstan, go!" a voice says, one that's achingly familiar, only I can't quite place it.

"Cor, do you hear that?" I say to him below the sounds of us hacking our way through. The brush is thick here, we all have swords out, cutting a path where there isn't one.

318

"Hear what, love?"

"I heard my name. I think it happened last night as well, but I thought I was hearing things."

He stops and takes up a defensive stance as he uses his other senses to scan the area. "I'm sorry, I don't hear anything." He's concerned though. "C'mon. Let's make you an Elf. Not much we can do about strange voices for the moment anyway."

There are a lot of twists and turns and I know I'm only able to continue on the right path because I'm with them; a human would simply be lost within the dark landscape. I've already seen the boney remains of a few who did manage to make it in here.

While I'm hesitant, I can feel the pride peeling off Corrik. I watch his wavy blond hair, the brightest thing in this place. I don't hear the voice again; I focus on hacking the brush. Finally, the path opens to a vast lake. It's a brilliant pastel blue, which is a stark contrast to the darkness that surrounds it.

In the center is a pillar. "The pillar of Varys," I say.

"That's right." Corrik smiles moving over to the lake.

Alrik watches over me carefully and I'm reminded of his obligatory responsibility toward me.

"How do we summon her?" I ask. There is nothing in the books about this. It must be taught, just like learning the directions to get here.

Corrik smiles and starts removing his clothes. "Undress, my love."

It's been a long time since I've been shy about nakedness, but for some reason now, I flush with embarrassment even though Corrik's undressing too, with no shame whatsoever. Wanting to get this over with, I do so quickly, leaving only the necklace the king gave me around my neck. It's a magical amulet that says he's sanctioned this. I'm not sure what I'm supposed to do with it.

There's also the cuff from Strobavik. I've been good about keeping it on. Mostly good. There was that time I removed it during practice because despite Strobavik's assurance it would be fine, I was worried it wouldn't be. I lost it for an hour. When I found it, my relief was short-lived. Somehow, he knew as soon as he saw me—that was not a pleasant spanking.

But this is going to involve water and I'm to take it off to bathe. That's mostly for cleanliness reasons but what will this water do to it?

"I'll hang onto your cuff for you, Tristan," Alrik says.

That's not suspicious at all. But it's not like a can refuse him in front of all these Elves. Corrik could say something, but it's a pick your battles situation. Corrik nods for me to do it. I remove it and toss it to him.

Alrik and Diekin perch on either side of the lake, for protection. We are fairly safe since we are permitted in this area by the creatures who live here, but no place is without some danger.

Corrik wades into the water, without acclimatizing himself to the cool temperature—*Elves*—but I'm not so ready to dive in after him even though I would like to cover up. Partly because I know how cold that water's going to be, but also because this feels even more intimate than sex. "Come, my darling," he says beckoning me.

The sun shines into this place, but it's minimal, shining only on the water where Corrik is. His golden hair is that much more golden with the white streaks popping, making him look like a good spirit. He's also starkers, and there are few things in this world more miraculous than Corrik's naked body. He's strong and powerful and I'm drawn to him. *Some days I still can't believe he's mine.* Other days I want to knock him off a bridge.

I dip my toe in the lake; it's cold, it's freezing, and I wonder if I'll die of frostbite before I become an Elf. Corrik doesn't seem to be struggling, a creature made for this kind of cold, but I shiver, even with my long hair to surround me. He pulls me into his arms when I get close and his body heat helps, but let me tell you, I'm looking forward to this being over. "Ready?"

"As I'll ever be."

Corrik nods, keeping me securely to him with one arm, he holds the other out and lets it hover over the water, just touching the surface. He releases energy as 'magic' I know he draws from the world, murmuring some words in Elvish. White light spreads across the water and thankfully, the water heats up enough to take the bone-numbing edge off. The light gets so bright, I can no longer see Diekin or Alrik.

But I can see something gliding to the surface from where the pillar disappears into the water. As it gets closer, I see that it's a naked Elven woman with long red hair and she's glowing as brightly as the water. She towers over both me and Corrik, by at least a few feet. Her eyes are too blue, and a chill runs through me that isn't because of the cold water.

She looks like she could eat me, and she might. "Tristan Arcade Kanes," she says, her voice sounds like tinkling glass.

"Y-Yes," I say and turn in Corrik's arms to face her.

She uses her large hand to grab my face from either side of my jaw, it's as ice-cold as the water was before Corrik heated it with magic. Her fingers scratch as she grasps onto the medallion the king gave to me, it seems to satisfy her. "You want to become Elf," she states.

Corrik isn't scared, which gives me courage and it's not like I've never been a sassy so-and-so while scared before, I don't see why that should change now. "No, I just like submerging myself in freezing cold water, in the buck, for no reason."

Her eyes frown. "I was warned about you. I suppose you cannot help your fiery dragon spirit, but I ask you to temper it for now if you would like your request granted."

I can feel Corrik burrowing his eyes into me. I'm going to pay for that later. So far, she is amused enough not to send me packing. "Yes, ma'am."

She runs her cold hand along my bare skin and trails it down to my penis, which she takes interest in. "This is nice," she says gripping it in her icy palm.

I glare at her. "If you don't mind."

She smirks. "Not to worry, Tristan. I know you have three other men in your life, none of whom would like me doing much with this."

Three...?

I count two possibilities she could mean and one of them is out of my life forever. "Are you going to make me an Elf, or not?"

"You pass the test. You do have the required magic." I do? "Your destiny is in this realm, but will you pay the price?"

"Price?" Corrik says. "I was not told of any price."

She laughs. "Oh Highness, you know better than that. There's always a price for magic."

Corrik grips me tighter. "What's the price?" I ask.

"I don't know Tristan. The universe will ask it of you at some point and you will have to pay it, or you will die. Becoming an Elf will take a large amount of energy from the Earth."

"Can I pay it for him?" Corrik asks.

"No. It must come from Tristan." She looks at me. "Are you willing to pay the price?"

I hope my future self doesn't regret this. "I—"

"—Tristan wait. Don't do it," Corrik says.

I spin around and study him with exhausted eyes. "I know you don't forget I *have* to, Cor."

He's regretful. "I shouldn't have done any of this. You were happy in your old life."

"There was a time I would have agreed with you and while I'm still terrified to do this, I know I'm in the right place. I am happy in my new life, it's where I'm meant to be." It still feels like I'm leaving my family even further behind, but facing responsibility is part of growing up. From the outset, I've been told that this was my destiny, and I fought that because *I create my life.*

But I understand more and more that while there is some accommodation for free will, I can't escape this path. All roads keep leading in one direction. I still create my life, but there's destiny too, a sort of combination between free will and predestination—*Freedestination.*

Corrik nods, but I can feel the guilt in him. He knows there's no turning back.

"I will pay the price when it is presented to me," I tell her.

"Very well, Tristan. Come with me. Your part is done, and you will remain here," she says to Corrik.

He's not happy about that. He stiffens, but remains standing, while she grabs my hand and yanks me under the water. She's a slight woman; I didn't expect her to be so strong, but I'm not getting out of her vice-grip.

I don't have much time to pull in a breath before I'm swept underwater. "Breathe the water in," she says, but she's not speaking to me with her mouth, her voice is in my head.

Naturally, the thought of breathing water is terrifying, but I'm Tristan—fool—Kanes and I won't let her see that. I take in a breath. As anyone would expect, I struggle and for a moment I think I've been had, but then the water seeps into my lungs, somehow oxygenating them, without drowning me. I don't know how; I can only guess magic is at work. We swim into the pillar, which is dark and hollow at first, but we're quickly transported elsewhere.

We go to another realm, one that is a lot brighter than the place where we summoned her, but we're still under water and it's a lot warmer here—thank fuck. I'm naked and I'd like to put something on, but it's not to be. At least she's naked too.

I can see everything down here. We swim through the brightly colored lake plants and the schools of little fish. I sense there are other creatures here too, but they don't bother us. I think they're afraid of her and I don't blame them. I can't wait to be done with her and this place and hopefully never return to it.

For now, I'm thankful I've got her to pull me along. She's got quick, snappy movements, her long red hair like a flame streaming behind her. I wouldn't be able to keep up on my own.

We swim a long way. There are so many twists and turns, I'm lost and I'm sure even Corrik couldn't find his way around in this place. It's hard to pick landmarks in such unfamiliar territory.

When we get to a large tree, with a pink base and glowing purple leaves, she lets go of my hand and beckons for me to follow. The only other life nearby is marine creatures who are curious but too scared to come forth, reminding me that my trust in her is only due to Corrik's which I didn't think to ask about. But Corrik wouldn't have allowed this if I weren't going to come out alive.

That doesn't mean this is going to be pleasant.

I try to put the others at ease by sending them calm energy as I also work to calm myself. The big moment is here. "I have checked you over and am satisfied that you meet the requirements, you have agreed to pay the price when it's asked of you, but the final step is getting The Mother's permission. I will give my blessing. My powers come from the core of the planet, the place from where all energy is ultimately extracted and I will use this source as an information network to tell her. Then, once you lay down and offer yourself over with your intention, she will make the final decision."

I nod.

The tree doesn't look scary, just eerily out of place, like it should be on land and not underwater. It's magnificent and I'm drawn to touch it. When I do my fears and apprehensions melt away. I have something greater to fulfill.

"You need to keep your intention for becoming Elf suspended in your heart, so she can hear you. That is all you have to do." She reaches down to the base of the tree, where the roots are. White light releases outward from the tree and vanishes as bubbles into the water. "My part in this is over now, this is where we part ways, Tristan." The Lady is as cold in her countenance as she is with her touch.

I panic. "Wait. What if I'm rejected?"

"Then you must swim back quickly before the spell wears off or you will drown."

"How will I find my way back?"

"You will be shown the way."

"Thank you," I say. All I get is a curt nod in return before she's gone. I look around. Down here, my sense of consciousness is heightened, and I wonder if this has something to do with why we could hear each other in our minds…? In any case, I sense the curious presence again. "Come on out."

A creature does, unsure about me. When it gets closer, I understand what I was feeling. It's another dragon, but if a dragon were a fish. The little guy swims over to me but remains a little ways away, a lot less forward than the other guy I met in the desolate mountain space we rescued Corrik from. This one is purple-ish-black, and his scales shine iridescent when the bit of light from the glowing tree hits them. "I won't hurt you, my friend."

He seems to calm a bit but remains where he is curious about what I'm going to do. It's nice to have someone down here to talk to. I would be scared, but what would that do? I focus on my task. "I'm supposed to lay here," I tell him. "With an intent."

The intent seems simple—to be an Elf, but I don't think that's all there is to it. Elves, despite their arrogant nature have a particular thread that burns through them above all. It's something that says they are of the land and that they care about it deeply. To be an Elf is to embody this. They are creatures who have never forgotten what it means to exist as raw beings of the Earth, which is why they can connect to it deeply enough to harness its energy.

But I have another intent I want to take with me. I hold out my arm, inviting the little guy to perch. Finally, he darts over, his curiosity getting the better of him. "I intend to watch over the land as all Elves do," I say. "But Elves care little for humanity. I think dragons did, which is why the first Tristan was given dragon's blood, so he could watch over humanity."

I don't know how that will affect the process, but I have to be true to my heart. I know my intent.

"Right, then. Will you watch over me?"

He's too tiny to do anything of use, the whole idea of a water dragon is absurd—how does he blow fire?—but it's nice to have kin with me. I hear the dragon trill in my mind.

He hops away, and I lay at the base of the tree rooted into the bottom of this lake in whatever place we're in. I sit down carefully at first, but when nothing happens, I'm quick to lay down. The dragon takes up vigil nearby, suddenly invested in his mission to look after me.

I lay there for a time while nothing happens. I hold my intentions in my heart and close my eyes, but still, nothing. I open them to look over to my friend who's got his head tilted to the side, curious about me, probably thinking I'm the oddest thing he's ever seen. After all, I'm not a creature of this place, but I showed up with a terrifying if beautiful Elf, and then laid down beside a tree, *not the behavior of sane people.*

When I think I've been bamboozled and am contemplating as to whether or not I should ask if the water dragon can lead me back to Corrik, that's when I feel it crawling up my leg, slithering like a snake. But it's not a snake, it's a tree root. The roots climb down my arms, up to my legs, surrounding me, burying me.

Roots poke *into* me.

By this point, there's nothing I can do about it, all of it is happening too quickly. I struggle, yanking hard, but I barely move, and the roots continue to overtake me, piercing into every part of me, straight into my organs, my face. Being underwater, I can't even scream. I try, but it comes out as bubbles. It doesn't take long for me to be covered in a casket of roots, sewn to the lake floor by them, even though it seems like an eternity. It hurts every bit as much as you would imagine being pierced by multiple tree roots growing into you would hurt.

First, they prick sharp like rose thorns through the skin, then there's a piercing sensation deep into my insides, a sickening sluice that carves and stabs as it goes. Through the nerves they burn and when the vines hit bone, it's a bruising pain as they chip and shatter forcing their way through. I can't think; I'm close to passing out.

And then I can't breathe.

This whole adventure has hinged on the fact that whatever Scary Lake Lady did, it allowed me to breathe underwater. Now, with each movement, a bit of magical help wears off. My lungs ache for breath like they should have in the first place as they fill with water. I panic. This was a mistake. We were idiots and I'm going to die down here. I can only, just barely see my little friend. He's crying out, unsure what to do, but he knows I'm in distress.

I don't know how long I have before the spell wears off and I drown, trapped, tied down by roots that have grown into me, but even if I could manage an escape, with the rate the magic's wearing off as I move, I'm not sure I'd make it. Will I even be shown the way back?

I stop fighting and surrender to it if only to calm the little guy down. Nothing can be done now. I'm dying and will soon be part of this tree. My lifeforce slips away as the water takes me, but I get moments to be with some final thoughts.

They are thoughts of love, and how grateful I am to have been so loved. As I go, I'm calmed, no longer afraid. An essence takes over and I know it's from whatever power lives inside this tree and it hits me— if I want to become an Elf, first I have to die.

So be it. To die shall be a fantastic adventure.

The human known as Tristan Kanes dies.

CHAPTER 22

I open my eyes.

When I sit up I have to tug at roots that are still attached to my body, ripping them out of the ground the same way you pull out a carrot. It's surprisingly easy to do, the roots no longer constricting me, their strength no longer a match for mine. All of the roots are external, none of the ones that found their way inside me remaining. I don't know how long I've been here, just that some time has passed. I look to where my dragonkin is watching over me. He's still here.

For a moment he's scared, but then he tentatively makes his way over to me, swimming in front of me, happy I'm still alive, and I can see he's proud of himself for having watched over me so commendably. "Thank you, my friend, you've done well."

My voice sounds different in my head. Deeper, like it comes from the Earth. I remember I must be changed. I look down at my naked form. I've increased in size, my muscles thicker, with more veins. I reach up to my ears and have to pat up, way up to the tall points that reach high.

It worked. Mother Earth said yes. I am an Elf now.

Before I can explore my new self too much further, I feel a tug in the direction I came from and there's a sense of urgency. I'm able to 'breathe' underwater again, but I have a feeling that's not going to last much longer. I've got to get out of here. "Are you coming with me?" He's not. "Well then, this is goodbye."

The little guy saddles up next to my face, rubbing his snout into my cheek. He gives me a last once over, admiring me, and then he swims away. I follow suit after I take a quick moment to thank the tree.

Swimming is easy. It's never been so easy. I travel back quickly and without a struggle. I'm fast and it doesn't take long for me to reach the white pillar. I understand something about Elves, no wonder they think they're better than everyone when it's so easy to do stuff. Not that I agree they should think themselves better, but I can see how one might get carried away with such gifts.

When I rise from the water, back to the place I came from, I know something is wrong. I've always had a keen sixth sense, but now it's *more*. Corrik isn't here but there are a few fallen bodies of another kind of Elf, one I could identify in my sleep, but there's one fallen body, in particular, that has my immediate attention near where I left my clothing and sword.

It's Diekin, and he's bleeding out. "Diekin!"

"... Tristan?"

He's groggy and fading. He needs magical medical attention fast. "It's me."

"You look good, brother. I'm glad I got to... got to see you before I go."

"No. You're not going, fuck that."

"What are you going to do about it, uh?"

"I don't know." Just that I need to do something. Instinctively, I put my hands on the area bleeding out and apply pressure. I have no idea what I'm doing, but I close my eyes and pray, asking for the answer. Diekin can't die.

There is light under my hands. Diekin gasps for air as the wound knits back together. His eyes widen. "Tristan, you healed me."

Did I? I think I might have. Couldn't tell you how. He's full of blood but no longer bleeding. "Are you okay to stand up?"

He is, but I can tell he's weak. "We need to get out of here he says."

"What happened? Where is everyone?"

"We were attacked by Rogue Elves. We spilt off, Corrik and Alrik went that way," he says pointing out of the forest. "More went in the other direction. I took care of these guys. The last one spliced me."

He's still staring at me like he's never seen me before and I guess he hasn't. I remember I'm naked and start throwing on my pants and boots, grabbing my sword. "Come, we'll have to get moving fast and hope there's a horse for us."

"I would tell you to go without me, but I know you won't have it, Warlord." He pauses. "Tristan, you have always been something divine and special, but now you're... *wow*. I have no words. You're stunning. Corrik might be possessive, but he's not the jealous sort, that might change."

I flush, embarrassed. *Am I that beautiful?* I don't have time to find out. We head away from this place.

---

*E*ven with Diekin in his weakened state, our journey out is a lot faster than when we came in and I realize how much I was slowing them down as a human. It's even more than I imagined it to be. And I'm strong. Holy shite am I strong. My sword is no longer the right weight, too light in my hand. I will need something stronger, which is a shame; I love my sword.

We make it out of the forest without encountering anymore Rogue Elves. There are horses, fallen Mortougian guards but no one else. It's tragic. I knew a few of these men and women. I help Diekin onto a horse. He's more exhausted now than he was before, I need to get him to a place where he can rest safely. "Which way do you think they went?" I ask.

He smiles. "Put your hand on the ground and look for the tracks.

You'll see them. Look out especially for Corrik, you'll have a sense of him."

I do as he's instructed, and he's right. With my improved sight, I can see the various tracks and the direction they're headed. From the mess of hoof and footprints, I get a sense of which ones are Corrik's. "There was a battle here and then they got on horseback and went off that way, not long ago."

We follow through the brush as fast as we can, keeping all our senses peeled. We stop at a few places when we come across fallen bodies and continue to follow tracks. It gets dark and we have to stop for the night. "Get some rest Diekin. I will keep watch for a few hours and then we'll keep going." He's about to fall off his horse.

"You're not tired, Warlord? I would think becoming an Elf would take a lot of energy."

I shake my head. "No. I've never felt so awake and alive."

He smirks. "Now you see why being an Elf is the best. "

"There definitely are perks, I'll say that."

"I will rest then, brother. Even just a few hours will help me a lot. I should be nearly full health and we can move faster."

I set up a watch by a tree with my bow and sword. I should be freezing, but I only feel a mild chill. The light's not all gone yet, and I finally have time to look at what I can see of myself without a mirror. My skin is still the same copper shade it was, which means I'll still stand out among the Mortougian Elves who are alabaster white, indicative of the winter climate they come from. I have the deep red tones I've always had, but they're more vibrant than before. My hair is still black with the colored streaks Bayaden gave me, but it's impossibly glossy. I hold my sword in front of my face, two eyes stare back, bluer than ever before, fiercer. I can't see my whole face, but I still see my father's eyes staring back at me, and I sigh, relieved. *I am still of my father.*

And my ears. I run my hand along them again, they're so tall; that's going to be something to get used to. My hair's already getting caught on them.

It's dark when I *sense* something nearby with a new sense of intu-

S. LEGEND

ition that seems to come from an ancient place. Quietly, I get up and creep over to where I'm being pulled. Things are different now and it's easier not to make a sound as an Elf.

Out of the darkness, a large form slams into me and we tumble away. I know it's a massive, male Elf, a lot bigger than me, even with my newly added size. As we tumble away, I manage to keep my sword, but I'm not sure I'm going to be able to fight this guy. I consider calling out to Diekin, but there's something familiar in the feel of him and it distracts me.

I fumble for my sword and have it just in time to hold it over my head and stop his form slicing me through. In the moonlight, I look up to see his eyes. Is that... but I don't have time to finish my thought. I have to pull out every skill I've ever learned to fight him and it's in the fighting of him, I confirm who it is—I'd know his style anywhere.

My heart flutters weakening me briefly but I'm quick to regain my fire. Finally, we'll get to fight in a real way. Bayaden never used his full force with me, knowing if he did, he would kill me. If I tell him it's me, he'll stop, and I want to see what he's really like. It's my only opportunity.

I have to fight like my life depends on it, because it does. This very well might turn out to be stupid—is this how I'm run through with a sword, like in Corrik's vision?—but I want it. I'm able to get off my knees and anticipate his next swing, which comes at me full force. From there it's his sword slicing through the air intent on killing me in the dark. We can't see well enough to recognize the other by sight, we have only our other senses and our blades glinting in the moonlight.

I'm almost insulted he doesn't recognize my fighting style as I do his and it distracts me long enough he's able to knock my sword out of my hand. I'm about to let on it's me, but he tosses his sword down and pounces on me, slamming me to the ground and pressing his lips to mine. "Still allowing my magnificence to distract you, I see?"

Bastard. He knew it was me all along.

I attack his lips, kissing him back, sucking him in like air.

It's not that I love him anymore than I do Corrik, Bayaden and I understand each other in a different way is all. I need both, I wish I could have both. With the polyamorous nature of Elves, I feel it should be possible somehow, the only kink in the chain being the whole war thing. "Tristan," he whispers. "I knew it was you the moment you lifted your sword."

I smile. "Same. I'm surprised you'd fight me so ferally."

"I saw the ears, I wanted to see if I was right about your skills as an Elf."

"And?"

"You need a lot of work."

"Hey!"

I whack him, he laughs. "I'm not kidding, you can improve, but you are still the finest swordsperson I've seen. I wish I could see what you look like, properly. I can only see some of you." He presses his hands around my body, feeling me.

"You might get the chance. Baya, what happened?"

He rolls onto his back, bringing me with him and I'm reminded of how we used to lie in his bed back in Aldrien. He sighs. "Ando ordered us to lay siege on you. His goal this time was Corrik."

"So, he doesn't care about me anymore? I'm devastated."

He laughs. "For a long time, he thought you were dead, but when he found out you weren't, he knew you had to have had help to get through the veil. He suspected me for a time, but Father played a hand in convincing him it must have been Corrik."

I hate how their father manipulates them, even Ando who I've always been on the fence about. "So, you've come to take Corrik." It's not a question.

"Yes. At least, I'm here to *try* to take Corrik. I attempted to warn you, best I could."

"That voice … it was you."

"Yes," he says, smiling at how clever he is. "Saving that, I was hoping I'd run into you first. Alone."

I nod nuzzling into his hair, wanting to bury myself into it for a long time. I know that's not to be though. "I came from the lake, everyone was gone."

"These are some of your first moments as an Elf then. I can't help being happy I'm one of the first."

"You are." I notice there's a new tattoo glowing under his eye. I squint, pressing carefully there. "This says—"

"—Tristan."

"But how?" We spent so much time worrying about who would say what and who would think what.

"I got it done, and I dared any fool to say a thing. One did. He lost his head, and no one's spoken your name since."

"And your father?"

"Understood. It's a silent thing between us."

I've always suspected the king's feelings for Tom ran a lot deeper than they let on. They were better at hiding it than Baya and I were.

"I like it." It makes my heart clench. I finally have a permanent mark on him. My brain is wild with questions for him. "How is, Uncle Taj?"

"He made it back and he will never forget the only human in his memory to survive an Elemental Death Wolf."

Right. That.

"Not without his help," I say, and he tenses but I don't want the mood to be serious. We only have so much time. "So? Do you have green babies yet, Baya?"

"Soon. My husband is pregnant."

"You did marry the prince then."

He nods. "I had to. Father made the decision. He's not you, but I find he's not so bad. There are things I like about him and sometimes he even likes me."

"You must drive him horribly insane." I laugh picturing it. I wish I could see them together, even once.

"A bit. He's soft and I have to say I like getting to protect him."

"Wow, I'm almost jealous. That must be your thing. As a human, you had to protect me."

"I have discovered, yeah. It is a thing, but Tristan, I've never stopped loving you. I have missed you. Some days it's more than I can bear."

I tear up. "For me as well." We lay there for a while on stolen minutes. We weren't supposed to have these, but we get them and I'm grateful for every second. "What now?"

"Zelphar's warriors gave a good fight. I was separated from my crew, but when I didn't see you with them, I took the opportunity to hang back. If you can get to Corrik, and convince them to head back to Mortouge, I can do the same with my warriors. It will be nothing more than a failed mission."

"Good plan. Should work. What about the war?"

"That's harder. Ando is hellbent and Father is behind him with dreams of strengthening the realm."

"And you?"

"I'm a soldier, Tristan. I'll do what my family asks of me, but I would prefer it if it could be stopped. It won't be easy though. C'mon," he says pulling me off the ground. "I want to look at you before I go."

Right. For a moment I forgot that our moments would end. He takes my hand, dragging me out of the trees and into the moonlight. "Tristan you're … something else. You were magnificent before, but now you don't seem from this world. Corrik is a very lucky Elf."

I get shy. I've already had so many Elves enamored with me, what's going to happen now? I push him. "Stop it. It's just me."

He secures his hand over mine. "I should spank you for that. It's never just you. You'll always mean a great deal to me. Tristan tell me, are you happy?"

I know this Elf. He doesn't have to say it for me to know his concern. I feel it like wind pouring off him in gusts. He's been worrying about me. He's lost sleep over it. He's still not sure he shouldn't cart me off to live in hiding, keeping me safe. "Things weren't easy at first. I didn't understand Corrik's actions—he locked me in my room."

Bayaden inhales a sharp breath. "You can't cage a dragon."

I shake my head. "No. But then when I lost him, I saw from a new perspective, I discovered I'm not so different, also wanting to lock my loved ones up to keep them safe. I have forgiven him. I am happy, Baya."

He smiles. "Then he may keep you."

"Arse. You like knowing it's because of your generosity."

"Of course, wouldn't be me if it were otherwise."

"I'm an Elf now. Maybe that's not up to you anymore."

He's gentle, raking a hand through my long hair, rubbing my new Elven ear between his thumb and index finger. "You and I both know that will never be true."

I press myself against his solid torso, nuzzling into his neck. An overwhelming urge to mark him rises up. Is this what it feels like? I knew of this urge in Elves, but this is the first time I'm experiencing it. It's the same discomfort as needing to move a limb after being immobile for some time and stretch away the stiffness. I refrain. I don't know how much his new husband would appreciate that. Him kissing me is one thing, markings are a much bigger deal. "It'll never be true."

He nuzzles me back—marking when you can't mark. He presses a meaty hand over my heart. "Truthfully it's not up to me either. I have been tasked with this and you know I always look after what I am responsible for."

I can't help the thought that he's like Alrik that way. "You do." I blink tears.

"Please, stay safe." He kisses the back of my hand and I have to say goodbye to him again.

"Be safe too and know, I'm going to stop this war."

"If anyone will do it, it will be you, little human."

I'm no longer human, but I still like the nickname and it holds meaning for me. My eyes fill with tears and I lean in for a last kiss to his soft lips, inhaling his scent of blood and dirt and musk, taking all of him I can with me.

*W*hen it gets light enough, I rouse Diekin, but it's hard. No wonder he slept through all the racket Baya and I must have caused last night, he's still recovering. "Is it time already, Tristan?"

"Afraid so."

We only get to packing when thick hooves sound against the dirt floor of the forest, echoing against the trees. Both Diekin and I pull swords, standing back-to-back, taking up a fighting stance. We relax when we see it's Corrik, Alrik, Jagar, Aldagir, Zelphar, Brylee, and what's left of our warriors.

Corrik hops off his horse.

The large Elf is speechless, eyes wide, breathing carefully. He walks over slowly, drinking me in; I get shy again—this is going to happen a lot isn't it? "Tristan?"

"It's me."

His smile glows and something else, his body relaxes. I see now how much me being human worried him. This doesn't get me out of danger, but it helps. A lot. He runs one of his large hands up my bare arm, to my neck, and up my long ear. I wiggle it and bites his lip. He spends so long not saying anything, I get self-conscious even though I have no reason to be. I know Corrik, I know he's pleased, but I need him to say something. "Is this okay?"

"Tahsen. It's more than okay. I'm just trying to convince myself that what my eyes are seeing is real. You're too beautiful to be real and I can't believe the Gods made you for me." He yanks me to him. "My cock aches for you, my darling. I need to get you home and to our bed. I'd take you here, but this deserves the time for worshipping." His lips ghost over mine and then we kiss deeply.

Alrik clears his throat. "We need to be on our way, we don't have enough protection against Rogue Elves to lollygag. Put your pretty wife-to-be over your horse Corrik and let's go."

It's hard not to openly scowl at him.

Unfortunately, Corrik does put me on his horse, but it's because we're low on horses and his happens to be one of the larger ones that can fit two. Plus, he wants to be near me. "Don't pay him any mind Tristan. I told you, he's grown affectionate for you."

I might finally believe Corrik on that one. "He has a funny way of showing it."

We ride for a long while before he says more, but I practically feel him ruminating on something. "Out with it Corrik."

"You won't like it."

"I have to deal with many a thing I don't like."

"Even your voice has changed, it's sexy," he says beginning to nibble on my neck.

"*Corrik.*"

"Fine. What about subbing for my brother now and then? I would not bring it up again, but I sense the energy between you two has grown and not that you have to appease his jealousy, but he is jealous."

"Reward his nasty behavior? Forget it. I am open to it if you are, but he can treat me kindly."

He smiles against my neck. "You were worried about your dragon blood leaving you. It has not, and it's fiercer than ever."

I laugh, but then I get serious. "Are you worried he won't cancel the engagement, Cor?"

"A bit. And I don't mean to imply you should sell your body for it, I only bring up you subbing for him at all because I think it would be good for you with the side benefit of ensuring he will call the engagement off. No, you're not *slave*, but you are *brat* and an intense session with Alrik would be beneficial for you now and then."

"You couldn't do it?"

"I could, but it's not my preference. I realized when your father came how strict he was with you. You may not have liked it all the time growing up because you need some room to roam free you weren't likely to get from him, but when I saw how his care of you calmed you instantly, I knew you contained that faucet." I can't deny how much my father's way helped, and I know the truth of what he's saying. "I have it in me to give you what you need, and if it's a no for you with Alrik, I will do that for you, but if you've got the energy with Alrik, and you're amenable, why not? I know how electric it can be with the right energetic pairing."

"What about Strobavik? He specializes in slaves." I have not forgotten that Alrik still has my cuff. I remain optimistic I'll get it back.

"He could too but it still wouldn't be the same. It's—Tristan? He can't help it, you know. He's bonded to you. He didn't ask for it to happen, sometimes it is the wish of the Gods and so it is. He's struggling."

As a human, none of that would have made sense. Those are not things that can be comprehended cerebrally. It's an Elf thing. Now that I'm Elf, I already feel the truth of what he's saying. I feel the pull to him greater than I did before.

Doesn't mean I like it.

"I will think about it. But he's such a dick."

"*Tristan*," he scolds. "You can't say that about him ... even if it's true sometimes."

We laugh together and then turn to other things. I tell him all about my underwater journey and the water dragon I met. I'll have to tell him about Bayaden, but I'd rather do so without Alrik watching over us.

Alrik doesn't know how deep my relations with the Aldrien Warlord run, beyond that I served him for over a year, and it may be best to keep it that way.

CHAPTER 23

We make the long journey home without anymore trouble. Everyone has the same level of shock at seeing my transformation, they're all impressed. Alrik won't talk to me, won't even look at me. I let him sulk for a bit. If there's anything I know about Cyredanthem men, it's that they need time to cool off and process.

This leaves time for Corrik and me as we prepare for our upcoming re-nuptials. I'm excited and it feels good to want to marry him this time with no apprehension. I am Elf now, I have already said goodbye to my old life, I'm ready to move forward into the new.

I continue to converse with my family via the set of books, like Corrik and I did. I tell Papa everything. He wishes he could be here for our second wedding, but they'd never make it in time. I consider asking Corrik to wait but don't. I'm just as anxious as Corrik is to be married as soon as possible. If I've learned anything over this past year, it's not to take the present moment for granted.

"You've been quiet, Tristan," Corrik says coming behind up me, nibbling my neck as he does.

I'm at the large table in our quarters reading a book on Elvish laws. I'm able to savor learning about the aspects of Elven culture I would like to, now that I've been given some free time. "I don't like this war, Corrik. I'm trying to find something here to convince both my father and yours it can be called off." After that, I'll have Bayaden's father to worry about, but two problems at a time.

He sighs and shuts my book. "You need to get out of here. You're free you know, or have you forgotten?"

I sizzle at him, for shutting my book. "I am free, which means I can do what I like and what I would like to do is study every law I can find to outwit our parents."

He spins my chair around, staring at me, drinking me in. "Okay fine, but what about the other thing on your mind, uh?"

I look at my hands, glance at the door to make sure there are no other ears to listen and then face my first husband, who will soon become my second husband. "Bayaden found me. We schemed to bring our respective parties home. As it turned out, Alrik had already made that decision, but had he not, I would have done what was necessary."

"And? Why do you look like you want to throw yourself off a bridge for that?" He moves the hair out of my eyes and tucks it behind one of my new, large, Elven ears—his new favorite thing to do. I wiggle it for him to show affection the way Elves do. I do try to be an Elf sometimes.

"I keep betraying you."

"Perhaps by your standards, yes. But you haven't, you're just being yourself. My Tristan, he's filled with a deep-rooted sense of justice. You think it's wrong and you can't help standing up against it."

I nod. "We kissed, Corrik. Had there been time, I would have let him do more. I would do it again."

I'm not as used to this poly thing as others are, but I think … no I *know* I am that way. Just like I'm a brat who likes being submissive for Corrik sometimes and someone who could maybe, perhaps see himself subbing for someone who required a deeper kind of submissive. I've come to realize, I wasn't acting when I did what I did for Alrik that one time before I left. I was responding to Alrik's energy.

I have many aspects to my sexuality. It's not a 'this' or 'that' phenomenon. The Lady of the Lake said I would have at least three men in my life and I know who they are now, I know how each of their energies affects me and I want them all. I don't want to choose.

But these kinds of relationships weren't normalized in Markaytia, and I still have some shame over it. It didn't help how Corrik was when we first married. I got the sense that I was to be his one and only, that he would murder anyone who suggested sharing. Now, I have a clearer distinction between possessiveness and jealousy. I also understand that while he does mean to keep me for himself, that doesn't extend to those who are dear to me. Because Corrik loves me, ardently so, and he can't resist giving me anything that makes me happy—even if it sometimes takes a little while when he's worried about my safety—it makes him happy to see me happy.

He sighs. "Did it have to be the Aldrien Warlord, Tristan? We have a perfectly handsome and dominant Warlord here in Mortouge if you like."

"Zelphar? Ugh. *Hard* no. And okay yes, he's my type, but he's a true arsehole, Cor. I don't know how Brylee stands him." Plus, the energy I feel with Zelphar is that of an annoying older brother. It makes me glad I was an only child.

Corrik laughs big and pulls me toward him. I encircle him with my strong arms. "I can feel him you know? In your hair. I could feel him since the moment you came near. At first, I didn't know who the Elf was. As you have now experienced, we can pick up on magic that comes from another Elf, but without knowing who the castor was, we can't tell who it was. I had my suspicions, but it wasn't until you confirmed it for me that I knew that this magical signature belonged to him."

"So, every time you touch my hair, you feel him?"

"Yes," he says like he's had a bad joke played on him.

It dawns on me. "This wasn't just a nice gesture, it was also an ownership symbol like marking."

His eyes delight with something playful. "It was that but also a few more things. It was a reminder for me, one I'd have to face daily, and accept if I wanted to accept you. Most importantly, it was a warning—he is in your heart and if I don't treat you right, he'll come for you. That broke me the most because he sensed something in you that spoke to your unhappiness. He sent you back with a hefty amount of hesitation." Tears fall from Corrik's eyes. "I hated that, and I knew it was true because he made this hair with deep love for you, that's what makes the spell possible and near unbreakable. He was worried about you, but despite all that, he sent you back to me because he knew you loved me too."

"That wasn't the only reason, Cor," I rush in to say, hating seeing the massive Elf cry like this. "His father was going to kill me."

"Maybe. But he would not have sent you to me knowing he was sending you to a life of misery. He would have shipped you back to Markaytia. He sent you here for you, Tristan."

Now I'm crying.

"Oh, my darling. It's okay. It's really okay. There's also one more thing it was. This is a thing Elves do with shared partners. Almost … like a fun prank."

"He pranked you, with my body? If I ever see him again, he's a dead Elf."

Thankfully, that makes Corrik laugh, I can't take his crying—it's too heartbreaking. "It's not so bad as it sounds to someone who might be of Markaytian decent. You like being marked, don't you?" he breathes into my ear.

"Yes."

"There you go. For you it's a mark you can wear with pride—he would not have done this if he didn't know you'd adore it, for me it's a 'so there, he's mine too'."

"Barbaric Elven behavior is what I call it. By the Gods, you two."

"Wait until my brother gets involved. It will seem barbaric then."

"Why would your brother get involved?"

He bites his lip. "Forget I said that. The point is, I've long accepted Bayaden. Don't feel guilt over what you do with him. He loves you and that's enough for me."

Part of me wants to follow up with the Alrik comment, and part of me doesn't at all. Not right now anyway. I leave it. "Why haven't you marked me in some barbaric way?"

"I have. The location spell, remember? That's a mark. I know where you go, which is why I knew you were at the healing center more often than you let on."

"I've been a lot less since I've become Elf."

"Do you see me complaining? Plus you heal a lot faster. I'm less concerned." He nuzzles into my hair.

"It doesn't bother you to feel him when you do that?"

"No. He made it with his love for you, which could only be possible with your love for him. It still contains your love. It's still you."

"Which must mean you can't kill him either."

"Correct. Not when you love him so. I've always said you are wise."

"Then you must have known he was in the area and that he would seek me out."

He kisses down my neck. "Yes."

I get an idea. "Could the same happen with Alrik?"

"It could, but that depends on him, and before you do what you're thinking don't. That's a dangerous game to play with Elves, my love. Only go to him if you want him too."

"But it could stop a war, Corrik."

That draws him up short, and he loses his playful edge. "When will you learn you're not an item to be traded for peace? And yes, I know I'm guilty of it too, but I should not have done that. No one should have."

"I made a choice too, Corrik."

"Maybe, but you had little choice. It was more coercion than choice. You could have run off, but that would have made you a traitor to your homeland."

"I was upset about the marriage, but I also saw the wisdom in it."

"Fine then, until you can see the wisdom in what I'm saying I forbid you to go to my brother unless it's for *you*. You will not use yourself as a political weapon anymore. No one will. Do you understand me, Tristan?"

"Yes," I say. "Fine."

"It's like that is it?"

"Like whaaa—no! Corrik, put me down." He slings me over his shoulder and carries me to the bed. It's annoying as fuck that he can still lift me so easily.

My pants are down too fast and I'm over his knee, squirming and kicking because my arse is set aflame from swat after swat from his hand. He's a lot more liberal in that department now that I'm Elf, knowing I'll heal quickly. He makes it count, and it hurts so much more than it used to. My jaw tenses and my face scrunches. "I won't use myself as a political weapon. I promise!"

He keeps spanking though until I'm sure I won't be sitting for a week even though I know that's not a possibility from just his hand. He'd need another kind of implement for that— they make special Elven spanking implements, just for that instance here.

I'm panting heavily and feeling very sorry for myself when he finally stops. "Are you going to behave yourself and obey me?"

"Yes, sir. I won't do it. I'll find another way to end the war," I say with a cheeky grin.

He gives my arse a final whack, and it's one I can feel the hand-print of and then he's helping me stand up and removing the rest of my clothing. I work on pushing his white jacket off and trace over his hard skin like I always do. "I no longer have to be gentle with you, Tristan. I look forward to being the one to take your Elven virginity too."

"When, uh, when exactly is that going to happen?" I ask as he pulls me into a hot kiss. With all the comments he made upon seeing me for the first time as Elf, I thought he'd ravage me as soon as we returned home, but he did not. There's been a lot of these little teasing sessions and I don't know how he holds back; I am Elf now, I feel the primal urges and they're intense. I'm not a dominant lover and even I've wanted to pin Corrik down and fuck him, or somehow make him fuck me.

He knows. Bastard! "On our wedding night," he says.

"You've got to be kidding me. You're going to re-enact our first wedding?"

"Sort of. Only I have an addition." He reaches over to the nightstand on his side to fetch the horrid contraption. It's a lot like the one I wore at our wedding. "New and improved, for an Elf."

I take the cock cage from him and inspect it, my cheeks flushing at the sight of it. "Does that bit go inside my cock, Corrik?"

"Yes. This one locks on with magic and if I put it on now, think about how aroused you'll be by the wedding."

"Corrik, please. That's cruel," I whine. But he knows I won't refuse him. He's kind of an adorable sadist, the way he looks like a little boy being told he's getting a new puppy isn't something I can resist.

"And yet I find it delicious. We'll put it on tonight after I've taken care of this," he says referring to my too hard cock, his face smug. "See how nice I am?"

I want to tell him just how nice he's not, but he doesn't have to take care of anything, and I know that cheeky boys don't get orgasms. Plus, I know well I'm not getting any orgasms after a spanking that was not just for fun. There's a spanking spectrum and while what I just got was not punishment, it was a warning—which is too close to punishment on the said spectrum. "You're the nicest there is, sir."

"That's a good boy," he says ghosting a hand over my balls and leaning into kiss me again. I whine into his mouth and my cock feels like it might burst. *Good boy* does something to me. "Looks like you can be well-behaved when you set your mind to it."

"I can, sir. I can suck your cock too if you'll let me."

Corrik groans. "I want that, I do. But I'm going to wait too."

My eyes widen. "You sure that's a good idea." It's one thing for me to be stupid, horny, but Corrik will be an animal by then.

"You are Elf and a menacing one at that, you can handle me."

"It will be savage."

"You live for danger, much to my dismay. It will practically be a wedding gift."

I laugh. "You know me—no more boats though."

He rubs noses with me. "No more boats."

*L*ife as an Elf gets better, which surprises me. Halflings have always been part Elf, I was a full human, *turned* Elf. But one does not simply become Elf, it must be permitted by the king and the Gods. Getting both permissions is enough for most Elves to accept that you always were an Elf in terms of spirit, you just had the 'misfortune' of being born in a human's body.

That's how they see it.

I think it's a load of shite. I still feel like a Markaytian, I'm Tristan in every way, I'm just more badass. Yes, I'm an Elf, I'm bigger and have unimaginable strength, I have the ability to harness magical energy, but I determine what I will do with these gifts, not the gifts themselves.

Zelphar the Elven Warlord is about the only one in my immediate circle of concern who doesn't believe I deserve full Elf status, but unfortunately for him, I have more status than he does, even if I have no jurisdiction on the field. The only thing he had was that he could have me beat daily and have it look like it was just my frail human form to blame. Now, I can keep up and sink some of his warriors to the ground. Bayaden was right, I still have a lot to learn, but now I have hope of learning it.

The king commissions a new sword for me as a gift. All of the swordsmiths in Mortouge fight over who gets to make it for me. It will be given to me at the ceremony, the one that should have happened long ago to officially introduce me to Mortouge, though Corrik claims I need no introduction with all the trouble I've caused.

He's probably right about that.

But we do have a gathering to honor all the children we lost to the witch wyrms with the royal family's solemn vow not to allow another child to go missing.

With the wedding approaching, I need to speak with Alrik. He hasn't made the necessary arrangements to end of our engagement and that's concerning.

He never returned my cuff. I knew not to ask about it. If he planned on giving it back, he would have by now. I've already gone to Strobavik. His vivid blue eyes turned down in time with his ears when he saw me without it. "The prince has withdrawn his permission," I said. My lip wobbled.

He knew which one. Somehow and in some way, I'm beholden to Alrik. My eyes filled with tears.

Strobavik wiped them away with his thumb. I almost meet his height now, about half a foot shorter but close. "Don't fret, sweetheart. Come. I promised you would meet my children. D'ayawin has a new kitten she'd like to show you."

"They know of me?"

"Of course, they do. You're quite famous with having been turned Elf and all. Heads up, she's called the damn thing Tristan. It's as stubborn as you are."

I know where to find Alrik, he's so bloody predictable and no I don't have a guard bring me down like I'm supposed to. That was meant to end once I became an Elf but to my dismay, Corrik relayed to me that Alrik insisted the rule remain in place. Bet Alrik was too chicken to tell me himself.

"How long were you planning to ignore me?" I say taking a seat preparing to watch him polish his sword for a bit.

"What did I say would happen next time you came here without a guard?"

"We need to talk Alrik, and you're avoiding me."

He sets his sword down. "Come here."

"No."

"What did you say to me?"

"I said no. We need to talk, Alrik." I keep my body hard, not giving an inch.

"If you've come to plead your case about the engagement, you've wasted your time. I'm planning to make the official announcement that we are no longer engaged at the ceremony. Happy?"

Of all the…! Elves are frustrating, especially this one. I vow never to be so frustrating. "I'm not happy. You're not being honest with me." Corrik's right and I feel the truth of it in my Elven body—there's an energy between us and denying it isn't good for either of us. I want to, for me, nothing to do with Aldrien wars. Besides, Alrik is Alrik. I doubt very much he would be swayed even by love if that were to happen between us. If we don't handle this thing between us, we'll both explode—especially if he's restraining half as much as I am.

"I'm not being dishonest either. I just don't want to chat further. Now get your arse over here. I promised you a spanking if you disobeyed me again and I mean what I say."

Ugh!

I stomp over to him. "I don't want a spanking. I won't do it again."

He pulls down my pants and underthings anyway, undeterred by my complaining. "If you don't want a spanking, obey me."

When I'm over his knee, facing the floor, I hear him take a sharp breath. He pauses to rub my bare arse, but then I'm attempting not to bite through my lip as his hand connects to my backside, painfully. "Why have you earned this spanking?"

"For disobedience, sir."

"Indeed," he says, as he lays down another crisp set of whacks that ring out and echo off the walls of the armory. I grimace and my jaw tenses. Alrik never messes around, his spankings are always fucking exacting from beginning to end. "What have you to say for yourself?"

"I will get a guard to bring me next time, promise. Ow!"

"Who says you're invited for a next time, hmmmm?"

But I can't answer that yet. I'm busy trying not to move out of the target range. Spankers hate when you squirm excessively, they add for that, but to willingly remain in front of that which is blistering your bottom is work. I grunt and wince. I wish I'd obeyed him in the first place. When he pauses, I release the breath I was holding. "Am I not invited back, sir?"

He doesn't answer, unless you call him spanking my arse an answer. In that case, he answered for several minutes. My eyes watered through the pain and I fought the urge to struggle. Strobavik taught me well—Alrik doesn't like a lot of reaction, if you've earned a spanking from him, you take it stoically. And he's unyielding, his hand falling over and over. I have to work to pull a breath and grip his pant leg for support. I'm probably not supposed to, but he doesn't correct me.

I shut my eyes tight, the bright, magical lighting overstimulating as tears drop to the floor and I stifle many a groan, feeling very sorry for myself. He slows his onslaught of swats, finishing with a loud smack I know will leave a hand-sized print in dark red. "Ahhhh, sir!"

He helps me up, pulling me between his legs. "I do not negotiate with brats. I will allow the company, but you will have a guard bring you down, Tristan. I shall return you." His eyes are blazing, and he might be thinking about slicing me in two, but he's gentle when he helps return my clothing to rights.

His dark eyes pierce me. "Corrik said we should—"

He stands abruptly, sliding a hand to the nape of my neck, gripping the roots painfully. "I know what Corrik thinks we should do. The problem, Tristan, is I'm a lot more possessive than my brother." He breathes like he might be aching. "I want you so badly. But I want you to be *mine*."

His lips are close; they're hot.

Our foreheads touch and he closes his eyes, collecting himself. He releases me. "Go. And if I catch you out past curfew without guard or permission again, it will be my thickest strap to your bare arse."

That angers me. I get his position, I'm lowest in the chain of hierarchy, so I can be disciplined by anyone, but Alrik's the only one who regularly disciplines me other than Corrik. I hate that he gets to when he's so bloody awful. "Don't worry, you won't have to see me again. I'll stay away, I'll stay *far* away from you. The nerve. And another thing—"

I don't get to finish my sentence, Alrik's lips are on mine, searing and heavy. It's fast and we break away surprised that it happened, both of us panting, me with rage, him with passion. "You see? It's stuff like that—"

"—by the Gods. Tristan, *shut up!*"

He shuts me up with his mouth on mine but this time it's not a quick thing. Our lips are secured, and his tongue is down my throat. He inhales me as he uses one of his strong hands to knock his sword, along with all his polishing equipment, off the table. He grips my thighs, lifting my arse onto the table.

I'm kind of in a lot of trouble now. I wanted to kiss him, but once you ignite the feral nature of an Elf, there's every chance it won't stop there. But part of me didn't believe Corrik with all his Alrik talk. Yes, I knew there was an energy, but not this kind of energy. I thought it was purely on a Dom-sub level, this is different. There's real passion.

And I can't stop either.

I'm fueled by my Elven nature now too. I want him as much as he wants me. I wrap my thighs around him, squeezing his pelvis toward mine. "You are so much better when you're pliant underneath me like this," he breaks away to say. "You'd look awfully pretty with a large, red, ball gag in your mouth."

Arse! "You won't do that, not for long. I suspect you like kissing me too much." I smirk at him.

He growls between kisses, slamming me onto my back, leaning over top of me. He knows I'm right.

"I like kissing you too, Alrik," I say in between yet more kissing, looking up at him sweetly.

He pauses, staring down at me like I'm a wonder of the world he's trying to figure out. "Why are you so addictive? I have tried to stop thinking about you. I can't." He nuzzles his face into my neck. "I didn't mean to get excited about marrying you, but I did."

"I can't say I was ever thrilled about marrying you," I get a death glare for that one, "but I like the way you protect me. It's different. I don't want to let it go." I know that's selfish, but it also says a lot—I protect myself, that's not an honor I would bestow onto just anyone. He knows it.

"You'll always have my sword, Tristan." He presses another kiss to my lips, we breathe each other in and then he helps me up and off the table. I detect the smidgeon of a smile.

"So? Do you like me better now that I'm an Elf?" My legs still hang off the table. I'm tempted to wrap them around him again, but I refrain.

He runs a hand through my hair. "You are something unworldly now. I can't help but think you more beautiful, but your inner spark hasn't changed, and that's what truly drew me to you."

"Are you saying you liked a human?"

"I'm saying I was attracted to *you*." He smirks and interlaces his hand in mine.

"I'm way too much of a brat to be your full-time mate, Alrik. You'd want to kill me daily."

"How's that different from now?" I lean my head to his torso, he cups it with the back of his hand.

"Trust me, I'm on my best behavior around you."

"Not likely. All right, you came to proposition me let's have it."

"Corrik thinks I need more, at least sometimes; an energy like what my father gave me," I explain.

"Corrik is no slouch in that department."

"No, but it's not his preference. It's not just that, he says we have an energy."

"We do," he agrees pressing a kiss to my lips. "So you sub for me when I call for you?"

"Yes, sir," I say.

"I spank for teasing like that," he tells me tilting my chin up. "Okay, I'm in, but I want something of you too—your obedience."

"You have that."

"Oh really? And what are you doing right now?"

"This was the only way I could talk to you!"

He takes a breath. "I will make myself more available to you."

"Stop avoiding me you mean."

"You don't let me get away with a thing."

"Neither do you," I say.

He smiles. A real smile. "I want my mark on you too. A tattoo on your right ankle, the crown prince symbol, which will mean a piece of you belongs to me."

"You'll have to run that one by Corrik, but I'm fine with it."

"Wasn't asking, Tristan."

"You utter arse."

He arches a sharp brow. "Just be grateful you didn't have to marry me."

I stare into his dark eyes. Dare I ask? I don't want to anger him but my brat's curiosity has to know. Why did he take it? Why hasn't he given it back?

"Don't ask about that," he says.

"Have you become a mind reader?"

"No. But while sometimes you're a puzzle, other times you're an open book."

"I want it back."

"No."

I put a hand on my hip because I'm not sure what else to do and Papa did it to Father sometimes when he wanted his way, and Father was being an impossible brute.

He closes his eyes and opens them again, taking a scrupled breath. "Give me a little time and we can revisit it. At that juncture, you can ask permission like you're supposed to."

"Is that what this is about? Permission? I'm happy to ask for permission, sir."

"That's part of it. But I already share you with my brother. I don't think I can handle a third person just yet."

Right. He doesn't know about Bayaden. "You do recall you're the one who introduced me and Strobavik in the first place, yeah?"

"I didn't say I was being rational or reasonable. I just know seeing the cuff on you made me want to cleave Strobavik in half a little bit more each day."

An ocean-sized wave of tingles wash through me and I flush head to toe. Do I rile him that much? Is it wrong that I find it hot? "You're a jealous beast."

"I'm Elf. It's how we are. Strobavik will understand. Now to bed with you."

"Do I have to? I'll bet we could have a lot more fun if I stayed," I tell him trailing fingers up his thick arm.

He inhales my scent. "The thought of getting to use you while you're in chastity is highly attractive to someone like me, but I'm going to wait."

"What is it with you *and* Corrik waiting? I'm not chocolate cake."

"Don't pout." He's contemplative. "I need to digest this. I wasn't planning on sharing a mate, but the Gods help me, I need you Tristan."

I nod. It must be confusing for him. I think Alrik's hardened himself to the world. I bite my lip, not wanting to go, needing something from him too, something only he can bring. He's already spanked me and boy was it a good one. My cheeks are hot and aching some, but there's something in his energy that I need to be near.

"I'm already getting to know that look. Fine, you may stay for a little longer, if you promise to sit there and behave."

"All the way over there?"

His mouth forms a line. "You'll be the death of me." He heaves a sigh, collecting his sword and polishing tools and then collecting me as if I too am an item. He sits me on his lap, efficiently working around me as he finishes up with his sword.

"*W*ill you mark me again?" I ask Corrik. We get a lazy day in the sun. It's still a cold day, it's always cold here save for two months of the year they call summer, which pales in comparison to summers in Markaytia or Aldrien. We've spread out on a blanket under a tree with food and drink. Corrik's insistent we do more date-like things as per Markaytian tradition.

"Do I not mark you enough, my little Markaytian?"

I smile. "You do. I mean something permanent like this stupid thing." Alrik made true on his tattoo threat. I had hoped Corrik would be upset about it and fight him, but he wasn't. He was amused.

"You complained about that 'stupid' little thing or was that just for show?"

My face heats. "Maybe mostly for show." I can't help it. I love signs of ownership, it's gotten worse now that I'm Elf. "But it's a bit ridiculous."

"Maybe I want my own tattoo, bigger than that one, hmmmm? What would you say to that?"

"What could I say? You three do what you will with me, no one cares about what Tristan wants." I cross my arms. Yes I'm pouting.

"You have three alpha men who worship you, my darling. We all care a great deal about what you want. And what you want is *Property of Corrik Cyredanthem* tattooed on your arse."

"Over my dead body, Corrik!"

"Alrik will hate it. He'll want to do something even grander. Maybe you'll become a giant tattoo."

Okay, he's teasing. Right? Yeah, he's teasing. Still, I have to make sure. "Is that really what you want?" If so, I already know I'll do it. I have a hard time denying any of them anything.

"No. I get to marry you—*again*. You'll wear my ring on your finger, you'll call me First and Second husband. That's a big deal to me. I'll get to make all the final decisions about us and you."

Right. I won't be marrying Bayaden or Alrik. And even if I did, Corrik is my first and second husband. The ways of Elvish laws are interesting. "Alrik won't want to marry me at some point too?" They have no laws around the number of marriages in any of the Elven realms like we do in Markaytia.

"I thought you did not want to bear the responsibility of Crown Prince Consort? His title overrides mine by far. You would have to take his."

I nod. "I don't want that."

"However, if he finally marries someone, they will take the title. You could become a later husband, which would give you some of his status and you would be expected to follow the rules under that status, but you would escape the full responsibility."

"That sounds more like what I'd be comfortable with, but it's too soon to say. I don't know that I want more than one husband. What about you?"

He takes a breath. "Tristan, I hope you won't take this the wrong

355

way, but I don't know that I want another. Maybe it will happen, but so far, I just want you." My face crumples. "That's exactly what I didn't want. Sexuality is a tricky thing, not everyone is the same. That doesn't make any of us better or worse. Me not wanting more than you doesn't make you bad for wanting others."

"How can it not? Surely there's someone else. You need someone more submissive than me. Let's get that person."

He pauses and goes very quiet. "If it will make you happy, Tristan, I will, but it would be for you."

I can't help the tears that fill my eyes and teeter over the brim. "I'm terrible, I'm a terrible person."

"This is what I didn't want, I don't want you upset over something you can't help. I'm just different Tristan. Different sexuality. I think I might be Tristan-sexual."

I laugh through my tears at that because it's so ridiculous. "You are my first love. That holds a special place in my heart."

"I know that now. Are you ready to marry me again in three days?"

"Yes. I'd marry you now. I'd marry you a hundred times."

"Maybe we will. We could remarry every ten years if we like. By the time you are a thousand years old, we will have married one hundred times. We can keep going too."

"That is the most ridiculous thing I've ever heard, but I kind of love it."

"Then it shall be done."

EPILOGUE

"*W*hat does it say?" I know full well I'm being a pest and I know how Alrik deals with pests, but I *have* to know.

Alrik yanks me into his lap. "You need a spanking and I'm about to give it if you don't settle."

We're in the Great Hall, but it's growing late and no more people are to come in today which is the only reason I'm allowed to be so casual. Corrik is away. That always makes me fucking nervous. I'm not over the witch wyrm incident and no one would allow me to go with him to hunt the next one saying I wasn't ready yet, never mind that I helped off the last witch wyrm we encountered. Corrik was for allowing me to come along, much to my surprise. He's kept his promise about me being at his side and was personally willing to look after me, but Alrik was against it and while Corrik is my direct Head of House, Alrik has a say in all things military, which is the category this instance fell under after much debate (it's complicated). Apparently, I'm ready when Zelphar says I am, which is seeming like more of an impossibility with each passing day. There was an incident. I became convinced Zelphar wouldn't approve me out of spite. I complained enough that Alrik did attend practice as an observer only to agree with Zelphar.

I got spanked for being dramatic. I might have been.

In any case, I am here and Corrik is away and so I stick close to Alrik. I spin the ring on my finger. At least we were married before he left. I'm grateful he is my husband once again. I pout in Alrik's lap even though I know it won't buy me any quarter with him, but that I get to sit in his lap at all is a privilege and a sight people aren't used to seeing. Alrik has not been public with any of the lovers he's taken in a long time. "They are fine, my delinquent one. They did find another witch wyrm, and it has been destroyed. They will be home in a week."

That relaxes me some, but I'll feel better when Corrik is home.

Alrik shoves his hand down my pants and I whine as he tugs on my heavy balls. "How are these, Tristan?"

Corrik. Evil, sadist Corrik decided it would be oh so fun to put me in chastity while he was gone. "To remember me by, my love," he said as he locked me in the thing.

He left the key with Alrik for safety reasons, and it can be removed with magic but Alrik is having too much damn fun to take it off. "You'll just have to learn to come on my cock, dear Tristan," Alrik keeps saying night after night, but so far it has not happened.

My balls *ache*.

"Please, Alrik. *Please.*" I can't take it anymore.

"I have a good feeling about tonight," is all I get, which means no.

But whining will get me nowhere. *Ugh.*

He removes his hand, patting my poor, caged cock outside my pants. "I'll get you there. Not to worry."

"Fine. May I be excused? I want to go for a ride." I am not generous. I'm growing agitated with everything; a witch wyrm hunt I'm *not* part of, talk of war with Aldrien I want *no* part in and a case of blue balls from the ninth realm of hell.

"It's getting late."

"I won't be long."

"Fine. You may go but I'm not removing your collar, Tristan."

I touch the sturdy leather. It's not the one from Corrik, it's from him. I agreed to become Alrik's submissive. For a moment I forget that I'm angry and stare at him with utter worship. "I wouldn't want you to, Master." Maybe in another life I would have minded but I love belonging to my men. It's just better for their egos if I don't belabor that point too often and make them work for it.

"So, you do remember how you're meant to address me." Yeah, I break the rules sometimes. Shocking, I know. "Go, make sure you're back by curfew." He lifts me and smacks my arse.

I glare at him. "I'd also like to sleep in my own bed if you don't mind very much."

He twists his lips in a way that says he does mind, but he is getting fed up with me. "Sleep in your own bed then, but you'd better have a new disposition by morning."

I storm away equally fed up with him for no good reason.

I ride down to see Jagar and Aldagir, which is as far as I'm permitted to go without a guard though I wonder how long that will last. Alrik doesn't care for it much. I drink mead and complain to them. It feels good to get stuff off my chest. "If there is a way we can help you with the war, Tristan, let us know. We're happy to help as always. My army is at your service," Jagar says.

I return to the palace, bathe and slip into bed, but I can't sleep. I know Corrik's on his way home, but I won't sleep soundly on my own until he is. Now I'm going to have to eat crow, but I suck up my pride, slip on my robe and creep into Alrik's chambers.

I'm the only one permitted by his guard without an invitation, so they let me in without question. I enter the anteroom and use my panther-like movements to go into the bedroom without waking him. Once I'm there, I stare at him for a few moments. The guard was quiet enough with the door, he's still asleep. It's about the only time he's peaceful, the only time all the heaviness in his face disperses. I don't want to disturb him, I have learned how much he does for the kingdom he loves, how much responsibility he bears. I know what it's like to feel responsible for everything and everyone.

I should not have come here.

I turn to leave. "Come," he says opening the covers for me.

I run to hop in with him and mold myself his much larger body where I cry. I'm silly for doing so. My problems are so small compared to his, but he's just such a good rock to cry on. I never expected him to be, not with how unrelenting he was when we first met, but maybe there's something to what Corrik says about my ability to open people up. He's not soft by any definition of that word, but he's softer with me than with anyone else.

"Now, now. Is your cock hurting you that bad? All you had to do was tell me."

"Alrik," I whisper-yell, laughing too.

He smirks, but it flips into a frown as he pulls me in by the nape of my neck to kiss my forehead. "I know you miss him, but please don't cry anymore, Tristan. I don't take it well. Zelphar's tired of me taking out all his warriors in one afternoon."

"I can try, Alrik."

"I thought you wanted to sleep in your own bed tonight, hmmmm?"

"We both knew that was nonsense when I said it." But a good example of letting the brat in me run free. He's better at sensing that than he thinks he is but not as good as Corrik or Bayaden. Still, I love him every bit as much. We give each other different things. I squeeze him tighter as if he might disappear.

He hums in agreement. "Do you think you can sleep now?"

I nod, yawn, and shut my eyes. I sleep like a rock.

The next day Alrik informs me how things will be. "You will serve me today. You need it and frankly, so do I."

I'm supposed to be a good little Elf and say, 'yes sir', but then I wouldn't be me. "The whole day? No way. Half is all you're getting."

That is *not* how one talks to Alrik, let me tell you.

He grips me hard by the hair at the nape of my neck. "You're worse than I thought. Do you make the rules around here?" he asks, fire lighting his silver eyes.

"N-No, Master."

"Better. On your knees, no I don't care that you haven't bathed yet.

You don't need to worry about things like that today. You worry about what I tell you to do and nothing else. Undress."

I do undress, but I worry about a lot of things I'm not supposed to like, what if he takes me out there to serve him naked? I'm still shy about it. I also worry about how long I'll have to kneel. Will it be for more than I can handle? There's a list of stuff like that seven parchments long and it's not what I'm meant to be thinking of. It's distracting me from my much larger dilemmas, which is why I'm supposed to think about nothing save for pleasing Alrik. *Focus on that one thing, Tristan.*

Slave and Master is the ultimate power exchange. We chose submissive as the official role I would serve for him (there was a collaring ceremony and everything) because there is some flexibility in a submissive role—we can move between extremes.

We don't do this often, which is a stark change from what it was meant to be, in the twenty-four-seven deal, had we married. Alrik knows this isn't me, not to that extent anyway. I've learned I have the capacity for it, but a permanent role like that that would drive me crazy. I know when Alrik chooses this, I'm spinning wildly out of control. Doesn't mean I won't fight him every step of the way. He wants me to yield? He can make me yield.

"I see you're going to be stubborn," he says. "We'll start with an hour."

"Alrik," I plead.

"An hour and a half," he says, brows furrowed, looking down at me. "Forget the appellation again and it's two."

I want to cry. An hour and a half is a long time to kneel like this. Sure I did two as a human and sure it's easier physically as an Elf, but I don't do peaceful silence well. "Yes, Master."

Yes Master is the only answer he's looking for.

The hour and a half is torture. He won't allow any small breaks in form. Each lapse is met with a whack from his special toy. Elves have special implements made for Elves. They're magical and have an effect on Elven flesh unlike the non-Elven counterparts, which would no longer have enough impact on me. It's a single, leather whip, attached to a thin stick; a delicate-looking item, but it packs a sting.

"Mmph," I grunt, trying not to cry out when he lashes the top of my arse for slouching. "Thank you, Master."

"You're not focusing on what you should be focusing on. Tell me, what should that be?"

"On you, Master."

"Very good. Unfortunately for you, I know how good you are at this. Your time starts over."

Ugh! But he's right. I'm not doing this properly and as much as this is for him, it's equally for me. A total power exchange is a two-way street. There is something amazing that can happen for those who are wired like me when we surrender completely. I know as well as he does how it works, in part focusing on serving him is to take my mind off other heavier things. As much as Alrik can grind my gears, I trust him completely; this is something I can give to him.

"Breathe, Tristan, remember to use your breath."

"Yes, Master. I can do better, Master."

I still earn lashes, because he's a strict bastard, but now that he sees I'm trying, he doesn't begin the time over again and I make it to the end. I get so many stripes after the hour and a half, I'm surprised when he tells me, "You have done well, Tristan."

Hotness creeps across my face. "Thank you, Master."

"On your hands and knees. I would like you to take ten of these to your arse because it should please me."

I want to shout at him about how unfair that is when he claims I've been good, but I know that will only add to my total. I also know it's not about how well-behaved I've been, it's purely about submission; about taking what he gives me because he wishes it. Whatever he should wish—it's the only place I have to give my energy to right now.

Of course, sadism is a bloody Cyredanthem trait and that plays in too. Diekin confided in me that Ditira is the same. "Two, you have committed to two Cyredanthems?" he said laughing at me when he found out I would also have a something with Alrik. "Now I know you're insane."

I stick my arse out ready for Alrik. The first lash falls and sends a sharp sting through my body, head to toe, even though the pain begins in my arse. "Ahh! One. Thank you, Master."

"Good boy."

Again, I flush at the praise, which is a kink all its own and I only want to take more for him already feeling the floaty bliss of subspace taking me away. He carries on with another, and another and another, each leaving hot lines across my arse, each radiating through me, and by the time we've reached ten, I'm sailing. I could take a hundred more, but he stops.

His large hand runs through my hair. It's a reverent hand and I absorb the care—he's so much different than I expected him to be than he threatened he'd be. I've come to realize his bark is bigger than his bite. Crossing him is still not advised. "Get on the bed, Tristan. On your back."

I comply quickly, as he removes his pants and he's on top of me in one swift motion, his long white hair a curtain drawn around me. My arse is already leaking for him, the new secretion of a slick-like substance signature to Elves is flowing. "I had so much more planned, but I'm sorry Tristan, I need to be in you."

I nod staring up at him with adoration. I've grown fond of Alrik, despite my best efforts to keep this relationship somewhat business-like. Originally it was lust, energy and designation. I would sub for him when he called for me, we would have passionate hate-sex, but as seems to be the way in the relationships I cultivate, things changed before I could stop them and there was real worship developing during our sessions from both sides.

In the beginning, I would leave as soon as he was done looking after me and go on with my day, or night as the case may be, but soon I was staying longer, nestled into his chest as he ran kisses along my neck and spent time doing innocuous things like brushing out my hair and massaging lotion into my sore muscles; pretty much anything he could think of to keep me with him a moment longer. "If you want my company, Alrik, all you have to do is ask," I said to him one day.

I got the standard Alrik grunt and smack to my arse and yes, I was being a bit cheeky, but I was also serious. Alrik didn't like his feelings for me anymore than Bayaden did at first. He did end up inviting me to sit with him while he did his work in the Great Hall after that. I kneeled at his feet, of course, but it was no small thing. That day began to crystalize my place in his life.

I wondered all kinds of things, like how they would share me. It wasn't like that though, I'm not a toy they fight over, even if I sometimes (willingly) am a toy. I also thought they might fight *about* me, but while they do disagree from time to time, it's never a fight over me thing, even with their barbaric ownership markings, which…

…well I kinda love them.

Corrik did give me a tattoo, of a "C" on the back of my neck in Elvish and I was equally drawn to asking him if he would get a "T" on the back of his neck in Markaytian. I didn't realize I could mark my men too, not permanently anyway, but I can and I'm wild about the idea. I think about Bayaden's tattoo of my name under his eye often.

I don't know if I'll ever see Bayaden again, but I like the thought that he has something of me on him forever.

The head of Alrik's large, Elven cock lines up with my entrance, it's so hard it's purpling; he wants me. He begins to slide in slowly, allowing me to adjust to this size. It's different adjusting as an Elf than it was as a human. It happens faster, my passage relaxes and Alrik can slip into the hilt, brushing up against my prostate immediately.

I moan, my cock trying to get hard but failing, caged as it is. "That's it, take my cock. You like that, don't you, my delinquent one?"

"Love your cock, Master," I say smiling up at him, delirious. My arse still stings from his nasty little implement, same with all the places on my body that suffered the treatment, but the sting mixes with the pleasure his cock brings and it sends me reeling.

"*Good boy.*"

I moan. Fuck. I love being called "good boy." Not that I'll ever admit to that out loud, but they know. Alrik slams his cock into me at a steady pace, all the while looking into my eyes. "You going to come around my cock, sweet boy?"

I nod lost in the bliss. For once I don't even care if I come or not. I'm enjoying his responses and seeing *his* pleasure. The large Elf has sweat breaking across his brow and over his ears, dripping into his white hair. Alrik is an old Elf. Thousands of years old, but you wouldn't know if not for his silver eyes that are pure pools of an ancient story. His eyes crinkle with happiness as he gazes at me all the while fucking me, getting closer to me, hitting my prostate over and over.

"C'mon sweetheart, come. You can come for me like this can't you?"

I think I can today. I know I want to, I've *wanted* to all month. "*Please*," I cry. "Please, Master."

I can tell he's straining, holding back his orgasm for me, which is unheard of. It's usually, '*if you want to come, you'll do it before I do or not at all*', but he wants me to win this one today. The sensation of his cock against my prostate is overwhelming, combined with just the right amount of pain and I finally fall over the edge.

And it's exactly like that, a falling versus an explosion. Come does dribbles out of my cock, but the orgasmic sensations come from my arse instead, casting out and vibrating through me as I squeeze around his dick. When it's over, I'm boneless as he pumps sticky come into me.

Still on top of me, his hands pressed into the mattress, he cranes his head down to kiss me, his tongue slipping over mine, tangling and caressing. "You did it," he says, proud of me.

I'm still far away in subspace, I nod everything around me buoyant.

"Come. Time for a hot bath and then we've got work to attend to today."

He makes sure I'm cleaned up and that salve is rubbed into my lash marks and then he helps me dress in the world's smallest pair of shorts, which I make a note to complain about later, even deep as I am into my sub-haze. I kneel for him as gracefully as I can at his feet in the Great Hall as he works, enjoying how my hair surrounds me as he places it just so. He occasionally runs his hands through it and tells me what a good job I'm doing, encouraging me, "just a bit longer, sweetheart," when my endurance begins to wane.

At the end of the day, he carries me back to his bed and massages my feet until I return to the land of the living. I stretch and smile, feeling a world better. Fuck. I always fight it but surrendering brings me freedom. "Fucking hell, Alrik. That was intense."

"Not as intense as it was going to be," he says picking up my foot, to press a kiss into the wrinkles on the bottom of it. "But you're too irresistible for your own good."

"I can't believe you made me wear tiny little pants. I'd like to veto these."

"But you look so delightful."

I grumble rolling my hot face into the pillow. I'll never see the last of them, will I?

"Tristan, you sure you don't want to take my title? You could do a lot of good for the realm. You're good with people and you would make a good mate for me. I have come to realize, I'm happy with a part-time husband, I'm too busy for someone full-time. What you and I have works for me."

A pit forms in my stomach. I'm drawn to make him happy, to please him, it kills me when I have to turn him down. Plus, doing things for the good of the realm is my weakness.

"It won't interfere with you and Corrik, I'll make sure," he continues. "We would need at least one child, but I'll bear the responsibility of raising him or her and I'll find a partner to satisfy my other, deeper, total power exchange needs."

Wow, he really wants this. I bite my lip.

"Don't answer now," he says when he sees I'm about to. "This isn't a proposal. This is just me putting it out to you for consideration. There's no rush at the moment, it can be a hundred years from now if you like, but I want you to know that is my intention. Your fault. I told you if I kissed you, I would need you to be mine."

"You'd be my Third Husband," I muse. Most Elves are four hundred before they have a second of course I'm an exception in that too. "I thought Crown Princes didn't marry their first husband as a third husband."

"They don't," he says pressing his thumbs into the spaces in between my toes on the tops of my feet. "But even Mother and Father agree, you're something different and special. You were meant to come into our world and do something great. You'd have more power to do that with my title."

I know he's right. My heart clenches and I'm reminded of my intent when I asked the Mother to make me Elf.

I remember there was a price. Is this the price? Service to the first Elven realm for the rest of my days? I don't know. "I'll consider it, Alrik."

He relaxes, crawling up the bed to lounge beside me. I pick up one of his large hands and smoothen a thumb over the crease between his wrist and hand, palm-side down. "I want a tattoo here."

"Oh? What would you like me to get?"

"The Markaytian dragon, like on my chest." In fact, I want one on each of them. I own them as much as they own me.

"Possessive are we?"

"And if I am?"

"You are in good company. I'll have it done tomorrow."

"Good and now I'm sleeping."

"Because you make the rules now?"

"No, because you've exhausted the fuck out of me, and you know better than to run me into the ground or Corrik will be furious."

He laughs. "I know better than that for more than because of Corrik, but it's true. You're staying here then?"

"Mmmmhhmmh," I mumble closing my eyes.

He wraps me in his arms, nuzzling into my hair and my neck. "Sleep, Tristan."

And I do.

*C*orrik will be home today, or he *should* if all went well. Alrik was annoyed with my buzzing around the palace, more specifically buzzing around him and he sent me out to the market-place. "Go wait for him down there where you won't bother me."

I'm glad to be away from him when he's grouchy like he is, even if I know it's only because he's worried too—he just expresses it differently than I do. I pull on my cloak so I can hide my face, preferring not to take a guard into the marketplace, and wait in the shadows until I see the entourage pull in. Corrik is one of the leads, just behind a few of Zelphar's warriors.

Corrik's eyes are stuck wide like he's seen too much. There's blood smeared across his face and soaking his clothes. A quick assessment tells me it's not his blood and I sag, relieved, and able to rejoice in Corrik's homecoming.

I love all my men, but there's an unnamable thing between Corrik and I that pierces me unlike the others. The other two keep me grounded, Corrik moves me. Sometimes a plot has to force us into action, Corrik is my plot but also my story. I would never have chosen this life as the person I was before; I *had* to be pushed into it and I had to have a guide. I'm eternally grateful Corrik came to steal me away. I am a new person and the same, oddly. I've become more of my own person than I ever would have at home in Markaytia and it's because of Corrik. No, I'm not officially Warlord (even though many still refuse to call me anything else), but I'm needed here, I feel it. I don't know what that looks like yet, I just know it's big and it's coming.

But it's Corrik I'll look to first before the others, and that is the way it will always be. I can't have the rest without Corrik. Somehow, he makes the other two in my life make sense.

I race out to him and when the guard sees it's me, they allow me to hop onto the back of Corrik's horse. "Tristan," he sighs. I squeeze and inhale him at the same time, feeling like I'm home now even though I've been 'home' the whole time. "I'm full of blood."

"I don't care. Never leave me again."

"It is never my choice to leave you. I expect you to be ready to travel with me next time."

"Is something wrong, Corrik?" He feels all wrong. Happy to see me but concerned.

"Ditira was badly injured." My heart clenches. "She is still alive, but we need to get her to the Healing Center now."

I nod. "I'm coming with you." Diekin's going to be beside himself. He was needed here and not permitted to join them either.

The rest of the Elven entourage rolls in and they are carting someone in on a stretcher. *Ditira.* I can't look. I look forward to where the Healing Center is, to where we're headed. When we arrive, we watch as they bring her in. Corrik jumps off his horse pulling me into his arms for comfort. Ditira is his twin. He must be going through a range of emotions.

"Corrik, what happened? From what I was told, it sounded as though all was well, and that the trip home would be easy."

"Yes, we were," he says, "and I'll tell you all about it, but I have to do this first." He tilts my chin up and our lips meet. He's gentle when his tongue drifts into my mouth entwining with mine; he takes his time, savoring me and I go lax allowing his tenderness.

Because even though it's an affectionate kiss, Corrik is in charge of it, putting the stamp of ownership into it, claiming me as his once again, always, and forever. "There. Better. I've missed you, my darling."

"I've missed you too."

He tucks my hair behind my tall ear, as he does. "You were right Tristan. The Aldrien Elves did not create the witch wyrms. We should have listened to you. We were ambushed days ago by creatures none of us have ever seen before. Creatures that were undead. These could not have been created by an Elf."

"Then who?"

He licks his lips not wanting to say. "The Sephkharis, Lyklor. Emperor of the underworld."

"That sounds bad."

"It's very bad. And I'm still not sure King Caer Guy hasn't played a part in this even if he did not create the witch wyrms. He opened the veil, so either they're working together, or Lyklor is working on his own. I suspect the latter though, not because I trust the Aldrien king, but not even he is foolish enough to allow Lyklor dominion here. This is the problem opening veils. There is much about the powers of the underworld we do not understand. His arrogance in doing such a thing could be the undoing of us all."

Corrik is wrecked inside and out. This is a lot. More often it's the Toppy-type taking care of their brat, but brats also have a responsibility to take care of their Top. "Come my love. We will sort out what to do about the Emperor of the Underworld another day, together," I say pulling him along, leaving his horse who someone will look after.

"Oh?"

"Yes. For now, I'm going to get you into a hot bath and we'll wash this blood off you." It's probably Ditira's blood.

"A bath sounds nice."

"That's not all. I'm going to take you to bed. You can use something whippy on my arse, you'll like that. I've a list of naughty things I've been up to while you've been gone to be taken to task for."

"I knew it," he says lacing his hand into mine. "Can't leave you alone for a minute."

"You'll do well to remember that. Then we'll make love. First hard and rough, then slow and tender."

He yanks me around by my hand, so I can stare into his violet eyes. "Tristan, I love you most." It's the most earnest thing he's ever said.

I move a bloody strand of hair out of his face. "I love you most." He beams. "Now, let me tell you about the tattoo I want you to have." We start walking again.

"Another one?"

"Yes, a dragon this time. The Markaytian one like on my chest. Maybe yours will have *Property of Tristan Kanes* under it."

"You aren't a Kanes anymore, you're a Cyredanthem," he points out. "And I intend to keep you that way."

"Makes no difference."

"It makes all the difference," he says.

"Anyway, point being, everyone will know you're mine."

"Don't they already?"

"Probably, but one can't be too sure," I say.

"Possessive thing."

"It's been said."

He laughs. "I will do whatever you wish, my darling. Now, I have some spanking to do." He throws me over his shoulder, easily carrying me squealing toward the palace, complaining, and whacking him on the back.

This is my life as a brat, as husband to an Elven prince and lover of two more, as Elf in the first realm and I wouldn't have it any other way. I am Tristan Kanes. I can't run away from my destiny, but when we meet, I will be ready.

LOOK FOR (PROBABLY) THE FINAL STORY

TRISTAN BOOK THREE: DRAGON'S BLOOD 2022
Sign up for my newsletter and never miss an update!
www.mockingbirdpublications.com

SIGN UP HERE

SURPRISE STORY FREE

Did you notice some unanswered vagueness in the Epilogue? Well that's because ... TA DA! BOOM! Free story.

Wanna see Corrik and Tristan's wedding night? Wanna see Alrik collar Tristan? Wanna see Tristan get spanked?

Head over here to join my newsletter and get a FREE story. It's PWP, that's porn without plot but hey did I mention? it's FREE.

CLICK HERE TO GET YOUR FREE COPY! Or go to www.-mockingbirdpublications >More >Free Content

LETTER FROM MOCK

Dear Readers,

"Kink" is not a gimmick I use to sell stories. I may be writing fantasied versions, but the themes I write are real; the feels are real. I write to represent a group of us I know exists to whom which seeing themselves represented could mean a great deal.

Spanking is not usually thought of as its own kink. It's often thrown into the BDSM category. When spanking is mentioned, people usually think "sexy times". And yeah, that's a thing. Spanking is a turn on for some people, but it's so much more. Spanking is its own fetish.

Years ago, I noticed a hole in the market for spanking books. *Real* spanking books that focus on the many nuances having this kink means. I found this hole because I was looking for specific kinds of stories about spanking that just weren't there. I want to read them just as much as I want to write them.

Seven years ago, I began posting my works for free on the internet with the hope I'd meet more people like me. Never did I imagine how many people I'd meet who were looking for the same feels I do. They wanted to connect to their authentic selves, an aspect they might not be able to share with the world. There are tons of us!

I know the feeling when you read a story that speaks to your soul. I am filled and I feel like I belong somewhere.

So, while I write these stories for me, I also write them for you. I want you to feel seen. I want you to know you belong somewhere. I want you to know that the craving inside you is shared by many and that it IS okay. You are perfectly "normal" (whatever normal means) and if you look up to the sky, I'm out here doing the same thing and wondering if stars ever get spanked.

If you feel so inclined, please leave a review on Amazon and/or Goodreads They help me out. *Huge.*

All my love,

Mock

(S. Legend)

www.mockingbirdpublications.com

ACKNOWLEDGMENTS

I would like to say a special thank you to all my betas. You helped make this book better with your loving feedback. I'm grateful for each of you.

ABOUT THE AUTHOR

Some of you know her as Mock, others as S. Legend, or Miss S. She welcomes all names but will often go by Mock, a name given to her by her readers.

Mock is an ambitious creative, weaving the most precious aspects of her soul into stories. She is an architect, building fascinating worlds, designed from inquiry, rooted in worldly wonderings. It's an intuitive process where she is the scribe, the translator, the conduit.

It helped that storytelling was the language spoken at home. One simply didn't say, "We have an ant infestation. " In Mock's family it was, "I was on my way to the living room, when a peculiar ant crossed my path. I looked to my right, a suspicious line of them marched toward the pantry. In that moment I knew; my kitchen was under siege." The natural flow of conversation always took this form.

And so.

When Mock wrote her first novel, she didn't plan it chapter by chapter, there was no outline, no "plotting" to speak of. But she didn't "pants" it either, she didn't make it up as she went along. She knew how the story felt, where it curved in places and hollowed in others; she knew the destination it rushed toward. Instead of orchestrating, she let the world inspire her, and held space for the words to come, trusting the characters knew what they were doing. All she had to do was tell a story, as she always had done; like breathing.

This is her peace, her healing and solace: Gifts better shared.

Mock's works are the comfort you seek when you need to come home. Her unique writing style will take you, wayfaring reader, to unexpected destinations.

She always says, "I'm not in the business of making up stories, I couldn't if I tired. I'm lucky enough to get picked to share someone else's story when I ask a question to the universe. Someone answers; I write it down."

Printed in Great Britain
by Amazon

63085409R00234